Described in the *Irish Times* as 'one of our foremost writers for young people', Sheena Wilkinson has won numerous awards for her eight novels, including the Children's Books Ireland Book of the Year for *Grounded*. Her historical trilogy about young women coming of age in the Ireland of a century ago has been praised for its 'formidable narrative and . . . acute sense of historical justice' (*Belfast Telegraph*). Her short stories and memoirs have won or been shortlisted in many competitions, including the Fish and the Bridport. *Mrs Hart's Marriage Bureau* is her first novel for adults. Sheena lives by the shores of Lough Neagh.

SHEENA WILKINSON

Mrs Hart's Marriage Bureau

HarperCollins*Ireland*

HarperCollins*Ireland*
Macken House,
39/40 Mayor Street Upper,
Dublin 1
D01 C9W8
Ireland

a division of
HarperCollins*Publishers*
1 London Bridge Street,
London SE1 9GF
UK

www.harpercollins.co.uk

First published by HarperCollins*Publishers* 2023
1

A catalogue record for this book is available from the British Library

ISBN: 978-0-00-856479-7

This novel is entirely a work of fiction.
The names, characters and incidents portrayed in it are
the work of the author's imagination. Any resemblance to
actual persons, living or dead, events or localities is
entirely coincidental.

Typeset in Sabon by Palimpsest Book Production Ltd, Falkirk, Stirlingshire

Printed and bound in the UK using 100% Renewable Electricity by CPI Group (UK) Ltd

For my darling husband Seamus

One

The trouble was, Martha thought, as she bade goodbye to the final applicant with relief – poor Miss Ewart's breath had not been all you might care for – you simply couldn't choose a plain woman, or a poorly groomed one, however efficient. Miss Ewart's references had been excellent, and her qualifications and typing speed superior to any other candidate, but the reputation of Mrs Hart's Matrimonial Bureau (discretion guaranteed) was at stake. And hers was a business – Martha disliked the term but had never found a better one – where appearances counted. At least Miss Ewart had not had dyed hair like the previous interviewee.

Martha sighed, pinched the top of her nose and looked sadly at both her list and the teapot, the former full of scored-out names and question marks, and the latter empty. Well, that at least could be remedied: this was Manchester's Midland Hotel, not the Teaspoon Café in Easterbridge. The merest glance at the superior-looking waitress, and fresh tea was ordered. Earl Grey, since she need please only herself.

'Two cups again, madam?' asked the waitress, gathering up the detritus of the previous tea with calm dexterity and frowning slightly in the direction of the window table, where a girl in a grey hat had been sitting for ages.

1

'Just one, thank you.'

'Very good, madam.'

In the Teaspoon Café the waitress would say, 'A'reet, then, love,' and sniff. Miss Ewart, droopy of hem and bosom, had looked as though she would be very much at home in the Teaspoon Café. Mrs Hart's Matrimonial Bureau might be provincial and – her lips tightened at the memory of the perfidious Hilda's parting insult – *passé*, but there were standards to maintain.

It had been an affectation, perhaps, to arrange interviews in Manchester instead of at the office, but she had hoped that by casting her net wider, seeing the candidates in grander surroundings, she might attract the right sort. But she had liked none of them, not enough to imagine sharing her small office, poring together over registration forms to match Miss X with Mr Y, or wonder how on earth to tell Mrs Z (widowed) that there was still nobody suitable on the books. You needed someone *sympathique*.

Hilda had not been *sympathique*. Hilda had been, it was not too dramatic a word, treacherous. But never mind. Martha was not one to dwell or hark back. Whomever she chose now would help her take Mrs Hart's Matrimonial Bureau forward into a brighter future. But oh dear, how hopeless they had been!

The Earl Grey appeared, with two cups, she noticed, but said nothing. The waitress was only human, after all. She busied herself with the strainer, approving the supply of milk *and* lemon (she preferred the former but liked being considered one who might choose the latter). The first waft of bergamot when she gave the pot a surreptitious stir restored her to sanguinity. She scanned the list again. She had seen six women and it was natural that they should have blurred; a recap might reveal something overlooked.

She had to squint to make sense of it. Years of jotting down rapid notes without looking at the page – it didn't inspire confidence in clients if she broke eye contact – had made her handwriting spidery. And all those ticks, underlinings and symbols! One name shone out virgin and un-scribbled over – Miss April McVey. She had not turned up at all. How rude, but from what she remembered from her application, Miss McVey, though well-enough-qualified, was Irish and therefore possibly congenitally unreliable. There had been an odd testimonial from a priest, if she remembered rightly.

Now what on earth did that angry-looking squiggle mean beside Miss Fowler? Was she the one with dyed hair? No, she had been the girl with the lovely skin and the second-best typing speed. Martha closed her eyes, the better to recall what was wrong with her. She had been well-spoken, confident, delightful little mauve hat, but there had been something . . .

Ah! Of course! No, she would not have done. Political enthusiasm was all very well – Martha had been a committed suffragette in her day, or at least she had once had a copy of *Votes for Women* confiscated at school – but the gleam in Miss Fowler's eyes when she told Martha about her jolly weekend rambles with her chums in the British Union of Fascists – no! It might be the thin end of a rather unpleasant wedge.

The girl who'd been working in the newspaper office was likely enough, but she had kept flashing her engagement ring. Another six months and Martha would be looking for a replacement. Oh dear, perhaps if she advanced Miss Ewart a small dress allowance and encouraged her to consult a dentist . . .

'Miss Hart?'

'Mrs,' Martha said automatically and opened her eyes.

The girl from the window table was standing in front of her. A young woman, she should say, but now that she was thirty-eight, Martha saw anyone younger as a girl. She was perhaps twenty-five, tall and fair, with bobbed hair peeping from under a tilted grey felt hat. She was twisting the handle of her brown leather bag and must have been doing so for some time because the fingertips of her gloves were stained, though there was nothing slovenly about the rest of her appearance. Running a matrimonial bureau had made Martha swift to note details and she saw with approval that this girl was well turned out in a modest way. That is, the clothes were well worn, but the quality good, apart from the hat, which was a little modish for Martha's taste. Still, the grey felt collar of her tweed coat exactly matched it, and as the tweed looked old and the felt new, Martha guessed she was a resourceful girl. But who was she? Could she be—

'I'm April McVey,' the girl said in what sounded to Martha like a Scottish accent. But hadn't she said Irish? And her appointment had been for one o'clock – it was after four now.

April rushed on. 'I know I'm late. I got lost. My Aunt Kathleen said the hotel was just by the station, she said you couldn't miss it, only I went to the wrong station.' She sounded close to tears though she faced Martha with a jaunty chin.

'I can see that would be easily done,' Martha said. 'But, my dear, you're three hours late.'

'Och, I know. But when I got here and I worked out you were you, if you know what I mean, I could see you were busy and I didn't like to interrupt, so I waited till you were done. I never knew I could make a pot of tea last that long. It's great the way they bring you fresh water, isn't it, but I didn't like to ask more than twice. And' – she lowered her voice – 'it's awful dear. You could get dinner for a family of six for that in Lisnacashan. But it's gorgeous, isn't it?' She looked round with evident satisfaction. 'And it was worth it to watch all the people. I hardly got ten pages of my book read. It's the new E.M. Delafield. Do you know her? She's awful funny. Very English – mind you, everything here seems very English to me.' She smiled for the first time, a wide smile that hovered between confidence and uncertainty, the mouth a little big for beauty,

4

the teeth crooked, but the overall impression very attractive, and Martha found herself smiling back.

'I was ready to come over a minute ago,' Miss McVey said, 'but you looked like you needed that cup of tea so I was biding my time. But you might not want to see me? Maybe you're already suited?'

Martha bit her lip. This girl wouldn't possibly do. Nobody in Easterbridge would understand her accent – Ulster, was it? That bit of Ireland that wasn't really Ireland and, thank heavens, was no longer in the news all the time. And yet . . .

She was personable and as well-turned-out as she could manage. Resourceful – she had not given up and gone home. Literate. Sensitive – she had not barged in on another interview but had waited for Martha to be free *and* refreshed. It was hard not to warm to someone with such a respect for the power of a good brew. And she was interested in people – a most necessary qualification.

'I have to say,' Miss McVey went on, 'and it's not my place, but sure I might as well, that none of those women looked like the kind of person you'd want in a marriage bureau. That last one, God love the cratur.' She shook her head. 'And your woman with the purple hat – she was in the rest room at the same time as me, and she gave me a look would wither you when I asked her would she pass the soap for there was none at my basin. And thon thing with the dyed hair' – Martha winced at the memory – 'sure she'd steal the fellas for herself.'

'Funnily enough that's what my last assistant did.' She added *insightful* to the girl's qualifications.

'Och well, you'd be safe with me,' Miss McVey said comfortably. 'I've no notion of getting married.'

'Everyone says that,' Martha said, 'until they do.'

'Is that right?' She looked surprised, her grey-blue eyes wide. 'All the girls at home are near dead to get married. It's all they

5

talk about.' She sighed. 'I've hardly any friends left. They go all boring, talking about their husbands' socks and how they like their meat cooked, and then sure it's babies and nappies and you never see them. I don't see the appeal. I'm more your career girl type.' She perked up, with that little tilt of her chin. 'I ran Daddy's office like clockwork. I'd be well able for your bureau. I'm very bossy. I'd love matching people up.'

'Let me see, you ran the office at a garments factory, isn't that right?'

'I did, aye. I couldn't get a reference from the boss because Daddy died last month.' She rushed on before Martha could express any condolence. 'But sure it mightn't have counted anyway, him being family. That's why I asked the minister.'

She was impossible. But there was something irresistible about her, something honest and charming and fresh. She was, Martha was sure, everything that was ever meant by *sympathique*.

'Why don't you sit down?' she said. 'Some of the other candidates were excellent but it wouldn't be fair not to give you a chance when you've had such a long wait.'

April – impossible now to think of her as Miss McVey – beamed and sat down at once. 'Grand,' she said. She glanced down at the teapot. 'Would you be fit to squeeze thon pot?'

Two

Martha had started up her bureau in 1924, ten years ago.

'It wants modernising,' she admitted. 'I was so busy with Mother that I've sort of let it run itself in recent years – or rather, I let my assistant get on with it. Only she kept snaffling all the most eligible chaps for herself and her pals—'

'I wouldn't do that,' April said, taking a sip of tea.

'—and now she's jolly well gone and got herself engaged to one – a solicitor, no less – so I've had to sack her. She'd have left anyway of course but at least *I* decided when. I shouldn't have put so much trust in her, but what was I to do, with Mother so poorly? Anyway, you don't need to hear all that. Fact is, I let things slide. And now Mother's passed on . . . Well, everyone says, "Take a bit of time for yourself at last, Martha," "Have a rest, Martha," but I'm not the sort to rest.'

'I know rightly,' April said. 'I'm the same myself. When I—'

'I like to be busy,' Martha went on. 'I *need* to be busy. And I can't pretend the bureau makes a fortune, but it pays its way and I do think we provide a vital service. In 1926,' she reminisced, 'I went to seventeen weddings, all of my own making.'

April's eyes widened. 'Ah now, you wouldn't make me go to weddings, would you?' she asked as if Martha was expecting her to visit an abattoir in the course of duty.

Martha ignored her. 'Three blind chaps that year if I remember right. And seven amputees. And poor Freddie Lowther – we didn't think we'd ever get him suited, but we found him a smashing girl, Louise. She'd grown up in a prison, her father was the governor, so nothing bothered her, and she was awfully good with Freddie, quite turned him round. He was neurasthenic, poor chap, and rather given to wandering about in his unmentionables, but she has him keeping hens and when he does have a lapse, which is very seldom these days, the hens don't mind. I don't suppose they even notice. I'm not sure Louise does any more.'

April looked puzzled. 'So a lot of your fellas, I mean your gentlemen clients, are . . .'

'War veterans. But of course! That was how it all started.' Martha settled down for a good long monologue. 'I was a VAD in the war – what did you do, dear?'

'Sure I was no age. Thirteen when it ended.'

'Forgive me.' The war loomed so large in Martha's life that she was apt to forget how long ago it was. So April was twenty-eightish – older than she looked. 'Well, I nursed abroad, in field hospitals mostly.'

'I'd say that was quare hard work.'

'Oh, it was. Back-breaking and heart-breaking, but I loved being useful. I'd been brought up to be an ornament to society and not much else. You know the sort of thing: helping Mother with the flowers, and dances at the tennis club and hoping to be noticed by some half-decent chap. And then all the chaps went off to war.'

'My daddy was at the Somme,' April said, which made Martha feel very old indeed. 'And had you a fella yourself— I mean, a chap?'

'Gordon Hart.' How long since she had said his name aloud! She had not told the others any of this. 'Killed at Passchendaele.

We were married when he was on leave in 1916. We had eleven days together all told.' She glanced down at her left hand as if to reassure herself the thin gold band was where it always was. 'I'd have liked to keep on nursing after the war, there was no shortage of work with so many convalescent homes and that, but Father died in the great flu . . .'

'God aye, wasn't it desperate?' April said. 'Mammy had it too; she was never right after.'

'Terrible.' Martha shook her head. 'He was a doctor – hadn't a chance. And then my older brothers came home from the war. They were *lucky*.' She imagined quotation marks around the word. 'Mark was practically deaf – damage from a shell, and his nerves weren't all they might have been. And Thomas' – dear Thomas! – 'was fine from the neck down but his poor face was horribly disfigured. For a while I just kept things going at home, looking after everyone – as women do.'

'Sure don't I know rightly,' April said.

'Father left a little money—'

'Lucky you; mine left debts.'

'—enough to live on, quietly, for Mother and me, for a few years. The boys went back to work. Mark had been a reporter on the local paper, the *Easterbridge Recorder* – he's still there. He does the typesetting now – he wasn't quite up to the reporting. But he's happy enough. And Thomas kept on with his plan to be a schoolmaster. I don't know how he found the courage, standing up in front of little boys all day long, with his face how it is. And it was worse then, the scars aren't so livid now, but they never seemed to mind.'

'They'd have seen him as a hero,' April said. 'Jamesie McAlinden in Lisnacashan was the same; he'd the face blew off him, but nobody ever looked sideways at him.'

'Yes. Children can be cruel, but they can be very accepting too. By 1922 he was a housemaster. But he wanted to wed.

9

Mark had married his fiancée Beulah, but Thomas had joined up straight from Leeds University and he hadn't been keeping company with anyone. Or nobody important. There was a girl, but he broke it off.'

'*He* did?'

'Didn't want her to feel an obligation.'

'Och, God love him.' April sounded indignant. 'What about' – and with a shift of tone that charmed Martha, she quoted, '"love is not love which alters when it alteration finds"?'

'This clearly wouldn't have been "the marriage of true minds".' Martha smiled her approval. The girl was clearly not uneducated despite being prone to such phrases as *the face blew off him* and *the poor cratur*. 'Esme was very young. But when Mark married, Thomas really felt left behind.'

April nodded feelingly.

'Saw himself growing old as a bachelor schoolmaster and though he was grateful to have come through – so many didn't – he knew he'd be lonely with that kind of life. But he couldn't see a girl being interested, not with him looking as he did.'

'Aye. Poor Jamesie never found a woman.'

'It was Mark, in a way, who came up with the idea,' Martha went on. 'He was talking about an advertisement he'd typeset – I hadn't seen it, I never bothered with the personal columns – from a lady wanting to marry an ex-serviceman. And she said, and I never forgot this, *any disability considered*. She said she was kind and capable.'

'Did Thomas reply?' April was leaning forward, lips parted, eyes wide. Her interest and empathy seemed genuine.

'Oh no. He was too shy. But Mark said they published something similar every month or so. And I started to think, for every lady who'd go so far as to place an advertisement there must be others who'd like to meet someone but prefer to be

10

introduced in a more, well, conventional way. It's not everyone, especially ladies, who'd advertise for a man. I wouldn't, myself. Would you?'

April shook her head.

'There was such a lot of talk about *surplus women*, and how few men there were, and encouraging spinsters to go to the colonies. You won't remember. You were too young.'

'Phemie MacMenamin went to Canada. She said they were crying out for women to go there – to the back of beyond. To marry farmers.' She screwed up her face. 'It wouldn't be for me.'

'But some women would go anywhere for the chance to marry and have children. I can see why.' Martha looked down at her left hand again. 'Some of my own pals were keen to meet chaps. But we all felt too old. The young folk, the ones who'd missed the war, were having a gay time, even in Easterbridge, but there didn't seem to be chances for people like us – not me, I wasn't keen, not after Gordon. It wouldn't have seemed right. After all, I'm a war widow, not a spinster.'

'So how did you start—?'

'I thought of that poor woman and how she might attract the wrong sort, men who might take advantage. She'd described herself as *a lady of means*. I wanted to write to her myself, advise her to be careful, but I worried that she might think I was a busybody. Or if I mentioned my own situation, she might think me one of those terribly bitter women who don't want anyone else to be happy. I couldn't have borne that.'

'Aye, I know rightly. There was this wee woman in Lisnacashan—'

'So I sent the advertisement to some of Thomas and Mark's pals, and to two of Gordon's cousins who had come through. All decent chaps. All damaged in some way – a leg missing here, an arm there – but able to offer kindness and good spirits. I didn't share her details with anyone I thought wasn't quite the thing. And several of them did respond and, well, I won't bore you with the details and it wasn't all plain sailing, but it did eventually result in a match. A chap from Thomas's regiment.'

'Fair play to you.'

Martha nodded. 'It was terribly gratifying. Jean was a lovely person, full of love and longing – her chap had come all through the war only to die of that dratted flu – and Gerry was blinded and didn't imagine he'd ever find a wife.' She touched the teapot and said, 'Shall I ask for fresh tea?'

'No, go on with the story.' April wrinkled her nose. 'I know this is a classy hotel but that tea tastes funny to me.'

'What I learned from those chaps was that they wouldn't have thought of reading the personal column. And as I've said, most decent people wouldn't advertise. What we do is very different. And I did love knowing that I'd brought together two people who'd never have met each other, who may never have met anyone. They were both lonely and now they're happy as sandboys. They've even got a little girl. They called her Martha!' She beamed.

'Och, isn't that lovely. I'm called after the month I was born in. April Fool's Day – but after twelve o'clock, so it doesn't make me a fool.'

Martha smiled. 'I can see you're no fool, Miss McVey – and April is a lovely name.' It suited the girl; there was something springlike about her, despite the tweed coat and the grey March day at the window, a suggestion of daffodils and skipping lambs.

'I suppose I caught the matchmaking bug,' Martha went on. 'And I wanted to keep going. It was terribly discreet. Really very private at first. I wrote to a few of my pals and asked Thomas and Mark to enlist some of theirs – and we got them to pass the message on to friends of friends. Gradually we got a list together of men who'd like to meet women, and vice versa. Not the sort of people who would advertise, but also not the sort to sit at home feeling sorry for themselves. People with a bit of pluck who only needed a helping hand. I matched them up as well as I could.' She smiled at the memory. How preposterous it had been. And yet it had worked. 'It wasn't easy – we only had nine people for weeks, and only three of them were men. Ladies were much more likely to come forward. But then the *Easterbridge Recorder* did a little story on Jean and Gerry's wedding – sporting of them to talk openly about how they'd met – and after that I had so many enquiries that I had to set up properly. I took an office in town, right in the centre of Easterbridge, and by the end of 1925 I was able to employ an assistant. It's the most satisfying work, April. Well, you'll find out for yourself.'

April's face relaxed. 'You mean I've got the job?'

'I think you would suit,' Martha said. 'Shall we say a month's trial?'

'Och, that's grand. I'm glad I waited. Mammy always says what's for you won't go by you.' For a moment her face seemed to darken and then she said, 'And what about your Thomas? I hope he got a happy ending.'

Martha smiled. 'At first I used to go through all the applications to find the perfect girl for him. I found it best to be honest about the sort of gentlemen we had on our books – and we did have plenty after the *Recorder* ran that story. So if a lady didn't fancy the idea of a facial disfigurement or a missing limb, she could make that plain at the outset and no harm done. But I couldn't get Thomas to sign up. I think he was still shy about his face. Oh, it did rile me! He was the reason I'd started the bureau. Or at least,' she added honestly, 'a big part of it, and he jolly well wouldn't join in.' She knew she sounded like a child disappointed because her big brother wouldn't play dollies. But it had been vexing! 'And then, just like that, a new matron started at the school and they fell for each other. And of course she was used to his face – they were chums first – and now they're married too, with three little boys. He's moved on to a bigger school down in Devon. I miss him but I'm so happy for him.

'I do think,' she went on, 'and I'm only admitting this to you because we're going to be working together, that it's ideal for a man and woman to be chums first if possible, and let the love grow, but not everyone can meet that way. And that's where we come in.'

'It's sensible,' April said. 'Everybody who applies to you knows they want to get married. There's less chance of misunderstanding.'

Again that slight shadow crossed her face, so Martha said gently, 'Indeed there is, my dear.' Had April been the victim of a misunderstanding? Could that be why she protested so much about marriage? Why had she come to England?

'And you've never remarried?' Martha started at the question and April blushed and said, 'Sorry. People always tell me I'm too nosy.'

Martha shook her head. 'Oh dear no! People assume I will. Some people, unkind people, have even suggested I set the whole thing up just to audition for the next Mr Martha Hart. But nothing could be further from the truth. I can't forget Gordon. And then I was so busy with Mother – she had a stroke in '31 and was bedridden until she died. I still kept an interest in the bureau, but I couldn't be involved with all the day-to-day business. And I don't mind admitting that it's seen better days. Hilda, your predecessor, wasn't very efficient, nor was she as understanding as she should have been with our more challenging clients.'

April looked alarmed. 'Challenging?'

'We have one or two who are not easy to suit. But you'll be all right. I can see you're resourceful and sensible. I think you might be just what we need.'

And if she wasn't, Martha thought, as she gestured for the bill and started to gather up her belongings, she would certainly stir things up.

Three

In the crowded juddering tram, April began to shake. Hunger, maybe – her budget had not allowed for a bun to go with the gallons of tea she had drunk; or reaction – she had done it, actually got herself a job! Or fear. Because now she would have to tell Mammy and Aunt Kathleen the truth, that she'd no notion of staying in Manchester with them; she was off to some town called, what was it? Something bridge. Easterbridge. She wasn't even sure where it was. That nice Mrs Hart had tried to explain, but April's geography of England was sketchy. It was east of here, she believed, and she had a notion it was in Yorkshire, but more than that she didn't know.

She rubbed a lookout hole on the steamed-up window – och dear, her gloves were destroyed! – and gave a wriggle of anticipation at the thought of Easterbridge. Wherever it was, whatever it was like, it was much too far to come back to Eupatoria Street in the evenings. No more sharing a bed with Mammy and trying not to annoy Aunt Kathleen. No more listening to endless chat about Lisnacashan in Aunt Kathleen's parlour, which had so many fringes and antimacassars and doilies that April felt she inhaled velvet with every breath. If the Lisnacashan April and Mammy had left a fortnight ago was dull, the Lisnacashan of forty years ago sounded worse: *What about the Breens over the bridge? The ones with the child that wasn't right? Didn't Dan Breen marry Jeanie McCann or was it Jenny McMahon? What end did old Mrs McMahon take? Och, Kathleen, sure you know well she died in the Russian flu. Was that 1889 or 1890? It was 1890 because remember the Galbraiths sold the barren cow?* . . . And on and on up every road and loaning and into every dreary house. If Aunt Kathleen was so interested in Lisnacashan, why had she left it and never gone back?

She knew why, of course. The usual: to get married. She had fallen for a Manchester shoe salesman and that was her away over the water for good. Not exactly for good, because the shoe salesman had drunk himself into an early grave in 1910. But she had never come home, so she can't have missed Lisnacashan that much. Or maybe she was too mortified. April could understand that now. Though whatever about Daddy, and despite where he met his end, at least he never drank.

She peered through the hole she had made in the window. Was this her stop? Everywhere looked similar; rows and rows of red-bricked terraces and tall factories and everything clogged with soot. She *thought* this was the end of Eupatoria Street, but it might not be. Och well, she would get off anyway. If she had to walk a bit, so be it. Hadn't she been sitting on her b-t-m all afternoon? Oh, but it had been in a good cause!

She emerged from the tram and clutched her bag to her. Yes! There was the fish shop – her stomach growled – and the Methodist chapel and the Red Lion. You could have fitted the whole of Lisnacashan into the six or seven streets that seemed to be Aunt Kathleen's world, but Lisnacashan was more spread out, with gardens merging into fields merging into gentle hills. Here everything seemed bricked-up and smoky, and you had to look up above the buildings to see a smudge of sky, like in

17

a child's painting. Church Street in Lisnacashan, where April had spent her whole life, was in the very centre of the town, but even so, you were only a skip and a jump from the fields and the woods and the banks of the River Blackwater.

Aunt Kathleen lived at the far end of Eupatoria Street, the better end, as she was fond of reminding them. The house was tall and thin, the front door opening directly on the street; there were three bedrooms but as one of them was where Aunt Kathleen did the dressmaking that was her living, April and Mammy had to share the small attic. But beggars can't be choosers. Aunt Kathleen didn't say that – she had said, right from the start, when it became clear that Daddy's death had left them in unfortunate circumstances, that they were welcome, and what she had was theirs, but she had a way of making April feel like a beggar. *You've a great appetite, April, dear; it's a wonder you stay so slim.* But no longer! This was Wednesday, and on Saturday she would take the train to Easterbridge.

April checked her wristwatch: half past five. Aunt Kathleen put tea on the table at five; would she have kept hers? Dear, but she was starving. She started to half run along the street, and two small girls paused their skipping game to stare at her, open-mouthed, and then nudged each other and giggled. One of them stuck her tongue out. April did the same. She wouldn't have done it in Lisnacashan, and of course she wouldn't do it in Easterbridge. But she felt reckless and skittish, the way she and her pal Evelyn used to feel running up the school lane on Friday afternoons, ready for what Evelyn's mammy called *divilment*.

The reaction in Eupatoria Street was not encouraging.

'*Easterbridge?*' Aunt Kathleen, taking her plate of dried-up rissoles out of the oven, looked disbelieving, as if April had made the place up.

'It's in Yorkshire,' April said, hoping it was. It did not take long to clear her plate; Aunt Kathleen's portions were small,

18

her appetite, and Mammy's, birdlike. April supposed that not being hungry was something you grew into in middle age, like high lace collars and an appreciation of sermons.

'But you'll have to pay for lodgings,' Mammy said, her eyes big with anxiety. 'That won't leave you with much.'

'I'll send you money every week,' April promised. *You won't be beholden to Aunt Kathleen*, she tried to say with her own eyes.

'But if you got a job here in Manchester—'

'I did try.' She had not, in fact, tried very hard. 'There's over two million unemployed in this country.'

'Plenty of jobs for those who want them,' Aunt Kathleen said. 'I heard they were taking on at the dogfood factory. You wouldn't even need to take the tram.'

April bit her lip. 'Aunt Kathleen, at home I was more or less running McVey's. I can't take a job as a factory hand. I'm trained for office work. I went to night school.'

Aunt Kathleen sniffed and lit the gas under the kettle. 'So what sort of office is this?'

April placed her knife and fork neatly in the middle of her plate and took a deep breath. She had deliberately kept the details vague. 'It's a' – she was about to say *marriage bureau* but remembered the posh word Mrs Hart had used – 'matrimonial bureau.'

Mammy clutched her lace collar. Aunt Kathleen's brows shot up towards her grey hairline.

'It's very respectable,' April said. 'The woman who owns it, Mrs Hart, she's a real lady. You should have seen her furs. People come from all over to her.'

'A *matchmaker*?'

April shrugged. 'I suppose so. She set it up to help people after the war. Veterans and such.'

Mammy, who knew more than anyone could want about war veterans, having put up with Daddy all those years, shook her head. 'It doesn't sound the kind of thing—'

19

'It'll be grand,' April said. 'You know I like sorting people out. Sure weren't the girls in the factory always asking me for advice?'

Mammy had no idea what sorts of things the girls consulted her about, and April wasn't about to break any confidences, but Lisnacashan was by no means as God-fearing as it appeared on Sunday mornings, with half the town in the parish church, a quarter in the Presbyterian and another quarter (though April didn't know many of them) doing queer things in Latin in the Catholic chapel over the bridge. The McVeys were Presbyterians, but April didn't intend to keep going now that Daddy couldn't make her. Sure they mightn't even have a Presbyterian church in Easterbridge. The thought pleased her. Since Daddy's death she had given in to many of these small rebellions. After all, they were nothing to what he had done.

Aunt Kathleen sniffed and poured out the tea, strong and peat-coloured, the opposite of that funny tea in the Midland Hotel. While she and Mammy speculated about the dreadful sorts of people April might be dealing with, April was making a list of what she would need and wondering if there would be time to make over her green linen; Mrs Hart had said she must be smart. Aunt Kathleen might have some scraps she could make into new collars and cuffs.

She imagined herself in an elegant, high-ceilinged office overlooking a street of gracious buildings. The Easterbridge of her imagination owed much to Jane Austen; though, being in Yorkshire, maybe she ought to be thinking more along the lines of the Brontës. She must be sure to finish her library book before Saturday, and maybe Mammy would return it for her if she hadn't time. She hoped there would be a public library in Easterbridge. Och, there would surely – a town big enough for its own marriage bureau must have a decent library. She could read all evening with nobody to tell her she'd ruin her eyes. Mostly, at home, she hadn't let herself escape to her own room. When she was in the sitting room, Daddy was nicer to Mammy. Mammy never *said*, 'Don't leave me alone with him,' but she didn't have to. April seemed to have spent her whole life keeping the peace between them simply by being there. And now he was dead, and Mammy had Aunt Kathleen, who wasn't a ray of sunshine, but at least she wasn't a bully, and she did seem to like having Mammy; she hadn't hesitated about taking her in. Mammy would be grand in Eupatoria Street, away from the shame.

And you, my girl, can start your own life at last, April told herself. She'd be twenty-nine in a couple of weeks' time. Not too late.

Four

Easterbridge revealed itself to April gradually as the train hissed and huffed to the station. The buildings were mostly pale yellow-grey stone, some fancy Victoriana with gargoyles and turrets, and a lot of steep stone terraces, some modest, others tall and grand like the houses in her imagination. It was far smaller than Manchester, of course, and Belfast, which she had only visited a couple of times. But huge compared to Lisnacashan, with suburbs ribboning up the hills as far as she could see and the promise beyond of rough moorland. Lisnacashan was low-lying, in a river valley; it might be good to have some upland air – what the magazines called *bracing*.

Mrs Hart had booked her into a hotel for the first week, until April could see about lodgings. 'I imagine you'll want to choose your own rooms,' she had said in her low, pleasant voice as they had walked out of the Midland Hotel together, 'but I can certainly advise you on suitable areas.' Her voice had grown warm. 'It's a very pleasant town, Easterbridge. And I do think you'll suit splendidly.'

She had offered to meet her at the station but April had demurred. 'Och, it's grand,' she had said. 'I'm a big girl. I'll see you on Monday morning.'

Now, a spiteful rain starting to needle her face, and her suitcases having somehow gained a couple of stone each since she had left Manchester, she wished she had been less independent. She supposed there would be taxis at the station; she wouldn't have a notion how to find the Blossom Private Temperance Hotel. Anyway, she was here, she had made it, and even if her arms felt like they were about to snap in two, as she lugged first one case and then the other off the train, and stood flexing her aching muscles on the platform, people's arms didn't actually break from carrying heavy loads. Just as, she and Mammy had already discovered, you didn't actually die of shame. She rammed her hat more securely onto her head; it was an eejit of a thing, tilting like a drowsy bird. She wished she hadn't bought it.

The station formed one side of a sloping square, flanked by tall stone offices and a grand-looking hotel, the Royal Oak – not the one she was booked into. The fourth side was open to the street and, yes, there was a taxi, a big black one. Thanks be to God. She started towards it, waddling like a duck, her hat tipping further and further over her eyes until she was obliged to stop for a moment at the marble fountain in the middle of the square, whose low wall was handy for resting her suitcases on. She took off her hat and rammed it back on more firmly. At home she'd have worn a woollen tam on a day like this, but you needed a decent hat to go halfway across England in a train and she'd bought this in the best shop in Lisnacashan. It struck her that Lisnacashan was no longer home. Was home where you came from, or where your people were, or where you lived? Well, Easterbridge was where she was going to live now, and it would be up to her to make it home.

Taking a breath, she looked up at the figure on top of the fountain: a determined-looking woman holding a sword and a wreath. There was an inscription at her feet: *In Memoriam: The Natives of Easterbridge Who Fell in the War in the Crimea. Erected AD 1865.* Another war. Was that the Charge of the Light Brigade one? She thought they'd probably been fighting about something else in Ireland at that time; sure they usually were.

Never mind that – someone was about to pinch her taxi! A man was bearing down on it, looking determined, and unencumbered by suitcases or a wayward hat – his trilby sat smugly on his head. How dare he! April grabbed the handles of her cases, jerked her neck to persuade her hat to a more secure position, and marched taxi-wards. She arrived at the car at the same time as the man and thrust out her hand to claim it. As did he. Rage filled April. She'd been on three trains, had had to run for the last one so she'd missed getting a cup of tea, she was drenched and tired and water was running down her neck and she'd be damned if she let this man take her taxi.

'Oi! I got here first,' she said.

The man raised his hat and smiled. 'Indeed you did, miss. Please, allow me.' And he opened the car door, just as the taxi-driver, a short, big-bellied man, came shuffling round. He looked at the man.

'Taxi for *you*, wasn't it, Mr Carr?' The driver looked at April as if she was no better than she should be.

The man shook his head. 'I can walk. I thought I might have my daughter with me, which was why I booked you, but no, please, take the young lady to . . . well, wherever she's going.' He smiled at April, who could feel her cheeks burning and for once could think of nothing to say. 'Good afternoon,' he said, and set off along the road, tall, rather spare, in a dark tweed overcoat, as April settled herself into the taxi.

24

'Eh, you're a lucky lass,' the driver said. 'Not many as would give up their taxi on a day like this. Proper gent, Mr Carr is.'

April bit her lip. 'Em, the Blossom Temperance Hotel,' she said, and hoped the journey would be a short one.

Five

I thought I might have my daughter with me. Fabian Carr, setting out to walk home, wasn't sure whether to be relieved or disappointed that, for now at least, he had another reprieve. On the one hand, life was simpler when Prudence, with her sulks and sudden blazing rages, was safely away at school. On the other, he didn't seem to be getting used to an empty house. And it always seemed especially empty at weekends. He had imagined, when he moved back to Easterbridge – he had grown up about ten miles away – that he might see more of Felicity. He was alone; she was alone – in her case from choice. But though quite happy to see her big brother sometimes, and not too proud to ask him to help with manly tasks in that ridiculous house she'd insisted on buying – fitting new lino in the bathroom, sorting out the attic he had encouraged her to let out – she made it clear that she considered her time and her home her own. And being a writer she worked at odd hours, so he had learned never to call without checking first.

Anyway, he was forty years of age, respected senior partner at Easterbridge's most established solicitors; he shouldn't need to rely on his little sister for company. Or his child. He crossed his fingers inside his coat pocket and hoped that Prudence would settle now. St Lucy's was her third school in three years. No headmistress had gone so far as to publicly expel her, but he was always asked, politely but firmly, to make alternative arrangements for the following year. He had fully expected today's interview with Miss Willard to go the same way.

He turned out of Station Square to begin the long slow climb up Parkgate, past the park to the big semi-detached villa in Parkgate Avenue that still didn't feel like home. He had thought leaving London would be helpful; he had always preferred his native north country, and there were no memories of Serena here apart from furniture and of course photographs. But maybe he was too old for a new beginning.

A fresh start. That's what Prudence's headmistress had called it. *We'll say no more about it; Prudence and you can have a fresh start.* Prudence, bulky in the unbecoming brown gym slip, had stared at the floor, picked at her fingernails and shrugged and mumbled that she supposed. Miss Willard had taken this as acquiescence and packed her off to prep.

'Don't worry too much, Mr Carr,' she had said. 'Sometimes they take longer to settle and of course, losing her mother . . .'

It was what they always said.

'It's three years since my wife died,' Fabian had said. 'I'd have thought Prudence should be, well, trusted to behave like a civilised human by now.'

Miss Willard had inclined her head wisely. 'It was a minor infringement of bounds,' she said. 'Let's not treat her like a hardened criminal.'

If it was so minor, why drag him fifty miles across England on a bleak March day? But he was grateful, really; Miss Willard was the first headmistress *not* to treat her like a hardened criminal.

'Girls are funny creatures,' she had gone on.

'I won't disagree.'

'Does she have . . . I don't wish to pry, Mr Carr, but does she have any female role models? That makes such a difference to a motherless girl.'

He had tried not to wince at the word *motherless* – it was a statement of fact. He felt that he was being put on trial and found wanting. But wasn't part of his reason for sending Prudence away a desire to give her exactly those female influences he couldn't supply? St Lucy's was full of terrifying-looking big girls in long slim skirts; the one who had shown him to Miss Willard's office had been as capable and formidable as his own secretary. And much more elegant.

'I have a sister,' he had said. 'Felicity.' He almost told her who Felicity was – they were bound to have her books in the school library, but he didn't like to show off. Also, Miss Willard might expect Felicity to visit St Lucy's to give a lecture, and Felicity would hate the idea. 'She lives nearby. But Prudence doesn't see a great deal of her.' Felicity had made it clear from the start that she would not be any kind of surrogate mother. Children bored her; at least, she preferred imaginary ones.

'You have no plans to remarry? Forgive me, Mr Carr, but often widowers—'

'No,' he had said. 'No plans at all.'

He felt squirmy now at his recalled embarrassment, actually sensing his cheeks burn, though that might have been the steep pull of Parkgate Road – he wasn't as fit as he had been. Too many heavy lunches, not enough exercise. It was a reasonable question. When Serena had first died, after a year of the most horrible suffering, nobody would have dreamed of asking such a thing, and even now, Miss Willard was the first person actually to give voice to it. He supposed headmistresses rushed in where angels feared to tread, or maybe he was out of touch with modern women, having fallen for Serena before the war. And Serena had been the gentler, pre-war type of woman, not the modern sort who smoked and wore trousers and had opinions.

That made him think of that funny fierce girl who had hijacked his taxi. *Oi! I got here first.* Face screwed up in determination. Unusual accent – but he had heard it before, in the war. He had spent some time at a field hospital near Étaples with a shrapnel wound, and the chap in the bed beside him had talked just like that: Lieutenant Gilbert Ryan from the 36th (Ulster) Division. They had played chess, setting out the board on a chair between their beds. He wondered what this girl was doing so far from home. Easterbridge was not the sort of town to attract many outsiders. He wondered too, as he did from time to time, what had happened to Ryan; he hoped he had come through.

The rain had worsened; water dripped off his hat brim and made him hunch his shoulders and build up speed so that he was jog-trotting up Parkgate Road and round the corner into Parkgate Avenue. Number four was in darkness as usual. He would have liked a live-in housekeeper – at least there would have been someone to answer the door and keep a light burning. But getting staff in Easterbridge was no easier than in London; he was lucky enough to have a daily woman, as Mrs Perry, who fulfilled that role with limited enthusiasm and much surreptitious reading of magazines that she stuffed behind cushions, never tired of telling him.

Maybe, he thought, opening the gate and starting up the flagged path to the white door, he would get a little dog. Prudence was always begging for one. Though he supposed then she would be even less keen to stay at school.

Six

The first thing April said when she walked into the office on her first day, in the same grey coat and hat, but with a bright orange woollen scarf tucked into the collar was, 'Oh.'

It was the shortest utterance she had so far made in Martha's presence, but no less expressive for its brevity. Martha understood perfectly.

Oh. It's quite small.

Oh. It's not very fancy.

Oh. It's a bit of a mess.

But no sooner had Martha registered this disappointment than April crossed to the coat stand, took off her outdoor things, hung them up and said, 'We'll need to give this place a good redd out.' She looked down at her neat green linen frock and touched one lace cuff protectively. 'Have you a pinny?'

Martha shook her head dumbly. 'Unless Mrs Atkinson left hers in the storeroom. She's the char.'

April's face said clearly, *She can't be much good*, though all she did was stand politely while Martha looked in the tiny store cupboard just outside the door and came up with – hooray – a voluminous purple floral pinny. She looked at it doubtfully, but April said, 'Sure that's grand. It'd go round two men and a wee

30

fella.' She stuck her arms through the armholes and wound it round her. It did go round twice, and she looked very odd, but at least it covered her frock.

'Actually, Mrs Atkinson doesn't seem to have been in lately,' Martha said. 'I think perhaps Hilda hurt her feelings. I must see about getting her back.'

'I don't mind getting my hands dirty.' April took off her lace collar and cuffs and laid them reverently on Martha's desk.

'I'd thought you might feel yourself above that kind of thing,' Martha said. 'Hilda always did.'

'Hilda sounds a bit of an eejit.'

'Oh, she was by no means a . . . an eejit.' The word sounded strange on her lips; should she have said *idiot*? Were they the same thing? 'But she knew what she wanted and she used my business to make sure she got it.'

'Well,' April said, 'I'm not too proud to clean. I mean' – she seemed to remember her dignity – 'just this once.'

'We don't have any appointments today,' Martha said.

'No harm to you, but it's just as well.'

'It's not as bad as it looks. And this isn't where I interview clients.' Martha tried not to sound defensive. 'I have another room downstairs.'

She led April down the steep stairs and showed her the interview room on the first floor. Back in 1924 this had been all she could afford, a small back room above a jeweller's shop, and it had had to house everything. When she had the chance to expand a few years later, she had been delighted to move all the more businesslike paraphernalia – filing cabinets and desks and typewriter – upstairs into what she called the private office, leaving this as the public face of Mrs Hart's Matrimonial Bureau. She had always been proud of the room, which was small but cosy, with a little cast-iron fireplace and four easy chairs grouped round a low table. Photographs of 'her' weddings hung over

31

the fireplace, and she made sure there were society magazines on the table, though the clients were generally too nervous to read. Still, it was a nice touch, she thought, as were the aspidistra on the mantelpiece and the good clock.

April sneezed. 'Sorry,' she said, riffling through layers of pinny to find a handkerchief. 'It's awful dusty in here.'

'Is it?' Martha ran a finger over the nearest chair back. 'Oh dear, it is, isn't it?' For the first time in a while she heard Mother's voice in her head: *Look at those curtains! Ragged all around the bottom! Really, Martha!* How had she not noticed? When was the last time she had used this room? Last Tuesday, the regular depressing interview with poor Mrs Lewis, whom she had been trying to match for almost a year now. How embarrassing. Still, at least she wasn't a new client. But she must write to Mrs Atkinson today, reassure her that Hilda was gone and beg her to come back. Offer a small raise.

'Right.' April sounded businesslike. 'I'll get stuck in here. Maybe you'd start sorting out the office while I'm doing it? Now, where's the hot water? And I take it you've a mop bucket?'

'I'll fetch what you need.' And Martha scuttled back up to the cupboard, wondering who was in charge of whom.

It was no surprise that April was one of those people who sang while they worked. Both of them had their doors open and the strains of an unfamiliar song – Irish, she supposed, something about the Banks of the Bann – drifted up the stairs. . She had a good voice, strong and sweet and high. Martha, taking a pile of papers from her desk and starting to sort through them, wondered if she might like to sing in the choir at St Margaret's. It would be a good way for her to meet folk. It couldn't be easy, moving to a new place at her age, and Easterbridge was not like Manchester or Leeds, full of people from all over. It could be standoffish. Martha must make sure April wasn't lonely. The only time she had left home herself had been during the war, and there, in the nurse's hostel, it had been more a question of too much company than too little. She had not, like most girls, left home to marry; the eleven days of married life with Gordon had been spent partly at his home, partly in a boarding house in Whitby, but mostly, it seemed now, on draughty station platforms, determined not to cry until the train had left.

She lifted a sheaf of the bureau's registration forms and blew a little dust off the top one to see if it was all right. No, it looked dog-eared and shabby; Hilda never would put them back in the drawer as she was supposed to. Such a waste, Martha thought, preparing to screw the form up and put in the waste-paper basket – or no, it would do to show April.

April was a grafter. The singing – fair comely maids and sweet flowery vales and heartbroken exiles – continued, but with a reassuring backdrop of bangs and clatters and more than one trip to the cupboard to replace dirty water with clean and to rinse out her cloth at the sink.

'I'm nearly done,' she said on her third trip. 'No harm to you, but that room was bogging. I mean, it looked grand enough on the surface but when you dug down . . .' She was hot and dusty-looking, a smear across one cheek and a cobweb misting her fair hair. She had her arms full of a grey froth that Martha recognised with shame as the curtains. She shook her head, the cobweb flying out and sticking to her cheek. 'Ugh!' she said, her hands too full of curtain to investigate. 'What's that?'

'Keep still and I'll get it.' Martha leaned over and swept her finger over April's cheek. The girl stayed very still, arms clasped round the grey lace, squinting as though undergoing a medical ordeal. She smelt, Martha noted, of fresh sweat and a sharp floral scent and her skin was soft and faintly pink. I haven't been so close to another person since – well, since Mother died, Martha thought. She felt April's warm breath on her hand.

'I think you've earned a cup of tea,' she said. 'You've been working like billy-o.'

April grinned. 'You're not to come and inspect it till I've done. Now, I was going to ask you should I steep the curtains in the sink here? Or will you take them home and give them a good wash? They'd come up lovely with a wee bit of Reckitt's Blue. And then I can mend them – unless you want to do that yourself?'

'Oh dear,' Martha said. 'I hadn't noticed how bad they were. I suppose seeing them all the time . . .'

'Och, sure don't I know rightly,' April said. 'Mammy was as good a housekeeper as you'd get but when we had to clear all out to leave she was disgraced at the state of the place – all the wee nooks and crannies you don't see.' She closed her lips over her teeth, as if she had said too much, and Martha thought again that there was something about that removal from Ireland that she was not keen to share. Still, it wasn't her business; working in the marriage industry made you very discreet.

After the tea, and another half hour's singing, April announced that the downstairs room was ready for inspection.

'Oh, it's lovely!' Martha's delight was genuine. The room shone as it had not done for years. April had dusted the aspidistra and the glass on the pictures, and the 1920s brides beamed out, their low-waisted frocks and orange-blossom bouquets restored. 'It looks so much more welcoming,' Martha said. 'All we need are some new clients. Now, let me take you out for lunch, my dear; you've worked like a Trojan.'

The Teaspoon Café in St Margaret's Lane was not the finest establishment in Easterbridge but it was two doors down from the bureau, next door to Ackroyd's Country Outfitters, and its soup, though indeterminate in both colour and flavour, was hot and satisfying. April, hands scrubbed pink and lace cuffs re-attached, ate with enthusiasm, but daintily, and her manner with the waitress was pleasant and gracious, much less familiar than Martha would have expected. Her faint concern that April would not be polished enough started to diminish, and she felt something like fervour for this new dawn for Mrs Hart's Matrimonial Bureau. A fervour she had not felt for years.

It lasted about ten minutes. Settled back in the private office, tidier now, but not so shiny as the downstairs room, they had their first professional, well, nothing so vulgar as a row, but a strong difference of opinion. It was over the registration forms.

Martha was very proud of her forms. She had laboured over them when the bureau opened, keen to ensure that her clients were getting the best chance to – she wouldn't say *sell* them-selves, but present themselves and their needs and hopes honestly and fairly. Seated at her desk she passed the form over to April to approve.

'This is what people fill in,' she said. 'Let me know if you think it needs tweaking.'

Martha knew the form did not need tweaking by a single syllable. She merely wanted to reassure her new assistant that she did not intend her to limit her activities to scrubbing floors and cleaning windows. She did not expect her to snort and clasp her hands to her mouth in undisguised horror – she was beginning to suspect that April's reactions would gener-ally be undisguised.

'Oh dear bless us!' April said. 'Is this . . . no, I can see it's not a joke.'

'A *joke*?' It was Martha's turn not to hide her reaction: extremely offended.

'Och, Martha. It's . . . it's . . .' Words seemed to fail April, which Martha knew already to be an unusual occurrence. 'Look at it,' she demanded, thrusting the form back at Martha. 'Read it out loud to me.'

'But you can see it.'

35

'Aye, but I want you to hear it.'

Martha reached into her bag and took out the old-fashioned wire-rimmed reading spectacles which she suspected made her look like a Victorian governess. Of course she knew every word on the form, but she supposed she should humour her assistant.

'Well,' she began briskly, 'there's the usual questions about name and age and address – I take it you don't object to those?'

'Ah no, they're grand, so they are,' April said. 'Go on.'

'*What sort of spouse are you hoping to meet?*'

'Fair enough,' April owned. She didn't comment on the questions about background and education and income except to say, with a deep sigh, 'Ah, you're quare and lucky over here. You don't need to worry about religion. Back home that'd be the first question; in fact you'd have to have a Catholic bureau and a Protestant one.'

'Most of our people tend to be C of E,' Martha said, this being something to which she had not given much thought, but of course the Irish were famously obsessed with religion.

'It's the next bit that needs to change,' April said. 'The bit about the arms and legs.'

Martha read aloud, '*The war has left many of our fine heroes incapacitated to some degree. We may introduce you to someone with a war disability. What level of impairment are you prepared to consider?*' And then the list she knew so well, every item calling to mind someone she had brought happiness to: '*Blindness (one/both eyes); neurasthenia; amputation (arm[s] or leg[s]).* What's wrong with it?' she demanded. 'We have to be honest.'

'It's awful depressing. It assumes all the men will be damaged and the women will be desperate.'

'Damaged and desperate!' Martha felt stabbed in the heart. 'Nothing could be further from the truth. But I did tell you

I set the bureau up to help people who needed rather a specialised service. I told you about my brothers. And there are so many—'

'Even now?'

'Well, we could adjust it slightly, take out the bit about amputations. Actually, people don't always fill in that section, they can ignore it if they want.' She knew she sounded defensive.

'Martha,' April said patiently, 'I see what good work you've done in the past. But what do you want from the bureau *now*? Today? In 1934?'

'I want to keep up that good work. I don't want to change—'

'And how many clients are on your books at the moment?'

Martha bit her lip. 'I did explain that Hilda hadn't been quite—'

'How many?' April demanded.

'I'd need to double-check but—'

'Fifty? One hundred?'

Silly girl! She clearly had no idea how many clients a marriage bureau in a provincial town was likely to have. 'More like twenty.' She sighed and admitted, 'and some of them have been with us rather a long time. Poor Mrs Lewis, the Colonel, that nice little chap with the stammer . . . We haven't been able to suit them. Yet.'

'And what's the average age?'

'I see what you're getting at,' Martha said, 'but when you consider that most of our gentlemen have been through the war . . .'

'Och Martha! D'you not want the bureau to prosper? D'you not want new blood? *Young* blood?'

That sounded positively vampiric, and Martha's eyes widened. 'But we were set up to—'

'I know!' April banged her fist on the desk and Martha jerked back in alarm. She lowered her voice. 'Look, you can limp on – you said yourself you'd let things slide – or you can bring the bureau up to date, relaunch it for a wider clientele.' She blinked, as if surprised to hear herself sound so business-like. 'It's 1934; people don't want to be defined by an old war that ended years ago. God, Martha, I should know, I grew up in a place that can't forget its ancient fights. People don't want to hear words like *war damage*. People want romance and promise and hope and' – her grey-blue eyes sparked and she suddenly laughed. 'Och, listen to me! I haven't a romantic bone in my body, but I know what people want. The girls in the factory talked about nothing else. And Evelyn, my best pal, got married a few years ago and she was all biz even though her fella's about a hundred with a paunch on him and hardly any hair. So you need to sound more positive. More up to date. You need to appeal to young people.'

'But young people don't need this kind of service. Their parents introduce them to suitable partners. They meet at dances and tennis parties and church.'

'Some don't.' April sounded confident. 'Some don't want the partners their parents would choose. My daddy, God be good to him, always had a notion I'd take up with Jacky Mulholland from the chemist's.' She shuddered. 'And lots of young women now leave home to work in shops and offices in big towns. They don't know how to meet other people outside work. It's all very well for the sociable types, who want to go to church socials or dances. But there must be lots of shy, lonely girls out there – in offices and factories, living in hostels or rooms – who would love to meet decent fellas. And you, we, could really help them.'

'I don't think that's the sort of person we really have in mind.'

'Och, for God's sake! Don't be such a flipping snob!'

Martha looked at her in horror. How vulgar! And then, because she was a fair woman, she made herself look at what

April had said. And, well, might she have a point? Was one of the main issues with Mrs Hart's Matrimonial Bureau class rather than age? All the ex-servicemen on her books were officers. They might have been unsound in wind and limb, and occasionally in mind, but they did not lack education and what Martha still thought of as *the right background*. Not gentry, on the whole, they had their own networks, but teachers, doctors, the better kind of civil servant – she had recently matched a local veterinary surgeon with the daughter of a successful racehorse trainer. April was talking about people of the clerk class, office workers, girls like herself. Martha would have to be careful not to say anything to offend her. After all, she had employed her knowing she was several rungs down the social ladder from Hilda. Hilda had been distinctly top-drawer in how she looked and spoke, but she had not been honest or decent. April, Martha felt, for all her bluntness, would always be both.

She was also very indignant. 'It strikes me,' she said, waving a hand over the desk and knocking a ledger onto the ground where it landed with a thud, 'that you don't really want me. You said assistant, but I think you just want a wee skivvy.'

'Of course I—'

April held up a hand. 'No, let me finish. You say you want the bureau to thrive, but it sounds like you'd rather it kept on along the same old grooves. And I won't say you won't keep it ticking over, though I honestly don't see how you'll afford to pay me.'

Martha bridled at the mention of money. 'I assure you—'

'Look, Martha, I've left my home, my mammy, my *country*' – this was below the belt; the girl had already been in England when Martha had interviewed her, but she was in full flow, her cheeks flushed and the words tumbling out as fluently as the songs had done before lunch – 'because I believed you'd a really

39

challenging role for me, bringing the bureau up to date and helping you run it. That's what I thought I was being hired to do. And like I said, like I've *proved*, I don't mind doing the dirty work. But just doing what I'm told, saying yes to everything even if I disagree, och, I couldn't do that. I'm nearly thirty, I'm a career woman, not some wee girl wanting to fill in the time before I get married.'

She paused for breath but was back in harness before Martha could interrupt. 'You did say when you interviewed me, that you knew the bureau needed modernising.'

Martha felt ashamed. 'I meant a fresh coat of paint, perhaps some new brochures, draft a new advertisement for the *Recorder* . . .'

'Och aye, all that,' April said, 'but that's only the start.' She counted on her fingers. 'A big story in the *Recorder* – maybe your brother can give us a hand there – and in the big papers too. Isn't it *The Times* you have over here? New literature; new—'

'I honestly didn't anticipate anything so . . . so wholesale,' Martha said faintly.

'Well, you should.' April stood up. 'I'm going to tidy this other desk. I take it this was Hilda's?' Martha nodded mutely. 'I'll give you a shout if I'm not sure about anything.'

She didn't sing this time, but busied herself with the detritus that had gathered on Hilda's desk, sorting it into piles. She kept up a muttered commentary, which was irritating but, Martha guessed, was her way of showing that there were, as far as she was concerned, no hard feelings. 'Three copies of the *Tatler* – it's well seen she wasn't killing herself with work. You could put those downstairs.' She moved on to the drawers. 'Seven, eight, nine pencils. I hope there's a sharpener some-where. A wee book of Papier Poudré, that's handy stuff, so it is. Would you mind if I took that? Oh no, it's sort of peachy.

Not right for me, I'm too pale. Celtic complexion, Evelyn used to say.'

'You're right.' Martha didn't mean about the Papier Poudré or the complexion.

April was so busy that she seemed not to hear. 'Here's a few hair pins, they'll not go amiss; I might grow mine. Here's a photo of Clark Gable, or maybe it's Cary Grant; sure all those boys look the same. Ooh, a packet of toffees.' A rustling ensued and the next words were indistinct. 'Aye, they're grand. Sure toffees don't go off, do they?'

'You're right,' Martha repeated, louder this time. *Good girl*, said Mother, and Martha wasn't sure if she meant her, or April.

'Oh, sorry, d'you want one?' April held out a Mackintosh's Toffee.

Martha shook her head. 'I mean this place.' She swept her arms round to encompass the office. 'I'm scared of change. I've been jogging on, letting Hilda have her way, and really, she'd already taken the bureau away from what I originally intended, in the sense that she let things become slack, and whatever else we were – old-fashioned or . . . or snobbish – we were always well-run and efficient. At least until Mother became ill. That's when things started to slide. That would have been the time to modernise, but I was so bound up with Mother.' She smiled sadly. 'All right, dear, I know what you mean. And your passion, that fire, it reminds me of how I used to be.' She grabbed a jotter pad from her own desk and handed it to April. 'Let's start straight away,' she said, and briefly she felt the zeal that had made her run away to be a VAD. 'We'll draft an advertisement together.'

'Why don't you change the name?' April suggested. 'Mrs Hart's Matrimonial Bureau's a wee bit dull. And *matrimonial* sounds out of the arc!'

'It's discreet,' Martha said. She remembered choosing the name, deciding on *Mrs* Hart because it was important that people knew she was – had been – married herself. 'You wouldn't want to call it, I don't know, Love Hart or something?' She shuddered and April giggled, then looked thoughtful and somehow older.

'I think you should get away from hearts and romance,' she said. 'What about something to do with hands? You know, hands joining in marriage?'

Martha felt, and doubtless looked, unimpressed.

'I know!' April cried. 'You could call it True Minds!' When Martha frowned again she said, 'You know – like the poem. We talked about it at the interview? The "marriage of true minds".'

'It's not terribly romantic.' And it was dreadful of her, but she couldn't bear the idea of the bureau losing *her* name. Maybe *matrimonial* was indeed old-fashioned so why not simply Mrs Hart's *Marriage* Bureau?

But April's face was shining with vehemence, and after all, hadn't she just reassured the girl that she was prepared to make real changes? 'It's modern,' April went on before Martha could say any more. 'It's saying that marriage today is about mutual respect and sympathy and shared interests and, well, minds, and not just something women have to do to escape their families or being old maids. Not that there's anything wrong with old maids,' she added. 'Sure I'm one myself. But it's also Shakespeare so it's traditional too. And classy.'

'True Minds.' Martha turned the phrase over. 'Isn't that deceptive? I mean, it's not clear what it's for unless people know their Shakespeare.' And despite the possibly reasonable charge about snobbery, she wouldn't prosper with a bureau that catered only for the literati. In Oxford or London, maybe, but not Easterbridge.

'True Minds Marriage Bureau? Sure, that'd make a great headline. And it needn't sound like you're touting for business,' she went on. Martha made a concerted effort not to wince at the expression. 'You said the bureau is ten years old this year.

You could relaunch by the way you're celebrating its anniversary. Have a birthday party. Invite all your successful clients.'

'I don't think so,' Martha said. 'People don't tend to want to admit they met through a marriage bureau.'

'Well, invite the *un*successful ones. Give them too much sherry and hope they all pair off. Sure you could get rid of them all at one fell swoop.'

Martha smiled, slowly. 'Perhaps we could run to a cake,' she said. 'A small one.'

Seven

Cleaning and arguing fairly gave you an appetite. April had her evening mapped out: find a tea shop – nicer than the Teaspoon – and have a good stuff before tackling the list of possible lodgings.

Martha had gone through the Rooms to Let column with a pencil and marked up several which she considered possible.

'These are all in the best part of town,' she had said. 'Parkgate. *Room to let to lady only.*' She nodded approvingly, the old-fashioned earphones in which she wore her dark hair bobbing up and down. 'Obviously I can give you a reference.'

'What about this one? *Studio Room to let; suit artist or writer.*' She couldn't help feeling a thrill – so bohemian!

'Oh my dear!' Martha scored her pencil through it. 'It's in Riverside Road!' April looked at her blankly. 'I couldn't send you *north* of the river; it's always been . . . well, you know' – April didn't know – 'and it's gone downhill even more since Shaw's Mill shut down.' Martha shuddered, as if the north side of the River Easter were the ghettos of New York or a Dickensian slum. She peered closely at the paper. 'Laburnum Villa. I'm sure that's dear little Miss Hudson from the church choir – now she would look after you like a mother. I wonder why she has a

44

room to let?' Her face clouded. 'Oh! I suppose poor Miss Semple has been taken into St Vincent's again.' She lowered her voice. 'Nerves, poor thing. And they mustn't expect her to leave this time if her room's to let. Still, it's an ill wind. You'd do very well with Miss Hudson. I'd go there first if I were you. Would you like me to ring her up for you?'

'Och, I'd rather just rap the door and see for myself,' April said, pocketing the list. Martha's matchmaking clearly did not stop at the romantic. April would have to be careful that her boss didn't try to find *her* a fella. She must lose no chance to remind her that she was a career woman with no thoughts of marriage at all. Ever.

Life looked much more promising after a good tea with an egg, and a thick slice of fruit cake to finish. She'd had it in a tea shop called The Copper Kettle, round the corner from the bureau, beside a very new-looking cinema. She'd check that out once she was settled; she loved a good picture and there was no cinema in Lisnacashan – you had to go all the way to Cookstown. Now, fed and watered, she felt ready for the business of room-hunting.

She looked at the map Martha had sketched. The streets she recommended were not far away, beyond the station and on the other side of a small park that presumably gave the area its name. They were attractive streets, rising steeply uphill from the park; well-spaced solid Victorian villas, mostly semi-detached in the soft yellowish local stone, only slightly sooty round the edges. All three houses advertising rooms looked the soul of respectability, with starched lace curtains at shining windows and polished brass door-knockers on freshly painted doors. They all had gardens, bare now apart from neat crocuses and the occasional burst of daffodil, with views over the park. April had feared having to live in a garret in a rooming house with smelly dark passages and a terrifying bathroom. Even standing on the pavement and looking in, she knew these houses would smell of lavender and furniture polish. In every one of them, she guessed, was a motherly genteel landlady, a widow trying to make ends meet. Someone like Aunt Kathleen – though hopefully not *too* like Aunt Kathleen. Someone who would make April comfortable and watch out for her coming home in the evenings. Someone who would tell her the gossip of the town and take a great interest in her job. Someone who would encourage her to feel at home. Someone who would never want her to leave.

Laburnum Villa was at the top of the hill and had a conservatory at the side which reminded her of a baby version of the Palm House at Belfast's Botanic Gardens, which she had visited on a Sunday school excursion. A small white-haired woman – dear little Miss Hudson she supposed – was winding wool round the back of a cane chair and April saw herself, year after year, helping to wind that wool. It was what spinsters did. And she would be so lonely that she might be glad to stay with dear little Miss Hudson and wind wool and hear about what the vicar had said and who was dead and how the bread hadn't risen this morning. It might be better than going upstairs to a room furnished with Miss Hudson's parents' Victorian furniture that was too good to throw out, and the ghost of poor Miss Semple, who had clearly gone mad as a rat. I'm only twenty-eight, she thought. I'm not old enough for this. I want . . . I don't know what I want, but not this.

She pulled out the advertisement for the despised Riverside Road: *Studio Room to let; suit artist or writer.* Of course she was neither, but it sounded so romantic. She and Evelyn, before Evelyn had started walking out with the impossible Maurice Kenny, used to imagine sharing a flat in a big city – Belfast or even Dublin – and having their own front door, and eating chips and knowing interesting people, the sort of people that didn't live in Lisnacashan. Only Evelyn hadn't *really* wanted it, not enough to say no to Maurice's promise of a new bungalow behind his daddy's farm on the Cookstown Road. 'It was just a silly dream,' she'd told April when April accused her of reneging on their plans. 'It's not what real grown-up people do. And sure when are you ever going to leave your mammy and daddy?'

Well, I have left them, April thought now, and I am a real grown-up person.

She turned and walked down the hill, through the park and over the bridge to the wrong side of town. And immediately felt better even though it was all higgledy-piggledy and throughother and the smoke hit the back of her throat and made her cough. A jungle of crowded terraced streets led uphill from Riverside Road in a maze of blackened stone and rough cobbles. Martha's description of Riverside Road had prepared her for a prostitute outside every house and maybe a gangster hiding in every alley with some rioting unemployed mill workers to add to the craic. In fact it was a long, straggling road, separated from the riverbanks by dilapidated black iron railings.

April looked through the railings down to the water below. It was murky, but no more so than the Blackwater, which nosed through Lisnacashan on its way to Lough Neagh. A moorhen flicked its tail in the water and made her smile. There were buildings only on the right-hand side of the road, some tall houses which must once have been grand, and a few low-rise industrial buildings. Two shrieking girls swung on a lamppost outside a shabby public house, The Queen's Head, plaits flying round their heads, and a gaggle of small boys took noisy turns with one bicycle doing wheelies in an alleyway. I wonder could I get a bicycle? April thought. She and Evelyn used to manage with one between them, giving each other backies. She felt for a moment the solid roughness of Evelyn's woolly jumper in her fingers, Evelyn's silky red hair blowing back into her mouth. How much would a bicycle cost?

It was obvious which building was the former Shaw's Mill; it loomed over the street, behind a brick wall, dark and huge, five times the size of McVey's in Lisnacashan, its rows of windows blank, the lower-floor ones roughly boarded up. April shivered as she passed the rusting iron gates. Was she daft to think about living here? It was a good few steps down the ladder of respectability from Church Street in Lisnacashan, lower even than Eupatoria Street. But maybe the room would be taken already and that would make up her mind.

Number eleven must be that tall, thin house with the bright yellow door inside an open porch, just past the mill. *Studio* had sounded bohemian, and she was disappointed at the ordinariness of the house. The only encouraging thing was the welcoming yellow door. Number eleven must once have been the same mellow sandstone as the houses in Parkgate but was now streaked with black. She crossed the road for a better look. The house was very narrow and she guessed there would be no garden behind, just a yard. She rang the doorbell. For a long time there was no response, but she wasn't one for giving up, so she pressed harder and longer and was at last rewarded with the sound of battering footsteps on wooden stairs, and from behind the door a very cross voice.

'I'm coming! For Christ's sake! Give me a chance.'

The door was yanked open.

'What?' The woman standing in the doorway pushed an impatient hand across her face. The hand was inky and now the face was too. April thought it wise not to mention this; the woman looked flustered enough. She was maybe thirty-five, with brown curly hair twisted into a loose knot on top of her head, and wore a rough sort of homespun-looking djibbah in a colour April wouldn't have been seen dead in and would struggle to name. Mud, or baby's boke. It contrasted with the bright paisley scarf in reds and rusts twirled round her neck.

April looked down at the newspaper cutting in her hand. 'I've come about the room?'

'Oh. Gosh. The room. I'd forgotten. Is it still in?' She squinted at the advertisement. 'I must have paid for a month. Or maybe Fabian did. He's desperate to keep me from penury.'

'So it's gone?' April said, with more relief than disappointment. Maybe she would indeed cross the river again and call on dear little Miss Hudson. Winding wool wasn't *that* bad.

'What?' The woman seemed to come from a long way away to focus on April. 'Oh. No. It's still there. Nobody wants it. You won't want it.'

'How d'you know? I often want the things other people don't.' She heard Evelyn's voice: *Honestly, April, why do you never just want what normal people want?*

'Really?' The woman blinked and looked at April with more interest. 'Well, I suppose I can show you. You won't take it though. There's not much of a view and the stairs are a killer.' She had a husky voice, as if getting over a cold. 'I'll show you the room, but I haven't dusted it or anything,' she went on. 'Mrs Gibney, my char, won't go above the first floor. Says she gets dizzy. I did dust at first, but nobody came, and then the ones that did didn't like it, and I hate dusting so I thought, bugger them, I've got better things to do.' She turned and led the way down the dark, narrow hall, which smelt faintly of damp, and up the uncarpeted stairs. She walked briskly, as if the sooner to get rid of this interruption.

I don't have to live here, April thought. I can go and be coddled by dear little Miss Hudson. I bet *she* dusts every day – och, no, sure she'll have a maid, or at the very least a better char than this Mrs Gibney. Eleven Riverside Road was not dirty, and the walls were newly distempered – April could smell fresh paint – but it didn't *shine*. There were bookcases on the landing, stuffed with all sorts of books. She recognised some of her own old favourites, Jane Austen and the Brontës as well as a whole shelf of modern novels and some children's books: *Swallows and Amazons*, and a whole set of the Forest Fay books. So this woman had children? She had mentioned a man – Florian? Husband presumably. She didn't wear a wedding ring. Maybe she was too advanced in her ideas. Well, April didn't want to live in a family house. Bad enough living with her own family. There were a lot of paintings in a squiggling, scribbly style. Modern art, identified April wisely. She didn't think there was anything like this in the whole of Lisnacashan. She wondered if the woman had done the paintings herself; maybe it had been paint on her hands, not ink. Not that it mattered; she wasn't going to take the room.

At the first turn of the stairs the woman threw open a door. 'Bathroom,' she said. 'I don't get up early so you could have it to yourself in the mornings. I like a good soak at night, but I suppose we could have a rota.'

April peered round the door with trepidation, but the bathroom was perfectly respectable, with a new-looking shower attachment over the bath and faded but pretty green tiles on the walls.

'The WC's next door,' the woman said, opening that door too. Again, the facilities were modest but clean. April had a feeling dear little Miss Hudson would have had a crocheted crinoline lady to cover up the lavatory paper, like Aunt Kathleen.

'How many people live here?' April asked.

She looked surprised. 'Oh, just me.' She smiled for the first time and rubbed her forehead, leaving another faint smudge of ink. 'Sorry. I'm like a bear with a sore head when someone disturbs my writing – not your fault. I'm Felicity. Felicity Carr.'

'April McVey.'

'From – is it Northern Ireland?'

'It is, aye.' She was impressed; mostly the English thought she was Scottish or just screwed up their faces and said they couldn't understand her.

At the bottom of what were clearly the stairs to the attic, Felicity paused. 'You go ahead,' she said. 'It's ridiculous for me to stand breathing down your neck and pointing out the facilities. You've got eyes in your head. Rent ten shillings a week; that includes hot water and light but no meals.'

I'm not taking it, April thought, but I might as well go and have a wee nosy, see what ten shillings a week buys you in Easterbridge. The stairs were steep and creaky; she didn't hold out much hope for the room. An attic, probably once a maid's room, would be small and cold, crammed with unwanted cast-off furniture and peeling floral wallpaper in a pattern too big and dark for its poky size. It would be redolent of chamber pots and ancient sweat.

But as she opened the door she remembered that the room had been described as a *studio*. And it looked like one. It was large, painted a gleaming white that made it seem even bigger. The floorboards were scrubbed and polished, and there was a minimum of furniture, also painted white – a large bed with a new-looking striped mattress, humped in the middle, an easy chair, a bedside table and a large desk. A tiny fireplace was furnished with a gas ring like the one at the office. You couldn't cook on it beyond boiling a kettle but presumably she could use Felicity's kitchen? There was no wardrobe, but louvred wooden doors, painted the same clean white as the walls, made a basic but serviceable cupboard into the eaves, and the wall facing it was shelved from floor to ceiling. Plenty of room for books and clothes.

She crossed the room to look out of the single dormer window. Not much of a view, Felicity had said, but being two flights up and near the river there was sky and a sense of space and air as well as rooftops and chimneys. If she got the angle right, she could see a bit of the river. She imagined herself writing to Mammy and Aunt Kathleen and Evelyn: *I have the top floor of a big house by the river*. Now didn't that sound grand! This was not a room where she could slide into being Poor Miss McVey.

She ran down the stairs to where Felicity was waiting.

'Och, it's lovely; I'll take it!' she said. 'I mean' – she tried to sound businesslike – 'I like the room and I can furnish you with references. I've a letter from the minister. I've only just moved to Easterbridge; I'm helping to run an office' – she was suddenly shy about saying she worked in a marriage bureau – 'but my boss, my business partner I should say—'

Felicity waved that aside. 'Don't worry. As long as you're quiet when I'm writing. Can you pay a month in advance?'

April nodded. She wouldn't be paid until the end of the month, but she'd been saving a shilling here and half a crown there ever since she'd started work. *Running away money*, she thought of it, though not even Evelyn knew, and when it turned out that Daddy had ruined them, she'd been glad of her own stash sewn inside a cushion on her bedside chair. And God forgive her, but she hadn't let on about it even to Mammy.

She thought of something else. 'Oh, your advert said *writer or artist*. I'm not exactly either. Does that matter?'

Felicity shook her head. 'I said that because I didn't want some shopgirl who would hang stockings over the bath and leave rouge stains on the basin, or some sad middle-aged typist who would want to make a pal of me. I want someone who can just do her own thing. Actually, I was rather hoping for a man.' She laughed at April's face. 'Oh, not as a *man*. But I thought a man would be more likely to keep himself to himself, not want to bother with me.'

April looked at her. She was untidy, with her messy curly hair and inky face, and honest to God that djibbah did nothing for her figure, but her skin glowed and her eyes were a clear cool blue with thick dark lashes. Was she really so unaware of her appearance that she thought a male lodger would be too?

'Fabian will be relieved, though,' Felicity went on. 'He's terribly old-fashioned.'

April remembered that this Fabian had paid for the advertisement and was keen to keep Felicity solvent. 'Is Fabian your fella?'

Felicity laughed. 'Good lord no! My big brother. Very sweet, but thinks it's about 1910. I don't know how we managed to come from the same family. He's the one who sorted out the room for me: painted it and put the shelves up. He's handy that way.'

April forbore to say that that might be why the attic looked better than the rest of the house.

They made arrangements for her to call back with the rent next day and to move in as soon as she'd bought what she needed. Felicity made no mention of linen, clearly she was expected to provide that for herself, but was sure it would help the room feel more like her own. Felicity showed her the kitchen on the way out, a cavernous room where she could easily make herself an egg in the evenings without being in the way. There was even a refrigerator.

Isn't it wonderful, she thought, walking back through the dark streets to the Blossom Temperance Hotel. A room of my own!

Eight

Riverside Road!

Martha, tearing up old invoices from 1928 – why had she kept them so long? – didn't try to hide her horror. What on earth would the neighbours be like? April was such a puppyish type, too; no doubt she'd be best pals with all sorts of unsavoury characters before the end of the week. And it wasn't snobbery; she felt responsible for the girl, and she couldn't bear the thought of her having to walk past that awful old mill every evening. Anyone could be lurking.

But April was stubborn. 'It's grand,' she said. 'I like it.'

'But who is this Miss Carr?' Martha did not know everyone in town, especially not that side of the river, but still, she couldn't help feeling that that those she did not must be somehow unknowable.

'She's a writer,' April said. 'I don't know what of, I never asked, but I'm sure it's something respectable. Maybe she'll write an article about us and make us famous.'

'There'll be no need for that,' Martha said stiffly.

'Och come on, Martha.' April grinned. 'Remember those seventeen weddings in 1926? What if we beat that in 1934 – well, 1935, I suppose they'll hardly marry immediately – would you not like a nice big spread in the *Recorder*?'

'Oh, she writes for the *Recorder*? I must ask Mark what she's like.'

'Well, no, not as far as I know,' April admitted. 'Sure I was thinking more of *The Times*, anyway.' She grinned, and Martha, a little uncertainly at first, grinned back.

No, it wasn't snobbery, and it wasn't just a sense of responsibility. She liked the girl. She was so much younger, it was almost like . . . well, of course not like having a daughter, she wasn't that young, but maybe a little sister. And she would not have wanted her sister walking up Riverside Road.

She had decided to close the bureau for the rest of the month, or rather, to tell any prospective clients that their list was full just now, but that they would be in touch at the start of April, immediately after Easter.

'That makes us sound very successful,' she told April, 'and it keeps them keen.'

April sounded unconvinced. 'What if the notion goes off them?'

Martha laughed. 'The *notion*? It's not as if they wake up one day and think, *Ooh, what shall I do today? I know, I'll contact a marriage bureau and potentially change my whole life. Oh dear, it's closed today; oh well, I'll not bother then. As you were.*'

April giggled.

'When people come to see us,' Martha explained, 'they've often been thinking about it for months. Years.'

'I suppose.' April's face brightened. 'And it will be properly spring then. And my birthday.'

'And "In the Spring a young man's fancy lightly turns to thoughts of love",' Martha quoted.

'Och, I was thinking more that the place'll look better in the sunshine. And if you let me paint the door to the street like I want to, there'll be better drying.'

By Thursday the telephone in the now-spotless office had rung only four times – two wrong numbers and one woman, Bertha Bell, asking to be removed from the books because she had met the loveliest chap at a Baptist convention, and really it was as well she had because the so-called men the bureau had suggested for her had been impossible, quite dreadful, and if she had known she would never have wasted her money, and she would be grateful if Martha would destroy all her records because if her Norman were ever to know that she had signed up to a marriage bureau she would be absolutely mortified. In fact she would prefer it if Martha would return any information and she would see to its destruction personally.

'Honestly,' Martha said, replacing the receiver after telling Miss Bell firmly and politely that this was against company policy – she had not needed to relay the conversation to April because Bertha Bell had a most carrying voice – 'does she think we publish our old files in the *Easterbridge Recorder*?'

'What do you do with them?' April had started going through the filing cabinets by now, which had pink index cards for the women and blue for the men. 'I mean, this isn't everything, is it – all the way back to 1924?'

'No. I move anything over two years old to that old filing cabinet in the corner,' Martha said. 'I never quite like to destroy them. If you look under *B* you should find her.'

April riffled quickly through the *B*s and came up triumphantly with a pink card. 'Miss Bertha Adeline Bell,' she pronounced. She scanned the card and gave a snort of laughter. 'No,' she said. 'You definitely can't send that back to her.'

The card for Miss Bertha Bell said, in the space for *Notes/ Office Use Only* at the bottom: *Not greatly troubled with either personal hygiene or self-awareness.*

'Was that Hilda?' April asked, wide-eyed. 'That's a bit pass-remarkable.'

'Er, no, I believe that was me,' Martha said, remembering the notes she had made about the applicants for April's job.

The fourth call came when Martha was downstairs using the small lavatory they shared with the jeweller on the ground floor. She heard the telephone ring from the bottom of the stairs and forced herself not to hurry despite the little niggle of anxiety it sparked. What if April's telephone manner failed to prepossess? What if the caller didn't understand her? It wasn't always easy to make voices out on the phone and whoever was calling would not be expecting an Ulster accent. What if April tried to engage them in inconsequential chatter and told them all about Lisnacashan? Well, she would have to learn.

She entered the office just as April was replacing the receiver. 'Och, you just missed the poor wee woman,' she said. 'I'd say she was bad with her nerves, that one, no harm to her.'

Martha managed not to groan. 'Who was it?' she asked.

April handed her a scrap of paper. 'I've it all written down here,' she said. 'A Mrs Primrose Lewis. She nearly ate me because I said *Miss*. Sure I never heard her right; she'd need to speak up.'

'Oh dear, yes. Mrs Lewis is soft-spoken. She's been on the books for – oh, it must be a year. But we just can't get her suited, though I don't think Hilda tried very hard. Maybe you'll have better luck.'

'Fussy?' April asked.

Martha hesitated, caught between honesty and kindness. 'If it were only that!' she said. 'No, she's the opposite of fussy. Gosh, that sounds as though I'm suggesting she's of easy virtue. I don't mean that at all. She's a widow in her fifties. Only child out in Australia. She's desperately lonely and thinks another husband will be the answer. And that's . . . well, it's not a very good starting point.'

'But sure isn't that what they all want? Isn't that what yous—I mean *we*, are all about?'

'Of course they all want to meet someone and eventually marry. But some people – some women I'm sorry to say – give off a sort of aura of desperation and it puts men off. I haven't many men on the books who are looking for someone like Mrs Lewis, someone older that is, and I've introduced her to all of them. She claimed to like all of them – well, apart from the poor old Colonel – but . . .'

'They didn't like her?'

Martha spread her hands. 'That's about it. She's too eager to please, too obviously desperate. And she's not' – again she chose her words carefully – 'overburdened by physical charms.'

'Nor financial ones, I assume,' April said drily. 'If she was a rich widow she'd be beating them off with a stick.'

'Well, no. She's just a nice, ordinary, lonely middle-aged woman. I'll wait and ring her up tomorrow.'

'Och, get it over with or she'll think I never gave you the message. You don't want your clients thinking you've another assistant that's as much use as a chocolate teapot. And talking of tea, I'll make us a wee cuppa and you can look forward to one of these nice Eccles cakes I bought.'

The conversation with Mrs Lewis went much as it always did, leaving Martha in great need of that wee cuppa.

'Maybe we'll get an influx of nice widowers when they see our story in the *Recorder*,' April said when Martha reported back to her, accepting a cup rather wearily.

'Even if we do, they aren't going to like her unless she, well, changes,' Martha said. 'But people don't, do they? Not at that age.' She wondered, as she said it, if she had changed much herself since the days when she had married Second Lieutenant Gordon Hart. Sometimes she felt exactly the same inside; at others she barely recognised that hopeful young woman.

'Anyway,' she said. 'You told me you wanted challenge and responsibility so I'm going to let you have a go with her.'

April perked up like a dog hearing its name. 'Do you really want me to?'

'You can't do worse than I have,' Martha said. 'I've booked her in for an appointment once we reopen, and you can do your best.'

'Fair play to you, Martha. I won't let you down.' April refreshed both their cups – Martha had never drunk so much tea in her life; even when she had been in the office with Hilda, which had not been often in the last year of Mother's life, there had been a great deal less chatter and tea – and changed the subject. 'Martha, could you tell me where I could buy bed linen? Not too dear.'

'You mean this Miss Carr isn't providing linen?'

'She said her brother sorted out the room.'

'Her brother? How very odd.' How very unseemly, but what could you expect from Riverside Road? 'But her brother doesn't live with her?'

April shook her head.

'He must be a bachelor,' Martha said.

'How d'you know?'

Martha smiled wisely. 'Think about it, dear. A married brother would have asked his wife's advice. And *she* would not have omitted such a detail. Men aren't quite as practical as women, poor dears. Their minds are on business affairs and the like. But I'd have expected better from this Miss Carr.'

'Och, being a writer, Miss Carr's mind is likely above sheets and bedside rugs,' April said.

'Well, it ought not to be. Though perhaps she would be well suited to a rather down to earth, practical sort of man? You did say she was unmarried? We had a delightful fellow, a Mr Henry Barrett, a cabinet maker, sign up in the new year – that's always a busy time – and we haven't managed to suit him yet. I did think of introducing him to that Bertha Bell as it happens, but she said she wouldn't consider a tradesman. Silly girl. His work is exquisite; he sells to Hepton's on the Coaldale Road, which is very high-end. I imagine writers and people like that are not so bothered by class distinctions.'

'I don't think she's looking for a man of any class,' April said. 'She seems happy as Larry the way she is.'

In Martha's experience, women on their own were seldom as happy as Larry; the more content they seemed, the harder they were working at pretending. But April was younger and less experienced. Look how she insisted herself that she had no interest in marriage. *The lady doth protest too much, methinks,* Martha thought, but she hoped April would go on protesting at least for long enough to help her get the bureau back on an even keel.

'My house is coming down with unused bed linen,' Martha said. She hesitated and went on, 'Even though Gordon and I never had the chance to set up home together, people gave us wedding presents, and an awful lot of those were sheets and pillowcases. I have enough linen to furnish a small hotel. I'd be delighted to give you what you need. You save your money.' Her assistant might be living in Riverside Road, but at least she would be sleeping in the best linen. There was a lovely blanket too, knitted for Martha by her Aunt Maisie, which she had never used. She would give that to April too. She liked to think of her snuggled up in it. For all her enthusiasm for it, an attic in Riverside Road didn't sound suitable at all.

Nine

Somehow, with her things unpacked, the attic looked more, rather than less, bare. April tried not to feel disheartened as she made up the bed. This is what you wanted, she reminded herself. The white, which had seemed so bright and fresh, struck now as cold and stark, the little colour provided by the spines of her own few battered books on the shelf only accentuating it.

Martha's bed linen was plain and serviceable but of the very best quality, carefully packed with tissue between the folds, and smelling faintly of lavender. Even now, with the bed made up and the spare sheets and pillowcases on a shelf in the cupboard, the lavender scent hung in the air, sweet but melancholy. She imagined Martha, younger than April was now, married and widowed within months, packing away all her hopes for the future along with the sheets, protecting them with lavender and tissue. She thought of the sheets sitting in a linen press in Martha's home all through the years, while her brothers came home from the war and her father died, and she looked after her mother and ran her business and then buried her mother too. God love her, it was sad when you thought about it.

The blankets were thick and serviceable, the colour of dun ponies, except for one, hand-knitted in squares of pink, mauve and blue. It would be, April thought, spreading it over the bed, like having bluebells in her room. She had not brought any pictures or photos except a little framed snap of herself and Evelyn at the harvest fair the year after the war, which had sat on her bedside table since she was fourteen. Evelyn had one similar. At least, she had had; she probably didn't now. All she seemed interested in was her bungalow and her wee son Robbie.

She had expected Felicity to be there when she moved in, but Felicity had left her latchkey in a flowerpot by the front door with a note in violet ink and a dashing hand: *Out all day, but see you this evening – or maybe not*, she had added, signing herself *FC*, and it was unclear whether she considered it to be herself or April who might have better things to do. Well, April reminded herself, you didn't want dear little Miss Hudson fussing over you and making you tea and straightening your counterpane, so you needn't whinge. And fair play to Felicity, she had left a kettle, a blue china teapot and a few cups on the hearth so at least she could make tea – or she could once she had bought tea, milk, and a few things of that sort. There was bound to be a corner shop. She grabbed her bag from the hook on the back of the door, lifted her coat and umbrella – it had been threatening rain all morning and now bad-tempered squalls rattled the window. She shoved an old red woollen tam over her hair, noting that she would need it cut soon, it was losing the 'bob' shape she had worn for years, and started down the steep stairs.

She was tempted, though she didn't give in, to push open the two doors on the first floor, one of which must be Felicity's bedroom, and one, she guessed, a study. She remembered that when Felicity had answered the door on Monday, she had been writing and had come down the stairs. Miss Marple, she thought, and then, distracted by the bookcases that lined the landing, she had a proper look. There were some new novels she hadn't read yet – the latest Agatha Christie, maybe that was what put

Miss Marple in her head, and a few Dorothy L. Sayers, and some earnest tomes about politics and economics that April couldn't imagine wanting to read. One bookcase was mostly children's books – that was more like it! She recognised some of the school stories she and Evelyn had been obsessed with, Angela Brazil and Elsie Oxenham; and the Forest Fay series by Cicily Rafter – Mammy liked those, said they were sweet and wholesome, and April had bought her the last one for her birthday. She flicked through one now, but it looked too whimsical for her taste. She preferred something with more action or a bit of a laugh.

A heavy banging on the front door made her start. Probably a salesman or a delivery. But such an impatient bashing! And then, as she reached the top of the stairs, the letterbox opened and a high imperious voice shouted in.

'Aunty Fee! Stop pretending you're out! I can see your feet. Let me in. It's raining a monsoon out here. I'll catch pneumonia. I probably already have.'

April ran down the stairs and opened the door, and a small girl in a brown school uniform burst in. She stared at April with wide greenish eyes. 'Who are you?'

'I'm the lodger.'

'Oh.' She dismissed this as beneath her notice. 'I suppose Aunty Fee's scribbling?' She went tearing towards the stairs, shouting, 'Aunty Fee, you have to come. It's an emergency and I don't care if you're writing.'

'She's out,' April said. She was not in the least fazed by high-handed wee madams. She had been one herself and had spent most of her working life with girls. In fact she felt quite at home when the girl stamped her foot and said, 'Well, the beastly mean cow has no right to be out! I need her. I *need* her!' Her face crumpled and she burst into noisy, snattery tears. The tears evidently mortified her because she turned her back on April.

'Here.' April fished in her pocket for a handkerchief and waved it over one shaking shoulder. 'It's clean.' As the girl took it, April said, 'Isn't it funny how people always say that? You'd hardly hand someone a dirty hanky!'

'I would.' She blew her nose noisily. 'I'd jolly well give this one to Aunty Fee and serve her flipping well right.'

'I was on my way out,' April said. 'I've just moved in and I'm dying for a cup of tea. I suppose I could leave you here, or' – the girl looked up with a sudden flash of hope – 'you could come with me and tell me what the emergency is. Or not.' She shrugged. 'You could just have a cup of tea.'

'And a bun?' The girl gave a sudden grin that transformed her sullen face and made her look like an expectant kitten, all wide eyes and pointed chin. 'You talk oddly. Are you Scottish?'

'Northern Irish. I take it you know the area? Is there a wee corner shop nearby?'

'A corner shop?' She drooped in disgust. 'When you said a cup of tea I thought you meant a tea shop. Not a dull old cup of tea *here*.' She looked round the hallway of number eleven as if no girl had ever been so ill-used as to be expected to drink tea in such an establishment.

'I suppose I meant in my room,' April said, 'but you're right, a tea shop would be more festive. You'll have to lead the way though.'

It was not, as the girl had claimed, a monsoon, but the rain was sufficiently unpleasant for April to say, 'The nearest place will do. It needn't be very nice.'

'Really?' The girl looked delighted. 'Can it be that place on Townsend Street that smells of cat and keeps the tea boiling in an urn all day? Aunty Fee always says you could catch God-knows-what from there.'

'Well . . . Maybe not that one. I don't want to catch anything.'

The girl sighed. 'I do. I long to catch scarlet fever or . . . or diphtheria or . . . I don't know, galloping consumption. Do people still get that or is it just in books?'

'Och, I think they do. But sure why would you want to catch anything?' She summoned all the dignity she had had as Miss McVey of McVey's, or indeed Miss McVey of the True Minds Marriage Bureau (formerly Mrs Hart's Matrimonial Bureau), and tried to sound severe. 'That's a silly way to talk. What's your name, anyway?'

'Prudence.'

April laughed. 'Is it hard having a name that's a virtue? Living up to it, I mean?'

'I don't try,' Prudence said with scorn. 'What's yours?'

'April.'

'Were you born in April?'

'I was.' And Felicity's name, she thought, meant happiness. Not so much a virtue as, well, what was happiness? A state? An aspiration? 'Anyway, Prudence, why would you want to catch something?'

'School,' she said, as if the answer were obvious. 'If I caught something I wouldn't have to go back for simply ages.'

'Here we are,' April said, stopping at a tea shop on the bridge and ignoring that silly remark. 'It doesn't look like you'd catch anything here.'

'The Bridge Tea Rooms,' Prudence read from the sign above the bow window. 'It looks grannyish.' Then she saw April's face and said quickly, 'I mean, lovely.'

Installed at a table in a steamy coffee-ish fug, April passed Prudence a slightly squashed iced bun which she broke into with enthusiasm before the tea had had a chance even to think about brewing.

'Sorry,' she said, through a mouthful of crumbs, 'but I'm starving. I left before brekker; I couldn't risk being spotted at the station if I'd left it any later.' She smiled with satisfaction. 'I should think they're all frantic with worry by now, wouldn't you? Serve them right. Serve Daddy right too.'

Light was starting to dawn. 'Prudence, d'you mean you've come here from your boarding school? That you've run away?'

'Yes.' Prudence sounded very proud. There was no trace of the tears now.

'But people will be worried about you.'

'Good. I want them to worry. I did warn them,' she said patiently as if April were rather stupid. 'I said I wouldn't stay and I didn't. I never do. They should know by now.'

'You mean you've done this before?'

'Heaps of times. Well, last time I only got as far as the end of the hockey pitch. Stupid old Miss Belcher caught me.' She made a little moue of distaste and poured out her tea without asking April if she would like hers poured. Whatever they taught her at school it wasn't manners, April thought, and then wondered how she had come to have such middle-aged thoughts.

If only she had headed out to find tea five minutes earlier; if she hadn't stopped to nosy at Felicity's bookcases! Prudence would have found the house empty and been obliged to go somewhere else – home, April supposed – and she wouldn't have had to bother with her. Now she was involved, whether she liked it or not. Should she contact the school? Or Prudence's family? That would be better, let them deal with it. She was only the lodger.

'Why did you go to your aunt's home?'

'I knew she wouldn't flap,' Prudence said, 'because she wouldn't really care. I mean she'd care about being disrupted – she hates having her work disturbed – but she wouldn't fuss. Daddy always fusses. He's hopeless. He hasn't a clue how to bring me up.'

April was tempted to agree. 'What about your mother?'

'Dead.'

'I'm sor—'

'It was ages ago. I was only eleven.' Her eyes dared April to sympathise, and April remembered how much she had hated people fussing when Daddy died.

'What age are you now?' She looked about twelve and April was surprised when she said fourteen. 'And why did you run away?'

Prudence looked down at her empty plate. 'I'd love another bun,' she said hopefully. 'That one was minuscule.'

'If you're hungry you can have toast and an egg,' April said firmly. 'That'll stick to your ribs better. And before you have anything you can tell me why you ran away.'

'You'll think it's silly.' For the first time since they had left the house, Prudence seemed unsure of herself.

'Sure it's no odds what I think. *You* mustn't have thought it was silly.'

'No. It was unfair. It was beastly unfair.' She had a carrying, cut-glass voice which made one or two women at adjoining tables look round.

'You don't have a local accent,' April observed.

Prudence sighed. 'I've mostly lived in London. We only came here last year after Aunty Fee did. Daddy thought we should have some family around. Daddy grew up nearby, but Mummy said she wouldn't live in the provinces for anything.'

'Are you close to your aunt?'

Prudence gave a huge sigh. 'Not really. When I was little she was mostly travelling. She looked after me for a little while when Mummy was sick but then she buggered back off abroad.' She looked up at April from under lowered lashes to see if she would react to her language, but April was used to girls' bravado. 'Don't you think that was mean? She said she had to go, but she could write her soppy old books anywhere.'

April merely raised an eyebrow. 'And you ran away because . . .?'

'The hockey team.'

'What about the hockey team?'

'Well, I'm on it. At least I'm in the third eleven which is jolly good for a lower fourth – all the others are lower fifth at least.' April tried to look impressed. 'And I'm the best player. Last week, against St Monica's in the semi-final of the county shield, I scored four goals.'

'Fancy.'

'And today's the final and they wouldn't let me play.' Her voice rose in a wail of indignation and April hoped she wouldn't start to cry again.

'Why not?'

Prudence waved her hand with a dismissive air. 'Oh. They said I bullied one of the lower seconds. Wendy Beechcroft.' Her face twisted in scorn. 'Silly little ass. I didn't bully her. She sits at my table and honestly, April, she's such a cry-baby. I teased her a little – saying the tapioca was frogspawn and the jam was blood – the sort of thing everyone says, only she believed me, and she stopped eating and she started fainting in prayers and being sick – honestly, such *fuss*! – and then she blabbed to Matron that it was because of me, and I got a bad conduct mark, which means you're automatically out of matches. I went to see Miss Willard – she's the head, awful old thing with a moustache. Ugh. Anyway, I pointed out that I was the best on the team and that it was punishing the school to leave me out – Nina Roberts is reserve and she's hopeless – and she said, oh, a lot of nonsense. Anyway, I wasn't going to watch the silly old match and cheer for Nina Roberts, so here I am.'

April shook her head.

'I knew you'd think it was silly.'

68

'Not so much silly. I think you behaved very badly. I wouldn't have let you play either.'

'You sound like a teacher.'

'I used to be in charge of factory girls. Your age, some of them. I ran a wee club for them. You'll need to give me your phone number. I can ring up your father – I'll ask to use the phone here – and he can come and collect you.'

'No! I mean,' she added quickly, 'we aren't on the phone.' But she blushed and looked down at the table and April knew it was a lie.

'I'm not giving you a choice. Your aunty won't be home till late. I'm not looking after you, and I can't let you loose in her house. I'm sure she wouldn't like it.'

'So?' The pointed chin was up. 'I could just run away from here and go . . . anywhere.'

'You've no money.'

Prudence narrowed her eyes. 'Who says?'

'You were hungry. If you'd had more than your train fare you'd have bought something to eat at the station.'

'I might not have had time.' But it was obvious April had guessed right and Prudence tried a different tack. 'If you get Daddy to come here I'll scream the place down.'

April gave her a withering look. 'Really? At your age? Och, in that case I'm taking you home right now.' She drained her cup and stood up. 'Come on. Nobody knows me in Easterbridge, but they will soon, and I don't want to be associated with anything so undignified.' She shuddered at the thought of Martha finding out. Those women at the next table, with the prim hats, looked just the sort she'd be friendly with.

The fight had gone out of Prudence, possibly she realised that she had no option, and she trailed along beside April in the rain, silent apart from giving directions. Over the bridge they trudged and skirted the park railings; April recognised the area as the one Martha had been so keen for her to live in. She couldn't help being curious about Prudence's home. She assumed her father was the brother who had fixed up the white room. Old-fashioned, Felicity had called him, but it was not an old-fashioned room.

'What does your daddy do, Prudence?' she asked as they turned into a short avenue of solid detached houses in the local stone. Up here, above the smoke of the town, it was still warm creamy yellow with only the faintest edgings of grey.

'He's a solicitor. So dull.'

'But important.' She remembered Martha saying that Hilda had snaffled herself a solicitor.

Prudence shrugged and pointed over the street. 'It's that one,' she said. 'With the white door. You don't have to stay,' she added. 'I can explain myself.'

It was tempting. She'd seen the wee madam home; she could always watch and make sure she went in. But she still didn't trust her, and anyway, part of her was curious to see this Fabian.

'Ah no,' she said. 'You won't get rid of me that easily.'

Ten

The doorbell never rang on Saturdays. It rarely rang on other days either, but at least he was in the office then, busy and focused, with the small noises of his secretary and the junior partner punctuating the quiet. Still, Fabian warned himself, don't expect it to be anyone really. He had grown up not far away, but his hopes of reconnecting with old pals had not been realised and he had not seemed to make new ones. It could only be Felicity and she never stayed long. Fabian thought she called from a sense of duty. Well, it would break up the day. Odd of her to walk in the rain, but she had always been a queer fish.

As he made his way up the hall he could see not one, but two figures through the frosted glass door panels. One was too tall to be Felicity and one too small. Collectors for the church jumble sale, then, or someone selling charity flags door-to-door. He was already putting his hand in his trouser pocket for the loose change that accumulated there – a habit which had driven Serena mad – as he drew open the door.

'Oh!'

It was Prudence, looking mulish, her hair unravelling from its plaits and her stockings splashed with dirty water. And, good

71

lord, was that a mistress with her? Had she been sent home in disgrace, under guard? Panic surged in his chest. What was he going to do with her? He was running out of schools.

'Prue?' He looked at the young woman beside her. She was tall and fair, in a red woollen tam and a slightly shabby grey coat. She didn't look like a schoolmarm. 'I'm sorry, I don't—?'

She pushed Prudence forward into the hallway. 'I'm April McVey,' she said, as he stood aside to let her in. Her voice tickled the edges of his memory. Unusual accent, but he had heard it recently. He looked closer. It couldn't be . . . Good lord, it was indeed! The girl who had snaffled his taxi. She smiled at him, a wide, frank, slightly toothy smile, without recognition. Should he say they had met before, or would she think it strange? She had clearly been mortified when she had realised her mistake over the taxi; it would be unkind to remind her. But what on earth was she doing on his doorstep with his daughter?

Before she could explain, or he could ask, Prudence herself burst out, 'I said I wouldn't stay at that rotten school – I *told* you. And you're not to send me back, and I don't care what Miss Willard says, and you know I wouldn't bully anyone. It's not fair; they always pick on me far worse than anyone else; they just don't like me – nobody likes me.' And she so far forgot herself as to stamp her foot.

'Well, no harm to you but would you blame them, carrying on like that?' The girl bit her lip and looked Fabian in the eye. 'Sorry, I shouldn't . . .'

Prudence gave her a sideways glance where, he thought, dislike fought it out with grudging respect.

'Right,' Fabian said. 'I'm sorry, Miss . . .?'

'April McVey,' she repeated. 'I'm your sister's lodger. At least I was in the middle of moving in when Madam here arrived. I just wanted to deliver her safely. I'll head on here.'

'I can't let you go. You've been so kind. You must let me—'

Her nostrils flared. 'Ah, now don't be offering to pay me for my trouble. D'you think I want a tip, like a . . . a chambermaid?' She backed away a few steps, and he cursed his habit of jingling the change in his pocket when he was nervous. And *why* was he nervous? It was ridiculous!

'—give you tea,' he finished. 'I can't let you go straight back out into that.' He nodded at the rain which was increasing in intensity. 'And it was very kind of you to look after Prudence.'

'I don't need looking after,' Prudence cut in. 'Daddy, we had tea in The Bridge but I'm awfully hungry. I only had a tiny bun.'

'You had more than you deserve.' He was careful to make his voice frosty. 'Go to your room and I'll see you later. I'd like to talk to Miss McVey.'

'In fairness,' April said, 'she is probably starving. Apparently she left before her breakfast. And it was only a wee bun, right enough.'

Prudence looked grateful, and annoyed to have to be grateful, all in one sulky expression.

'I'll send up some bread and butter,' Fabian said. 'Miss McVey, I can offer you something better than that. There's Madeira cake.' Mrs Perry baked a cake every Friday to make up for leaving him to his own devices all weekend.

'Grand.'

He showed her into the sitting room, a large, tidy, formal room in which he had never felt quite at home. The walls had been freshly painted before he had moved in, and though he might not have chosen that particular mushroom shade, he had not bothered to change it. In fact, he realised now, it was not a room on which he had impressed himself much at all. The furniture had been chosen by Serena for their London home. The only sign of his recent occupation was *The Times* folded on the small table by the settee, the crossword half done and a pen lying beside it. He saw April noticing the portrait of Serena above the fireplace. It wasn't a great likeness; Felicity had commissioned one of her artistic pals to do it, and he had been touched by the gesture without warming to the painting. It was awfully modern; there were orange streaks in her dark hair and her face was weirdly elongated. He preferred the wedding photo which sat on top of the piano – a piano that was never played these days, but that he had not been able to get rid of. A chess set sat on top of the piano too, a fine dust blooming on the heads of all the pieces – he must speak to Mrs Perry about that.

April shivered in her damp coat and Fabian said quickly, 'You must let me put a light to that fire. I hadn't bothered, just for myself.' Oh gosh, he thought, I don't want this young woman to think I'm one of those men who can't cope alone. Because I'm not. This room is pristine, not a speck of dust, apart from on the chess pieces. Yet it never seemed to welcome him home. He couldn't say what made it different from the house he had lived in with Serena, apart from the obvious absence of Serena herself. The furniture was the same, the arrangement of the room was more or less like their sitting room in London, but there was definitely something called a woman's touch. He hadn't appreciated it when Serena was alive but he knew it was missing now. He wished he had a different room to show Miss McVey into. Somewhere warm and homely and inviting. She would not want to linger here; she would drink a polite cup of tea and leave. And then he thought, honestly, how silly! If this young woman was lodging in that cheaply furnished attic at Felicity's, she couldn't be used to luxury.

The fire whooshed into life and he pulled up a chair to the hearth. 'Warm yourself, Miss McVey. I'll sort out tea. The housekeeper doesn't come in on Saturdays, but it won't take me a minute.'

It took considerably longer. He decided to bring up the promised bread and butter to Prudence; she would certainly come down and demand them if he did not. At the last moment he added a slice of cake to her tray. He was no longer used to carrying trays upstairs; there had been a good deal of it when Serena was ill. He left the tray outside Prudence's bedroom door. He could hear her within, opening drawers, probably changing out of the despised gym frock. Anxiety squeezed his heart – what had she done? What could he do with her?

'Tea outside your door,' he called. And then, when she didn't respond, 'Prue? Do I need to telephone the school? I imagine they don't know you're—'

'I don't care what you do,' she said from behind the door. 'But I'm *not* going back.'

It could wait. Perhaps Miss McVey would have some light to shed.

'I don't know how to thank you,' he said, when he returned to the sitting room bearing a tray daintier than the one he had carried up to Prudence. He had used the good Royal Albert and had remembered to rinse it first. Goodness knows when it had last had an outing. He was proud of himself for thinking of this.

'Sure I hadn't much choice.' She smiled at her cup. 'My granny had this china. No, what could I do? She arrived and I was there. It was nothing much. I'm used to girls.'

He looked at her with interest. 'You're a teacher?'

She shook her head. 'Dear lord, no, I wouldn't have the patience. I managed the office at my daddy's works – a garment factory. But that meant dealing with the machinists and their dramas. I started a club to keep them off the streets in the evenings.' She smiled reminiscently. 'They were a quare crowd.'

He noticed that her eyes were grey-blue, and one cheek softly pink in the warmth from the fire, though the other was pale.

The hair that peeked from the red tam was fair and shortish. She must be too warm in that woollen hat; it wasn't made for indoors. He wanted to ask her to take it off, but he didn't know how to without sounding silly. Or worse. Oh dear, when had he become so awkward?

'I'm not,' he said. 'Used to girls, I mean. I sometimes think it would be easier if she'd been a boy.' Or if she had stayed eleven. It was this growing up business that was so difficult.

'Rearing her on your own?' He must have looked startled at her frankness as she hurried to say, 'I'm sorry – she did say her mammy died.'

'Prue was only eleven,' he said. 'But Serena was ill for over a year. Felicity helped out for a while, but she's not maternal, it didn't work, and she didn't stay long. Prue was left to her own devices a good deal. We had a nurse so Serena wouldn't have to go into a nursing home. It was what she wanted, and I couldn't deny her of course. But I sometimes think it wasn't the best thing for the child. I've a feeling she saw a good deal more of Serena's suffering than we'd have wanted.' He shook his head as if to shake away the memories and offered April a slice of Madeira cake.

'My daddy died a few weeks ago,' she said. 'Heart attack. We'd no idea there was anything wrong, and I'd say that made it worse for my mammy. At least' – she frowned, as if anxious to get this right – 'Prudence hadn't that shock. She knew her mammy was sick. It might have made it easier. Not to bear, but to accept.' She bit into the cake. 'This is lovely. And sorry, I've only met you; I shouldn't be talking about people dying. I'm an awful eejit some-times. It's like talking about religion, isn't it? Mind you, they'll talk about religion at home at the drop of a hat. Or death, come to that. They love a good wake in Lisnacashan. But I know yous aren't like that in England. My boss keeps me right.' Before he could ask what she did, she went on, 'So you've brought

Prudence up on your own? Fair play to you. Mind you' – she looked at him from under her lashes as if trying to work out if she should go on, and then went ahead – 'if you were a woman, nobody'd think anything of it. I mean, you'd just be expected to get on with it.'

Fabian decided not to be offended. 'If I were a woman,' he said ruefully, 'I'd have made a better fist of it.'

'Och, she's not that bad. It's a desperate age. I was a demon. Me and my pal Evelyn – we'd our mammies tormented.'

Our mammies. He felt suddenly bleak at the enormity of trying to deal with his daughter alone. He rubbed his hands over his face, noting that he had not shaved as carefully as he would have done had he expected a visitor. 'Prudence is dreadful. It doesn't matter what I do. She's rude and ungrateful and she seems to hate everything. She's been asked to leave two schools already. And now she's started this running away caper. Oh lord, I suppose I'd better ring up the headmistress and let her know she's safe. I had no idea.'

'The school should've contacted you. If Prudence left this morning before breakfast . . .'

'I suppose they hoped she'd come back. She did the same thing only last Saturday and they rang up at once and I went straight there. I was frantic but it turned out she was hiding in the grounds all the time, just wanted to give everyone a fright. Maybe this time Miss Willard thought she wouldn't bother me for nothing. I don't blame her. *I* wouldn't want to be in charge of all those girls. One is enough!' He sighed and changed the subject. 'Miss McVey, let me freshen your cup.'

She held out her teacup. 'I'll take a wee heat.'

'What a charming expression. I do like your voice. I had a pal in the war from Ulster, he spoke rather like you.'

'Daddy was in the war,' April said, which made him feel very old.

'I just got in at the end,' he said, which was not strictly true, but he found himself wanting her to think of him as young. Or if not young, then not too old. 'So what brings you to Easterbridge?'

'I needed a job,' she said simply.

'And what is it you do? You said you weren't a teacher.'

She tilted her chin rather grandly. 'I'm an office manager.' She didn't say what kind of office, but if she had run the office at her father's works, then he supposed she did something similar here. Easterbridge was more of a market town than a manufacturing one, and both its mills were now closed, but there were a few factories, especially on the Coaldale Road; probably she worked in one of those. He wouldn't have minded someone like her in his own office, instead of Miss Cooke who always made him feel that his collar wasn't pressed.

'Well, I hope you settle in,' he said. 'It's a decent town. I grew up not far away and I was happy to move back to the area when Felicity did. I thought it would be better for Prudence than London. Healthier air and what have you.'

'Sure if she's away at school she doesn't get the good of it.'

He felt himself rebuked. 'She does have holidays.' And, oh dear, the Easter holidays were only a couple of weeks away.

'Is there not a school in Easterbridge?'

'Quite a good girls' high. Miss Cooke, my secretary, is always telling me how happy her nieces are there, but I don't think I could cope with having Prue home all the time.' He rushed on. 'She misses out on so much, not having a mother. At least at school she has women around – the female influence.'

April frowned, her forehead wrinkling like a perplexed puppy. 'But what about her aunty? I mean, she went there first today. Is she close to her?'

'Oh, Prue worships Felicity,' he said. 'But Felicity's no more interested in her than she would be in a kitten. Amusing enough for a while, but she wouldn't want to have to clean its litter box. She's a fearful shirker, Felicity. Oh, I shouldn't say that to you.'

'We aren't pals,' April said. 'I mean, she's only my landlady.' She looked thoughtful. 'But I got the impression she worked hard. Though in fairness I'm only saying that because she was writing the one time I met her; she was covered in ink.'

'Felicity works at the things she wants to work at,' Fabian said, 'but she does things very much on her own terms.'

'Sure who else's terms should she do things on?' She sounded suddenly fierce and he saw, fleetingly, the girl who had nabbed his taxi. 'And would you say that if she was a man?'

He raised his hands in a gesture of mock self-defence. How funny. He had thought of her as a quaint, old-fashioned Irish lass, unpolished, fresh from the farm, but she was clearly what his late mother would have called *one of those new women*.

'Maybe not,' he admitted.

'And you moved here to be closer to her?'

He nodded and gestured towards the teapot. April shook her head. 'Felicity's lived abroad a good deal,' he said. 'I hoped she'd make her home with us after Serena died but she wouldn't. She said that wasn't what she wanted to do with her life.'

'Good for her.' She sounded fiercer than ever and again he felt the need to defend himself.

'I didn't expect her to give up her writing. But she could write anywhere, and we were in London then; perfect for literary life.'

'And how much literary life would she have had rearing your child?' She looked for a moment as if she was about to place accusing hands on her hips. 'Sorry! None of my business. I should go, really. And take no notice of me. I'm a desperate one for rushing in and giving my tuppence worth.' She set her cup down and fidgeted with her skirt. 'I suppose you hit a raw nerve.' He raised an interested eyebrow. 'Och, it's nothing – nothing out of the ordinary. Just . . . I was expected to stay home and keep the home fires burning. You know, spinster daughter. I'm the *only* daughter,' she admitted, 'but nobody ever asked me what *I* wanted.'

He wondered if there had been someone she had wanted to marry. She was very attractive, despite the fierceness – or perhaps because of it. And when she left, leaving behind a faint scent of something floral and a depression in the cushion she had leaned against, he wondered if she might ever return.

Eleven

April had forgotten how wonderful it felt to be cycling! Her brand-new Raleigh, a birthday present to herself, had three gears – Sturmey-Archer, state of the art. The young man in the bicycle shop yesterday had assured her she would soon get used to them, and moreover that she'd need them round here, and he had been right on both counts. On foot, she hadn't realised how hilly Easterbridge was. But once she got into the way of it, she would be taking this slope up from the river in her stride. How glorious to *whoosh* down the other side instead of stopping halfway up at number eleven.

But why stop? It was Easter Sunday, *and* her birthday and nobody was waiting for her. Not like in Lisnacashan. *Where are you going, April? Would you not stay and keep me company, April?* Actually Mammy didn't have to ask out loud; April had felt the asking, the needing, seep from her. But now she was her own woman. It was a dry bright evening, and the clocks had gone forward last weekend so it wouldn't be dark for another hour; she might as well go for a wee spin. She turned into Townsend Street and zigzagged uphill through the terraced streets until they petered out and the road ahead was narrow and meandering, with only a few cottages on either side, small fields and drystone walls reminding her of home. Even in bottom gear she had to pedal hard, but she could feel the air in her lungs grow sharp and clean.

Above the fields loomed the moors, rough and bruise-coloured. She stopped at the top of the hill, panting, leaning over the handlebars, wishing she had a drink of water. How long was it since she had cycled? Ten years? More. She wasn't as fit as she'd been then! She manoeuvred the bike into a field gateway, pushed her damp hair back and looked down over the town, its dark roofs and the skeins of smoke rising from its chimneys. The river snaked through it just like the Blackwater at home. But she didn't know where it went, or what direction it flowed in.

This was where she lived and worked now, but that didn't make it home. Yet. The feeling she still got several times a day, that she had no real business here, flickered in her heart, but she suppressed it. After all, she'd never lived anywhere but Lisnacashan; she'd only stayed in Manchester a few weeks. She'd have to give herself time. Maybe someday Easterbridge would feel more homely, but in the meantime, she had a room she loved, a congenial business partner and a stirring of interest in her work, which was about to start in earnest. And freedom. Freedom for the first time ever. Right now not a sinner knew or cared where she was. Sure wasn't that a birthday gift worth having? She turned the bike and flew down the hill in top gear, hardly needing to pedal anyway, and arrived at number eleven with her cheeks glowing, absolutely starving. She might open a can of pilchards and add them to the omelette she had planned for dinner. It wasn't very festive, though she supposed eggs were appropriate for Easter. Mammy was disappointed that April hadn't come to Manchester for the holiday weekend, but she would have to be careful about budgeting if she was to keep sending Mammy what she had promised.

There was a shed round the back where Felicity had said she was welcome to keep her bike. As she had imagined, number eleven had only a small yard, but Felicity had made it pleasant with things in clay pots. April wasn't sure what they were; at the moment they were fairly bare, but the pots were clean and well weeded and gave every appearance of being well looked after. She couldn't have said why it surprised her that Felicity should have green fingers; she supposed because she gave the impression of caring mainly for her writing, which was silly. April knew you could care for a lot of things at once, she did herself, and it wasn't as if she *knew* Felicity. The shed was tidy, stacked with old pots and cans of paint, but there was room for her bike. She put it away and patted its lovely new sprung saddle. It was the most expensive thing she had ever owned.

She rarely saw her landlady; they had tacitly worked out a system whereby April made her evening meal early – something simple and cheap, eggs or tinned soup – and had her things cleared away and the kitchen restored to order before Felicity cooked. She ate late, which April in her mind linked with being literary and sophisticated and having lived abroad. But tonight they reached the kitchen about the same time.

'Oh,' April said. 'Sorry, I won't get in your way.' She was annoyed with herself for being apologetic – she was a paying lodger; she'd no call to creep and apologise as if she were Poor Miss McVey! But maybe she would take her meal upstairs for once – though she could skip the pilchards; they were grand and tasty but you wouldn't want the smell of them in the room where you slept. Even eggs could be a bit whiffy. Maybe she would just have a cheese sandwich tonight. And then she squared her shoulders: *Catch yourself on, April!* Let Felicity take her meal elsewhere if she didn't want April's company.

The two women bustled about, inevitably getting in each other's way. Felicity stood at the table, chopping up vegetables and some kind of aromatic herb – she must have taken to foreign food when she was abroad – and checking on the pan from time to time, where some meat was sweating. She didn't seem to mind April sitting down with her omelette.

'I'd take it upstairs,' April said, 'but I don't want my room to smell of pilchards.'

'Lord, no.' Felicity wrinkled her nose. 'I ought to have put that in the lease: no pilchards above ground-floor level. Or any fish. Prawns are the worst.'

'Ugh,' April said. 'Even the look of them makes me want to boke. All pink and slimy.' She gestured at the chopping board. 'What are you . . .?'

'Pichelsteiner. A German stew.' She pronounced it in what sounded to April like the proper way.

'Have you been to Germany?'

'I lived there for years. In the Bavarian Alps mostly.'

To April the Bavarian Alps sounded very exotic; she had only a vague idea of where they were. 'What were you doing there?'

Felicity looked bored. 'Oh, first I went because of my silly chest – the doctors thought I had a weakness; it was nothing really, but they thought I'd be better in the mountains, and I was. And then I liked it and I made good friends, so I stayed. I can write anywhere, and I gave English lessons to make ends meet.'

It was not quite the story Prudence had told – that Felicity had gone abroad to get out of looking after her, but then people never did see things the same way. Daddy, for example. He couldn't have seen what he had done in the same way everyone else in Lisnacashan did.

'Of course I had to come back to England sometimes to see publishers and things, but I always went back. Until . . . well, until now. For obvious reasons.'

Felicity didn't look remotely tubercular now; she was sturdy and rosy. She looked as though she had been tramping over the moors all day, not bent over her typewriter. And maybe she had for all April knew. She wondered what the *obvious reasons* were, but before she could ask, Felicity said, 'You seem to have scored a hit with my big brother.'

'Fabian?' She was annoyed to feel herself blush.

'He insisted on taking me out for lunch and talked about you at length. I take it you've met Prudence.'

'Oh yes. Lucky I was here, I suppose.'

'Serve the little beast right if she'd had to walk the streets,' Felicity said austerely. 'She needs a good spanking. Always did. Her mother spoilt her, silly woman. And when Serena died, everyone spoilt her. Fabian's too soft on her. And now her school says she's on a final warning, so he's terrified she'll get kicked out altogether. I hope she doesn't. She'd run rings round Fabian if she were home all the time, and they'd be forever bothering me. I don't know why people think if you're a woman you want to have kids around all the time.'

'I don't mind kids,' April said, though in principle she approved Felicity's stance. She would have liked to tell Felicity about her factory girls, but Felicity didn't give her a chance.

'And of course if you're single,' she went on, 'it's meant to be the dream of your life to take on someone else's brats.' She looked at April closely. 'Do you like it?'

April was taken aback. 'What?'

'The single life. Being a bachelorette.' She used the word wryly and April grimaced.

'I think I'm a bit old to call myself that.' She was about to say, 'Twenty-nine today,' but didn't like to, in case Felicity thought she wanted some kind of acknowledgement. *Bachelorette.* Nobody in Lisnacashan would use such a word! Imagine writing to Evelyn, *I'm enjoying the bachelorette life-style here in England.* Evelyn would imagine her with a cigarette holder and maybe slacks.

'Better than spinster, though?' Felicity broke in on her thoughts.

'Maybe. I don't feel old enough for that.' And it wasn't just a matter of age. Spinsters were despised and pitied. Not by April; when she looked at what Mammy put up with and then compared her to someone like Miss Martin from the lower road who answered to nobody, or Miss Connaughton who kept the haberdasher's shop in Main Street and lived happily over the shop with her pal Miss McGlone . . . well, she knew which she'd prefer. Which was why she'd decided a long time ago she was never getting married.

'Oh, I embraced spinsterhood years ago,' Felicity said. 'And I intend to be the fearsome kind. Like Aunt March.'

April grinned. Wasn't it grand when someone else talked about people in books like they were real! Only Evelyn had ever done it with her, and that was when they were kids, sharing whatever stories they could get hold of. 'Was Aunt March not a widow?' she argued.

'You could be right. I haven't read *Little Women* for years.'

'The film's coming to the Odeon,' April said. 'I saw the posters today; it's just round the corner from my office in town.' She liked saying *my office*. She imagined going to the pictures with Felicity, stopping for chips on the way home, arguing about the film.

'Oh yes. You do some kind of clerical work, don't you?'

Indignation flared in April and killed the image of herself and Felicity eating chips. 'Actually,' she said with dignity. 'I'm co-director of the True Minds Marriage Bureau.' It was her own fault, of course, that Felicity hadn't known that, and *co-director* was a slight exaggeration, but she was sure she had not said *clerk*.

Felicity looked intrigued. 'A marriage bureau!' And she actually laughed, which made April tilt her chin and climb, mentally, onto the highest horse she could find. A horse, she thought, appropriate to her status as co-director. *Office manager*, she had told Fabian. *Assistant*, the advertisement had said. Ah well.

'It was set up to help people after the war,' she explained in lofty tones. 'Martha Hart, my co-director, sees her work as a sort of mission.' She didn't know why she wanted Felicity to see what she did as serious; perhaps because she was slightly in awe of the cleverness of Felicity being a writer, or perhaps because *some kind of clerical work* was very close to being poor Miss McVey. She wanted Felicity to see her as an equal, even if she did rent a room from her. 'It's not a silly romantic thing.'

'Well, I'd like to hope it was slightly romantic,' Felicity said, still looking amused, 'though I suppose it is rather a business-like approach to marriage. Must they declare what they earn and all that? Is it all frightfully Jane Austen? You know, working out what people are worth.'

'Why not apply to be a client?' April said. 'And then you can find out.'

'Oh, I'm not the marrying sort.' Felicity lifted her chopping board and added the vegetables to the pot on the stove. April remembered Fabian saying she liked to do things on her own terms. 'I told you – fearsome spinster. But maybe you could find someone for my brother.'

April didn't say that she had been thinking that very thing herself. If ever a man was in need of wife, it was Fabian Carr. If ever a girl was in need of a stepmother, it was Prudence Carr. Someone sensible, April decided, maybe older, not some silly wee girl. Indeed, she may already have had a look through the files, just to familiarise herself with the clientele. There wasn't anyone *quite* right, but sure they'd be signing up in droves after the relaunch. For a moment she imagined herself and Felicity plotting together to sort Fabian out. She was about to say all this when she caught herself on. She wasn't sure if Felicity was serious and, in any case, you couldn't go round saying personal things like that and touting for business. She decided to laugh it off. 'Well, we're having a sort of relaunch next week, so he's bound to see our notices in the paper and that sort of thing. I'm sure Martha would be pleased to have him – she says it's always harder to get decent men.'

Felicity turned down the gas under the pot. 'Isn't it always! But he'd be much too shy. And I think he'd consider it, you know, *not quite the thing*.'

'It's very discreet.' April felt offended on behalf of Martha and the bureau. 'Nobody'd ever know a thing about it, only the women we matched him with, and of course it might only be one woman. Martha's often managed to find a match on her first attempt. She has a genius for matchmaking.'

Felicity raised her eyebrows. 'And do you?'

'I don't know yet,' April admitted. 'But you needn't worry about your brother meeting the wrong sort of woman. Martha's very fussy.'

'I really can't imagine him . . . but it would solve a lot of problems. He needs another wife. And he's very much the marrying sort. Gosh, I wish he would join your bureau – I'd pay his fees myself.'

'Well, maybe you'll persuade him,' April said. 'I'm sure we could find a nice lady. Someone who wouldn't be put off by a stepdaughter. I think your stew's boiling over.'

Felicity did brisk, competent things with her pot, and lord, it smelt delicious, much better than April's lowly omelette. She was hungry all over again – she had forgotten how cycling sharpened your appetite.

'So, what exactly do you write?' she asked. Felicity seemed to be in an expansive mood and April was keen to keep the subject safely away from Fabian.

Felicity shrugged. 'Whatever will sell. I'm just a hack.'

'For the newspapers?'

'Story papers mostly.'

April was disappointed; in her head she had been thinking of Felicity as a cross between Virginia Woolf and Katherine Mansfield – not that she had ever managed to finish anything by the former. 'Prudence said books?' She had said *soppy old books* actually.

'For kids. They don't bring in much money.'

How unexpected, April thought; Felicity didn't even like children. Still, it was no odder than April running a marriage bureau. *Helping to*, she reminded herself as she went up to her attic room. Don't be getting notions, now.

Twelve

Martha was worried that April was getting grandiose ideas about the relaunch. All this talk about parties and newspaper stories! She'd even asked Martha if she thought they'd be invited to talk about it on the wireless.

'Can you imagine the business we'd get?' she said, her eyes sparkling. 'They'd be queued down the stairs and out the street. We'd have to battle through them.'

It wasn't quite like that. The Wednesday before Easter there was half a column on page eleven of the *Easterbridge Recorder* – 'Ten Years Of Happy Matches!' – which sounded, April complained, like an advertisement for Swan Vestas, though Martha thought it struck a nice note. The new brochures arrived from the printers bearing an illustration of a smiling middle-aged couple walking hand in hand (all limbs present and correct at April's insistence) along a country lane of almost indecent picturesqueness.

April had sniffed at these. 'They won't appeal to younger people,' she complained. 'Those two look about a hundred and ninety. And what's your woman *wearing*?'

'Oh, April! Don't exaggerate.' She thought the illustration charming. Mark had put her in touch with a lady artist who did sketches for the *Easterbridge Recorder*'s weekend story page. The brochures were to be given out only to those who wrote or rang up for information, not distributed, as April had suggested, to libraries and launderettes, where young women might gather.

'I don't think so, dear,' Martha had said kindly – she did not like to squash and there was no doubt that the office looked much brighter since April had started. Even the door to the street was resplendent with a fresh coat of paint and a new (but discreet) brass plaque. 'We don't need to tout for business.'

In the days after the *Recorder* came out, seventeen people wrote or telephoned asking for appointments, and eleven less brave souls requested brochures 'for a friend'.

Martha had not yet had a chance to show April the work of the bureau face to face. But now they started to book in appointments. Not the hordes April had gleefully predicted – the diary was designed so that no client would overlap with another.

'After all,' Martha pointed out, 'if a man and woman get chatting on the stairs and hit it off, they might both leave without paying a fee.'

'Aye, that'd give you a quare dunt.'

Martha hoped that April would be able to engage with the clients without saying things like *a quare dunt*.

'You do remember,' she said, 'that we open late on Tuesdays and Thursdays, so that men in business can come in after work?'

'And women.' April's chin tilted in the way Martha was getting to know so well. 'Plenty of women in business. Like me. And you.'

'Well, yes, but we don't get many career-minded women. Think about it. Women in most lines of work have to give up their positions on marriage. If they've really chosen a career, they don't come to us. The women we see mostly have mere jobs – things they don't mind giving up.'

April sniffed. 'Plenty of married women in mills and factories. They've no choice.'

'Well, no, but they don't tend to consult us.'

Martha asked April to sit in on her interviews for the first week.

'I know you're terribly competent,' she said apologetically. 'The office has never looked better. But interviewing clients takes a certain diplomacy.'

April grinned. 'Och, my best friends have never called me diplomatic,' she said. 'I'm happy to watch and learn.'

Over the years, Martha had fine-tuned the bureau's application system. The clients filled out the registration form, which included, if it could be managed, a photograph, and then she went over the details with them, adding a few notes, asking for clarification. It was important not to seem prurient, she explained, and yet she liked to feel that the clients left having revealed more of themselves than they realised.

'And what I enjoy most, of course,' she said, 'is looking at all the details and thinking about what sort of match would suit and, if possible, actually matching the client to an existing one. But sometimes you have to be patient and wait for someone to come along.'

April sighed. 'I'm not the best at that.'

The first Wednesday in April their ten o'clock client was a tall young woman with a BBC accent, though as she relaxed, so did her vowels. She looked vaguely familiar to Martha from the society page of the *Easterbridge Recorder*.

'Sybil Postlethwaite,' she announced. She was dressed in an exquisite jade-green costume and her light-brown hair was beautifully Marcel-waved. Beside her, Martha felt dowdy and April looked positively schoolgirlish, though she was wearing what Martha knew (because she knew the provenance of every one of April's four office outfits by now) was her best frock, bought for her father's funeral. Sybil Postlethwaite's blouse looked like it cost more than April's yearly dress allowance. She was not pretty, her nose was long and her eyes protuberant, but her face was so expertly made up and her bearing so poised that the general impression was attractive. Martha wondered why she was seeking their help; she must meet plenty of men in the normal social round, and she had said she was twenty-four, surely not old enough to panic about being left on the shelf.

Sybil had been to a finishing school in Switzerland which had specialised in the domestic arts. 'I learned cordon bleu cookery and terribly fancy tapestry,' she said, 'and how to interview servants and, oh, you know, all of that.'

'And since then?'

'Helping Mother,' she said simply, 'at least when I'm at home. But I'm always being packed off to house parties with school friends. Tennis in the summer, hunting in the winter. Those terrible cold big houses.' She shivered and April nodded as though she herself spent every weekend in the stately homes of England. Sybil smiled back. 'Meeting lots of friends' brothers.' And then she seemed to droop. 'Only none of the friends' brothers seem to stick. The only one who really seemed interested was, well, I don't think he was quite sincere. I'll be . . . Daddy's going to settle some money on me when I marry.' She looked embarrassed, and now Martha saw anxiety in the large eyes. 'And I'm tired of going visiting. I want to stay here in Easterbridge and have, well, a nice husband. A home. Children. The same as any woman.'

'You've come to the right place,' Martha said calmly. 'When you meet men socially it can be hard to gauge their attentions but all our gentlemen are serious about marrying. And, to put it bluntly, Miss Postlethwaite, we'll make sure that we don't introduce you to anyone who's, shall we say, motivated by financial considerations. Now, tell me something about yourself – what fun to have learned proper cordon bleu. Do you like to cook?'

'I liked the tapestry better,' Sybil said. 'I embroidered four pictures for Mummy's fiftieth birthday – the four seasons. I framed them myself.' Her face brightened. 'I honestly think that's my favourite thing in the world, handicrafts. Working with wood especially.' She clasped her hands over her elegant knees.

'Isn't that gorgeous,' April cut in. 'What else have you made?' Martha smiled at her – she sounded so much warmer than Hilda ever had, and Sybil waxed enthusiastic about pictures and chair seats as if she were talking to a pal. When Martha stood up to indicate that the interview was over, she told her she was very confident of being able to set up an introduction very soon. Of course, she always said that.

Sybil's footsteps were no sooner dying away on the stairs down to the street than Martha opened the filing cabinet and looked through some of the blue cards. She hesitated over a couple and took them out to read more carefully. 'Hmm,' she said. 'Too old? And there's that nice Mr Ainsworth, but he's a little . . . I'm not sure; I think she needs someone with a bit more get-up-and-go.' She frowned. Something was still nudging at the edge of her memory. 'Postlethwaite? Why does that name – of course!' Her mind cleared. 'Bernie Postlethwaite's daughter – has to be. Those eyes. And clearly dripping with money.'

April looked puzzled.

'Bernie's one of the richest men in Easterbridge,' Martha explained. 'He came from a two-up two-down in Townsend Street and went into the paper factory at fourteen. Ended up making a fortune developing soft lavatory paper.'

April giggled. 'Fair play to him. There was this wee man from the back road at home who—'

'Oh, absolutely.' She had overcome any squeamishness about interrupting April's stories of Lisnacashan. 'Clever chap, and he's done well for himself. Look at Sybil. Best schools, talks like Queen Mary herself and seems a thoroughly nice girl. But . . .'

'The posh boys don't want to marry lavatory paper.'

'It would be different if she were prettier. It always is.'

'Martha!' April's mouth fell open and she flapped her hands in front of her face in excitement. 'Oh my word! I know exactly the right person!'

'Who?' Martha was sceptical. April had done an impressive job of familiarising herself with the profiles on file, but she didn't yet have Martha's forensic knowledge.

'Sure it's obvious.' She sounded impatient at Martha's stupidity. 'Mr Barrett!'

'Mr—?'

'The cabinet maker! The one you told me about. That Bertha Bell rejected for being trade.'

'But—'

'You heard Sybil, she loves making things. Wood – she loves wood. Just like him!'

'Oh April, I don't think—'

'Och, I know what you're going to say. But if her father's a self-made man, surely he'll respect Mr Barrett for his skill.'

'He might think he's after her money.'

April snorted. 'I bet he's no more after her money than some of those idle fellas she meets at house parties. Och, Martha, give it a try. Please.'

'I wouldn't want them to think we didn't consider her worthy of introducing to a professional person or . . .' How could she make this eager girl see the impossibility of her scheme? She had a notion the Irish were less class-bound than the English, but even so.

'Martha, it's 1934! What's the point in being called True Minds? Och, please let's introduce them.'

Martha flicked the blue cards in her hands and then took out Henry Barrett's. She read it carefully. 'All right,' she said at last. 'I don't suppose there's anything to lose. I'll have to choose my words carefully, though.'

April hugged herself. 'I think it's a hat you'll be choosing carefully,' she said.

Martha laughed. 'Oh, April, you're getting ahead of yourself!'

The child was impossibly naïve, but once again Martha was reminded of herself in 1924, carried away with the success of her first match. It had been like playing with her dolls, making them do what she wanted them to. Or chess, which she had played with her brothers. And back then, with Gordon gone and the world unrecognisable without him, that little bit of control had probably saved her from becoming bitter. And she must have had some daft ideas then herself, but there had been nobody to squash her.

'Maybe it's not such a bad idea,' she said. 'He's a good man, artistic and clever, and she's clearly artistic too. If her family have any sense, they'll recognise that.'

'Exactly!'

'All right. I'll write to Mr Barrett now; you can take it to the post when you go for lunch and he'll get it in the morning. If he likes the sound of Miss Postlethwaite, and if she likes the sound of him, we can introduce them by the end of the week. And if not, there's no harm done. We can try someone else.' She gave a smile of satisfaction. 'Let's have a cup of tea to celebrate.' She looked at April keenly. 'I've a feeling you're more romantic than you admit.'

'I am not indeed,' April said hotly, as if accused of some great moral failing. 'It's just common sense.'

Whatever it was, her confidence was not unfounded. Sybil Postlethwaite and Henry Barrett did like the sound of each other. At least, they were both agreeable to meeting, and came in on Friday afternoon as suggested.

'Why not just give them the details and let them get on with it?' April asked. 'They're grown adults. They shouldn't need a chaperone.'

'People like it,' Martha said. 'It's more personal. They feel they're being introduced by mutual friends rather than merely set up because they ticked certain boxes on the registration form.'

April prepared a tray of tea and for the first ten minutes they all sat together in the interview room. Barrett was a tall, thin, serious-looking man with beautiful hands. Sybil was as well presented as she had been on Wednesday, but a tiny smear of lipstick was smudged beyond the limit of her mouth, suggesting she had nervously replenished it before coming in, which touched Martha. She was desperately protective of both these strangers, and even more protective of her new assistant whose idea this had been. Let it work!

Any instinct that this was a preposterous match fled when she saw Sybil smile, with relief, Martha imagined, that Barrett was so personable, but also anxiety that she herself might meet with approval. How awful to feel so vulnerable, so desperate for approval. How comforting that she herself was content with her life as it was. They were both shy and awkward at first, trying to examine each other without its being obvious, but before long they were talking amiably about Mr Barrett's work – it turned out that Sybil's mother had bought two of his chairs. The more animated she became, the more Sybil's accent relaxed, and Barrett lightened up too, describing how he had served his apprenticeship in Leeds.

'I'd a wonderful mentor,' he said. 'Mr Nicholls. He taught me everything. Not just about wood but, well, life I suppose.' He looked self-conscious. 'My own father died in the war.'

97

Martha nodded her sympathy and April did too. She was being very quiet, but her eyes were fixed on the couple with what looked like determination to be proved right, but also a warm sympathy which, Martha thought, augured well for her future at True Minds.

'It's important for young people,' Barrett went on, warming to his theme, 'to have someone to give them a hand. I see some of the kids these days, hanging about on corners, nothing much to do, even here in Easterbridge, and I think, well, it reminds me how lucky I was.'

Sybil was looking fascinated. 'I know exactly what you mean,' she said. 'That school I went to in Switzerland . . . it was nonsense in some ways, but learning handicrafts, tapestry and that, was wonderful. So satisfying.' She described how she felt when she had done a piece of tapestry that turned out well, and Barrett nodded in delighted agreement.

'That's how I feel,' he said. 'And you say you make your own frames? Tell me how you do that. I've never met a girl who was interested in wood.'

Martha smiled at April. 'They can take it from here,' she said quietly. She raised her voice. 'Miss McVey and I will be upstairs. Do feel free to have another cup of tea and take your time getting to know each other. You might just let me know as soon as you're able if you'd like to be taken off the books for now.' This was her discreet way of reassuring them that if they decided to meet again she would regard them both as unavailable until they told her otherwise.

'Of course it doesn't always end in marriage,' she told April as they went upstairs together and April started to get ahead with some invoices, 'but we generally find that they have a good sense of whether or not they would like to pursue things after a couple of meetings. You don't get that awful situation of walking out for ages with no understanding. Which is very hard on a girl especially. They can be perfectly frank with each other about whether or not they think they might be suited. And I have a good feeling about those two.'

'I'd never say I told you so,' April said.

On Monday morning there were notes from both Henry and Sybil thanking them for the introduction, saying they had enjoyed meeting and would continue to do so. Sybil's was businesslike, but Henry let himself go so far as to say he was 'thrilled to have been introduced to such a talented lady'.

'Well done!' Martha handed both notes to April and told her to file them in the *Settled For Now* cabinet.

'What if one wants to pursue it and the other doesn't?' April asked.

'It happens,' Martha admitted, thinking of poor Mrs Lewis, who had yet to meet with a man's approval. 'It has to be mutual. If not, then it's back to the beginning and try again. But with those two I shouldn't be surprised if I *do* have to buy a new hat. Gosh, look at the time. A Miss Murrell is due – another new client. Would you like to interview her yourself?'

April jerked her head up from the files. 'You trust me?'

'I think we can say your instincts are admirable.'

'Ah, Martha, you're an angel. I won't let you down.'

Thirteen

Miss Florence Murrell was a plump, pretty, dark-eyed woman who told April she had been a nurse but had to give it up after her parents' death to look after her invalid sister. 'And now Delia has died and I miss having someone to care for.' She looked down at her hands in her lap. 'I'm thirty-nine,' she said. 'Maybe I've missed the boat. I didn't seem to mind when I was busy, but now . . . I saw your article in the paper, and I thought, well, why not give it a chance? Life can be' – she paused, choosing her words carefully – 'I wouldn't say lonely. Not lonely exactly. I have the church and some good pals and my cat, but, well, it's quite an *effort* not to be lonely.' She frowned at her brown tweed skirt, as though she had admitted to some terrible shame.

'I know,' April said. Of course, *she* wasn't lonely; she was free. She thought of Fabian Carr not lighting his fire because it wasn't worth it for just himself. Och, drat her squeamishness in not insisting that Felicity made him sign up! This woman would be perfect for him – everything about her exuded kindness and motherliness, and she would take no nonsense from that bold strap of a Prudence. *I miss having someone to care for.* Sure, Fabian and Prudence were crying out to be cared for!

100

Now, could she get Felicity to persuade him to sign up before this lovely wee Miss Murrell was snapped up? Maybe April could somehow engineer a meeting without Fabian signing up? Or if she introduced Miss Murrell only to hopeless cases, in the meantime working on Felicity to persuade Fabian . . .

She became aware of Miss Murrell's hopeful, slightly shy dark eyes and dismissed such a treacherous and unprofessional thought. *Not lonely exactly* – and she'd been planning to get the poor woman's hopes up only to dash them with impossible matches! There was no guarantee that Fabian would ever sign up, and in the meantime poor Miss Murrell would feel she had been silly to try to find happiness. Worse, she might settle for one of what Martha called *our more challenging gentlemen*. April imagined meeting her in the street, pushing an octogenarian in a bath chair, or walking the Colonel's spaniels. Even Primrose Lewis balked at that. Martha had a soft spot for the Colonel, but he was over sixty and looked every minute of it, besides smelling of spaniels and pipe smoke. Miss Murrell deserved better.

'We'll see if any of our gentlemen seem like good matches,' she promised. 'But if not, we have new clients signing up all the time. You might have to be patient.'

'Oh, I know.' Miss Murrell looked a little ashamed. 'I'm a middle-aged spinster; I don't expect—'

'Och, you're *lovely*,' April said sincerely. 'And as for being a middle-aged spinster, what do you think I am?'

'You're just a girl!'

April knew she was not, but she also knew that, to thirty-nine, twenty-nine probably did seem young. She was fiercely determined to make Miss Murrell happy. And she would speak to Felicity tonight – or, no! Why not send Fabian one of their brochures? He might guess it came from her, if Felicity had mentioned where she worked, and he would think her bumptious and interfering, but she could live with that. She hummed a jig as she saw Miss

Murrell out, and before she settled to anything else, put a brochure in an envelope and addressed it to Fabian. It was the work of a few minutes to look up his office's address. It was only in the next street, beside the Odeon; she could have delivered it in her lunch hour, but she put it on the pile for the post – better be businesslike. Pleased with herself, she leaned over the desk and opened the window. It was a beautiful day; cycling over the bridge that morning she had sensed warmth in the breeze. St Margaret's Lane was a quiet street – what traffic noise there was would be worth it for the fresh air coming in. She looked down through the blinds. A man was walking along towards the bureau, checking the numbers on the doors as he passed them; probably their next client. She consulted the diary. A Mr Young was due, a schoolmaster. She wondered how he had got out of school on a weekday, but she supposed the holidays must still be on. He looked exactly like a schoolmaster: tweed jacket and trilby, neat gingerish moustache, about thirty – too young for Miss Murrell. How funny if they had passed in the street.

Mr Young paused at the door, and then April lost sight of him. He must be in the hallway. She expected steps on the staircase – the stairs creaked – but there were none. Was he perhaps stopping to light a cigarette, or more likely put one out? Had he been smoking? She hadn't noticed. But no steps came, and soon she saw Mr Young's trilby appear beneath her again, and then Mr Young was walking back down St Margaret's Lane, much faster than he had walked up it. He looked back once and scurried on.

April drew back. Had he seen her looking out? Had she frightened him off? Surely not. The blinds were adjusted for maximum privacy. Well, maybe it wasn't Mr Young at all, just someone who had lost his way, or had stopped in the doorway for some reason – to tie a shoelace, to light a cigarette, to fix a troublesome sock.

But no Mr Young appeared for his appointment.

'How strange,' Martha said. 'His letter – we arranged the appointment by post – sounded very keen.'

April told her what she had seen, and Martha looked wise. 'Shy,' she said. 'Happens from time to time. Mostly they just don't turn up. It's not as if there's anything off-putting about our doorway; it's perfectly discreet as you know. What a pity. We don't have many younger men. Shame if he's too shy to make the first move. Never mind.'

April was not one to be satisfied with *never mind*. Cycling home that evening, taking a turn over the moors, delighting in her growing confidence on the bicycle and the sense of freedom it gave her, she thought about Mr Young. All right, if he was as shy as that, he might never cope with meeting a stranger, but often people just needed encouragement to make the first move. Look how awkward she'd felt in the Midland Hotel, how she'd almost been too shy to approach Martha. Thank goodness she'd got over that. Well, Young had made the first move. It was the *next* move, walking up the stairs and knocking on the office door, which he had jibbed at. How could they make that step easier? She screwed up her face in thought and had such a brilliant idea that she lost concentration and had to skid to a stop to avoid a fat tabby cat which was taking its life in its paws by sitting in the middle of the road outside a cottage. It arched itself with disdain and blinked at her with cold golden eyes.

'Sorry, puss,' she said.

'It's his own fault,' said a voice, and a woman looked over the cottage wall. 'Thinks he owns the road.' She was fair and smiling, her arms full of purple tulips. April smiled back and said what a pretty garden, and she was glad she hadn't hurt the cat.

It was the slightest of encounters, but it cheered her. She freewheeled down the hill, the spring sun warm on her shoulders, feeling for the first time that Easterbridge was a grand place to live and that she was very well suited to her new job.

Next morning, she told Martha her brilliant idea.

'Why don't we offer clients the option of being interviewed at home? Not everybody of course, just people like Mr Young. The more sensitive ones.'

Martha frowned over her spectacles. 'I'm not sure,' she said. 'Mightn't it seem rather intrusive?'

'But–we've seen what happens when people are shy about coming to the office.'

'Doesn't it smack a little of the means test, or health visitors, or—'

'Sure we already ask them about their means!'

'It's not quite *nice*, somehow. Going into someone's private home.'

But April held fast to her guns. She thought of Fabian's home – she was sure she had gained a much keener insight into him because she had seen him there with his unlit fire and his neat tea trays. Had he merely picked Prudence up from the tea shop, she would have seen that he was polite and presentable but not those homely touches that made him human and, yes, she didn't mind admitting it, quite appealing to the right sort of woman.

'It wouldn't be the standard service,' she said, 'and we needn't advertise it, but if we felt someone seemed a wee bit shy on the phone or reluctant to commit to a meeting . . .? Och, let me just try, Martha. I bet I can get Mr Young back for a start. You know we need more young men.'

And Martha sighed and said it was not how they had always done things but perhaps . . .

It was April's first big mistake.

Fourteen

Martha, though she seemed to feel Mother looking over her shoulder saying, *I really don't know if this is wise*, wrote to Mr Young to say she was sorry that he had not been able to keep his appointment.

If it would be more convenient, we would be willing to interview you in your own home, she wrote, and somewhat to her surprise he telephoned the very next day to say that would be agreeable.

'He sounded nervous,' reported April, who had taken the call. 'So you must admit, Martha, I'm a genius. Amn't I?'

'Well . . .' She still didn't like it, but maybe she was being a fuddy-duddy? April had been right about Sybil and Henry.

'I'm going to see him tomorrow at three,' April went on. 'I've written down the address – Oaklea Road; isn't that out past the tennis club? I've been that way on my bike.'

'*You're* going to see him?'

'Well, it was my idea. Would you rather go?' She bit her lip. 'Sorry – did I get a wee bit ahead of myself? That's like the time—'

Martha shook her head. 'You can't go to a man's house alone,' she said.

'Och, Martha! You don't think it's a ruse to have me carried off to the white slave trade?' April laughed. 'I saw him, remember – he's a weedy specimen. I'll be grand.'

'It's not that so much, though you can't be too careful. But it's not . . . well, it's just not very *comme il faut*, as the French say. Not quite the thing.' She sighed and looked at her diary. 'Luckily I'm free then,' she said. 'We have a Miss Jennings coming at five so it will be a rush to get back, but it'll have to be managed. Next time, check with me first.'

April nodded, pouting a little. A few seconds later she said, 'Ah, you're saying *next time*! So you don't think it's daft, do you?'

'Not *daft* exactly.'

'It'll be good to have you along,' April said generously. 'You're far better at putting people at ease than I am.'

'Well, I've been doing it for years.'

But not this. Not this going up to a strange house. The following afternoon, adrift from the haven of her office, her little queendom, Martha felt anxious and somehow exposed, though April tripped along beside her full of chat, passing remarks on most of the houses and gardens they passed. It was uncanny how many of the good citizens of Oaklea Road – and it was not a short road – had gardens which reminded April of Lisnacashan.

Cedric Young lived with his mother in a neat villa and taught English in the boys' grammar. His mother, a plump little lady in an old-fashioned long wool skirt, opened the door to them and put up her hands in glee. A small greyish dog of startling malevolence appeared behind her, teeth bared in yapping protest.

'I'm so pleased you've come!' Mrs Young said. 'Now, don't be naughty, Wriggles! I've been telling Cedric for years he needs a nice girl. But he's that shy. Up in his room with his poetry or walking the dog over the moors. Well, it's no life for a young man.'

Wriggles growled.

'What a protective little dog,' Martha said, keeping her hands close to her.

She wanted to rescue Cedric from his mother and Wriggles, a feeling intensified when they were shown into a hot parlour with all the furniture tasselled and skirted in faded green velvet, as it must have been when Mrs Young came to the house as a bride fifty years ago. She told them that Cedric was the last of her seven children, the youngest by some years and the only boy. Family photos lined the floral walls, and a bright fire burned in the grate. A little table was set for tea with delicate rose-patterned china. There were four cups.

'I'll call Cedric,' Mrs Young said. 'He must not have heard the door. Come on, Wriggles darling. You can stay in the kitchen.'

When she had left, April whispered, 'This isn't going to work. Not with his mammy here.'

Martha couldn't help agreeing, but they were here now, so when Mrs Young came back, accompanied by a mortified-looking Cedric – April gave her a look that told her he was indeed the man she had seen from the window – she said, sweetly but firmly, 'Mrs Young – it's very important that we talk to Cedric confidentially. If we're to help him, I mean.'

'Cedric has no secrets from me!' Mrs Young trilled. Cedric studied the flowers in the hearthrug and dug his toe into the carpet. He looked like a small boy dragged to the headmaster's study. 'And it was my idea to engage, well, professional help.' A fiery blush mottled Cedric's cheeks.

I bet it was, Martha thought. 'All the same,' she said. 'If you wouldn't mind leaving us?'

This was daring, in the woman's own home. Maybe even rude? She tried to catch April's eye, but April was carefully examining a beadwork lampshade, looking less at ease than Martha had ever seen her. Perhaps now she would understand why Martha had had such reservations – the office was a neutral, private space, akin to the doctor's consulting rooms. How on earth could anyone relax here, among the antimacassars and china shepherdesses and with Wriggles yapping in the next room? But Cedric said, in a flat voice, 'I don't mind if Mother stays. It's all the same to me, really.'

The interview began. After a few minutes, Martha was convinced that Cedric had no desire to marry, that he was everything that had ever been meant by *not the marrying kind*. He was doing this to appease his mother. Or for other reasons to do with respectability. He was polite and helpful, apparently frank, but seemed to be going through the motions. Yes, he was a junior master, but he had hopes of being head of department in a year or so when the senior chap retired. His mother had made the house over to him; his sisters were all married with families. No, he hadn't thought about what type of girl he'd like, just a nice one really. He might have been picking out a new suit. Children? Well, he didn't really mind one way or the other.

'And I shan't interfere,' Mrs Young said, setting down her teacup. 'I'd be very happy to stay in my own room. Cedric's wife could have things just as she wanted. Not that she would have any reason to change anything.' She looked with satisfaction round the velvety late-Victorian room. 'And I'm seventy-three,' she said. 'I shall be called home before long. But I would like to see my Cedric settled.'

She patted his pale freckled hand and he said, 'Now, Mother dear, you've years yet.'

Let us hope not, Martha thought, for the sake of the potential young Mrs Young. Young Mrs Young; how absurd. And yet it would not be the most absurd thing about Mr Young's marrying. Still, he wouldn't be the first chap like that she had helped.

It was a relief to get outside into the fresh spring afternoon. She let out a long *whoosh* of breath.

'Flip me,' April said, 'you'd think your man didn't want to get married.'

Martha looked at her closely. Her eyes were wide and candid. And if it wasn't up to Martha to refuse Mr Young's business, neither was it up to her to enlighten April. Hilda would not have needed to be enlightened; she would doubtless have had some vulgar modern slang word to describe him and his sort.

She chose her words carefully. 'I think some men aren't perhaps as keen on marriage as women are. They like the bachelor lifestyle.'

April gave a little snort. 'Aye, sure why wouldn't they? And they don't have to choose marriage instead of a career.'

'That's true.' Young would progress better in his career with the respectability of a wife by his side. As he well knew. She patted her bag, in which she had her notes. 'Well, Mr Young mightn't be terribly lively, but he's got his own home and a steady profession and decent prospects. There are several nice girls who would be very glad to meet him. I'm thinking of little Miss Robins. Oh, and the Jennings girl who's coming in later; she mentioned that she was especially fond of reading. An English master could be just the ticket.'

But all the way back to St Margaret's Lane, discomfort nibbled at her. On the one hand, Young had signed up; he had written a most welcome cheque; he had declared his intention to marry, and it was not up to her to question that, no matter what her instincts said. Instincts could be wrong. She was a business-woman; she did not deal in feminine intuition. But she thought of those hopeful young women, looking to her to give them futures they had been unable to find for themselves. Could she, in all conscience, introduce one of them to a man who was, at the very least, indifferent to marriage?

She sighed and April said confidently, 'You know what I think?'

'What?'

'I think he just wants to shut his mammy up. She's near dead to get him married. He's probably sick listening to her.'

'You could be right. Still, people marry for all sorts of reasons. I know that better than most.'

'Well, they should only marry for love!' April burst out.

Martha stopped and laughed, the faint anxiety about Young ebbing out of her. After all, she reasoned, if he were indifferent to marriage he would not have signed up.

'Oh, April!' she said, feeling much better. 'I knew you were more romantic than you admitted.'

Fifteen

April suspected that Mrs Primrose Lewis, who arrived early for her appointment bearing a tin of homemade biscuits, would disagree about her being romantic.

April knew she would need her most professional voice and manner. She had got up early to do her hair; she had experimented with clipping it back at the sides, which felt strange but looked the last word. She had kept dashing down to the lavatory to check it in the mirror, until Martha had asked if she was feeling quite all right, and she had been so mortified at the idea that Martha thought she had the runs or worse, that she confessed it was just the new hairstyle. Martha had laughed and said it was very becoming.

'I know you've been dealing with my partner,' April told Mrs Lewis now, 'but she – we felt that you might benefit from a change. Sometimes fresh eyes . . .'

Mrs Lewis looked her up and down; she seemed less impressed by the new hairstyle than Martha. In fact she looked distinctly unimpressed with April in general. 'I don't mean to be unkind, *Miss* McVey, but what can you know about marriage?'

'Och, not much, right enough,' April said cheerfully and, though she would never have wanted Martha to hear her say this, her frankness may have appealed to Mrs Lewis, because her mouth softened into a faint smile. She was a short, thin woman, the same age as Mammy, but Mammy wouldn't have been seen dead in such an almost girlish floral peach frock. Mrs Lewis's greying hair was arranged in sausage curls around a pink, anxious face. Clearly she was too respectable to tint her hair, but not confident enough for a more natural style. April felt that a simple bob or even a crop would have done more for her, but then, she suspected, Mrs Lewis would do anything to avoid looking like a middle-aged spinster. Or maybe she didn't want to look like the widow she was. She tried, and failed, to imagine Mammy seeking out another husband. Once bitten, twice shy. But sure everybody was different. What Mrs Lewis needed was a bit of what Martha called jollying.

She decided to continue being frank. 'We haven't been able to suit you yet,' she said.

'I'm afraid not.' Mrs Lewis looked apologetic. 'I know Mrs Hart has done her best. And so have I. I've met some lovely chaps. Really decent men. And I've chatted very nicely; I've shown an interest in their gardening or their cars or their families, because the men are often widowed too. I haven't gone on and on about my own concerns as some women do.' She looked at April as if strongly suspecting her of being one of those women.

'And what are your own concerns, Mrs Lewis?' April asked. 'I mean, your interests? What do you do with yourself? Apart from being such a grand baker,' she added gallantly, glancing at the biscuit tin.

Mrs Lewis looked taken aback. She frowned and played with the tassel on her belt. 'Well, my husband, Arthur, was a chiropodist; he died seven years ago, a sudden heart attack, such a shock.'

April nearly leapt in and said wasn't that a coincidence, the exact same thing happened her own daddy, but Daddy's death

112

wouldn't have contributed much to the jollying, so she merely murmured respectfully.

'And our daughter, Mabel,' Mrs Lewis went on, 'went to Australia to stay with an aunt, and she's married out there now. I don't suppose I'll ever see her again – six weeks, the journey takes. Arthur always said he would take me there when he retired but, well . . . He was only fifty-one. Of course I was a good deal younger; I'm not much over fifty even now.' April knew she had admitted to fifty-five on her registration form and smiled. 'Mabel's doing well out there; they go to the beach the way we would pop to the shops – imagine! She's got three kiddies. I don't suppose I'll ever meet them. I expect they have Australian accents. Funny to think about, isn't it? I've never heard their voices. Mabel speaks beautifully; she went to elocution. I'd love to hear Mabel's voice again.'

Her face was bleak, her tone resigned. April was reminded of Miss Murrell's comment about loneliness – what an effort it was to keep it at bay.

'But what about *you*?' she pressed on gently. 'What are your interests? You know' – with a flash of inspiration – 'True *Minds* we call the bureau now. What's in your mind? What do you do? Are you a member of any clubs or . . . or a church or . . . or anything . . .?' Her voice trailed away. The jollying wasn't going as well as she'd hoped.

'My *mind*?' Mrs Lewis looked as affronted as if April had asked what was in her underwear drawer. 'I look after my home,' she said. 'As I've always done.'

'And I'm sure it's a wee palace, but that can't take up all your time. And with your family so far away, surely you need to get out and about, meet other people, other women in your position. I hear there's a thriving Townswomen's Guild in the town? Mrs Hart is always telling me I should join.'

Mrs Lewis shook her head. 'I'm not a joiner,' she said. 'My interests are very domestic. Very natural. I haven't bothered about my *mind*.' She spoke as if the mind were some unmentionable part of the anatomy. 'That's why I'd like to marry again. I want to look after someone. That's what I was brought up to do. That's what any decent woman wants. Why would I want to go hobnobbing with a lot of silly bickering women?'

'It'd give you something to talk about. Something bigger than the home.' She rushed on before Mrs Lewis could tell her that nothing was bigger than the home. 'You say you're a good listener, but why should you do all the listening? Why not give yourself something to talk about? Even, I don't know, politics or—'

She could not have said anything worse. Mrs Lewis looked affronted. '*Politics*? I should hope I know better than that. Men don't want political women.'

'All right, not politics.' (Why did I say *politics*? she thought. I'm an eejit, sure I don't even like politics.) 'Maybe books? Or what about the cinema?'

'The cinema!' Mrs Lewis pursed her lips.

'Lots of men like the cinema.' She had no idea if this were true. 'Or a hobby, or what about some voluntary work? You could use your baking skills maybe . . .? She tried a different tack. 'I wonder if you might be coming across as a wee bit too' – not *keen*, that would offend her more than ever – 'desperate? And that maybe scares the men off a wee bit?'

'*Desperate*!'

'I didn't mean—'

'Miss McVey, this is a marriage bureau. Allegedly. You're supposed to cater for people who want to get married. Calling them *desperate* is, well, it's cruel! It's insulting.'

'Och no. I only meant—'

'What you *meant* was very clear, Miss McVey.' Mrs Lewis's voice was shrill. 'This is not the advice I have been paying for, and certainly not the attitude.' She stood up and gathered her bag to her. 'Where is Mrs Hart? I shall be telling her exactly what I think of—'

'I'm here.' And she was. Standing in the doorway, looking puzzled.

Of all the bad timing. Why in God's name had Martha to be walking past the interview room door at that very moment? Answering a call of nature, April supposed, but could she not have had the call five minutes earlier or later?

'Mrs Lewis?' Martha asked. 'Are you unhappy with—'

'Unhappy? *Unhappy?*' Mrs Lewis gripped her bag tighter. 'I should say I'm unhappy. This – this person you've employed seems to be a very self-assured young woman, but she has no knowledge of life. Of what women need.' She stopped, breathing rapidly through her nose. April wasn't sure whether she was close to tears or an explosion of rage. 'Telling me I need to get involved with politics, and go to the cinema, and calling me desperate! *Desperate*! I've never been so insulted.'

April scrabbled to explain. 'I'm sorry if I've been a wee bit brisk.' She turned to Martha. 'I was just suggesting to Mrs Lewis that maybe by building herself up a wee bit, making herself more interesting' – oh God, she shouldn't have said that; too late now, and the alternatives that flashed into her mind (*attractive, desirable*) – were worse – 'she'd be in a better position to attr– er, engage the attentions of a man.'

Mrs Lewis sighed and gave Martha a *You see what I mean?* look.

April rushed on, speaking directly to Mrs Lewis. 'I honestly think that if you forget about marriage for a wee while, and sort of shake up your life, get out and about more, you'll find that you meet people – not necessarily a man, but *friends*.

There's nothing like a good pal.' She thought of Evelyn, who hadn't written since April had left Manchester. And sure when she did write, it was all about how wonderful wee Robbie was. But she couldn't think about that now.

With great dignity, Mrs Lewis made for the doorway. 'If it were that simple, I wouldn't have sought your help in the first place. I don't want *friends*.' She turned back before going down the stairs. 'You won't be surprised to know that I no longer require your so-called services and shall be stopping my payments forthwith.' On the second step she turned back again and with an *and-another-thing* air, said, 'And I really would advise you to stop saying *wee*. *Wee* this and *wee* that. It's most irritating.'

When she had gone, April flumped back in her chair and fanned her face with her hand. 'I'm sorry,' she told Martha. 'She didn't seem to take to me.'

'What on earth did you say?' Martha's brow wrinkled in concern; it made her look much older.

April gave Martha a fair account of the interview. 'And I suggested,' she ended, 'that she try to get a wee—I mean, get something *more* into her life. Not to focus everything on getting a man.'

'April!' Martha sounded horrified. 'What aspect of *marriage bureau* have you failed to grasp?'

'Och, Martha, sure you said yourself it wasn't working. You said a fresh approach—'

'If this were a bakery and someone came in for bread, would you tell them they might be better off going to the greengrocer's for a nice green apple instead?'

'Ah, come on now, that's not the same thing.'

'It's exactly the same thing.'

April was furious to find her throat thickening with tears. 'But you said . . . you agreed to changing the name. True *Minds*. I was only suggesting—'

'I think it might be better if you didn't do too much suggesting for a while.'

April tilted her chin. 'Right you be,' she said. 'You're the boss.'

Sixteen

'Checkmate.'

'Eh?' Prudence's eyebrows drew together in disbelief. 'But—'

'Your king has nowhere to go,' Fabian explained. 'If he goes here my rook has him, and—'

'But he can go there.' She shifted her king diagonally and Fabian shook his head.

'Sorry, darling.' He indicated his knight, ready to pounce.

'I don't understand the horses. I never remember what way they go.'

'They can go one square in one direction and two in—'

'Don't tell me. I won't remember and I don't even like chess. It's a stupid game.' She pulled back from the table like a child refusing its dinner and began to chew the end of her plait.

Other fathers, Fabian thought, have daughters who are companions. Comforts even. But these Easter holidays Prudence had been impossible. For some time now she had treated him very much as *Silly Old Daddy*; now she seemed positively to loathe him.

'It's as if she can't bear to be in the same room,' he had complained to Felicity the previous evening. She had come to dinner, and Prudence, the minute the meal was over, had disappeared to her room citing 'my holiday task'.

118

'And these holidays have been endless,' he went on. 'It seems the more expensive the school, the less time the pupils spend there.'

'Fourteen's a ghastly age,' Felicity said. 'I was revolting. You were vile. She's worse because—'

'I know.' He cut her off before she could say *motherless*. 'But, Fee, I'm really worried. Miss Willard said when I brought her back that time that this would be her final chance. And if she behaves at school the way she does with me . . .' He shuddered. 'If it were just naughtiness, or even cheek, but it's the way she looks at me as if I'm, I don't know, ridiculous.'

'Oh, that's normal enough. I remember thinking Daddy was a frightful bore at that age. Didn't you?'

'No, I didn't.' His father had been a high-minded, slightly remote man, interested in maps and languages. Fabian had admired him hugely and, at fourteen, home from school for the holidays, had loved his father's company on walks and fishing trips. It was Father who introduced him to chess; he still remembered his incredulity the first time Fabian had beaten him. And then his proud delight. He had shaken his hand – Fabian had been overwhelmed by the magnanimous manliness of the gesture – and said that he would enjoy playing with him so much more now that he was a worthy adversary. It had been one of the high points of Fabian's adolescence.

'He was always wanting to teach me German,' Felicity said.

'Which would have come in jolly handy had you but known.'

'Oh, I picked it up soon enough when I lived there,' she said. 'His was medieval German anyway. Not much use in buying a kilo of apples and asking where the tram leaves from.' She looked at her watch. 'And talking of Germany, I must go. I have a meeting.'

'So late?' It was almost eight.

'Yes.' She never told you more than she wanted you to know. And she never spent longer with you than it suited her.

119

Fabian's father had never let him win at chess and Fabian had respected that. He wasn't going to let Prudence win either; it would be teaching her quite the wrong values. If only she weren't such a bad loser.

'Back to school on Saturday,' he said now, gathering up the pieces preparatory to setting the board back on top of the piano.

If this was intended to cheer her up, it didn't work. She heaved a sigh with more energy than she had put into anything since she came home.

'Holiday task done?' He sounded so falsely jolly that he was sure he must irritate her as much he annoyed himself.

'Uh-huh.'

'Maybe you'll get the chance to play a bit of chess at school,' he suggested. 'When you come home for the summer you'll be beating me in a few moves.'

She gave him a scornful look. 'Only very odd girls play chess,' she said. 'The ones who don't do games because they're outgrowing their strength or some footling rot like that.'

He leapt on the word *games*. 'Well, tennis term, isn't it? You'll like that.' She had been a physical, lively child and now, as this strange in-between half-grown creature, seemed to retain an aptitude for sports. Drill and games were the only things on her report marked *Excellent*.

'S'pose. I should have had my racquet restrung.'

'I'm sure it'll be fine. It's not so very old. Why don't we go up to the tennis club tomorrow? I can take the afternoon off. Have tea in a tea shop afterwards? Last day treat, eh?'

She looked as if an afternoon spent with him was the furthest thing from a treat she could imagine. 'We aren't members of the tennis club.'

'We can book a court as guests, and if you like it, we can join. Your mother and I used to play when we were courting. She was much better than me.'

This was not quite true, but he had taken to introducing Serena into conversations like this; he was worried that Prudence's only memories were of a sick mother, in bed or on the sofa, face twisted in pain, turning away from the child, unable to bear her romp and fuss. A mother who must have seemed to be rebuffing her even before the ultimate rejection of death. He wanted to restore a healthy Serena to Prudence's mind: a racquet-wielding, laughing Serena full of life and hope. A sort of heavenly role model. Prudence did not seem perturbed by these mentions, but nor did she show any interest. He did it, he supposed, mainly for himself, drilling down through the months of illness to what he had not then realised was the charmed time beneath, like a dentist drilling through a bad tooth.

He could not have pretended that Prudence leapt with alacrity on his tennis idea, but he took her *s'pose* as acquiescence and next day, sure enough, she was outside his office at one-thirty. It was the first time he had allowed her to go into the town unchaperoned, so he supposed there was an element of novelty in the outing. She was waiting on the low wall opposite, plaits tied round her head, white school tennis frock showing beneath her open gabardine, racquet in its wooden press leaning against her legs. He watched her for a moment before she saw him, wishing she could be happier, easier; wishing most of all that he wasn't so useless with her.

But the afternoon went better than he could have hoped. At first Prudence walked slightly apart, as if there were no greater mortification than being seen in public with her father, but gradually she edged closer and unbent so far as to say that she was hoping to get onto the second six that term.

'Which nobody in lower fourth has ever done before.'

He forbore to say that she had only been at St Lucy's for two terms so how did she know, or that she had not yet played tennis there; he said instead that that would be marvellous. As they walked up Oaklea Road he heard himself say, 'I'll buy you a new racquet if you get into the six.' And then he worried that that was wrong. Was he bribing her? Should he offer her a new racquet in any case? Or was he spoiling her? She didn't need a new racquet.

But she said, 'Oh, darling Daddy, that would be *miraculous*,' and began a long story about someone called Dottie and a hockey stick. He rather lost the thread but it didn't matter.

The tennis club was near the end of the road, surrounded by trees in blossom. As they approached its long wall, they could hear the plop of balls on catgut and the cries of 'Played! Oh well done! Mine!'

Prudence turned to him, her face bright. 'I wonder if I'll beat you, Daddy,' she said.

'Not if I can help it.'

But as they changed their shoes – he had changed into flannels and sports shirt before leaving the office – he wondered if, perhaps, it might be an idea to let her.

In fact they were fairly well matched. He was surprised at her strength and the way she darted around the court. She was fierce too, fighting for every ball, sometimes too hard. She went two sets up fairly quickly, even though he was playing his normal game – which, he supposed, wasn't saying much. He hadn't played for years. He had had to wipe his racquet down to get the dust off. But he was steadier; by the third set she was tiring.

'Don't waste so much energy,' he advised her. 'There's no point wearing yourself out for balls you'll never reach.'

She pouted. 'I won't wear myself out,' she argued.

One thing was sure: she did not play like her mother. Serena had played an elegant, ladylike game.

'You play like a boy,' he said after a long rally where she had returned every shot with a great deal of clout if not always accuracy.

Instead of being flattered she screwed up her face. 'Ugh, Daddy, don't be silly. I play like Dorothy Round.'

He was about to ask if this was a girl in her form when he remembered that she was a tennis player.

'Well, we must see about you joining the club,' he said. 'Would you like that?'

'S'pose.'

Oh, Daddy, darling, thank you – how kind you are. He often did this; made up the reply he liked to think she really meant. But it had been a good idea, the best time he had had with her since Serena died, and as they walked back down towards town, looking forward to tea in The Copper Kettle, he said, 'You can play as much as you like in the summer. That'll be something to look forward to, won't it?'

'S'pose.' She hit her racquet press against her leg. 'But I'll have nobody to play *with*. You're always at work, and anyway I'd rather . . .'

'Play with someone your own age,' he finished. 'But if you join the club you'll make friends.'

She humped a shoulder. 'They'll know each other. They probably won't like me.' He could almost see the doom descend on her.

'Of course they'll like you,' he said heartily.

'Daddy!' Her tone changed. 'Look, it's that lady. Aunty Fee's lodger.' She pointed down the road to where a bicycle was making its way slowly but determinedly up the hill. And on the bicycle, pink in the face, hatless, her hair blowing out behind her, was April McVey. She had her skirt bunched up out of the way and he couldn't help noticing the length of her brown-stockinged legs as they pistoned purposefully at the pedals. Beside him Prudence slowed her steps. 'What a lovely bicycle,' she breathed.

Would April see them? It was a steep hill; she had to give all her energy to pedalling, standing in the pedals at one point.

Maybe she would have to get off and push and then it would be natural to raise his hat, to call out to her even. He would say, *Good afternoon, Miss McVey. What a lovely afternoon. How energetic you are!* Or, no, was that rather personal? What about, *I'd rather be walking down this hill than cycling up it!* That would show admiration of her energy, and be charmingly self-deprecating, but no, she might think of him then as middle-aged and flabby. He carried his racquet a little more obviously, that she might see he had been playing tennis. And, oh gosh, she would be past in a second! Quick, say *something*! He whipped off his hat and called, 'Good afternoon, Miss McVey!' That was all he could manage. And, how embarrassing, she hadn't noticed, or didn't recognise them; she must think him one of those seedy fellows who make themselves nuisances to strange women. How much better if he'd said nothing.

But Prudence yelled out shrilly and waved her racquet. 'Miss McVey!' she called in such clarion tones that had April been riding a motorbike she couldn't have failed to hear. She looked up, gave a wobble, recovered herself and slid to a stop. She put one foot down on the pavement to anchor herself and smiled at them, gesturing that she was too out of breath to speak just yet.

If Fabian was shy, Prudence was not. She beamed at April. 'We've been playing tennis at the club,' she said. 'Is that where you're going?'

April shook her head. 'I've never played tennis in my life,' she said. 'But fair play to yous. It's a grand day for it.' She held her face up to the sun. 'I'm at my work,' she said and laughed. 'It might not look like it, but I am.'

'It's certainly not the afternoon to be in an office,' Fabian agreed.

Prudence was gazing at the bicycle. 'I like your bike.' She reached out a hand to touch the shining handlebars.

'Me too. It's got gears, look.' She showed them the little lever. 'Makes the hills a wee bit easier.'

The way she said *wee* – he had noted it before – was enchanting.

'Who are the flowers for?' Prudence demanded, and he noticed for the first time a bunch of daffodils in the bicycle's front basket, along with her battered satchel.

April laughed. 'For me,' she said.

'From an admirer?'

'Prudence! I'm so sorry, Miss McVey.'

April laughed. 'From a grateful client,' she said. 'And don't be calling me Miss McVey, sure didn't we sort that out last time? I'll be going home after this call and I didn't want to leave them in the office all weekend.' She hesitated, then reached forward and separated about half the blooms from the rest. She handed them to Prudence. 'There you go,' she said. 'Sure I've plenty here.'

'Oh, I can't let you . . .' he began but Prudence was already scooping up the flowers.

'Thank you so much!' she said, gazing up at April with adoration. 'Nobody's ever given me flowers before.'

April laughed. 'Me neither.'

'Which makes it doubly kind of you.' Fabian raised his hat again. 'We mustn't keep you.'

'I was glad of the break. This hill's a killer. I'm going on out the Belldale Road; I thought this would be a short cut, but I forgot how steep it was. Right, I'd better get on.' She pushed away from the kerb and shouted back over her shoulder, 'Bye-ee!'

She couldn't get a great deal of speed up, so he was able to watch her for quite a while, the straight back in the short wool coat, the bright fair hair, the strong regular pedalling of her slim legs. She was delightful. And then he was ashamed. She could only be about twenty-five. She wouldn't look at a middle-aged man like him, and he, well, he should not be looking at her. Not like that.

'Did you ever have a bicycle, Daddy?' Prudence asked as they continued down the hill.

'Gosh, yes. I cycled everywhere when I was your age,' he said. 'And at Oxford. And then, I don't know, I grew up and married Mummy and we lived in London and there was always the bus or the tube.'

Prudence's hands were full with her racquet and the daffodils, so she could not grab his arm, but she rubbed the side of her head against it like a dog. 'Daddy?' she said, giving the word about four syllables and a good deal of honey, and he knew what was coming.

'We'll see.' He remembered the bad report, the final warning, the desire not to spoil her.

'I could cycle to the tennis club,' she wheedled.

'I suppose you could,' he said.

And maybe he would buy himself a bicycle too. After all, she would need help to become proficient; he couldn't just send her out on the roads unsupervised.

Fabian was not generally given to flights of fancy, but all the way home he couldn't help imagining himself cycling along beside a straight-backed girl with bright hair and strong legs. And she was not his daughter.

Seventeen

April couldn't say that Martha did anything so undignified as to *sulk* after the ill-fated interview with Primrose Lewis. But disappointment tightened her lips and April could feel it prickling the air of the office. It was a relief at Friday lunchtime when Martha said she was leaving early to go to her nephew's birthday tea.

'I can trust you to lock up, can't I? Only Beulah's not very strong at the moment and I promised to help. Billy's whole class is coming and you can imagine all those little boys . . .'

'Of course.'

'And you will keep the keys safe over the weekend?'

'I'm not an eejit.'

Martha did not look absolutely convinced of this. 'There's not much to do this afternoon,' she said. 'Just a few brochures to send out and—'

April waved the to-do list she kept on her desk. 'All under control. Away you go. I'll be grand.'

'Leave early if you've got everything cleared up,' Martha said. 'It's a lovely day. Really feels like spring at last.'

She didn't say, *If you're not here you can't do any damage*, but April couldn't help thinking she meant it. And it wasn't fair; she'd given Mrs Lewis great advice. Martha was just being an old stick. *What aspect of marriage bureau have you failed to grasp?*

But she hated being out of favour. She'd fly through this and then give the office a really good tidy, give Martha a nice surprise on Monday. Let her see April wasn't the kind to leave early. And sure why would she? She didn't have much to do. Sometimes . . . it was silly, she'd longed for this freedom . . . but sometimes the weekends felt a wee bit long.

There were no appointments booked so she was surprised to hear a light, quick tread on the steps outside, and then a knock on the door. 'Come in,' she said, feeling important. Sybil Postlethwaite's face beamed over an armful of the most glorious daffodils – big yellow ones with orange trumpets, dozens of them.

'Miss McVey.' She thrust the daffodils across the desk. 'These are for you.'

'For me?' She gathered them up in glee. 'Why?'

'Henry,' Sybil said simply. 'He's perfect. I couldn't be happier. I've never imagined it could be like this. Like' – her face worked as she tried to find the right words – 'like having the best chum, only more so. Being able to make plans and . . . oh, it's wonderful, Miss McVey! I'm so happy. And Daddy and Mummy adore him.'

April swelled with pride. 'I'm sorry Mrs Hart isn't here,' she said, and she meant it. If only Martha could hear this! Because *she* hadn't been for giving that cratur Henry a chance at all with Sybil. *See,* she wanted to say, *I am good at this! My modern instincts are just what you need.*

'I'd tell all my pals to come here,' Sybil said earnestly, 'except I don't really want to admit how I met Henry.'

'Och, never worry.' Since Martha was not here, she said, 'We probably wouldn't have the kind of posh fellas they'd be after.'

'But it's precisely because Henry isn't a posh fellow that he's perfect,' Sybil said, and they both laughed and it felt, to April, just for a moment, like giggling with a pal, and as she said goodbye to Sybil and filled a jug of water for the flowers, she realised that she had not giggled with a pal for a long time.

She wasn't expecting the phone to ring – Friday afternoon was generally quiet – but it did so just as she was locking the filing cabinet. A Mr Johnson. He sounded good-humoured, rather chattier than prospective clients tended to be. He was a bachelor of forty, he said, a professional man who was minded to meet a nice lady. He was very busy and did not greatly care for the social round, which, at his age, was unlikely to introduce him to suitable women, as he mostly socialised with men at his club, who were in the main escaping their domestic fires for the evening. 'I don't want to miss my chance,' he said.

The words reminded her of what Miss Murrell had said. Of course, in an ideal world she wanted Fabian Carr for Miss Murrell, but in the event of his not signing up to the bureau – and she couldn't make him! – she had to have a contingency plan. This Mr Johnson sounded eminently suitable. She made the usual initial notes on her scribbler.

'May I ask where you heard of us?' she asked. Martha liked to know which forms of advertising were most worthwhile.

'Word of mouth.' He had a colleague, he naturally couldn't say who – he understood the need for discretion, especially in a small town – but a person he trusted, who had consulted them very lately, and had already been introduced to a jolly nice girl. 'Tell you the truth, we all thought the old chap would never settle down, bit of a mummy's boy – we used to tease him no end, and suddenly he's taking this lovely little thing to the pictures! Didn't think he had it in him.'

Lovely little thing was – April frowned and drew a mouse on the notepad (she had only two doodles, mice and daisies) – well, demeaning; still, some men did talk like this; she couldn't expect everyone who signed up to be as modern as she was herself. Maybe Miss Murrell wouldn't mind being called *a lovely little thing.*

'Let me make an appointment for you to come in, Mr Johnson.' She reached for the diary. 'My colleague is away on business today' – she wasn't going to say she was at a six-year-old's birthday party – 'but I can take the booking. Would Tuesday suit? We have evening appointments for businesspeople.'

He sounded downcast. 'I'd rather hoped to see someone sooner than that.' His voice became confiding. 'You know, it's Friday and I'm thinking of the prospect of another lonely weekend. It would mean so much to be able to set the wheels in motion at once.' He sighed. 'I might as well tell you: it's my birthday today. I know it sounds fanciful, but I feel if I could set the wheels in motion as it were, it would help me face it all so much better.'

'Och, Mr Johnson!' Fellow feeling crept into her voice. 'Sure don't I know all about it?' She remembered her own birthday, all alone in a strange town. And this poor cratur was forty! Sure, she'd felt bad enough being twenty-nine.

And she understood about Fridays. She used to think Friday nights in Lisnacashan, keeping the peace between Mammy and Daddy, were hard, especially after Evelyn got married and there was no chance of slipping down to her house for an hour's escape. But Friday nights in Easterbridge . . .

It was grand living alone; it was what she'd always wanted. But it was, well, quiet. Sometimes she went to bed about nine because there was nothing much else to do.

Sympathy for Mr Johnson grew. She glanced at the clock. 'I

could fit you in this afternoon,' she said, 'if you could come down shortly?'

He sighed. 'My car's at the garage,' he said. 'Problem with the gear box. But my colleague said two ladies came to his house, so I was hoping—'

'Och now, we only provide that service in exceptional circumstances.' So he was, as she had suspected, a colleague of Cedric Young's, and evidently Martha had gone ahead and introduced Cedric to some *lovely little thing*. Miss Robins or Miss Jennings presumably. Imagine her not even telling April! Was that because of her mistake with Mrs Lewis? If she managed to sign up Mr Johnson it might appease Martha. Bachelors of forty did not come their way every day. And a schoolmaster! Martha thought there was nobody like a schoolmaster. She would be delighted if April could round up the week's business by bringing in another. Martha wouldn't approve of her going alone, but the end would justify the means, and she needn't actually say she had gone to his house.

And Martha had said she could go home early today. Why not snap up this Mr Johnson on the way ? She would find out where he lived and if it were not too far out of her way . . .

He lived on the road she normally took to cycle onto the moors. In fact she knew the house as soon as he described it – that place where she'd nearly run over the cat. That nice woman she had talked to in the garden must be his sister. So no worries about going alone to a man's home. And Miss Murrell had lived with *her* sister until lately! She felt a pang for that friendly woman picking tulips, but surely her brother wouldn't just oust her from her home. And anyway, she might be the adventurous type. Maybe she couldn't wait to get him married off so she could join a circus or travel the world. She might have a gentleman friend who was pestering her to get married, only she didn't like to leave her poor brother to cope alone. Or she might be longing to set up home with a pal.

She was so lost in these thoughts that she nearly didn't see Fabian and Prudence Carr until she was past them. And they'd a lovely wee chat, and she shared her daffodils, and they were delighted, and it was like a sign, she thought, that this afternoon was blessed.

Johnson's house was a sturdy, well-kept stone cottage, gentrified and pretty, rose-gold in the afternoon sun, the moors reaching right down to its garden. April leaned her bicycle carefully against the wall, the daffodils sprouting brightly from its basket. Nigel Johnson answered the door so quickly that he must have been waiting for her arrival. He was a dark, heavyset man with a high colour – she hoped his florid cheeks didn't mean what they had for Daddy: that his heart wasn't in the best shape. Imagine if she found the poor man a wife and then he croaked! He ushered her into a tidy, homely parlour with modern furniture and walls crowded with photos, including some military ones. He had clearly served in the war; Martha would be beside herself with joy. He still had a soldierly look, with a thick moustache and a very upright bearing.

Johnson saw that her eyes were drawn to the pictures. 'Fought with the Yorkshires,' he said. 'Happy times.'

'Happy?'

'The camaraderie. Chance to prove yourself.'

Wasn't it marvellous, the difference in people? Daddy could never bear to be reminded, and Fabian Carr, when he had mentioned the war, had sounded almost awkward about it. Johnson must have had what was called *a good war*.

She was getting better at the usual small talk, designed to set the client at ease. How pretty his house was; she had often noticed it when she cycled out here; how nice the garden looked in the spring sunshine.

'Your sister seems fond of the garden,' she said. 'It must be lovely later in the year.'

'My—? Oh yes.' He beamed. 'She is. Very fond. Very fond indeed. She's away at the moment. Visiting her mother.' Johnson crossed to a table in the corner and took the stopper out of a decanter. 'You'll join me in a drink, Miss – er . . .?'

'McVey. Och, I couldn't. I'm at work. And I don't really—'

'Come, come! You wouldn't let me drink alone on my birthday, hmm?' She wasn't too keen on his hectoring manner, and his expansive maleness, the way he possessed the room, but that was daft, sure wasn't it his own room! It was Friday afternoon, it was his birthday, and if a drink helped him to relax, what harm could it do? And if he wasn't the kind of man she personally found pleasing, sure what odds. Miss Murrell, or any of their spinster clients, might well be attracted to him.

'I'm having whisky,' he said, 'but I'm guessing for a little lady like you, a sweet sherry . . .?'

April's chin went up. *Little lady* indeed! 'I'll have whisky too,' she said. (For the first time in a while she cocked a mental snook at Daddy.) She sat down where he gestured her to do so, on the green brocade sofa, and took out her notebook and a registration form. She set them in her lap and accepted the glass he handed her. The smell made her splutter, but she didn't want to look like an eejit, so she took a good glug. It tasted like medicine, and snaked hotly down through her, burning bits of inside she'd never been aware of before.

Johnson stood with his back to the window, his own glass looking small in his hand. He looked her up and down. 'My colleague didn't do you justice, Miss McVey. He merely said an older lady and a young fair one. He didn't say how pretty you were.'

April set her glass down on the coffee table. 'If we can just fill in the form, Mr Johnson? Now, some people find some of the questions a wee— I mean, a little surprising.'

'I'm hard to surprise.'

'I mean we have to ask about income, that kind of thing.' She repeated the words she had heard Martha say so often now. 'We find that people prefer to be matched with those broadly within their own social class.' She wondered how long his sister would be – did *visiting her mother* mean staying for a weekend, or popping into town? And why did he say *her* mother, not *our* mother? Stepsister maybe? And that flicker of confusion when she had said *your sister* – or was she reading too much into things? She could be an awful eejit that way. *Too much imagination*, Mammy said. She rushed on, 'But I can assure you everything is done with the utmost discretion. We only use your details to—'

'Utmost discretion, eh?' He raised his eyebrows in what she told herself was not a leer.

'Mr Johnson, excuse me, I must just check – you are a bachelor? Looking for marriage?'

'What else should I be?' Again that raised-eyebrows look and she worried that she had offended him. Maybe he was just a wee bit tight – it was his birthday, after all. She'd interviewed a few defensive, awkward folk and she'd reminded herself the craturs were lonely and probably embarrassed. And some people hid that with bluster, men especially. She must be careful not to become one of those man-hating spinsters people laughed at. She must strive to be fair.

'You can appreciate we have to be very careful. Now' – she uncapped her pen – 'let's fire away. So you're forty – today!' She made herself smile, and jotted that down. 'And am I right in thinking you're a schoolmaster?'

'For my sins. Mathematics,' he said. 'At the grammar. How did you – oh aye!' He wagged his finger at her. 'I see you're a bit of a Sherlock Holmes!' He stood up and came over to sit beside her, the sofa sagging under his weight. He smelt faintly of sweat, overlaid by cologne and whisky.

April swallowed and drew back as far as she could, but the sofa seemed to have shrunk. 'Mr Johnson, would you mind? I can't quite concentrate. Would you sit back where you were? I need space to . . . to write your responses. Or, if you want to sit here, I can go somewhere else.'

She half rose but he reached across and took the pen from her hand. Before she could stop him, he put the cap on again and tossed it down on to the coffee table. 'Come on now, missie.' He took hold of her arm. 'We both know you don't need to write down my particulars.'

'I don't underst—'

'Oh, I think you do. I think we both know that you understand very well. Marriage bureau indeed! True Minds, eh? I can see what's on *your* mind. I can see what sort of *bureau* you are. Coming alone to a man's house. Exceptional circumstances indeed!'

His other hand was on her knee. She stared at it as she might have stared at an insect that had landed on her, unsure whether to brush it off and risk angering it, or sit tight and hope to avoid the sting. She found, deep inside her where she hadn't known it could go, her voice. It was high and tight but steady. 'Please take your hand off me.'

In response he increased the pressure and leaned forward. She smelt the whisky on his breath and the sweat from his underarms; he was breathing fast. She knew almost nothing of men but guessed he was in a state of some excitement.

His voice was low and murmuring now. 'Come on; you wouldn't have come here if you didn't want it! *Bureau*! Don't you mean *brothel*?' His other hand squeezed her breast very firmly. She tried to scramble away but he had manoeuvred

135

himself so that he was pinning her against the back of the sofa. His face loomed – his hairy wet mouth against hers – ugh – she pressed her lips shut – his tongue tried to push through – should she bite? Could she bear to? No. She managed to free an elbow and raised it to fend him off, not caring where it landed, knowing that, though she was tall and strong, she was no match physically for him, would have to fight dirty. *Like a girl*. But she was not the dirty one!

Her elbow-punch connected with his nose. He jumped back. 'You little bitch,' he said. 'I was only . . . Christ! You frigid teasing Irish bitch.'

She grabbed her pen and her bag and dashed for the door. If he got there first, if he wouldn't let her out, if he had locked her in . . . Oh God, she breathed, please please let me out of here and I'll never ask for anything in my life ever again. But God mustn't have been listening, or wouldn't be bargained with by someone who hadn't been to church for weeks, because as she flung herself on the door, Johnson was grabbing her from behind, one hand reaching under her jacket at the waistband of her skirt, the other round her neck. She dropped her chin and bit that hand very hard and he let go with a shout of pain and she flung open the door and ran: down the hallway, front door – oh, let it not be locked, thank God – she was outside – oh rush of air, where was her bike, oh God oh God please, there it was, where she had left it – she jumped on it, legs shaking, feet grappling for the pedals, hands sweating on the handlebars, sweat running down her back too, pooling at her waist, pedal like mad, the wheels were spinning too fast, she couldn't get any purchase on them, but she was getting away, down the hill, thank God it was down-hill all the way, she could not have cycled uphill. She flew over potholes she would normally have avoided, shedding daffodils in ones and twos.

She didn't stop for well over a mile, when she was sure that he could not be following, and then she did not so much stop as let the bike run aground in a field gateway and collapse off it, her whole body shaking. She gulped for breath. When she remembered her teeth sinking into his hand and the taste of his skin and blood, she all but boked. She leaned over the gate, retching, tasting the whisky again, looking down to the town, trying to get her breath back to normal, determined not to cry – she would not cry because of that . . . that . . . monster. She thrummed with disgust and tension.

You frigid teasing Irish bitch. The words filled her mind and all she could counter them with was an incoherent *No. I'm not. I didn't.* But, oh God, what an eejit she had been! Primrose Lewis's words came back now to add their stings: *a very self-assured young woman, but she has no knowledge of life.*

Down in the valley, Easterbridge looked quiet; people would be coming home from work, the streets bustling with bicycles and cars and people, but from up here you could see only stolid unmoving buildings. The gate struck hard and cold under her hands, a sensation initially welcome and then uncomfortable. She stuffed her hands into her jacket pockets. Had she left her gloves behind? No, look, there they were – she had taken them off when she arrived and placed them in her basket. And she had her bag and her best pen – a present from Evelyn; she would have hated to lose that. What she had left behind was their brochure and the registration form on which she had only got as far as filling in his name and age. Incriminating to have left it, but for him, not her. He would surely have the sense to destroy it before his wife came home. Because of course the fair-haired woman in the garden was his wife. Probably she was indeed visiting her mother and would not be back for a day or so. And he had decided to take advantage of her absence – but what on earth had Cedric Young said? *Didn't think he had it in him.* Staffroom boasting, no doubt; Young couldn't resist the chance to brag, to prove himself one of the lads for once, show how normal he was, and whatever he had said about April and Martha had led Johnson to think . . .

What? That True Minds was a front for a – she hated to let her mind go back to that room and his hands on her body and his whisky breath in her ear but she had to. *Brothel*, he had said. Did anyone else think that? Maybe Mrs Hart's Matrimonial Bureau *had* sounded more respectable; maybe she shouldn't have been so insistent on changing to True Minds. Could there possibly have been something in the story in the *Recorder*, in their brochure, some sort of double entendre to make people think . . .? No. For dear sake, Martha had run the business for ten years. It gave her a good enough living to employ April. People contacted them in good faith. It was discreet and respectable. Only someone with a filthy mind and a complete lack of respect for women could have imagined otherwise. And Johnson clearly had both. His poor wee wife. She should go and find her, call on her some day when Johnson was at school, tell her what her husband was really like, rescue her.

But not everyone wanted to be rescued. And that woman, with her bulbs and her wavy fair hair, and her respectable schoolmaster husband, would not believe April; would think she had designs on her husband and had been spurned, and wanted to cause trouble. Nobody would believe her. She could imagine what they would say: *Spinster, you know, not quite natural. Fantasist. Needs a good seeing to. And you know the Irish . . .*

No. There was nobody she could tell. She gave a little moan, and then nausea swept through her, and she did boke, hot and sour into the ditch. Shivering, she turned back to the road, grasped the handlebars of her bicycle, and went to mount. But her legs would not work. She had to wheel the bicycle all the way home, looking into the empty basket, biting her cheeks to stop herself from crying.

Eighteen

Saturday morning. April stood at the back door and breathed in the cool promising air. Go on, she told herself. Go to the shed, get your bike, and go. You can't skulk inside all weekend. You'll go mad.

She'd woken at four, heart pounding, mouth sandy-dry and his whisky-sweat stink in her nostrils. Maybe she should go to Manchester for the weekend? Mammy was always asking her to. But the thought of dragging herself to the station, boarding a train – what if *he* were there? She would get into a carriage and close the door behind her and he would be there and it would be too late, and she would be trapped. And what if, when she got to Eupatoria Street and Mammy, she couldn't make herself leave again, couldn't make herself come back here to Easterbridge to her own life? The one she'd fought so hard for. She'd be disgraced forever. And she'd never be able to hide from Mammy that something was wrong. She knew her too well.

No. She pulled in a deep breath and forced herself to go to the shed. She wasn't going to let that monster keep her in. She was ashamed to see her poor bicycle slumped against the wall, mud on its frame and wheels. She had shoved it away last night without cleaning it. She gave it a wipe now with the cloth she kept for the purpose. She had to pick bits of daffodil stalk out of the basket. Wasn't it as well she'd given some to Prudence? Imagine if they'd all been wasted, scattered all over the Belldale Road like scraps of yellowed newspaper.

She had got into the habit of cycling up onto the moors on Saturdays, taking a picnic, exploring the hills and valleys and outlying villages, but she could not bring herself to cycle past *that house*. Well, no matter. There was another road out of the town, past the park and away on up beyond where Fabian and Prudence lived, so she'd go that way. She did, but it was much longer and steeper, and she had to ride for a long time along a trunk road which, even on a weekend, thundered with lorries that made her bicycle shake. The moors were there, just the same, glowering over the town, but no matter how hard she kept pedalling, she never seemed to reach them. And then the air darkened and it rained, and her sandwiches got sodden, and she was back home in number eleven by mid-afternoon, with the long evening stretching ahead. Never mind Sunday to follow.

It'd have been grand if Felicity had been around to have a cup of tea with, as they occasionally did these days, but the study door was firmly closed. Right. Well, she'd take a leaf out of her landlady's book, and do some writing herself – Mammy always liked hearing from her, and it wasn't her turn to write to Evelyn, but sure that didn't matter. Evelyn probably didn't have time for writing, she'd said in that last letter that wee Robbie was into everything, and it'd be a lovely surprise to hear from April again so soon. But when she sat down at the white table in her white room and uncapped her good pen, she remembered the last time she had used it and set the pen down. Sure what news had she? No new friends, no achievements; she hadn't joined anything or done anything except make stupid mistakes. She didn't belong here. She'd been better off in Lisnacashan.

141

Well, maybe so, but she'd never sat around moping in Lisnacashan and she wasn't about to start now. She would go to the pictures! *Little Women* wouldn't be showing for much longer, and why should she miss it just because she didn't have anyone to go with? She had never been to the pictures alone, but there was a first time for everything and she made her way into town with a determinedly lighter heart, even if it was thumping hard and she shrank inside her coat every time she'd to cycle past a man.

Catch yourself on, April McVey, she told herself. Don't be an eejit. Nobody's going to grab you and pull you off your bike in the street.

The Odeon was new and shiny, all chrome fittings and curved lemon-painted walls; it must surely be the most modern thing in Easterbridge. She had expected people to stare at her, a woman alone, but in fact she saw several others and made sure to sit near them. Were they spinsters like herself, or women whose husbands or sweethearts couldn't be dragged to such a sentimental picture? It didn't matter; their presence made her feel better.

She had to sit through the newsreels, and the first one was about Germany, which she paid more attention to than usual because of Felicity having lived there. April wasn't a great one for politics, though you couldn't really get away from them in Northern Ireland. Even in Lisnacashan there'd been trouble around partition, and only a couple of years ago there'd been riots in neighbouring towns. She'd heard people say this new fella in Germany was getting the country sorted out rightly, but she hadn't paid him much attention. Now he filled the screen, a funny-looking wee man, but he must have something in him – look at the thousands of people who'd turned out in support of him. His troops marched across the screen, arms raised in a stiff salute, and though they looked a bit eejity there was also

142

something sinister about their massed ranks. Something too intense. She shuddered. It's far away, she thought; don't worry about it, you've enough to think about. And it probably wasn't as bad as it looked; those big crowds were probably like the crowds Daddy had told her about in 1912 when he'd gone to Belfast to sign the Ulster Covenant. It must be nice to feel something that bound you together like that. She wriggled, wishing *Little Women* would start. At last the Nazis stopped marching, to be replaced by a much more restful scene of young Germans hiking through a pretty flower meadow, singing gaily, the boys in lederhosen and the girls in fresh dirndl skirts, looking jolly and wholesome. She settled down in her seat, arranging her skirt more comfortably under her so the prickly new moquette wouldn't scratch her legs through her stockings.

But, for dear sake, it still wasn't time for the main feature. A *Pathé Tutorial on Self-Defence for the Weaker Sex!* was announced and the screen was filled by a solid man and a willowy woman with an aureole of curly hair and a perfectly painted mouth.

'He's after her bag!' declared the narrator in his posh English voice, and the woman proceeded to overthrow the man with a neat judo throw. He grabbed her round the neck – she floored him again; he went for her waist – she rolled him over. When she had finished, she shook back her curls and calmly powdered her nose. 'And that's how seven stone can overturn fourteen stone,' trilled the announcer.

April's stomach contracted. It hadn't been remotely like that when Johnson had gone for her. He hadn't been after her handbag. He'd been after – ugh, don't think about it. And she couldn't have flung him over her head with one kick, even if she'd known how. There wouldn't have been space, for one thing. The young woman onscreen smiled nonchalantly and sauntered off, clutching her bag.

It was a relief when *Little Women* finally came on and she could lose herself – or most of herself – in Jo and her sisters, the story as familiar as her own life. She had a wee cry when Beth died, but not when Jo refused Laurie – she'd always understood why Jo wouldn't marry him, though Evelyn had argued that Jo was an eejit and nobody in their right minds wouldn't fancy Laurie. Of course people in films were never the way you imagined them, but Katharine Hepburn was so strong and passionate that soon, for April, she *was* Jo. And Aunt March was deliciously ferocious – she looked forward to telling Felicity. She stayed right through the trailer for next week's film, *The Lucky Loser*, which she didn't fancy, and couldn't help being proud of herself as she cycled home, aware, as she reached Riverside Road, of being exhausted, but of having made quite a bit of time pass. She could have a wee read now, and that would put the evening in rightly. Because when she wasn't consciously thinking of something else, the scene in Johnson's house kept playing through her mind. Except she wasn't like the nonchalant high-kicking woman in the tutorial film who kept hold of her bag – and, it was implied, her virtue – she was a silly girl who was no better than she should be and got what was coming to her.

On the way upstairs she scanned the bookcases. Felicity had said she could borrow anything she liked. There was a Carnegie Library in town, and she meant to join sometime – that might be a project for next week – but it was handy to browse the shelves in her own house. She would know what she wanted when she saw it – nothing too demanding. Maybe a reread of an old friend? Not *Little Women*, it was too fresh in her mind now, but she smiled to see it. There was all of Jane Austen, but she wasn't in the mood for Jane Austen. Too much about marriage. (*What aspect of marriage bureau have you failed to grasp?* It still stung.) Here were some foreign books – she squinted at the funny Gothic print, the same as the print on the newsreel. German. Well, that was no good to man nor beast.

Something a bit lighter? There was a bundle of magazines stuffed onto the shelves above the books. April pulled some out and started to flick through without much hope. She assumed Felicity would subscribe to highbrow literary journals, or maybe *Time and Tide*, which Martha liked. But actually most of the magazines were of the *Peg's Paper* type, the sort of thing the girls in the factory used to read. She looked at the titles of the stories: 'The Sheikh's Revenge'; 'She Was Only a Scullery Maid'; 'Virtue Forsaken!' She flicked through the last one and read of Molly the mill girl who had been kidnapped outside the mill by a brigand (what *was* a brigand, exactly?). He was a very handsome brigand, with dark curls and a cruel lip but things did not augur well for poor Molly's virtue. Definitely not what she needed right now.

She stuffed the magazines back. Aha – the children's books: *Rivals of the Chalet School* – now that couldn't wring the withers. What a strange book for Felicity, though. She opened it and a little slip of paper fell out. *With compliments. The Times.* It must be a review copy. Fancy living with someone who reviewed books for *The Times*! She took it upstairs, noting as she went that one of the scribbly abstract paintings had disappeared from the landing. Pity; she had grown fond of its red and orange swirls, but maybe Felicity was fed up with it? April wouldn't have minded it in her room, a wee splash of cheer.

She curled up on her bed and read doggedly for the rest of the evening, transported to the Austrian Tyrol, which, though she wasn't sure where it was, made her think of those smiling young German people in their alpine meadow. Och, it was just what she needed! Nobody in the Chalet School let their pals down and the few male characters were dotes. She even took the book downstairs with her when she made her evening meal.

She hoped she might see Felicity and perhaps use the book to start a conversation – and then tell her about the film – but there was no sign of her. April made an omelette and read while she ate. Tomorrow was Sunday, always a long day, and the only thing she absolutely had to do was to sponge and press her clothes for the week ahead. She remembered Miss Murrell: *not lonely exactly*. But the effort; oh God, Miss Murrell was right about the effort.

Nineteen

'I've been thinking,' April said on Monday morning, when Martha was opening the post. Her voice was casual. 'I believe you're right about home visits – far better to see clients here. After all, we've worked so hard to get the . . . the ambiance right. And sure, if they can't be bothered getting themselves down to the office, are they really the sort of clients we can help?'

Martha, paper knife poised at an angle, was amused. 'That's precisely what I've been telling you!'

'I know. I'm awful stubborn,' April said. 'Sometimes it takes me ages to admit I'm wrong.' She gave Martha a bright grin, and Martha smiled back, relieved. Thank goodness! She'd hated feeling so annoyed with April, uncomfortably aware that she might have been too hard on her. After all, Martha too had failed with poor Primrose Lewis.

But things were looking up! She waved the letter she had just opened. 'This chap sounds just the ticket for your little Miss Murrell. A widower with a daughter' – April perked up, and Martha tossed the letter across the desk – 'and a son,' she finished and April, for some reason, looked disappointed as she scanned the letter.

'A farmer,' she said with a sniff. 'He probably just wants a workhorse.'

Martha snatched the letter back. 'Don't be cynical, April – it doesn't suit us in this line of work.'

April sighed. 'Och no. You're right; he sounds grand. I can see that wee Miss Murrell churning butter and collecting eggs in a flowery pinny, can't you?' Without waiting for a response she said, 'She has a cat, so she must like animals. That's a start. Right, will I organise an appointment for him?'

'Please.'

As Martha dealt with the correspondence she noticed April watching her, as if she expected something, something not altogether welcome. Was she still anxious about Primrose Lewis? That was all forgotten now.

Still, the girl wasn't quite herself and as the week went on Martha became more and more aware of it. There was a brittleness to her; she smiled readily but warily. Martha could find no fault with her commitment; all week she worked as if for a wager, sorting the post almost before Martha noticed it had arrived, jumping up the minute a client left, attacking old files that were perfectly happy languishing where they were, and even getting out a duster to ensure every corner was sparkling clean.

On Thursday, Martha told her off. 'You don't need to do that, now Mrs Atkinson's back,' she said. 'You are allowed to sit quietly once in a while.'

'Och, I'm not one for sitting quietly,' April said. 'I don't want you thinking I'm lazy.'

'Hardly. I've known from the start you were a grafter. But there's no need to be quite so' – she spread her hands – 'agitated. We want this place to feel relaxed and welcoming as well as professional. You're the best assistant I've ever had. But lately, these last few days, you don't seem quite yourself. Is everything all right, my dear?' She softened her voice. 'I do hope you see me as a friend as well as a colleague. And I want you to know that business with Mrs Lewis is forgotten. I was rather hard on you. Ours is a strange sort of business; I can't expect you to get everything right immediately.'

To her shock, April's eyes blurred with tears. She bent lower over her desk and blinked them away. Gosh, Martha thought. What should I do? Surely she'd rather I pretended not to notice? Her instinct was to offer a handkerchief, a cup of tea and a shoulder but she made herself desist. Just because it would make her feel better to comfort April did not mean that April wanted to be comforted. So she did nothing and in a few moments, April looked up and smiled and her voice was hardly different from usual.

'Och, I'm grand,' she said. 'Just getting used to a new place.'

'Are your lodgings comfortable? I had my doubts about Riverside Road.'

'Ah no, it's grand. I love it.'

'And you're making friends?'

April shrugged.

'Do you have plenty to keep yourself amused with when you aren't at work?' Martha asked. 'I can't help feeling responsible for you – a young girl in a strange place. But I haven't wanted to interfere. I know your independence is important to you.'

'Oh God, aye,' April said. 'You know me – a busy bee.'

'Busy with . . .?'

'I'm out on my bike a lot. Getting to know the area.'

'And . . .?'

'Well.' She chewed her lip. 'Sundays can be a bit long.'

Martha leapt on this. 'Do you go to church? That's a super way to meet folk. I go to St Margaret's and—'

April shook her head. 'I don't think—'

'But you are a Protestant, aren't you?' She tried to remember the reference – no, it had definitely not been from *Father* anything.

'Presbyterian. I was made to go to church twice every Sunday, and Sunday School and all, but now . . . och, I can't seem to believe the same way. I used to think Jesus wanted me for a sunbeam, but now I think he can just do without me.'

How typical of the Irish, Martha thought – north or south, Protestant or Catholic, they had an open way of talking about religion that the English wouldn't dream of. They were the same about death. It must not be encouraged.

'Oh, that wouldn't matter in St Margaret's,' she said breezily. 'It's terribly friendly. And belief – er, *faith*, if you like – well that's entirely between you and God. The Church of England's very civilised that way.'

April looked unconvinced.

'And you've a lovely voice.' It occurred to her that she had not heard April sing all week. 'We could do with you in the choir.'

'No, thanks. I'm grand.'

'Well, you must come to lunch some Sunday,' Martha insisted. 'No shop-talk, I promise.'

'Thank you.'

'And you know I've suggested the Townswomen's Guild,' Martha went on. 'You'd be very welcome. They'd love to hear about Northern Ireland. There used to be such a lot about the Irish question in the newspapers, but not lately. And you have such a lively way with words.'

'Och, it's not really my sort of thing,' April said, and Martha gave up. After all, she argued with herself going home that evening, replaying the conversation in her mind, worrying that she should have made the lunch invitation more definite – *some Sunday* was what people said when they had no intention of committing to a date – April was just an employee. She had her own life to lead. Martha shouldn't try to make her into a friend, or run her life for her. She was a big girl.

In the meantime, and talking of running people's lives, there was the meeting between Miss Murrell and Farmer Yeadon to oversee. They were to come in tomorrow at ten and Martha suggested that April look after them on her own.

'She's your client, really. And once you've done this, then there's no aspect of the business you won't have managed alone – and very successfully.' It was her way of showing April she had forgiven and forgotten the Primrose Lewis affair.

But April bit her lip and said she would rather Martha were there.

At first Martha thought the meeting would be disastrous. Miss Murrell arrived first in what looked like a very new costume in a heathery tweed, and as the clock hands juddered past ten, she started to pleat and unpleat her handkerchief in her lap.

'I'm sure there's a good reason for the delay,' Martha said more than once, cursing Yeadon and sure that there jolly well wasn't. Honestly, men were impossible! Had this Joseph Yeadon no empathy with poor Miss Murrell, to keep her waiting, looking desperate and abandoned, like the heroine of a Thomas Hardy novel?

'Farmers be awful busy this time of year,' April said helpfully, and Martha decided to be grateful for her reassurance rather than appalled by her syntax.

It was so quiet that they heard the church clock chime the quarter hour. Miss Murrell looked up and sighed, as if she had heard the death knell.

'I should go,' she said. She patted down her lovely skirt. Martha couldn't bear to think of her buying it, full of expectation and hope.

'Och, don't,' April said. 'Give him a wee minute. I remember this one time—'

Before she could finish, footsteps thundered up the stairs outside the office and a loud knock battered on the door. Miss Murrell sat up like a naughty child and stuffed her handkerchief into her pocket. Martha ached for her.

'I hope he has a good excuse,' she said, before calling out, 'Come in!' feeling like a stern headmistress.

That feeling lasted for about three seconds. Joseph Yeadon was a heavyset man in a good tweed suit with his waistcoat buttoned up wrongly and his tie awry. His curly hair had not been adequately tamed by Brylcreem and fell into his eyes. He had cut himself shaving, twice, and he was out of breath. He looked like he was about to cry.

'I'm sorry!' he said, before any of the three women could say a word. 'I've been up with a calving all night. Poor little thing was arse-first, er, breech, I mean, and the veterinary was away at a foaling over Coaldale way. I called up my neighbour Charlie and he did his best, but he'd be more at home with a bitch whelping. Time we got it out and on its feet and suckling, it was gone eight and I'd the kiddies to get up and out to school and . . .' He ran out of steam.

Before he could apologise again, and before Martha or April could say a thing, Miss Murrell, her face glowing with under-standing and relief, said, 'And is the little calf all right, Mr Yeadon?'

He turned to her and smiled, his face relaxing for the first time. 'Aye, it's champion now. Bit battered but it'll do. I've a good cowman but these things always happen in the middle of the night.'

'It was the same when I was nursing,' Miss Murrell said. 'Are your children of an age to help?'

'If I'd woken our Sam he'd have given me a hand and welcome. But then I'd have had bother getting him off to school today. Sally's not much of a one for cattle. It's sheep she likes – always on at me to let her keep a pet lamb. But they don't stay lambs forever, that's what she won't see.'

'It was always cats with me,' Miss Murrell said. 'My late sister Delia was asthmatic so I couldn't have a cat of my own until she passed. Do you have cats, Mr Yeadon?'

Martha saw his face work, anxious to say the right thing. 'Maybe not what you'd think of as cats, Miss Murrell – they're farm cats. Half wild, living in the barn. We don't feed them – they catch mice and rats. Earn their keep you might say. No room for pets on a farm.'

'Well, no, I suppose not.'

'I've a grand sheepdog.' His face lit up. 'Old Nell. She's not meant to come in the house, but Sally sneaks her in and she creeps under the kitchen table and closes her eyes – thinks if she can't see us, we can't see her.'

Miss Murrell laughed, a warm burble, and April, catching Martha's eye, went to put the kettle on. They both knew they could leave them to it.

'All the same,' April said when she and Martha had retired upstairs to let them do just that, 'if anything comes of it, and if they get married – och, it still feels so peculiar to say this about two people who've only met! – I still say he's looking for a workhorse. You heard what he said, *no room for pets on a farm.*'

'He needs a mother for his children,' Martha said simply. 'He was very frank about that. The little girl especially – she's only seven. Hard for her to grow up without a mother. People marry for all sorts of reasons, that's something I learned a long time ago, and who's to say which reason's best?'

'Och aye, right enough.' She looked thoughtful. 'And he seemed a right cratur, didn't he?'

'I have only the faintest idea what *a right cratur* might be,' Martha said drily.

April grinned – for the first time, surely, that week. 'What you'd call a thoroughly decent chap.'

Twenty

Hope was the cruellest thing. When Fabian had taken Prudence back to St Lucy's the day after the tennis, he really believed that she had turned a corner, that she was determined to settle down this term. He wouldn't even mind if she didn't pass her exams – it didn't matter much for a girl – so long as she enjoyed herself and made friends.

'See you get on that tennis team!' he had said heartily, as he carried her suitcase up the steps to the front door where, he knew from the last two beginnings-of-term, it would be picked up by the school handyman and taken to her dorm.

'*Daddy*,' she said in mortified tones. 'People will think I'm swanking.'

'What people?'

'That's Mirabel Blythe,' she said. 'Getting out of that grey car. She's the games captain. She's super.'

'Well, unless she's also super-human she can't have heard,' he reassured her, but he smiled. He remembered so well the extreme self-consciousness of being fourteen, of parents erupting into your school world with the potential to mortify with you every utterance – or simply by wearing the wrong thing. He recalled a half-term visit from his mother in a hideous orange

154

frock; he had been terrified the fellows would chaff him afterwards. If Prudence cared about that sort of thing, well, it was normal, wasn't it? A sure sign that she was settling.

And he drove home full of hope.

Short-lived hope.

Miss Willard was very sorry. *Genuinely* sorry, she said on the phone on Friday evening, and her voice sounded suitably regretful, but St Lucy's could not countenance actual physical violence.

'It was much worse than last time,' she said. 'She actually hit a younger child in the face with her tennis racquet.'

'Unprovoked?'

He heard her sigh. 'Mr Carr, I can't pretend to have the full story. Girls can be duplicitous. But I do know little Mercy Somerville had to have three stitches on her lip and has lost a tooth. Her parents are not at all pleased. I've been lenient with Prudence before – perhaps too lenient – but I simply cannot keep a disturbed and violent child. You couldn't expect it.'

He did not expect it. He arranged to pick her up next morning.

Disturbed. Was she? Had he created a monster? What had he not done, not given her, for her to have turned out this way? Had he been too wrapped up in his own grief to notice her? He made himself think back to those terrible first weeks after Serena's death when he had had to force himself through every minute of every day, trying to keep things as steady as possible for the child. He had not broken down in front of her; he had not given in to drink or wailing or smashing crockery – and he had felt like doing all those things. He had not sent her to boarding school at once, though many people had advised it. Maybe that had been wrong of him. Maybe she would have been better away from the home where Serena's absence burned such a big hole. And then she might have got used to being away at school more easily.

She was not noticeably chastened when he brought her home. 'Have you sorted out my tennis club membership?' she asked. 'I don't think you should be expecting that just at the moment.' 'But you promised.'

'Prudence.' He tried to inject a warning note into her name, tried to make her see that she was in no position to expect treats.

She sulked in her room all weekend and when he complained, she said there was nothing else to do. He wondered if he should take her to church. Serena had been a believer, he less so, but when he suggested it on Sunday morning, she said it had been bad enough at school, all that compulsory chapel and prayer and she wasn't going to do it at home too.

'You'd have to drag me,' she said, with a flash in her eyes as if she wished he would try, as if she would relish the struggle. 'Kicking and screaming.'

'Don't be foolish,' he said, and left her – *To stew in the juice she got hot in*, as his mother used to say when Felicity, about the same age, had shown similar propensities to flounce and fling.

He would have to tell Felicity. He could ring her up, but it might be better to walk across town and see her instead – Sunday evening, she should be in. She was so damned evasive; so keen to assert that she was busy, and not interested in other people's children, but surely she would see this was a crisis? At the very least she knew how it felt to be a girl, whereas he hadn't a clue.

And talking of girls, her young lodger was likely to be in. He dressed with particular care, choosing a striped tie he had not worn since before Serena died, and taking trouble with his hair in front of the glass in his bedroom – luckily, he thought, as he parted and combed it, the springy brown curls he and Felicity had both inherited from their mother seemed to be as thick as ever, and though there were a few grey threads, you'd need to look closely to see them. But his face in the glass was serious, the mouth thinner, surely, than it had been? No, that was silly; your mouth couldn't get thinner. He made himself smile and his lips relaxed. That was better. He was forty, not sixty. *Widower* was an ageing word, but there was no need to go round looking like a stern, middle-aged solicitor.

The walk through town on the spring evening revived him. He had, on a whim, remembering the daffodils April McVey had given Prudence, gathered some pink tulips from his own front garden; even Felicity would soften at the gift of flowers.

He had never understood Felicity choosing to live in Riverside Road. And even if the area hadn't been dubious, the house itself was awkward and narrow and full of stairs. He had hoped, when he moved to Easterbridge, that she would move in with him – there was plenty of room in Parkgate Avenue, and with Prudence away at school she could not have accused him of wanting an unpaid mother substitute, but of course she had refused.

As he neared the house, slightly out of breath, he saw with relief that a lamp burned in the front room window. He rang the bell. Silence. For a long time. But he could see her: that shadow behind the curtains, moving around the room. Oh, for goodness sake, was she going to be pretend to be out? She really was the most infuriating sister. He rang again. And then – gosh, she actually twitched the curtain, the most un-Felicity-like gesture he could imagine – he saw her hand and a sliver of face as she checked to see who was there. For a moment he felt amused. Funny old Felicity. She made such a song and dance about doing things on her own terms, not letting anyone force her into the spinster aunt role, and here she was behaving exactly like a spinster aunt, and a nervous one at that. He would rib her about that! Or maybe not – he reminded himself he was there to ask for help – no point in getting off on the wrong foot. She could be touchy – artistic temperament and all that.

The door pulled back a mere inch, and she spoke from behind it. But it wasn't her! It was Miss McVey – April, she had asked him to call her – though an April who sounded very different from the perky girl he had met three times now. 'Is that . . . who is it, please?'

'It's me, Fabian Carr. I've come to see Felicity.'

'She's not in.' No face, just her fingers gripped round the edge of the door. Her fingernails were bitten. He had not noticed before.

'Will she be back soon?'

'She's away for a few days. In London.'

'Damn. I mean— Sorry, Miss McVey, er, April. I wanted to talk to her about Prudence. I wonder would you . . . Look, could I come in? I can't talk through the door like this, and you might be able to help.'

'Well . . .' The fingers shifted; the door was pulled slowly open. 'All right.'

She stood back – almost, he would have said, *shrank* back – against the wall, to let him in. And said nothing. Which, even on their slight acquaintance, he knew was unusual for her.

'I'm sorry,' he said. 'Am I disturbing you?'

She shook her head. 'No. But I couldn't think who'd be coming to the door at this time of night.'

She could not be used to being alone in a big house. No wonder she seemed nervous. A bud of protectiveness started to unfurl inside him. He thrust the tulips at her.

'From the garden,' he said.

Her face brightened. 'Och, they're gorgeous.'

'I can't claim much credit,' he said. 'The people I bought the house from were keen gardeners. Things keep appearing when I'm not looking – it's rather lovely.'

'I'll get a vase.'

He hung up his coat and hat on the old hallstand which he remembered from his childhood – Felicity had taken quite a few bits and pieces from their parents' house because Serena had preferred her own style – and followed her down the hallway to the kitchen. While she bustled about and found a vase – a gaudy, peasanty-looking thing, German, he presumed – then filled it with water, while he leaned against the table and sniffed the air.

'I'd know the smell of Fee's kitchen anywhere,' he said. 'Sort of spicy and different from other people's.'

'I know what you mean,' April said. 'She goes in for fierce exotic things.'

'Do you cook much yourself?'

'Och, not really. Mammy did all that.' She wiped carefully round the rim of the vase.

'But you do for yourself? I can't imagine Fee cooking for a guest.'

'I mostly have a good feed in town at lunchtime,' she said, 'so I can make do with something simple at night – a Welsh rarebit or something. Do they really come from Wales?'

'I've no idea.' He imagined running into her at lunchtime in town, inviting her to share his table. He wondered where she went. It would hardly be the Royal Oak. The Copper Kettle was nice, but perhaps the Teaspoon was more within her budget. He had no idea what she earned. 'I do the same,' he said. 'Lunch in town, I mean. At least I did.' He wrinkled his nose. 'I suppose things will have to change now with Prudence at home. I can't expect her to survive on toasted cheese and apples.'

'Is she not back at school?' Her voice was full of interest.

Fabian sighed. 'Long story. Any chance of a cup of tea?'

She hesitated.

'I'm sorry,' he said. 'I'm sure you have plans for the evening.'

'No, you're grand.' She set the vase down on the table. 'I'll make us a wee pot.'

It was not a wee pot; it was the big Brown Betty teapot he remembered from childhood, which was never used for company, but always at breakfast time. As she warmed it, he was reminded of Nancy, their cook-general, doing the same when he used to sneak into the kitchen to beg for an early morning slice of toast. It would have seemed the most natural thing in the world now to sit down at the table in the spice-scented kitchen with the teapot between them, but April set a tray, as he had done when she had come to his house, and they walked back to the sitting room, he carrying the tulips and she the tea tray.

'Felicity told me to use this room,' she said when she had set the tray down on a table beside the settee. The room was tidy except for a writing case on the table. He wondered whom she had been writing to. 'In case you think I'm making free—'

'Don't be ridiculous.'

'She said she'd rather the place was used and the lights on. Though not all evening.' April crossed the room and sat down in the armchair next to the window. The lamplight reddened her smooth fair hair. 'She's a bit mean about the electric. She's always reminding me to turn the lights out. Sorry – never let on I told you that.'

He smiled. 'Of course not.' He was never sure if Felicity were quite well off, or living hand-to-mouth. He suspected it varied; if he asked about money, she always said she was fine. They had sold their family home, which had allowed her to buy this house, but she had no income other than what she earned. He suspected she was grateful for April's rent.

Felicity loathed clutter, so the sitting room contained only a modern three-piece suite in green moquette, a couple of small tables, a wooden standard lamp, and a few paintings of the same sort as Serena's portrait. Lighter patches on the walls suggested there had, until recently, been more. Fabian wondered what had happened to those. The chess set he had bought her for her twenty-first birthday was on the table under the window. He noticed at once that it had been set up wrongly: the white queen and king were on the wrong squares and two of the pawns had fallen over. He itched to fix it.

'So where did you say Felicity had gone?' he asked, sitting down on the green settee.

'London. To see her publishers.'

'On a Sunday?'

April leaned forward and rested her elbows on her knees. She was wearing a skirt in a colour he thought he remembered Serena calling cornflower, though he would have said blue.

'*I* thought that was a wee bit strange,' she admitted. 'But sure what would I know about publishers and the like?'

'Hmm. She has friends in London. I suppose she might be seeing them too.'

'She never said.'

'I wanted to talk to her about Prudence.'

'Aye, you said she wasn't at school?'

He told her briefly what had happened. 'When you brought her home that day you said that you'd been, er, a demon yourself at that age ? But I can't imagine you did anything so . . . so, well, violent.'

She leaned back, running her finger round the top of her cup, and he could see she was considering the question carefully. 'Not violent,' she said. 'High-spirited. I got told off for being unladylike.'

'There's nothing remotely unladylike about you!'

She blushed and bit her lip.

'Sorry, I didn't mean to make such a personal remark. If only that were all it was with Prudence. She's not high-spirited; she's—'

'She's got no mammy,' April said simply.

'But Miss – April, I can't let that go on and on being an excuse!' He rubbed his hands over his face, through his hair and sighed. 'It's what everyone says, and it's true, but it makes me feel . . . it's not as though I can change it. I've done my best.'

'Course you have,' she said consolingly.

'But it's not enough. She needs something I can't give her. I thought sending her to school would give her that, well, female influence, but she hates it. St Lucy's was the third.'

'There must be schools in Easterbridge. I was at commercial college at her age, but some girls went to the high school in the next town. There must be something like that here.'

'There's a good girls' high, yes. I've an appointment with the head tomorrow, but she's already told me there are no vacancies till September. And I really think she's better at boarding school.'

'You mean it suits you better.'

Fabian was stung. 'It's not that. But everyone says a man can't bring up a girl alone. And I'm out most of the day.'

'So'd she be.'

'I suppose so. But I can't let her kick her heels at home for four months. A boarding school might take her sooner.'

'If I were you, I'd give up on boarding school. You can see it doesn't suit her.' She smiled a wistful smile. 'I always wanted to go to boarding school. I thought it'd be like the books: midnight feasts and bosom pals. But I suppose it's not like that in real life.'

'I went away to school, and it wasn't remotely like the stories.' He sighed. 'If only she were still young enough for a nanny.'

April looked thoughtful. 'That's not a bad idea. It's only a couple of months till the holidays. Why don't you find someone to tutor her? There must be a nice, retired schoolmarm somewhere in town.'

'I don't know anyone.' Then he perked up. 'Oh, I have an acquaintance at the boys' grammar. I wonder if he'd—'

'*No*. You need a lady,' April said so sharply that he was startled. 'You said yourself she needed a female influence.'

'But I don't know anyone,' he repeated, 'and I can't imagine Felicity does. She seems to mix with rather odd people.'

'Och, you just advertise.' She shook her head. 'No harm to you, but I'd have thought that was obvious.'

'But it would take time and . . .' He imagined having to interview squads of retired schoolmarms, terrifying spinsters who would want to turn his home into a schoolroom. And Prudence would hate them.

'And in the meantime, get her a bicycle. I saw how she looked at mine the other day. Sure there's no better way to explore. You said you haven't lived here long? Well, let her get to know the countryside. She'll tire herself out and have something to tell you in the evenings. It'll only be for a week or so if you act at once. You can get adverts into the *Recorder* up to Monday evening, for Wednesday's paper. Or if you miss that, you can telephone and ask for Bert. He'll usually let you slip it in.'

'You're very knowledgeable for a newcomer.'

'Och, I've had a few dealings with the local paper. In my professional capacity,' she added grandly.

'Ah yes, office manager, I think you said?' He realised that he had no idea what she actually did.

She looked him straight in the eye with a defiant wariness. 'I help run the True Minds Marriage Bureau,' she said. 'In St Margaret's Lane, next door to Ackroyd's,' she added, as if there were a proliferation of marriage bureaux in Easterbridge. Well, there might be for all he knew. He had never imagined such a thing.

'Good lord.'

'Did Felicity not tell you?'

'She never mentioned it. That must be interesting work.'

'Oh aye,' she said. 'And while I think of it, if you'd rather not advertise, there must be an educational agency in town, or maybe in Leeds or—'

'I suppose there must.' Never mind that for now! 'But, April, do tell me more about your work. What sort of people—?'

'Och, all sorts. But I don't suppose *you* discuss your clients?' she said severely. 'We have to be the height of discretion. All I'll say is that we have some lovely people. Especially women.'

'I'm sure you do.' He was embarrassed and not quite sure why. He cast around for a change of subject and his eye fell again on the chessboard.

'April,' he said, 'would you mind terribly? Only there's something I've been aching to do all evening, something that's been driving me mad.'

She widened her eyes in what looked like alarm, but could only have been surprise. 'What?'

In response he got up, went over to the chessboard, righted the fallen pawns and reversed the white king and queen so they were on the right squares.

April laughed. 'I wondered what you meant!'

'Silly, but they were annoying me. Do you play?'

She shook her head.

'That's a pity. Felicity's good. She played in Germany, in cafés with all sorts of people. And I'm trying to teach Prudence but she's rather impatient. It does take time.'

He imagined teaching April, sitting opposite each other over a chessboard; there was no concentration, in his experience, so intense. But she started to gather up the tea things and he took that as a sign that the evening was over.

Twenty-one

April was doodling mice on her notepad and wondering should she go to Manchester for the weekend – Mammy was nagging about never seeing her – when Martha, glancing up from her letters, said, 'This one's marked *For the attention of Miss April McVey*,' and held the envelope out to April.

She looked taken aback when April flinched as if the envelope were an unexploded bomb. Just when she thought she had banished her worries about Johnson harassing her! But if he was complaining, why address it to *her*? She swallowed, stomach clenched, and took her paper knife. No good in putting it off.

The letter was short, written in a quick, legible script in black ink. Before reading it, she glanced at the signature, *Fabian Carr*, and her stomach relaxed.

'Hooray,' she said, and Martha looked up with interest.

'What's making you so cheerful?'

'I'd a grand fella . . . I mean, a very nice chap in mind for the bureau and he wants' – she skimmed the letter – 'to see me as soon as possible. To sign up, I imagine, though he just says *Consult you on a professional matter*. Honestly, solicitors. So stuffy! I mind Mr McAdoo in Lisnacashan . . .' But Martha's eyes had adopted the glazed look that Lisnacashan seemed to bring on. April reached for her appointment diary. 'Tomorrow morning's free at ten. You don't need the interview room then?'

Martha shook her head. 'What's he like?'

'Och, Martha, he's *perfect*. Widower. Solicitor. About forty I think. Awful respectable. He's my landlady's brother, and to be honest with you I've been hoping he'd sign up. He's the type that needs a wife. I think the cratur's lonely. Are you sure Miss Murrell's suited to that farmer fellow?'

'Positive.' Martha said. 'Look what's just arrived.' She passed an envelope over to April. It contained a blurred snap of Miss Murrell feeding a pet lamb with a little girl with untidy plaits. A sheepdog with a motherly expression kept watch, while a sturdy boy, obviously Sam, leaned against a stone wall. There was a brief note too: 'Mr Yeadon and his family are very much to my liking.'

'Ah well,' April said. 'There's that nice wee—'

'Give him a chance to sign up first! You're getting as bad as I am!'

'You mean as good as?'

They laughed.

'*Perfect*, you said. Are you sure you're not going to do a Hilda on me?'

April felt herself blush, which was silly, because Martha couldn't have been more wrong. 'For dear sake! Haven't I told you I'm not interested?'

'You have.' Martha looked serious now. 'But in my experience, girls say that – think it, even – until they meet the right man, and then everything changes. And you did say *perfect*.'

'For us. For the bureau.' April picked up the phone to telephone the number Fabian had given her. His secretary sounded most reluctant to put her through. Probably, thought April, she had destroyed the brochure, otherwise Fabian wouldn't have looked so blank when she'd told him what she did; at least he'd have known the bureau existed. She imagined her to be the jealous type, protective of her boss, secretly in love with him, and then she caught herself on; for dear sake, probably the woman's mind was on higher things.

Before Fabian came in the next day, she looked through the women on file. He hadn't said yet what sort of wife he was looking for, but April knew very well what would suit him. Someone who didn't mind children, but not too mumsy; Prudence would be off his hands in a few years, and it was important to have someone then for companionship and shared interests. But not too young either; he wouldn't want to start in again with babies at his age. There had been a nice wee woman in last week, who bred fancy rabbits. There was plenty of room for rabbits at Fabian's house, and it would be an interest for Prudence. Though she couldn't help thinking the rabbit lady would have been better for Farmer Yeadon. As long as they could be kept from the cats . . .

She had not seen Fabian Carr in his working clothes before and she was taken aback at how handsome he was in the dark suit and sober tie. The weather had turned mild, so he had no overcoat. He moved furtively, glancing round in trepidation as he took off his hat, but by now April was used to clients being embarrassed and invited him to sit. He refused the customary cup of tea.

'My colleague is just upstairs in the other office,' April said formally. Let nobody think she would be anything less than professional just because Fabian was an acquaintance. 'I can see you alone, or you can see us together, whichever you prefer?'

He looked taken aback. 'Oh, just you. I wouldn't want . . . Look here, I hope you don't mind.'

'Of course I don't mind. I'm delighted you consulted me.'

'I mean, using your place of work. I know it's not quite . . .' He twisted his hat.

'I'm sorry? I don't understand. Where else would you see me only in my place of work?'

'Well, with it being not strictly . . . more of a personal . . . Oh dear, I'm not explaining myself very well, am I?'

She used her most reassuring voice, though uneasiness started to unfold somewhere deep inside. What did he mean, *personal*? She took a deep breath. Hell roast Nigel Johnson for making her anxious and doubtful about any man she encountered. 'Don't worry,' she said, and she said it, had he but known, to reassure them both. 'People often feel shy, but there's no need.'

'But I feel such an imposter.'

'Why should you feel an imposter?' She uncapped her pen and faced him across the low table.

'Well, it's not as though I want a wife.' He looked down at the hat now sitting on the chair beside him. 'Well, not today.' He gave a laugh that wasn't really a laugh.

'Excuse me?' The pen wobbled.

'But I thought it would be better to speak to you at work. Being a professional matter, I mean.'

She set the pen down. 'I think you need to explain.'

He crossed his legs, and clasped his hands over his knees. Nice hands, long fingers, very clean. 'When I said I wanted to consult you professionally, it wasn't as a director of a marriage bureau.' He said the words as though they hovered somewhere between ridiculous and disgusting.

'That *is* my profession.' She hoped she sounded dignified rather than defensive.

'I mean, I don't want to go on your books.'

Oh flip, she thought, what's he talking about? An absolutely ridiculous idea presented itself. Surely he hadn't a wee notion of *her*? Och no, he said *professional*.

'It's Prudence,' he rushed on.

'Prudence? But she's too young! It's over 21s only.'

'Don't be silly. I need someone to teach her. It was your idea.'

'I don't find teachers.' She thought, briefly, of what Martha had once said to her: *What aspect of Marriage Bureau have you failed to grasp?* Should she say that? No, it would be a wee bit cheeky. But for dear sake! And him meant to be a smart, professional man. 'I find wives and husbands.'

'I meant you could teach Prudence.'

'I'm not a teacher.' She fixed him with a cool look. 'I help run this bureau.'

'But you're good with girls. You told me you were used to them – the girls at your father's factory.'

'I ran a club, but I'm not qualified to teach.'

'You're qualified enough to teach Prue for a few months. Just keep her amused and busy. It doesn't really matter about lessons.'

April shuddered. 'A sort of governess?'

'If you like.'

'I don't think so.' She saw herself shut up in a schoolroom with a sulky Prudence, both longing for the hands of the clock to creep round to four o'clock. In her imaginings she was wearing a long grey frock of the sort favoured by Victorian spinsters and, though her eyesight was perfect, steel-rimmed spectacles. Poor Miss McVey!

She leaned forward and steepled her fingers, which she believed made her look stern and thoughtful. '*This* is my job,' she said. 'I like it.' Saying it aloud made her realise how true it was. 'I'm good at it. I'm hardly going to give it up for something temporary.'

'There must be plenty of office jobs. I could put in a word—'

'Mr Carr.' Anger swelled in her. 'There's over two million unemployed in this country, and I've no mind to join their ranks. I'm happy to help you find someone suitable, as a favour, but that someone is not me.'

'What about if you worked here in the mornings and taught Prudence in the afternoons? Or vice versa? Honestly, we'd fit in with you.' He looked eager; his eyes, so like his sister's, very bright. 'Perhaps if I had a word with your boss here—'

April stiffened her back and made her stare even harder. 'Mr Carr, I don't have a *boss*; I have a partner.' Sure that was nearly true. 'And if I wished to change my working hours, which I don't, I'd ask her myself, not get some man to do it as if I were a child.' She shook her head. 'Didn't I tell you to advertise?' For dear sake, *she* could have found ten governesses since the night he'd called in!

'I'm sorry. I didn't mean to offend you.' He looked deflated. 'I did try to draft an advertisement. But when it came down to it, I didn't know what to say. And the thought of a stranger in the house . . . And Prudence responded so well to you the times she's met you. She's asked about you several times. She doesn't always take to people. Since Serena, her mother, you know . . .' He broke off and started to fiddle with his hat again.

Damn, thought April. Don't you dare make me feel sorry for you, my boy!

She was beginning to rein in her eagerness to get Fabian signed up. He might be more trouble than he was worth. *She doesn't always take to people* – that would make life difficult for any prospective stepmother. It would have to be someone pretty strong-minded. The rabbit woman might be too gentle. Then she remembered Felicity: *Gosh, I wish he would join your bureau – I'd pay his fees myself*, she had said, and those cool blue eyes, so like the ones imploring her now, had grown wistful. Och, for dear sake, why hadn't she got a job managing a knicker factory or something with no feelings involved?

She doodled on the edge of her notepad and sighed. Fabian was looking at her like a puppy who thought it was being taken for a walk and now realises its owner is going out alone. Should she offer to help the little beast? After work maybe? They could do some reading together; sums – April was good

170

at sums – and she could pass on some clerical skills. It would be something to do in the evenings, somewhere safe to go, a purpose, and she would, of course, charge for her services, which meant she could send more to Mammy, maybe even save for a holiday in the summer.

Oh aye? Where would she go? And who with?

She squared her shoulders and capped her pen. This would not do! Easterbridge must be full of women who would be grateful for the chance of a couple of months' governessing. Some nice retired lady, missing her pupils and her sense of purpose and in need of the salary. Or, because she had read *Jane Eyre*, an attractive younger woman whom Fabian might fall for.

And since when, April McVey, she admonished herself, did you of all people start to think in the clichés of romantic fiction?

Since I started working in a marriage bureau, maybe?

She gave a giggle, which was not lost on Fabian, who looked up quizzically.

'Why not ask Felicity to help?' she suggested. 'Och, not the teaching.' Obviously *Felicity's* work was too important to interrupt. 'But she could help you advertise, and interview prospective clients. I'm sure that's the kind of thing sisters do for widowed brothers.'

'Which is precisely why I can't ask. You know what she's like about being put upon.'

Not for the first time April noted that Fabian seemed to imagine that she knew her landlady much better than she did. Felicity was home now, busier than ever, and had said divil the word about her time in London. In fact she'd been a bit rude when April had dared to asked her.

'Look, you said you didn't know what to write?' Which was pathetic; he was a solicitor, not an inarticulate schoolboy. '*I'll* draft something for you. Not now' – she looked at the office clock – 'I've an appointment shortly.' (She didn't, she had a Miss Jennifer Dunn in the afternoon, but he didn't know that.)

'And could you possibly bring it round this evening? Prudence would love to see you.'

She bit her lip. On the one hand, it would be nice to have something to look forward to after work. It was a damp day with no sign of the cloud lifting, so it would hardly be an evening for a cycle, though she felt uneasily that she might be making an excuse about that. She kept telling herself she *was* going to cycle past Johnson's house, but so far she had always found a reason not to. On the other, she wasn't that keen to see Prudence again. On the other – and she knew she had only two hands, but all the same, on the other – there was no reason to suppose that Fabian Carr might have designs on her, or that, if he did, he would be unable to control his base desires. She must not let Johnson spoil everything. She should test herself, agree to go, *make* herself go.

'All right,' she said. 'I'll call after work.'

As he was leaving, he half turned back and said, 'I'm sorry if I offended you about your work. I should know better.'

'You should, aye.' But she smiled, which he returned with evident relief. 'I'll see you at six. I'll come bearing the most exquisite advertisement you ever saw.'

In the event she did much better than that.

Clients came in all guises, and some April warmed to more than others. She liked Miss Jennifer Dunn on sight. Short and slim, with an aureole of bobbed fair curls, she looked younger than April, though she walked with a stick which belied her brisk schoolgirlish manner, and she told April early in the interview that she wasn't at all sure why she had come.

'But what else is one to do? I need *something*.'

April looked at the details on Miss Dunn's registration form. 'But you've had such an interesting life! Studied at Newnham and then – folk dancing?' She seemed, to April, like a girl in a story.

The rather anxious eyes brightened. 'Yes. I fell in love with dancing at Cambridge and then it became, well, my life! I taught it in all sorts of places, from palaces to pit villages – in the East End at first, then, when I came back up north, to unemployed miners' families. I taught dancing to the kiddies at first, then the older girls and boys wanted to join in. I had whole villages dancing!' She smiled at the memory, then drooped. 'Anyway, I can't teach now – not like this.' She indicated her bad leg, held stiffly in front of her, the stick resting against the chair. April tried not to look too nosy, but Miss Dunn explained that she had broken the leg badly in a traffic accident and that it had never set properly. 'So no more dancing. And I can't teach if I can't demonstrate.' She wrinkled her nose. 'Besides, if I'm honest, I can't bear seeing other people dancing when I can't join in. Does that sound dreadful? I should be grateful to be alive – there was a child killed in the same accident; a motor van lost control and ploughed into three of us – but I'm not very good at the gracious cripple act. When I see other people dancing, I want to join in so much I could cut their legs from under them.' She looked startled at her own frankness.

'I'd feel the same,' April said. She was having the thought she had often, that her work brought her into contact with so many other single women, most of whom were lonely, and with some of whom, like Miss Murrell and now this interesting Jennifer Dunn, she felt an affinity. If she had met these women in other circumstances they might have become pals. But you couldn't very well say to a client, *I'm a bit lonely and you seem nice – will you be my friend?* And of course they were all here to find husbands, after which, in April's experience, they became no good to man nor beast. Look at Evelyn – she owed April two letters. She wouldn't write again now, until – unless – Evelyn did.

She brought things back to a business footing. 'You needn't worry about your leg here,' she said. 'My partner set the bureau up partly to help injured servicemen after the war.'

Miss Dunn looked sceptical. 'I should imagine injured servicemen after the war were a more attractive proposition than a lame twenty-nine-year-old woman who isn't even sure . . .' She looked down at her hands.

'Isn't sure . . .?'

'Well, I never intended to marry. I loved my job too much to give it up. Not just the dancing, but the work; the challenge. Giving it all up to darn some man's socks and be the little wifey?' She shook her head and the bright curls bounced. 'I honestly don't think it's enough to compensate.'

'So why are you here?' April asked. 'Why not take another job instead? Even if you can't teach dancing, there must be plenty you could do. You've been to Cambridge, for dear sake!'

Miss Dunn, as April herself had done just a few hours earlier, said, 'Haven't you noticed the unemployment figures? Every job I go for there are twenty women, or young boys, competing against me. Clerical jobs, teaching, even typing pools – I'm tired of always being told the position's gone. It's my silly old leg, of course.'

'But that shouldn't matter in an office job, or even teaching. It's not like you're applying to be a games mistress.'

Miss Dunn laughed wryly. 'You'd be surprised. Of course they never say it's the leg. But I haven't worked for several years; the stupid leg took over a year to heal, or at least to get to where it is now, and my parents wanted me to convalesce at home – it's a village just outside town, Daddy's the vicar. I'm still there now and it's very comfortable, but I need something more. I don't want to be the vicar's daughter all my life, delivering the parish magazine and organising jumble for the fête.' She gave another of those wry laughs and stuck out the bad leg. 'Mind you, it takes me so long to deliver the parish mag that it's practically a full-time job.'

'So you'd rather marry?'

'I'd rather do *something*. I'd rather feel like a grown-up again, instead of *poor-little-Jenny-what-a-shame*.'

So they were back to the *something*. Clients, in April's limited but fast-growing experience, never said they were looking for *something*. It was always *someone*. But April knew the importance of *something*. Something worthwhile. Something important. Something to give you independence and a sense of purpose. She felt wistful; sure wasn't that what she wanted for herself? Wasn't that partly why she'd left Mammy and Manchester?

Her eye fell on the half-drafted advertisement she'd been working on while she'd been waiting for Miss Dunn in the interview room. You can't, she thought, it's unethical. And then, Och, you can surely. What about *True Minds*? If ever there was a woman who didn't really want to marry, here she was. And you have the means to make her – and two other people; three if you count Felicity – very happy.

'I wonder,' she said, 'if you've ever considered teaching privately?'

Twenty-two

It worked out even better than she could have imagined. Jennifer Dunn found herself very well suited to teaching Prudence, and Fabian was delighted with her.

'Even Prue thinks she's the cat's pyjamas,' Felicity reported. April had had to tell Felicity and Fabian how she had discovered Miss Dunn, but they were sworn to secrecy. Fabian said he knew she would come up trumps. Felicity said she was an evil genius and seemed to regard her with new respect. This evening she had asked April to share her dinner, some kind of dumpling stew with sausages, and absolutely delicious, though Felicity assured her it was terribly cheap. They were eating at the kitchen table and Felicity produced a bottle of German wine.

'I brought it back with me,' Felicity said. 'There aren't many bottles left, so let's enjoy this one. Or would you prefer something drier?'

April shook her head. 'It's lovely,' she said. But remembering the whisky she had drunk with Johnson, she sipped it very cautiously. Strange to think this bottle had come all the way from Germany. She did not let herself think, as she breathed in the herby, doughy smell of the dumplings, of those men marching and chanting. She banished them to the part of her mind where

176

she kept Johnson, and Daddy's death, and Evelyn not bothering to write. It was getting a wee bit crowded in there.

'What does Fabian say?'

'That she's bright and cultured, and very nice to have around.' Felicity salted her stew and passed the salt cellar to April.

'Och, well, she was at Cambridge,' April said, 'so she's bound to be bright and cultured. Fair play to her.'

One day in the middle of May, Jennifer called to the office as April was leaving. April, putting her hat on at the door, thinking that she must do something about her hair, heard the distinctive halting tread on the stairs and pulled the door open. Jennifer was almost hidden behind a huge bunch of bluebells, but her face shone out brightly above them.

'Miss McVey?' she said. 'Oh, I am glad I caught you. I came to say thank you.'

She thrust the flowers at April, and April buried her face in them in delight. Bluebells grew in abundance on the banks of the Blackwater at home, and the sweet heady scent made her nostalgic for that purple haze.

'Thank me for what? These are wonderful.' It was like the time when Sybil Postlethwaite had arrived with the daffodils, and April prepared herself for the same news: that Fabian had fallen for Jennifer already and she was coming to thank April for bringing them together. And she'd be delighted! She'd count it towards one of her matches even if Jennifer had never actually gone on the books. She and Martha had grown quite competitive about their respective targets. Felicity would be thrilled, and presumably Prudence wouldn't mind too much if she considered her prospective stepmother *the cat's pyjamas*.

'You saved me from making an idiotic mistake,' Jennifer said. 'I didn't really want to marry. I thought I did because, well, I had to do something, and I'd stupidly let myself think that I was good for nothing else. But I'd forgotten how much I liked teaching – not just the dancing, but the actual teaching; seeing someone make progress. Prudence is bright, but she wasn't thriving at school. She was always thinking people were being mean or didn't like her.'

April said nothing.

'But one to one, she's making splendid progress. I think half her problem is that she hated being away from home. She worries about her father, bless her.'

'So, are you going to keep on teaching her?' Prudence doing lessons at home with the vicar's daughter – very suitable. And in time surely Fabian would fall for the bright young governess – how could he resist?

Jennifer shook her head. 'No, she's going to the High School in September. She's resigned to it now, even looking forward to it. She's already planned which teams she's going to be on.'

'So you . . .?'

'I've signed up with a specialist agency.'

'*Not* a marriage bureau?'

Jennifer laughed. 'No. I've found I like working with girls who aren't at school – there must be lots who have to stay home because of illness or accident. I remember what it's like to be laid up for months: the boredom, the feeling that everyone else was getting on with life. I've got something I can offer girls in that situation. If I'd had someone . . . I mean, I was grown up, but even as a companion, it would have made life so much jollier.'

'Wouldn't you have to live in somewhere? I can't imagine Easterbridge is full of girls like that.'

Jennifer looked eager. 'Oh, but I'd like to live in. I want to be more independent. After all, before the accident I hadn't really lived at home since I was eighteen. No, I hope to find a position miles away – Cornwall or London or even abroad. There must be girls who're sent away because of their health, but who're well enough to do a few lessons. Imagine – I might end up in Switzerland or somewhere!' Her face lit up like a sunflower; even her bright hair seemed to shimmer.

April opened her mouth to say that living as a temporary governess, probably in an ill-appointed spare room, was hardly her idea of independence, and then she shut it again. Who was she to judge? Sure wasn't she only living in someone's spare room herself? And Jennifer was glowing at the idea. Maybe she would indeed get to travel. She might be like Felicity and live abroad for years.

'I'm staying with Prudence until the end of July,' Jennifer went on. 'I'll have a holiday in August and start work again in September. I can't wait.' She laughed again. 'And it's all thanks to you.'

'Och, it's really not. You might have seen the advert I was drafting for Mr Carr and applied anyway.'

'I might. But I was losing confidence. I really thought I'd just settle for marriage.' She bit her lip. 'Forgive me – of course you must believe marriage is the be-all and end-all, or you wouldn't be here.'

'I like matching people with what suits them,' April said, 'and in your case that wasn't marriage.'

It should have felt like a victory. All the same, discomfort nibbled at her, and she placed the bluebells in her bicycle basket to bring home. She told herself it was so she could share them with Felicity. The hall really did smell dampish, and Felicity said she must do something about that, but it would cost money. But mostly, April didn't want Martha asking questions if she displayed the bluebells in the office. It had been awkward that day a fortnight ago, confessing that both her appointments – Mr Carr and Miss Dunn – had decided not to sign up after all. Martha had looked bemused and far from overjoyed.

179

'Two? In one day? Good grief, April, what on earth did you do to put them off?'

April couldn't very well tell the truth – that she had, in a way, matched them to each other. She said airily, 'Och, their hearts weren't in it,' but her own heart pounded so loudly that she was sure Martha must hear it. Mammy always knew rightly when April was lying.

Maybe Martha did too, because she frowned. 'I wouldn't like to think you'd have many days like that, April,' she said. 'Would you like me to sit in on your appointments?'

'No!' April curdled with umbrage. 'They were just time-wasters. You've had them yourself from time to time.'

'But two in one day?'

'Just bad luck,' April said firmly, and crossed her fingers under the desk.

But nobody could deny that the bureau was doing well. They had always had clients from a wide area, but now they started to get enquiries from even further afield. At Whitsun Sybil Postlethwaite sent a card to say that she and Mr Barrett were engaged and planned to marry almost at once. 'We aren't both-ering with a long engagement as we have a perfectly splendid scheme we can't wait to start. We'll come and tell you in person as soon as we can!'

'They didn't waste much time,' April said.

Martha smiled, slightly wistfully, as she set the card on her desk. 'When you know, you know,' she said, a phrase which had always annoyed April and made her feel left out of some kind of club. She felt wistful herself, less about the marriage than at the sense of enthusiasm which seemed to glow from the blue ink. *That's* what she wanted. *That's* what she thought she'd find when she left home. Something big. Something to take up her time and energy; something worthwhile. And maybe when she found that, she would know.

'I knew I wanted to marry Gordon the first night I met him,' Martha went on. 'It was a hunt ball. I was dragged there with some horsey cousins and I hated it – all these hearty people whinnying at each other and blowing on a hunting horn. All talking about kills and quarry. Lots of red-faced old colonels dancing with you and trying to put their hands on your bottom. Men can be such beasts.'

April had a swift unbidden memory of Nigel Johnson and wrinkled her forehead in sympathy, even as her conscience scolded, it's not the same thing at all. Martha was an innocent wee girl, and you're a woman of the world who ought to know better.

'I sought refuge on the terrace and there was Gordon. His father was the local vet. And we got chatting and he was lovely and I, well, I just knew. My world sort of tilted and then righted itself. Only it looked brighter – sharper.' She bit her lip and huffed a little sigh. 'I know it sounds silly. But that's what it's like, April. At least, that's how it was for me.'

'What age were you?'

'Nineteen. And I know what you're going to say, that I was too young to know my own mind.'

'I wouldn't dream of it,' April said. 'I knew my own mind at that age.'

'A romance?' Martha sounded intrigued.

'Not at all! Don't I keep telling you I'm not that way inclined?'

'Everyone's that way inclined. Otherwise we'd be out of business.'

But not me, April thought. I really, honestly, properly never want to get married. Nobody could, who'd grown up with Mammy and Daddy tiptoeing around each other. Well, Mammy did the tiptoeing; Daddy stomped around wherever he liked. It hadn't exactly been a model of love and companionship, not like Evelyn's mammy and daddy who were sometimes, to Evelyn's mortification, seen taking a walk along the Blackwater on summer evenings, *hand in hand.*

As for the world tilting . . . the times that had happened to April's world – Evelyn marrying, Daddy dying, Johnson attacking her – it hadn't been romantic at all.

At home she liked the occasional evenings when Felicity was around and they would chat in the kitchen. Felicity seemed grateful for April's interference with Fabian and occasionally reported back favourably on Prudence's progress, but for the most part she seemed quite detached. Friendly, but busy with her own affairs. She had a couple more overnight trips and was evasive when April asked if she was seeing her publishers again, so April began to be fairly sure she had a lover in London. She had taken to heart Martha's comment that *everyone* was that way inclined – except herself. And maybe that was why Felicity hadn't bothered having the damp fixed in the hall; either she couldn't afford to, because of spending money on train fares, *or* she was planning to move away altogether. April hoped it was not the latter; though she often felt lonely in number eleven, she loved her white attic and didn't fancy having to move.

When Felicity was home, she worked harder than ever. April would see the light shining from under the study door late at night when she went down to the bathroom for her bedtime ablutions. One morning she was surprised to find her landlady in the kitchen, in yesterday's rumpled clothes, yawning widely as she waited for the kettle to boil. She blinked at April in surprise, eyes gritty with lack of sleep.

'Morning already?' she asked.

'It's after eight.'

'I must have worked all night.' She stretched and wriggled her shoulders.

'Inspiration must have been burning,' April said, feeling bohemian.

Felicity frowned. 'It's damn all to do with inspiration,' she

182

snapped. 'I have a deadline. Why do people always think writers have to be inspired?'

'Sorry. Sure what would I know?' She felt stung.

'No, I'm sorry.' Felicity sighed. 'I've been keeping myself going with coffee all night. It always makes me like a bear. Ignore me.' She gave another of those huge yawns, showing small white teeth which crossed a little in front, which April had never noticed before. She hugged her cardigan round her. 'Isn't it freezing? It's meant to be nearly summer.'

'It's because you haven't slept,' April said. 'Why don't you take a hot water bottle to bed and get a few hours now? I could bring you a cup of cocoa. You could pretend it was night-time.'

Felicity sighed. 'That sounds bliss, but I have to finish the dratted thing this morning.'

'A new book?' April asked eagerly.

Felicity hesitated. 'A story. I promised to do ten. I'm regretting it now, but this paper pays well. Ah well, nine done. I'm sure I can dash the last one off before lunch. Oh lord, but I must get to the bank. I have some cheques that have to go in today.' She looked hopeless.

'Could I help?' April offered. 'Which is your bank? I go past the National Provincial and the Yorkshire; I could lodge the cheques for you.'

Felicity perked up. 'Gosh, would you? It's the National Provincial. That would be a help. By the time I got into town and back out again . . .'

'Leave them on the hallstand.'

'You're an angel.' Felicity filled her coffee pot and slouched back to the study, still yawning.

She wasn't wrong about the weather, April thought, pulling her dressing gown tighter around her. Though it was almost the end of May, it had been a restless, blustery night, and the morning struck dank and chill. She washed and dressed hurriedly; she would deliver the cheques on the way, and she didn't want to be late. There was a pile of envelopes on the hallstand, one fat one containing cheques, and a couple of sealed and stamped letters – sure she'd pop those in the post for Felicity; it would be no bother. The fat envelope had – she couldn't resist counting – *five* cheques inside. Flip! Once safely out in the street, just before she put the envelope in her bag, she sneaked a look at the topmost cheque and saw that it was for fifteen pounds, from *Peg's Paper*. Nosily, she looked at the others – all for comparable amounts and all from similar weeklies. *Girls' Choice. Starry Stories.* How strange, April thought, when she had always imagined Felicity writing terribly highbrow things. But she remembered seeing those magazines in the bookcase. She hadn't noticed any stories by Felicity Carr, but probably she used a pseudonym. April had no pretensions to being intellectual, but she couldn't help feeling disillusioned. *Dash the last one off before lunch* . . . she couldn't imagine Virginia Woolf or E.M. Delafield saying that.

Another strange thing: the house was getting shabbier. The damp had not been fixed. The bath needed re-enamelled, or at least patched up in places. April's own room had a few issues – och, only wee things but they did her head in – the catch on the window was loose and the window rattled in the slightest breeze. The door stuck. The meals Felicity occasionally shared were tasty but, as she often told April, cheap. *Peasant fare*, she called it. And now she remembered Felicity saying, that evening she first saw the room, that Fabian was always trying to keep her from penury. Yet here was a lot of money. So she couldn't help wondering, as she lodged over seventy pounds into Felicity's bank account and carefully pocketed the receipt, where all the money went? Because very little of it was spent on number eleven Riverside Road. Certainly not clothes; April never saw her in anything but those shapeless old djibbahs. Maybe on the mysterious trips to London? Or could she be saving up to get married to some man in London? (*Everyone's that way inclined.*) And what had happened to the disappearing paintings? Had she sold them? And if so, where was the money? Which brought her thoughts full circle.

She nearly forgot about the letters, but as she turned into the High Street the postbox on the corner reminded her, so she fished them out of her pocket. And of course she had a wee nosy – sure, how could she not? One was for Germany – the address was gibberish to her, and the name something long and German; the other was – aha! – for London. To *Sir O.E. Mosley*. Well! A *titled* lover! But if Felicity was hobnobbing with sirs, why would she not get the bath fixed?

You know what, April McVey, you have too much imagination, April scolded herself as she cycled into town, and not enough happening in your own life. Probably Felicity had been waiting on that money for ages, and she'd use it to fix up the house; being a writer meant she didn't have a regular income like April. It was probably always a feast or a famine. As for thinking Felicity might have a lover . . . honestly, she had been far too long in a marriage bureau! Sir O.E. Mosley was probably a newspaper editor or something. Come to think of it, the name was a wee bit familiar. And she chained her bicycle to the railings outside the bureau and went up to see what True Minds had in store for her today.

Twenty-three

Martha's Sunday lunch invitation to April had had to be post-poned several times. Martha had a nasty cold; old Aunt Maisie came to visit; Beulah, who was expecting, wasn't at all well and Martha had taken Billy off her hands a few Sundays; but early in June, the promised lunch was made flesh. Literally. April said she hadn't seen such a joint of beef since she had moved to Easterbridge.

'Daddy loved his Sunday roast,' she said, and then, with a sigh, 'Och, well,' which Martha was not quite sure how to interpret.

There was Yorkshire pudding too, and several vegetables, and potatoes roasted in goose fat. Not to mention an apple tart with cream. And a huge pot of tea to follow with homemade lemon biscuits – which weren't as good as Primrose Lewis's, Martha admitted.

'They're delicious,' April assured her. They had hardly mentioned Primrose since the unfortunate interview. Martha knew she had been too stern with April, and even though she had apologised, she had never felt that things had been restored. Something awkward still seemed to hover between them. The lunch was partly to dispel that. And partly because, well, there was something up with April. Her bright bloom was wearing off, and Martha

186

wanted to be sure that it was not all anxiety about those few professional errors. It was strange to see her here, transported from the office, sitting on Mother's rose chintz armchair, drinking from Martha's own green Coalport wedding china.

'You must take some biscuits home,' Martha said. 'I don't suppose you have a chance to bake, in lodgings?'

'Och, I wouldn't be a baker,' April said.

She was looking slightly flushed; Martha had pressed a large sherry on her, and she had a feeling the girl wasn't used to strong drink. As if to confirm this, April yawned.

'Sorry,' she said. 'I'm so full. My granda used to say *I'm anybody's full cousin.* Mind you, he weighed eighteen stone. His name was James, but he always got Big Jim.'

Martha smiled. There had been fewer tales of Lisnacashan lately; it would not be absolutely truthful to say she had missed them, but she had been conscious of their absence, and she welcomed Big Jim with more warmth than she might have accorded him last month.

April leaned back in her chair. 'Lord bless us, I'll never move again,' she said, 'never mind cycle home.'

'No rush.' Martha poured out a second cup of tea.

'We've had a quare few cuppas together over the last few months,' April observed.

'Indeed.' Martha hesitated. 'I'm very pleased with you, April. On the whole. I know there's been a lot to learn. And I suspect Easterbridge is very different from Lisnacashan.' The name was strange in her mouth, sibilant; it sounded like slow rivers and old grey houses up dark dripping lanes.

April flushed deeper; it was very becoming, actually, the rosy cheeks, with her fair hair and the spotted mauve frock she was wearing – not new, but Martha had not seen it before, clearly Sunday best. She really was a pretty girl. For all her protestations about not wanting to marry – and Martha was beginning to suspect that a broken heart beat beneath those mauve polka-dots, however much April denied it – Martha was sure she'd be snapped up before long. And when she did fall in love . . . well, she was so wholehearted in all she did, doubtless she'd love with the same intensity she did everything else. Then Martha would have to find someone else. And she would miss April.

Stop borrowing trouble. She's not going anywhere! Mother's voice chimed in her head, and she glanced up at the mantelpiece, where faded studio portraits of her parents and brothers stood beside one of her own wedding. Martha saw April looking at that one too, and she picked it up and handed it to her. Young Martha smiled out, open-faced and happy, clutching her orange blossom, giving no indication of any fears. Yet dear Gordon, also smiling out with clear dark eyes, was in uniform. Had they let themselves worry about the future? They had barely spoken of it, had literally taken each day as it came.

Eleven. Eleven days. There had been their courtship before that, of course, but that too had been short, and, unlike those precious leaves, they had rarely been alone together.

April stroked the photo thoughtfully. Was she thinking of her own hopes? 'Och, nothing,' she said at Martha's quizzical look. 'I was just wondering – was it worth it? Was the happiness worth the pain?' Without the sherry, Martha suspected, even April wouldn't have asked.

Martha took the photograph back and set it gently down again on the mantelpiece. 'Oh yes,' she said quietly. 'You can't have loved anyone, or you wouldn't have to ask.' Again she heard Mother's voice, *Really, Martha, stop fishing*! And perhaps she too would not have asked without the sherry, but she took a sip of tea and said, 'I hope you don't mind my asking, April, but has there never been anyone? You say you're not interested in marriage, but you're such an attractive young woman, so vibrant and handsome, I can't believe you haven't had offers.'

April's face flamed even deeper, and – oh dear, Martha really shouldn't have been so prurient! – she gave a little shudder as if at the memory of something unpleasant.

Perhaps Martha should not have pressed her, but she did. Wasn't that was she was good at, pressing people to find out what they really needed, even when they didn't realise it themselves? 'In fact, my dear, I haven't asked you here just for lunch' – April's eyes sparked with alarm – 'I can't help noticing that you seem rather low in spirits. I wondered if it were, well, a chap. If you'd had to leave someone behind in Lisnacashan. Or if you've met someone here . . .?' After all, the girl had her evenings and weekends free. 'I can understand that being involved with the business of matchmaking every day could be challenging if one were feeling – slighted in any way.'

April shook her head. 'Not at all,' she said. 'I'm grand.' She smiled too widely.

'You used to chatter about your explorations,' Martha went on. 'You'd come in on a Monday full of your bicycle trips – you were getting to know our moors and villages better than I did myself! But you've not mentioned anything like that for weeks now. You're pale—'

'I'm always pale,' April said defensively. 'It's my Celtic complexion.' She tilted her head to one side and patted her cheek, which at this moment was far from pale.

'—and you've lost weight.'

'Not after this.' April reached for another lemon biscuit.

'Now stop it!' Martha sounded, she realised, quite fierce. 'I won't have it.' Her voice softened. 'You're not an easy person to help, April McVey. You're as bad as poor Primrose Lewis!'

'I don't need help.' April gave a bright laugh. 'I'm grand. I'm not one of your – our clients. It's a big change, coming here. I miss my old life more than I expected. Mammy and that. That's all.'

'I don't think it is all. I think something's happened. Something's weighing on your mind.' And her mother was only in Manchester; there was nothing to stop her visiting. But talking of mothers . . . well, of course she wasn't exactly *in loco parentis*, April was a grown woman, but she did feel protective of her. *You need someone to look after*, Mother said. *Why don't you get a little cat?* Really, she was getting very above herself today. Normally she kept her own counsel, up on the cloud where Martha vaguely imagined her, not playing a harp – she had been the most unmusical of women and would have considered it a foolish waste of time – but perhaps hemming handkerchiefs, dainty celestial ones, though one supposed there would be no need for handkerchiefs in heaven.

'It's silly,' April said, 'but yes, something, och . . . unpleasant happened a few weeks ago.'

'Unpleasant?'

She bit her lip. 'It was my own fault.' She looked down at her lap. 'Do you really want to know?'

'Of course.' She made her voice very kind and gentle – well, she *was* kind and gentle, and she was genuinely pleased April wanted to confide in her. It would be some scrape, some misunderstanding, perhaps something April couldn't have told her own mother, and Martha would be able to bring all her experience with the human heart to bear. Mother was right – she did miss having someone to care for; she would enjoy comforting April. She felt the same frisson she experienced when she made a really inspired match.

'D'you promise you won't be cross?' April sounded like a nervous child.

'Why on earth should I be cross?'

'I made a bad mistake.'

'We all make mistakes.'

'I know, but—'

'Just tell me, dear.'

April told her.

And Martha could hardly believe her ears. The most *ugly* story! How a man had inveigled his way . . . had tricked April, tried to take advantage of her.

Her horror intensified as April, hesitant at first and then with the words spurting like lemonade from a shaken bottle, spilled out a disgusting story: how he had grabbed her and pinned her against the sofa, how she had fought to free herself, how she had fled from the house. A house she had had no business in!

Later, Martha regretted her first words, and many of the subsequent ones, but at the time she could think only of the damage to the bureau, her precious life's work. 'You stupid girl,' she said. 'How could you have been so reckless?'

April stammered, 'Och, I-I know it was foolish.'

'Foolish? It was criminal! And you say you left one of our forms behind?'

April tilted her chin with something of her old spirit and Martha itched to slap her. 'Which he'll have disposed of,' she said. 'It's not going to do him any good if his wife finds it, is it?'

Martha shook her head. 'Even so, I can't believe you'd be so foolhardy. Risking our reputation.'

'My reputation too! He called me—'

'I don't wish you to repeat it,' Martha said coldly. 'It's *our* reputation. *Mine*. You were representing Mrs Hart's—'

'True Minds,' April corrected sulkily.

'*True Minds*! Indeed! I don't see much evidence of you using truth *or* your mind. To go behind my back; to go alone to a man's house; to put yourself in such a compromising position!'

'I'm not proud of it, Martha. I said to you the very next day it was a daft idea, going to their houses. I was only trying to sign up another schoolmaster for you. I thought it would be like going to Cedric Young's. I thought he lived with his sister.'

'You should never have gone alone. You were asking for trouble. For goodness sake, April, you aren't a silly young girl! I really would have expected more sense.'

April let out a long juddering breath and Martha forced herself to calm down, softening her voice slightly, at considerable effort. 'I can see it was a horrible experience. I'm just saying, what on earth do you expect when you put yourself at risk like that?'

'I *expected* him to be decent,' April said. 'You're always saying our business depends on trust.'

'Trust and discretion,' Martha said. 'And you can't say you exercised much of the latter.'

April jumped up. 'I know!' she said. 'I was an eejit. I'm sorry.'

And before Martha could stop her, she had flung herself out of the room and the house.

Martha should have followed her. Later, she wished she had. But she sat and let her leave, hearing the wheels of her bicycle *whirr* on the gravel outside and then, unexpectedly, Mother's voice again, sounding disappointed: *That was rather badly done.*

And she did not think Mother meant April.

Twenty-four

It was as if it was happening again. Every nerve in her body thrummed as if Johnson's hands were all over her. She pedalled furiously past the park, desperate to be back in number eleven. When she breathed in, it was not the mild June air with its hint of Sunday dinners and roses she tasted but Johnson's whisky breath. Her hands sweated on the handlebars.

Oh God, Martha's face! What she said! And she was right! Johnson had behaved badly, but she'd been an eejit in the first place. Going alone to a man's house to talk about something so intimate! Her stomach ached with overeating and what she now recognised must be the onset of her monthly. For dear sake, wasn't that all she needed! As she crossed the bridge and set off up Riverside Road, she gave way to a relieving if undignified belch, glad the road was deserted.

It was a relief to get home. She felt not merely full but bilious, a headache beginning to thump in her temples and her stomach cramping. Mammy would have said she needed a good dose of salts. Not that she could ever tell Mammy.

What she most craved, and she despised herself for it, was to curl up on her bed and have a good howl. She would just call at the kitchen on the way and make herself a cup of hot water to settle her insides.

She rarely saw Felicity at weekends, so she was startled when her landlady came in as the kettle was boiling.

'Making coffee?' Felicity stretched. 'I could do with it. That last chapter just wouldn't come right – and then it did.' Which sounded, to April, much more the kind of thing she expected from a real writer than *I'm sure I can dash off the last one before lunch.*

April shook her head. 'Sure when have you ever seen me making coffee?' she asked. 'I wouldn't know where to start.' It was a surprise to hear her voice sounding normal. 'I'm just having a cup of hot water, but there's plenty over for coffee.'

'Hot water. Ugh.' Felicity gave April a keen look and started bustling around with her coffee pot, pouring milk into a saucepan from a fat little yellow jug. 'You aren't slimming, are you? You certainly don't need to. Actually, you look a bit green around the gills, if you don't mind me saying.'

'I've been out for a big lunch,' April said. 'Overindulged.' She hoped this sounded racy and bohemian.

'Strong coffee's what you need,' Felicity said confidently. 'I'm having mine with warm milk – delicious.'

'No, thanks.' The smell of the coffee was nauseating. April took some deep steadying breaths and then, to her mortification, a stab of pain made her gasp and clutch at her stomach, at the same time as she felt a familiar surge down below.

'You poor thing.' Felicity sounded kinder than April had ever heard her. 'Look, can I get you anything?'

'It's just the curse,' April said, her teeth tight. She didn't normally suffer much, but maybe one month in six was bad. She wasn't due, but then she hadn't been regular since she left Lisnacashan. It would explain how rough she felt and how uncharacteristically mopey. And the heavy lunch and the scene with Martha were compounding the misery. 'Owww,' she groaned as another cramp stabbed her. 'Oh God, sorry.'

194

Felicity set her coffee pot down and put an arm round April's shoulders. The weight of it made April realise that she had not been touched by another human being since—

Ugh. She broke free from Felicity and leaned over the sink, sweating, trembling, praying she was not going to boke rings round her. Felicity would be disgusted, and who would blame her. But Felicity was rubbing her back and saying kind things – *you poor old sausage . . . beastly curse* – and after a while the threat passed, and she found herself crying instead, which was also mortifying though less messy.

'I'm so sorry,' she sobbed, when Felicity, with all the dexterity and kindness of a Chalet School prefect, though Chalet School girls never suffered from anything so ignominious, plonked her down at the kitchen table, yanked a large clean handkerchief down from the dolly over the range, and pushed it into her hand. 'I'm scundered.'

'What on earth,' said Felicity, 'does that mean?'

'Embarrassed,' April said. She blew her nose. 'But it can also mean fed up.'

'How confusing. Though I suppose you could be both at the same time?' She pulled out another chair and sat down.

I must get up and sort myself out, April thought, the flow's started, I don't want to stain my frock. But she was reluctant to move. It was so cosy here. And embarrassment had given way to resignation. So she had made a fool of herself in front of Felicity. What did it matter? She was an eejit. Martha had been right, and Martha didn't even know the half of it.

'What about a hot water bottle?' Felicity asked. 'I do find it just the ticket at my time of the month.'

'Aye,' April said. 'Lovely. Thanks. I'm so sorry, I don't normally . . .'

'Oh, everybody has a good bawl from time to time,' Felicity said easily. 'I don't hold with all this stiff-upper-lip nonsense.

That was one thing they understood in Germany; they're much more sentimental than us.'

'Really?' The recent newsreel marched through her mind. The harsh rallying shouts; the stiff-armed salutes. Everything so militaristic and regimented. The opposite of sentimental, surely? 'I wouldn't have thought that.'

'Gosh yes. Hanna, my pal there, was always blubbing because she'd seen a kitten out in the rain, or the because the leaves were falling. She was a regular waterfall.' Felicity laughed. 'Mind you, she's an artist and she's Jewish. I think they're more emotional than us stodgy Brits.'

'I never cry,' April said. She balled the soaking handkerchief and gave a damp giggle at this proof of the contrary.

'Is it really just your monthly?' Felicity asked. 'Tell me to mind my own business, I won't be offended – Fabian says I have the skin of a rhino – but—'

'No.' It was all very well this Hanna crying at kittens; she didn't want Felicity to think *she* was the sort of woman to be felled by her natural cycle. She had a wry memory of Daddy's factory, where she always struggled between wanting to sympathise with girls who genuinely suffered, and not giving in to the few lead-swingers who'd have done anything to skip work.

'Something happened,' she said. 'I mean, it was my own fault, I let it happen. And my partner – och, my boss, really – Martha, well, I told her today and she was raging, and it brought it all back, how horrible it was. And she said awful things about my judgement and' – only as she formed the words did she realise they were probably true – 'I think she'll sack me.' For how could Martha forgive this? And look at the way she'd run off like an eejit. She'd be bound to get her cards. And the thought of creeping back to Mammy and Aunty Kathleen in disgrace was desperate, but the thought of leaving the bureau without finding out what happened to Miss Murrell and Farmer

Yeadon, and the rabbit lady and even the poor old Colonel was almost worse..

'Sack you? What on earth have you done? Matched up a vicar to a lady of ill repute?'

'We don't have ladies of ill repute on our books,' April protested. Johnson had said something similar, implied the bureau was a cover for something else, but surely nobody as intelligent as Felicity could think such a thing? Then she saw that Felicity was grinning. 'It's not funny,' she snapped.

'Sorry. So what did you do? *Confess and shame the devil*, as my old nanny used to say. Oh lord, it's nothing to do with you poaching the wonderful Miss Dunn, is it?'

'No. She doesn't know about that, thank God.' Oh, what the hell? She might as well tell. 'A man' – April hesitated; what was the right word? She didn't want to be overdramatic, something Mammy was always accusing her of – 'molested me.' As Felicity's eyes widened, she went on, getting in before Felicity could say it, 'It was my own fault. I went to meet him alone in his house. I was asking for it.' She pursed her lips and screwed the sodden handkerchief into a tighter ball. 'As Martha was very quick to remind me.'

Felicity sat upright and made a huffing sound through her nose. 'Beast!' she said. 'No, silly, not you. *Him*. What did he do exactly?'

April wriggled and bit her lip. 'I'd rather not . . .'

'I know,' Felicity said, 'but you'd much better. It's like being sick: you'd do anything not to but you always feel better afterwards.' She grinned.

April sighed. 'I didn't feel better when I told Martha. I felt worse. She made me feel such an eejit!'

'Tell me what he did,' Felicity said calmly. She leaned forwards and patted April's arm. 'Take your time.'

For the second time that day she made herself go over what Johnson had said, how she had gone to the house alone, how

197

she had suppressed her qualms, how he had forced himself on her. It was easier than telling Martha, but then Felicity wasn't concerned about her business. Felicity was concerned about April. Felicity was looking as indignant as if . . . as if we were proper friends, April thought. It was like the time she'd told Evelyn that Daddy wouldn't let her take a job in Belfast, even though the pair of them had planned to do that together. Evelyn's face had gone hard and still like Felicity's now, and she'd said it wasn't fair. 'I could bust your da,' she'd said. Though a month later she'd been walking out with Maurice Kenny so they wouldn't have got to Belfast anyway.

'I drank his whisky,' April remembered. 'I didn't tell Martha that.'

'Were you drunk and incapable?'

'Of course not. I had a few sips. It was rotten.'

'Well then.' She touched April's shoulder. 'You didn't do anything wrong, April. He did. I suppose it was someone terribly respectable? Pillar of the establishment and all that?'

April nodded. 'A schoolmaster. But I shouldn't have put myself at risk. Like Martha said, I'm not a silly wee girl. I know how the world works.'

'Well, it shouldn't work like that.' Felicity sounded very fierce. 'Women held to higher standards than men.'

That sounded like something a politician would say. April looked at Felicity with respect. It must be great to be able to find the right words. April had no bother finding words, but not words that sounded like speeches.

Felicity went on. 'Men get away with these things. And worse. All the time. All the bloody time! And women get the blame.'

'I know.' April struggled to be fair. 'But it's not all men . . . probably hardly any, really. I mean, nothing like that's ever happened to me before. Well, there was old Manus McIlroy at home. His garden backed onto the riverbank, and he used to hide in his gateway and take out his, er, you know, when girls went past, but sure we all knew never to walk past that bit.'

She saw then a look in Felicity's blue eyes that made her say, 'You too?'

Felicity nodded. 'I was about Prudence's age,' she said. 'No, younger, thirteen. It was my music tutor, Mr Foster.' Her mouth made a little moue. 'He used to touch my leg under the piano. At first, I thought I was imagining it, or that he wasn't aware of it, or even that it was some kind of technique to help me play better.' She snorted. 'Honestly! I was so naïve.'

'Och, you were thirteen. You were meant to be naïve,' April said. 'Did you tell your parents?'

She shook her head. 'I was like you. I thought it was my own fault. He taught Fabian too, the hour before me, and he never touched Fabian's leg.'

Strange to think of Fabian and Felicity as children together! 'Did you ask him? Fabian, I mean?'

Felicity shook her head. 'Not exactly. I asked him if he liked Mr Foster, and he said yes, he was a decent sort and a good teacher. I said, *Don't you find him a bit creepy?* And he laughed and said, *What nonsense*, and if I didn't want to learn the piano any more I should tell Mummy and Daddy and not waste their money. So I thought, well, it's my fault, for being a girl. I was just starting to develop. I suppose in my mind the things were linked.' She shook her head. 'I never did learn to play the piano.'

'That's desperate,' April said.

'I wasn't a great loss to the world of music.'

'I mean desperate of him.'

'I know. It wasn't my fault. I know that now. But neither was yours. That's what I'm trying to tell you.'

'But I'm nearly thirty, not thirteen.'

'Doesn't matter. It was still his fault. I could, ooh' – she broke

199

off and gave a wicked grin that made her suddenly look very young – 'What's his name and I'll give it to my next villain?'

'You can't do that!'

'Well, not if he's called Higginbottom or Blenkinsopp, maybe. But if it's a usual sort of name . . .?'

'Johnson.'

'Perfect. Common as muck. I'll make sure he comes to a particularly sticky end.'

Maybe it was a trick, to make April say the name aloud, but she did feel better afterwards. In fact, considering that she might indeed lose her job, as she went upstairs with a hot water bottle, she felt surprisingly cheerful.

Twenty-five

Martha had never dreaded going into the office. There had been slow days, frustrating days when she hadn't achieved much, and awkward days like the time she had had to give the ghastly Hilda her cards, but not the actual, lead-in-the-pit-of-her-stomach *dread* that she felt unlocking the office door that Monday morning.

Come on, Martha, Mother said. *No shirking!* Mother had been a jolly sight too opinionated for her own good since yesterday lunchtime. And Martha was not in the habit of shirking. It was just that it was hard to know what to say. She had agonised and rehearsed through a restless, sheet-kicking, pillow-thumping night, perspiration seeping into her nightgown and gathering between her breasts, and woken with a heavy head. She would have welcomed someone to discuss it with, but there was nobody; she couldn't mention such a thing to her brothers, and though she was fond of Beulah, they did not have that kind of relationship. She had pals, of course, from choir mainly, but mostly of the spin-sterish type; they would have been too shocked. And besides, it would have been too much like airing the bureau's dirty linen in public.

201

As she opened the blinds and the window – the room was stuffy after being shut up for two days, and the morning promised heat later – she looked down the street and saw April approaching on her bicycle, wearing a straw hat Martha did not recognise and a red frock. She looked rather jaunty, considering, and Martha was unsure whether she felt admiring or resentful. This bicycling, red-frocked girl with the fair hair streaming out behind her did not look as though *she* had spent the night tossing and turning and tormenting herself.

Two minutes later and April was in the office. She did not take off her hat and hang it up as usual. Instead she stood in the doorway, looking as if she were dreading going to the dentist, but trying not to show it.

'Good morning, April.' Oh dear, why must her voice come out so cold and awkward when she did not intend it to? 'We should have a little talk. Why don't you sit down?'

'Martha.' April's chin was tilted, her eyes and voice steady, and she did not sit down. 'If you're going to sack me, go ahead. I don't want any wee talks. I've nothing more to say. I know you're annoyed with me, and I'm disappointed that you think women should be held to, er, to higher standards than men, because that's not one bit fair, so it's not. But this is your business and you're the boss, so you can do what you like.'

'*Sack* you?'

'Aye. Isn't that what—?'

'I've no intention of sacking you.'

'Oh.' This seemed to take a while to sink in. 'Are you sure?'

'Positive.'

April looked wary. 'So is the wee talk a sort of warning? To behave myself from now on?'

'April, you're not a naughty schoolgirl. I think we both know you wouldn't put yourself in such a position again.' And before April could jump in with anything about it not being her fault, she said, 'You were foolish, but I . . . well, I could have been more compassionate.'

'You could, aye.'

'And I'm sorry for that. I'd very much like to put it behind us.'

'All right then.' She took off her hat and hung it on the stand.

'That's a very pretty hat,' Martha offered.

'I know.' Martha waited to hear its provenance, and April's thoughts on summer hats in general, but *I know* was clearly all she was getting.

And that was how it was for a few days. They circled each other like cats. Very polite, domesticated cats, unlikely to forget themselves so far as to scratch or bite, but the former sense of understanding and mutual respect had evaporated. April was careful and unobtrusive and conciliatory, none of which, Martha knew, came naturally.

When Martha said that Cedric Young, having found no luck with Miss Robins or Miss Jennings, had settled on Miss Phoebe Grey, a shy typist who just wanted to be looked after by a nice chap, April did not opine, as she would have done the previous week, *He's not my idea of a nice chap*. She was not silent – Martha didn't imagine she ever could be – but she simply said, 'Is that right?' and that she would update the records accordingly.

When she told April that the Colonel had phoned to ask if they could step up their efforts, the summer shows would be starting soon and it would be capital to go along with a nice gel on his arm, she had not said, as she often used to, 'If you don't get that oul' cratur settled soon you may marry him yourself out of pity.' She had merely said that there was nobody new on their books who might do.

There was an encouraging flurry of requests for brochures and appointments. They had no fixed rule about who saw which potential clients, and in general they shared the workload equably. After the Primrose Lewis affair it was tacitly accepted that Martha had an especial affinity for older or widowed folk, while April was considered more in tune with the younger and livelier.

On Thursday April was filing when she gave a little cry that made Martha look up from her own work.

'What's wrong?' she asked.

'This.' April indicated the slips. 'Mr Meade! You normally give me the young fellas like him. And this girl, the one who doesn't like golfers, why was she not mine?' She sounded hurt.

'We don't have a law about it,' Martha said feebly. It was true that these clients – the young man home on furlough from the Indian civil service and determined to go back with a 'good sensible English bride', and the bright-faced girl who wanted help to find her own husband because her father kept bringing home all the single young men he met on the golf course – were the kind she normally gave to April.

'You don't trust me.'

'Nonsense! I just felt, after your bad experience, it was only kind to give you an easy week.'

'My bad experience was ages ago. I want to forget it.'

'As do I.'

'But you haven't, have you? Not if you're just giving me the donkey work.'

'Oh, April! I haven't been.'

Yes, you have, Mother said.

April sighed. 'Look, Martha, when I thought you were going to sack me, I was awful worried, but it wasn't just because I was scared of being without a job.' Martha listened, intrigued. 'It was because I like *this* job. More than I thought I would. I like matching people up. Working out who might suit who. And all I've done this week is filing and making out bills. The last person you let me interview was that Herbert Gee, and he never stopped telling me how he'd come especially from Leeds because there really wasn't a girl in Leeds good enough for him.' She sniffed. 'Not a girl in Leeds stupid enough if you ask me.'

'I'm sorry. You have a point.'

'So can I do the next new client interview?'

'Of course.' Martha looked down at the diary, praying that the next client wasn't an elderly or oversensitive person, but she was in luck. It was a Miss Angela Avery who had sounded, on the telephone, both young and buoyant. 'It's at four tomorrow.'

April looked mollified. 'Right you be,' she said.

She arrived next day looking very pretty indeed, in a blue shantung frock Martha had never seen and a white lambswool cardigan.

'You look lovely,' Martha said. 'That blue suits you. And what have you done with your hair? Have you had it set?'

'Oh.' April patted her hair and looked pleased. 'I set it myself on rollers last night and pinned the front up. I was worried it was a bit . . . *fancy*? It's not long enough to put up properly. But I'm a wee bit old to have it streeling about me loose now it's grown a bit.'

'It's very becoming. But is this all for Miss Avery?'

'Miss—? Oh! No. I'm going out after work and there isn't time to go home first.'

Martha raised her eyebrows enquiringly.

'It's not . . . I'm only going out for my tea,' April said. 'Dinner, I mean.'

'How lovely. With . . .?' She knew she sounded nosy, but April said readily enough, 'Just to my landlady's brother's house.'

'The chap who came in a few weeks ago? The one who wasted our time?'

'Yes.' She blushed and though Martha knew by now that the girl blushed easily, it wasn't hard to draw a reasonable conclusion.

205

'And I suppose he took a shine to you then and thought, what's the point in paying the middle-man – or woman?' She sighed. 'That's exactly what used to happen with Hilda.'

'Martha.' April took off her cardigan and placed it carefully over the back of her chair. 'I told you I wasn't like Hilda. I'm not interested in the clients. I'm a career woman.'

Martha shook her head as if she knew better. 'You say that now . . .'

'And if I'd any notion of marrying, which I don't,' she went on firmly, 'I wouldn't be going for Fabian Carr.'

'I thought you said he was eminently eligible.' Martha tried to think back to the day this Mr Carr had called. She had a vague memory of someone tall, with springy brown hair slightly threaded with grey, and a dark, well-cut suit. Better, she had noted at the time, than their average gentleman.

'Well, then, what would a man like that want with an eejit like me?' April grinned, Martha smiled back and the air in the office relaxed for the first time in what felt like weeks. 'Now, would you take a wee cuppa before we start, or will I wait and bring it in to your ten o'clock? I bought some gingerbread biscuits in that new bakery.'

All day there was a kind of shine about April; partly it was that she was so very well groomed, with the good frock and the new hairdo, but she chattered more than she had done for ages, and her return from lunch was heralded by a burst of song: 'That made me love Mary, the rose of Tralee,' she sang, hanging up her hat.

'Nice to hear you sing again.' The young bounced back so quickly.

'Och, sure there's nothing like wee song. And it's a gorgeous day.' She carried on humming while she sorted out the papers on her desk.

In fact the weather had turned dull and windy after early promise, and Martha had just been obliged to close the window, but she supposed, when you were young, and pretty, and looking forward to going out for dinner on a Friday night, it was indeed a gorgeous day.

Jealous? Mother asked. Which was ridiculous and it was just as well that the telephone rang then to cut her off before she really got going.

'That was Miss Avery,' she told April. 'She's had to postpone until half past five. Something about an unexpected family crisis.'

April looked up in dismay. 'What? But I'm meant to be at Fa– at Mr Carr's by six. I don't want to be late.'

'Oh dear, I hadn't thought. She was rather persuasive.' And what an early hour to be going out for dinner.

'It'll take me fifteen minutes to cycle there. And you know we need to give them a good hour. I can't rush her.'

'I'll take her. I'm not in any hurry.' Just a Friday evening with the crossword and a concert on the wireless.

'Och, Martha, are you sure?'

'Of course. You don't want to be arriving all hot and bothered.'

'You're an angel. I owe you a favour.'

Five minutes into the interview with Angela Avery, Martha was forced to agree, and the thoughts she sent spinning after April, who had spent ten minutes prettifying herself further before she left, were not kind ones. 'You look very nice indeed,' she had said sincerely as April had collected her hat, and had even helped her to place it carefully on the precious hairdo. She was not jealous, and she was delighted to see April having some fun.

All the same, there was only so much youthful bloom you could take.

As April had said, an hour was the usual allocation for new clients, but Miss Angela Avery had a great deal to say.

Confident, pretty, and obviously cognisant of both facts, Miss Avery simply couldn't understand why she wasn't able to find a chap of her own. Or at least, she explained brightly, tossing her head so her long golden curls – *she* clearly didn't worry about being too old to wear them loose – could be seen at their most charming, she could find them – gosh, when she went to dances and parties she was fending them off with a stick, not that she had an actual stick, of course not, ha ha, but a metaphorical stick, or did she mean a symbolic stick, anyway what did it matter, the point was, and she hoped Mrs Hart didn't think she was boasting, but really one had to be honest, she was popular. Jolly popular. A honeypot, her set called her. Why, she often had a crowd of chaps around her, fighting to bring her a lemonade or fill up her dance card, not *actually* fighting of course, ha ha, they were all terribly civilised chaps. But after the dance or the party, well, she couldn't seem to get a chap to stay. They never actually invited her to the pictures or a cocktail bar – not that she would *go* to a cocktail bar, not that there even *were* cocktail bars in Easterbridge, but Mrs Hart knew what she meant, didn't she? And all the while, other girls – she looked modestly down and stroked back a perfect golden ringlet – girls without her advantages . . . all right, if one were being perfectly honest, plain girls, were getting proposed to left, right and centre, which was a silly expression when one thought about it, wasn't it, but the point was, *all* her set, *all* the girls she'd been to school with – Enid Linden, Marian Carson, Pamela Jessop (she started counting them off on her fingers and Martha prayed that it had been a small school) *even*, she nodded meaningfully, Millicent Roland – were all married or at least engaged, and here she was, the belle of the lot . . . she was sorry to be so frank, but really, Mrs Hart should see Enid's ankles; and Marian's spots had never really cleared up, of course she didn't look after her skin, or indeed her, she lowered her voice, her bowels, which was half the trouble; and as for Millicent, well! All she could say was that she hoped imbecility was not hereditary. Oh dear, perhaps that was unkind, but honestly, such dullness! No conversation beyond her pony and her dogs, and not even that much about them; half the time she just sat like a cow chewing the cud. Yet *she* had just snaffled Peter Taylor-Scott! Yes, *the* Taylor-Scotts, who owned half the county. Imagine!

Martha, trying not to look at the clock, would have been very grateful for the taciturn Millicent.

'We do have some nice men who work overseas,' she suggested. 'Have you considered the colonies? I hear India has a great deal to offer. Social life and so forth.'

Miss Avery was not sure; didn't it depend greatly on which part of India? She had heard some dreadful things about the climate, and besides, she would be terribly missed if she went so far away. Her set really relied on her, not to speak of her poor sisters, who would be terribly bereft. Apart from Joan, of course, who had gone and got herself married last year, though as she was a year younger than Angela, she might have jolly well waited. Why, that's why she was late today: poor darling Susan, the baby of the family, had had a frightful disappointment at school, all to do with some team or other, and come home in *floods*, and though she had pretended not to want to talk about it, she, Angela, her adored big sister, had jolly well not rested until she had got the poor little duck to confide the whole sorry story.

If only, Martha thought, doodling a word and adorning it with curlicues and flourishes, trying to keep her face neutral and interested, Cedric Young had not settled on poor little Miss Grey. If he must marry, a wife as self-absorbed and, in fairness, as decorative, as Angela Avery, might have suited him. And she would restate the appeal of the colonies. Mr Meade had stipulated a *sensible* girl, but he was in a hurry and would not have too much opportunity to get to know her until they were safely on board the ship.

She looked down at the single word she had doodled: GHASTLY. She would look forward to telling April what she'd missed. Though it seemed a long time until Monday morning. For the first time in ages, she let herself imagine what it would have been like to be going home to Gordon. He had, like her, been fascinated by people's foibles; he would have loved her stories of the bureau – stories you could never share with anyone but a spouse or a colleague. But then, had Gordon not spilled his guts and blood into the Ypres mud, she would not have had a marriage bureau.

She would have had a marriage.

Twenty-six

Prudence straightened a fork and stood back to survey the table. 'You've gone to a lot of trouble, Daddy,' she said, looking at the dining table set for four, with the Royal Albert and the silver cutlery, both wedding presents and rarely used.

'It's nice to make an effort when people come to dinner.'

'You don't normally do all this for Aunty Fee.'

'No, but Miss McVey is coming too.'

Prudence's face brightened. 'And you promise to ask her advice about a bicycle for me?'

'Of course. That's one reason why I asked her.'

'One reason?' Prudence looked quizzical.

'And to say thank you. You know it was she who found Miss Dunn for us.' He had invited Felicity too because, well, it might be less awkward. Not that it was going to be awkward. Not that he was nervous. It was just that it was the first time he had entertained since before Serena's illness.

'Miss Dunn's a brick.' Prudence's face shone with hero-worship and he smiled at the change in her. 'You should have asked her too.'

'I think Miss Dunn sees enough of you without staying to dinner.'

'Daddy, have I time to re-plait my hair?'

'Of course. Felicity's bound to be late and Miss McVey has to come from work.'

It had been a silly idea to invite them so early; he had thought having the meal at their usual hour would make the invitation more casual, but as it was, he had rushed from the office, barely had time to check that Mrs Perry had left everything ready, and now he was wondering if he should shave again. And was the suit he wore to the office appropriate or rather funereal? He fingered his dark tie; perhaps he should change into something more festive . . . oh gosh, was that the doorbell already?

April McVey was almost hidden behind a bunch of purple and yellow freesias. She thrust them at him with a defiant air. 'I know what you're thinking,' she said.

He had been thinking how delightfully her blue frock skimmed her bosom, so he very much hoped this was not true.

'You're thinking it's strange to bring flowers to a man.'

'I'm thinking it's very kind of you. People don't bring flowers to men as a rule.' He held the bunch self-consciously away from his suit.

'Isn't it lovely weather?'

He tried to remember. 'Changeable.'

'I don't mind that. My uncle Hughie used to say it was never a bad day when you were fit to get up and put your boots on.'

Fabian smiled. 'You'll find Prudence much improved,' he said, showing her through the hall and into the sitting room, which was pleasantly cool this evening and, he was pleased to notice, gleaming, right down to the chess pieces on top of the piano. Good old Mrs Perry. It was a pity she wouldn't stay to serve the meal, but she had made it clear from the start that she would always have to be home for Mr Perry's tea. 'Miss Dunn has worked wonders – not just the lessons, but her influence; just having a nice young woman around.' April looked very interested and he rushed on. 'A young woman so obviously dedicated to her work. To her, er, vocation. I feel very happy, leaving them here together, and when I get home from work, Prudence is full of it: Miss Dunn this, Miss Dunn that. She's quite transformed. I only hope school works out as well. Honestly, April, you did a good deed the day you sent Jenny Dunn to this house.'

April gave a mock bow. 'I sometimes think I'd be better suited in an employment agency than a marriage bureau. But don't tell my boss.'

'I should imagine it requires similar skills.'

She laughed. 'You could be right. No word of Felicity yet?'

'She's often late. When she's writing she doesn't bother with everyday things like clocks and mealtimes. You must have noticed.'

'Our paths don't cross much,' April said. 'But aye, she does work hard – all day and half the night sometimes.'

'She said she was struggling with the new Forest Fay,' Fabian said. 'I'd the devil of a job to get her to come. She works so slowly; it takes a full year for each book though they aren't very long. She must only write about a paragraph a day.' It surprised him; in many ways so slapdash, in this one area Felicity was laborious and meticulous. She must hone and edit and agonise over every word. He supposed that was what it was like to have a real talent or, like Miss Dunn, a vocation.

'Forest Fay? *Those* books?' April sounded astonished. 'She never said!' She wrinkled her forehead as if trying to see the books in her mind's eye. '*Forest Fay Saves the Day* by Cicily Rafter. I bought that for Mammy. Cicily Rafter – Felicity Carr! Och, right enough! She has some of them in the house, but they're not in a special display cabinet or anything.'

He laughed at the idea. 'That wouldn't be her style. She's always secretive about her work.' And about her life. 'I think she feels she's not taken seriously as a writer, so she'd be damned if she's going to let anyone see her take *herself* too seriously.'

213

'But the Forest Fay books have been on *Children's Hour*! My mammy loves them and she's not even a child. She says they're lovely. Very sweet.'

'Exactly. I think Felicity feels it's a bit *infra dig* to be seen as a children's writer of sweet stories. People say things like, *When are you going to write a proper book?* and *That must be fun; my kiddies love the stories I tell them. I must write them down sometime if I have the time.* And of course children's writers don't earn a great deal so the wolf's never too far from the door. I don't know why she won't write something more lucrative, but what would I know? I don't pretend to be artistic.'

'But sure she . . .' April trailed off, her face puzzled. 'I mean I thought . . .' She stumbled over finishing the sentence. 'I don't suppose people can just write to order,' she managed. 'But I wouldn't know either.' She nodded at the freesias. 'You should put those in water.'

He went off to do so and returned a few minutes later with the freesias in a vase, and with Felicity, who had just arrived looking every inch the impoverished artist. She was his little sister, he couldn't see her as he saw other women, but he gathered she was considered attractive. *But she makes nothing of herself*, Serena used to say. This evening she was wearing a green cotton frock, much better than the shapeless sack things he had seen her in at home, but either it hadn't been pressed or she had travelled here on the back of a runaway donkey. Her hair needed washing, and she had bundled it into a sort of bird's nest affair and tied a blue scarf round it. Little curls escaped, framing a face that seemed not to have been checked in a glass before its owner left Riverside Road, because it sported a smudge of purple ink on the left cheek.

She kissed him – a fleeting contact that reminded him of how rarely he touched anyone these days, beyond a business-like handshake – and sank into an armchair with an air of exhaustion. 'I hope you're going to feed us well, Fabian. I forgot about lunch and, honestly, I think my back and front are stuck together – there is nothing inside me. I'd better not have a drink yet or I'll start committing indiscretions.' She grinned at April. 'Good day at the confetti-face?'

'I managed not to match up the bishop to the barmaid,' April said, and the women laughed, Fabian joining in with some relief.

It was going to be fine.

There was a pattering on the stairs and Prudence came in, her hair plaited tightly. 'What's the joke?' she demanded.

'*Pas devant les enfants*,' Felicity said, an annoying maxim Fabian remembered from childhood.

'I'm not an infant,' Prudence declared, 'and I do speak French. *Un petit peu.*' She grinned at April. 'Hello, Miss McVey. How's your bicycle?'

'It's very well, thank you,' April said gravely. 'It's outside.'

'Have you grown, Prudence?' Felicity asked. 'You look different.'

Prudence shrugged. Fabian didn't think she had grown in inches, but he did feel, watching her with the two women, that she had developed in confidence, and that made her nicer, easier to be with. She was less pert, less demanding of attention, less scornful. She listened politely when he told Felicity and April about the success of Miss Dunn, and interrupted only to say she wasn't just good, she was *goloptious*. Which led to some good-natured debate over whether or not that was really a word.

'April has some wonderful words,' Felicity said. 'What was that one you taught me the other night? *Scundered*?'

April shook her head. 'Och, you don't want to be teaching Prudence any of my silly old words.'

They went in to dinner, Felicity saying Thank God, she had been about to faint from hunger. The dining room had the same unaccustomed shine as the sitting room; perhaps that was why everything felt a little best-behaviour and everyone looked more sharply defined than usual. It was lovely to have four people at the table. It was especially lovely that one of them was April, looking round the room with a frank curiosity.

Prudence, breathing heavily through her mouth, served.

'I helped Mrs Perry with the soup,' she said. 'Don't salt it till you taste it.' She sounded very grown-up.

'It smells delicious.' April took a spoonful under Prudence's watchful eye and nodded and *hmmmm*ed. Prudence looked gratified and a little relieved and started spooning up her own soup.

There was a lamb casserole to follow – too heavy for June? He had had no idea what to serve and had let Mrs Perry decide – and then strawberries and cream. Felicity did indeed eat as if she had not eaten all day and was onto her second glass of wine before he was. Prudence asked when *she* would be allowed wine and Fabian said when she was sixteen, and Prudence sighed good-naturedly and said he was a stuffy old thing, but what could she expect. She had bet Miss Dunn tuppence that she wouldn't be allowed wine and she had been right. April caught his eye and smiled. She didn't, he noticed, drink much herself.

'Remember that wine you used to bring home from Germany?' Fabian asked Felicity. 'That was jolly good. No chance of your pals sending me over a case, I suppose?'

Felicity shook her head. 'I wouldn't ask. Things are hard enough for them.'

'I meant to pay, of course. I thought things were easier there now since Herr Hitler took over? Can't say I trust the chap myself, but there's no doubt he seems to be able to get people behind him.'

April widened her eyes. 'I think there's something creepy about him. All those people cheering and the way they stick their hands out – it gives me the heebie-jeebies, so it does.'

Felicity was looking at April with an expression Fabian couldn't read. 'Does it now?' she asked. She bit her lip and helped herself to more strawberries but said no more about the wine or Germany. When she did speak again it was in a completely different tone. 'These are jolly good, Fabian. Your own garden?'

'Yes. And how is Hanna?' Fabian turned to April and explained, 'Serena and I visited Felicity in Bavaria, and of course we met her friends. Hanna and – what was the young sister called, Fee? Eva?'

Felicity cleared her throat. 'Evie. She's Prudence's age.'

'That's right. Amusing little thing. Made quite a hit with Serena. She often said if we had another daughter, we might call her after her, but . . . anyway, that didn't happen.' Oh dear, he mustn't say too much about Serena. He wouldn't want April to think that he was dwelling on his dead wife.

'*I* wouldn't want a soppy name like that,' Prudence said. 'Miss Dunn says my name comes from Latin. And why did I not go to Bavaria?'

Felicity gave her a look which suggested she did not consider her as much improved as she might be. 'Because I didn't invite you,' she said. 'Tiresome child that you were.'

'That Erich was a good chap,' Fabian said, remembering a tall, quiet, thoughtful man. Poet or something. Keen on fishing. Very keen on Felicity, he had imagined, and Serena, with her superior feminine intuition had confirmed, but nothing seemed to have come of it. He had spoken English that would have put most Englishmen to shame. 'How's he?'

'Fine,' Felicity said. She held out her glass to April, who was closest to the wine. 'Would you mind topping me up, April?'

'I've never been abroad,' April said. 'Easterbridge is as far as I've ever got. What's Bavaria like?'

'Oh, very beautiful,' Fabian said when Felicity failed to respond. 'Munich's a fine city, and the countryside is spectacular – all mountains and meadows and lakes. Isn't it glorious, Fee?' He turned to his sister for confirmation, but she was chomping her way steadily through the last of the strawberries as if she wanted no further discussion of Germany. Odd – she used to be so keen to talk of her life there, her friends, German civilisation. Had been, occasionally, rather a bore. Perhaps Serena had been wrong and it was she who had been keen on Erich, not the other way round. And she had been disappointed. Was that why she had left Germany in such a rush?

That was the only awkward note in the evening. The talk turned to cycling. Fabian said he noted that April had come by bike; she must be getting used to Easterbridge's hills by now?

'I think so,' April said cautiously. 'The gears help.'

'I'm getting a new bicycle,' Prudence announced. 'Daddy said I'd need one for the High School and I might as well get used to it over the summer. We're going to buy it tomorrow. Only I don't know if I want a Raleigh or a Dawes. Yours is a Raleigh, isn't it?'

'It is.'

'And would you recommend it?' She leaned her head on her hand, looking serious and grown-up. 'I've looked at them both in catalogues but I can't make up my mind.'

'I can't pretend to be an expert. The only other one I ever rode was my pal Evelyn's, and I don't know what make that was. All I know is that it weighed a ton. Mind you, it could take the two of us – as long as we were going downhill.' She grinned and he saw her as a carefree girl laughing with her pal.

Prudence sighed. 'At least you had someone to ride *with*. *Poor* Miss Dunn can't cycle because of her bad leg.' She looked up at April hopefully. 'Maybe you could come with me, Miss McVey? Miss Dunn says I'm quite an interesting companion these days.'

Fabian cleared his throat. 'Actually, Prue, I was thinking of getting myself a bicycle too.'

'You, Daddy?'

'I'm not completely past it.' He was about to remind her that he was only forty, and then thought that to her, and possibly to April, forty might as well be sixty. 'And I don't want you on the roads alone until you're competent.'

'I'll pick it up easily,' Prudence said. 'I used to go everywhere on my Fairycycle, remember? And you know I'm good at anything sporty.'

'I don't know that it's exactly sporty.'

'It is when you're struggling up that hill to the tennis club,' April said, and they all laughed.

'I think you should get a bicycle, Fabian,' Felicity said. 'Get yourself in trim.'

'I am in trim!'

'You know what I mean. You could take Prudence out on adventures, like Father took us. Take a picnic. Show April the countryside. You'd like that, wouldn't you, April? Go right up as far as Shippards Hill. It'd do you good to get out. You don't want to turn into a stuffy old provincial solicitor.'

'I *am* a provincial solicitor.'

'It's the *stuffy* and the *old* you need to beware of. There are definite signs,' Felicity stated. 'I noticed a pipe on the table in the sitting room and that tie is lamentably dull.' His hand closed over the offending tie. 'I've also noticed a tendency to stoop' – Fabian immediately sat up tall, like a schoolboy told off – 'and a suggestion, just a *hint*, of cardigan.'

'Now that,' Fabian protested, 'is unfair. I have never owned a cardigan.'

'Yet cardigans seem to lurk.' Felicity half closed her eyes and stretched out her hands like a medium. 'Yes, I'm definitely picking up cardigans in the ether. But there's still hope of keeping them at bay if you take drastic action soon. I recommend cycling.'

'That's why I'm buying bikes for both of us tomorrow.'

'Oh, and you will come with us, won't you, Miss McVey? For a picnic like Aunty Fee says? *Please*.' Prudence was looking up at April kittenishly. Feminine wiles. Heaven knows what she would be like when she started getting interested in boys. Please God by then – no, he mustn't let himself imagine a wise and helpful stepmother. That was for the future. Just enjoy this evening. But that was a lovely idea, a bicycle picnic.

'Don't whine, Prudence,' Felicity told her niece. 'It's a revolting habit. Nobody will like you at the High School if you whine.'

Prudence sighed. 'All right.' In a measured tone, and without any coquettish tilts of the head, she said, 'Miss McVey, please will you come for a cycle ride with us?'

'April, I'm sure you're very busy,' Fabian said, 'but— '

'I'd love to,' April said. 'It's dull cycling on my own.'

Prudence asked. 'Aunty Fee, have you got a bicycle? You should come too.'

Felicity shook her head. 'I have to work. I'm all behind.'

'But you're always working. It can't take *that* long to write Forest Fay. They're quite short and you only bring out one a year.'

April said quickly, 'I read somewhere that a writer is someone who finds writing *harder* than other people.'

'That's silly,' Prudence said, at the same time as Felicity said, 'Yes, it does feel that way sometimes. Anyway' – as Prudence opened her mouth to protest again – 'I don't have a bicycle.'

'You could buy one.'

Felicity snorted. 'What with? I can't afford a bike.'

'I don't think I'll become a writer,' Prudence said. 'It doesn't seem very well paid.'

'What would you like to do, Prudence?' April asked.

'I used to say games mistress. But I don't like children—'

'How discerning of you,' Felicity said.

'—or schools. I'd rather be a tennis player. Or play hockey for England.' Prudence sucked her spoon.

April did not say, *That's not very realistic*, or *Don't be silly*. She said, 'I think you need to start very young for those things, but there's other ways to use your talent for sport. There was a girl from home, Mary Taggart, who was brilliant at gym and drill and d'you know what she did? She went off to Belfast and set up her own classes – not for children, but for working girls and women. She's had hundreds of women doing callisthenics and drill. Fair play to her.'

'Isn't that something like the Women's League of Health and Beauty?' Prudence asked. 'Miss Dunn's mentioned that.' She wrinkled her nose. 'Remember we saw them in Hyde Park, Daddy? Hundreds of girls all doing the same thing at the same time?' He did remember, and he had no wish for Prudence to skip around Hyde Park or anywhere else in the briefest of shorts. He was glad when she went on, 'I don't think I'd like that. All those beastly girls.'

'I think,' April said carefully, 'that you'll have a better idea when you go to the High School. You'll learn all sorts of new things. And I'm sure the girls won't all be *beastly*.' The word sounded comical in her accent.

'They were at St Lucy's. And at—'

'Aye, but that's boarding school,' April said. 'It'll be different at the High.'

'Miss Dunn did say that,' Prudence admitted.

'And she's right. You're lucky, you know. Being able to choose what to do.' She closed her lips over her teeth as if she didn't want to say more.

Fabian thought it might be time to make the coffee.

Twenty-seven

April and Felicity set off to walk home, April pushing her bike. Soon she found herself relishing the walk in the calm dusk: honeysuckle and jasmine scented the hedges all the way down into town, and it was a novelty to have company. Felicity swung along easily, her long stride matching April's though she was several inches shorter. They breathed in the hedges and gardens.

'Delicious,' Felicity said. 'I've been stuffing indoors all day. Bad for me, but what can you do? Deadlines are deadlines.'

'I didn't know you wrote Forest Fay.' April hoped it wasn't a secret.

'Oh. Yes.' April couldn't see Felicity's face as they were walking side by side, but she didn't sound cross, more self-conscious.

'My mammy loves them. I bought her the last one for her birthday. I got her the special edition with the coloured pictures and the gilt edges.'

'That was generous.'

'I'm a generous person,' April said idly. It was only something to say, to stop her blurting out what she longed to ask: *For dear sake, Felicity, where does all your money go? Why do paintings keep disappearing? And why does your brother think*

222

you write a paragraph a day when you write more words than Saint Paul?

Why did Felicity not tell Fabian that she wrote dozens of lucrative sensational stories? Surely he wasn't so prudish that he couldn't have coped with his sister writing about ruined shop girls and dastardly brigands? He didn't seem like a prude; he was quite funny when he relaxed. Clearly his image of his sister was of a struggling, perfectionist, impoverished artist, slaving for hours to hone every beautiful sentence of her wholesome children's books, with the wolf never far from the door. But April remembered the cheques she had lodged. The wolf ought not to be within miles of the door. The wolf flipping well ought to be in the next county.

So where was all the money going? A lover? Was Felicity planning an elopement? Or could she have a cocaine habit or something? She had heard about that kind of thing in artistic circles. Or even a wee problem like Daddy's? That was a sure way to lose money. But did women do that kind of thing?

She gave herself a shake. Honestly, she was becoming a snoopy old cat. She blamed the bureau; it made you far too interested in other people's affairs. *It's your affair when your bedroom window's broken and the bath scratches your b-t-m because the enamel's worn.*

'April?'

She became aware that Felicity was talking to her. 'Sorry, I was miles away.'

'Homesick? *Heimweh*, they say in German, but it can mean a kind of nostalgia too.'

She shook her head. 'Not for Lisnacashan. I was desperate to get out of it.'

'But you must miss people?'

She considered. 'I don't really miss Mammy. She's grand with my aunty and it's nice not to be worrying about her. I miss my pal, Evelyn.' It was strange to talk about Evelyn to Felicity. 'Mind you, I missed her before.'

'Quarrel?' She sounded interested.

'Och no. You couldn't fall out with Evelyn. It was just' – she struggled to explain properly – 'she started walking out with a fella, and then the next thing she was married. I remember saying to Mammy that Evelyn had no time for me now, and Mammy said what did I expect? Being pals was all very well when you were wee girls but she'd have to put Maurice first now.' She remembered the conversation clearly, Mammy looking at her as if she were an eejit. *And you'll be the same*, she'd said, *when you get married*. Evelyn finding a fella at the advanced age of twenty-six was supposed to have given hope to April. Then in the next breath Mammy had said, *But there's no need for you to get married if you don't want to*.

That was the thing with Mammy; she never said, *Don't leave me*. She never acknowledged that she needed April to protect her from Daddy; she never had to. And now Daddy was gone, and Mammy safe with Aunty Kathleen, and the scandal that had rocked Lisnacashan . . . well sure, what did it matter; they were miles away and they weren't going back. And if people were still talking about them, which she doubted, they couldn't hear, and what you didn't hear couldn't hurt you. And she was as free to get married now as anybody. Mammy would be thrilled; she would look forward to having grandchildren. She was always saying what a wee dote Evelyn's Robbie was.

But April had no notion of marrying.

'You know my brother likes you,' Felicity said, as though she could read her thoughts.

She felt her cheeks tingle in the cooling night air. 'He's a nice fella,' she said, and, hoping to change the subject, 'Isn't Prudence fairly improved?'

'Absolutely. She was the *most* aggravating child, and she was set fair to become an even more objectionable young woman, but it seems this Miss Dunn has stopped the rot. What luck that you found her.'

'But remember you can't tell anybody how,' April warned. 'If Martha knew . . .'

'You listened to what the woman really wanted. You did much better than merely introduce her to some feeble, two-a-penny chap.'

'I don't think Martha would see it like that. It's not really how it's meant to work.'

'So how exactly does it work? People write to you and then what?'

She explained about the registration form, and the interview.

'I'd love to see one of the forms,' Felicity said.

'You're not thinking of applying?'

Felicity laughed. 'No, but it might give me inspiration for a story. I write all sorts of nonsense really, and it's hard sometimes to get ideas. I wondered if seeing one of your forms might help.'

April was shocked. 'But they're— I mean, they're terribly private! People's hopes and dreams and . . . and what they earn and everything!'

'Oh gosh, I meant a blank one. My goodness, I'm not that bad!'

They giggled, clutching at each other in a hysterical way that made her fizz with remembering all those years of chumming with Evelyn, and reluctant to let go of Felicity's arm, though of course she had to.

They crossed the bridge and started the uphill walk along Riverside Road as dusk deepened. The riverbank side of the road was in shadow, and they instinctively crossed over to the shelter of the buildings. Warm light spilled from the windows of The Queen's Head and voices rumbled out as they approached.

Felicity turned to say something to April but before she could speak, the pub door flew open and two men fell out, tangled together in a flail of fists and yells.

'You're barred!' shouted a voice behind them and the pub door slammed shut.

The men sprawled, still scuffling, right in front of April and Felicity, forcing them into the road. April instinctively closed her hands round the handlebars of her precious bicycle, and Felicity tightened her grip on her bag, but the combatants had no interest in them, they probably hadn't even seen them, and as the women quickened their pace, the men kept fighting.

'Ugh. Beasts.' Felicity shuddered. April felt the shudder and realised that Felicity had taken her arm again. She glanced down at their sleeves, one white, one green, both faded to a similar grey in the dimming light. 'I'm glad *that's* not coming home to me tonight.'

'Martha did warn me about this side of town,' April said, keeping her voice light, though the sudden explosion of violence had shaken her and, like Felicity, she thought of the men's wives waiting at home. And their daughters. She thought about Johnson's wife, that nice friendly woman in the garden. It was awkward, pushing her bicycle with Felicity's hand through the crook of her arm, but she did not shake it off.

'Fabian too,' Felicity said. 'He couldn't understand why I wanted to live here instead of Parkgate. But I couldn't have afforded more than a tiny cottage in another part of town. And I like the river. But also, I'd rather live among real people.'

'The people in Parkgate are real.'

'You know what I mean: working people. Oh God, that sounds a bit patronising and do-goodery, doesn't it? Not that I *do* any good. When I came back from abroad I had all these schemes to, oh, I don't know, help people. Organise things.' The word *organise* made April think of those marching men on the newsreel with their outstretched arms, and then the League of Health and Beauty girls, drilling in unison. 'But I don't have the time.'

The brawl was well behind them now, and they moved back to the pavement just at the gates of the former mill. It seemed bigger than by day, a huge grey shadow lurking behind iron gates.

'In Germany,' Felicity began and then stopped as something sprang out of the shadows and streaked across their path. 'What—?' They both started and grabbed each other tighter, then, realising it was a cat, relaxed and laughed. Felicity didn't finish what she had been going to say. As they drew near number eleven and she reached into her bag for her key, taking her arm away from April's to do so, she said, as she had once said before, 'I didn't really want a lodger you know. It was only for the money. But I'm glad you came to live in my house. I wish I could, oh well . . .' She shook her head and opened the door, stepping aside to let April in first.

And April tried not to wonder what Felicity had been going to say as she undressed and went to bed in the white attic, the open skylight letting in a cool breeze and no sounds of the affray down the street.

Twenty-eight

'It's so kind of you. Again.' Beulah placed her hand protectively over her belly as Billy came hurtling down the hallway past her. 'Steady, Billy darling, or Aunty Martha will change her mind about taking you into town.'

Billy, all sandy curls and gappy smile, looked from mother to aunt to gauge the seriousness of this threat and decided it could be safely ignored. 'Can I take my trikecycle?' he begged.

'Tricycle,' Beulah corrected. Martha suspected that Billy, a canny enough lad, knew perfectly well how to say it. 'That's up to Aunty Martha.'

'If you're very careful,' Martha said, and Billy said, *Yesssss*, and skipped round the back of the house where, Martha assumed, the tricycle was stabled.

'I thought the novelty would have worn off,' Beulah said wearily, 'but he's keener than ever. He still has his birthday money and he wants to spend it on a bell. Could you bear to take him to buy one? I imagine they can fit it at the shop.'

'Absolutely.' She wasn't always sure how to amuse a six-year-old, so a definite mission made it easier. 'Go and rest, Beulah. You look all in.'

Beulah sighed. 'It's been hideous this time. But I hope . . .

well, it might be a good sign.' She said no more but Martha had always suspected that there had been other pregnancies, before and after Billy, which had not ended as they ought to have done. It was hard not to wonder, as Billy rode seriously in front of her, looking back every so often to check she wasn't too far behind, what it might have been like had she and Gordon had a child. Over the years she had swithered between relief and sadness that those eleven days and nights had left her without a baby. She would not have been able to start her bureau, would not have had the satisfaction of seeing her business thrive and bring fulfil-ment to so many people, but she would have had Gordon's child as compensation. A child now of – she didn't even need to calculate – seventeen. Old enough to be more like an aunt or uncle to Billy, old enough to be a companion to her. But she did not dwell. Dwelling got you nowhere; she had learned that a long time ago. Foolish to imagine a tall young girl with Gordon's dark eyes and soft hair, walking beside her chatting about, well, what did seventeen-year-old girls chat about? She had no idea.

Indeed, Martha. You have no idea. Keep your mind on Billy and count your blessings, Mother said, and she called, 'Billy! Stop when you get to the road and wait for me.'

The bicycle shop was on the edge of town, beside Hepton's on the Coaldale Road; she had not had occasion to go there before, but she remembered April telling her all about buying her own bicycle. She smiled. Dear April! She wondered how her dinner party had gone. She hoped she would tell her on Monday. Martha would be pleased, naturally, if it had gone well. And April might have a good idea about the ghastly Miss Avery. She would certainly laugh when Martha recounted the story.

The town was full of Saturday afternoon bustle, cars jostling and beeping; you could even smell them. She felt a pang for these streets in her childhood, when motor traffic was rare and people hadn't been in such a rush everywhere.

'Come on, Billy. Take my hand for crossing the road.'

She waggled her fingers at him and he said, 'I can't take your hand *and* my trikecycle.'

'True. Well, if you take one of my hands I can wheel the tricycle with the other.'

He thrust out his lip. 'I want to ride it across my own self. And I'm too old to take your hand. I'm six.'

'Six is *not* too old to take my hand. And six *is* too young to ride across the main road. But it's fine, of course, if you don't want to.' She spoke very matter-of-factly and he looked up at her in pouting suspicion.

'What d'you mean?'

'Well, we needn't cross the road at all. I want to go to the bookshop, which is on this side. And I rather fancy a cup of tea in the Willow Pattern Tea Rooms – also on this side. The only thing *across* the road is the bicycle shop. So if you don't want to cross the road holding my hand we needn't go there.'

He narrowed his eyes, considered this logic and then gave in with an exaggerated sigh that reminded her of Mark as a boy. It was awkward, negotiating the road with a six-year-old and a trike; she supposed if she were his mother she would have learned how to manage better. A couple – father and daughter she guessed – were crossing over at the same time, each wheeling, rather self-consciously, a brand-new bicycle. The girl smiled at Billy and said to her father, in a clear, carrying voice, 'Remember my Fairycycle, Daddy? I'm sure I haven't forgotten how to ride.'

'We'll see,' the father said. He too smiled at Billy and nodded at Martha. He seemed vaguely familiar but then so did many people in Easterbridge. So many lives she had completed. Though in fairness she could not have matched this girl's parents – the child must have been thirteen or so. Perhaps she had seen them at church.

Billy was entranced by the bicycle shop and gave his heart instantly to the pimply youth who screwed the bell to his handlebars. It was really, he said, a bell for a big boy's bicycle, and Billy looked as if he would burst with pride.

'A big boy's bicycle,' he kept repeating as they crossed back to the shops Martha wanted. She left him outside the bookshop with his trike, with strict orders to speak to nobody, while she dashed inside to pick up *The Nine Tailors*, the new Dorothy L. Sayers, but naturally she couldn't do that in the Willow Pattern Tea Rooms; the tricycle would have to take its chance in the street.

'But somebody might steal it,' Billy objected.

'Look, we'll take the window table,' Martha said, pointing to the bay window, 'and then we can keep an eye on it.'

'And if robbers come I can break the window and jump out at them?'

She suggested that he might simply run out of the tea shop while she rapped the window threateningly. 'But I don't think it will be necessary.'

'Aunty Martha!' He pulled at her hand. 'That lady's taking our seat!'

It was one of those awkward situations where two parties arrive at the same table at the same time. It being Saturday, the tea shop was busy and it was the last one.

'I don't mind sharing,' the other woman said. 'At least, I'm waiting for a friend but I'm half an hour early.'

'Oh, we'll be done long before that,' Martha said gratefully, setting her parcel on the table. '*Someone* isn't terribly patient.'

Billy beamed. 'That's my trikecycle,' he said, pointing out the window.

'Heavens, what a beauty,' the woman said, and only then did Martha recognise her.

'Mrs Lewis! How well you look!' She did not say that she had barely known her, and tried not to stare now. The sausage curls had been softened into a more natural-looking wave, peeping from under a pretty mauve hat. And her face was sort of shining. *Hopeful* was the word that came to mind. 'It's kind of you to share,' she said. 'Busy today, isn't it?'

Mrs Lewis inclined her head. 'Actually, I'm waiting for a friend,' she repeated. She looked at her wristwatch and gave a little chuckle. 'I'm stupidly early. He can't possibly be here for half an hour. He's coming from London.' It was not Martha's imagination, was it, that she was emphasising the *he*? But she would not be intrusive and ask.

They both ordered tea, with lemonade and a bun for Billy. Martha was peckish but decided not to have anything; she did not want to draw the encounter out, though Mrs Lewis seemed very happy chatting to Billy about his tricycle and guessing what age he might be. She guessed things like *eighteen* and *ninety-three next Wednesday*, which sent him into paroxysms of hilarity. The tea came quickly, and Billy gave the half of his attention which was not focused on guarding the tricycle outside to his bun.

'So how are you?' Martha poured her tea, though it was not drawn enough for her liking.

'Do you know, Mrs Hart, I'm very well indeed.'

'I'm so pleased,' Martha said. She had often felt bad about this woman, feared she had let her down even before the ill-judged letting loose of April on her, but here she was, smiling in her mauve hat.

Mrs Lewis leaned a little closer over the table. 'Mrs Hart, I've had some good fortune.' She lowered her voice. 'A little legacy – an aunt.'

'Good for you! At least, well, my condolences of course.'

It was clear from Mrs Lewis's voice that there was no need to condole. 'Poor Aunt Amaranth – she was a lonely old soul. Spinster, poor dear. I imagined she would leave everything to a cat's home. But it seemed she was fond of me. And it's made

232

such a difference. It's not that I wanted for anything especially, Arthur left me quite comfortable, bless him, but I had to be careful. And now, well, I can afford to have the house painted, and take a little holiday. I'm even planning' – she beamed at Martha, her face creasing up with joy – 'to take a voyage to Australia to see Mabel! Imagine!'

'But that's wonderful,' Martha said. 'You'll be able to meet your grandchildren at last!'

'I know!' She smiled indulgently at Billy. 'Little Johnny is just about the same age as young Billy here.'

'Ninety-three next Wednesday?' Billy piped up and they all laughed.

'It's a long way to travel alone,' Martha went on, 'but I hear the voyage is part of the experience – you'll make friends on board.'

'Oh but, Mrs Hart, that's the most wonderful part – I may not *be* alone.' She gave a girlish simper and Martha began to suspect that the man she was waiting for was indeed a gentleman friend. In which case, well, good for her of course, but how ignominious for the bureau.

'How lovely,' she said. 'You deserve things to turn out well.' It was a trite thing to say; people did not get what they *deserved* any more than they got what they *wanted*. She drank her tea quickly and made her farewells, Billy racing ahead. She did not want to stay and hear about Mrs Lewis's gentleman friend, still less did she want to be introduced to him when he turned up.

Jealous? Mother asked. She had developed this ridiculous bee in her celestial bonnet. And then, more to the point – and Mother could be very astute – she said, *I do hope the gentleman friend isn't just interested in the legacy.*

In the office on Monday she told April about the encounter.

'A legacy *and* a fella!' April said. 'Fair play to her!' Then her face sobered and, like Mother, she said, 'I hope the two aren't connected.'

'What do you mean?'

'Just that it's queer that we couldn't find a man that liked her, but now she's a few shillings . . . There was this poor cratur in Lisnacashan—'

'Oh, dear, let's hope not.'

'Och, now don't you be worrying,' April said soothingly. 'I'm sure it's grand. It's not like she advertised in the *Easterbridge Recorder*: *Mrs Primrose Lewis, formerly of modest income, would like it known that she is now a widow of means. Interested gentlemen should apply to box number—*'

Martha laughed, feeling better. 'You're right. And talking of that august journal, have you seen last week's? There was a photo of Sybil Postlethwaite's wedding.' She took the paper from her desk and read aloud: '*Sybil, lovely daughter of esteemed local businessman Bernard Postlethwaite, looked radiant in white bias-cut organdie with ruffled sleeves.* Splendid. I'll cut it out and stick it on the noticeboard.' Brides were always described as *radiant*, but they both agreed that Sybil, beaming from the grainy photo, looked delighted with herself and with her new husband.

'Already!' April said.

'Well, she did say they were in a hurry. And I haven't forgotten they're yours,' Martha said generously.

April laughed. 'Och, as long as they're happy it doesn't matter.'

'Talking of which, I'm jolly well giving you Angela Avery.' She told April all about her, sparing nothing, and April laughed as she had hoped. She seemed definitely to have recovered her spirits. Before Martha had even finished telling her the full ghastliness of Angela, she was flicking expertly through the files.

'There you go.' She wielded a blue card. 'Easy. Herbert Gee. *Made* for each other.'

Martha looked at the photo attached to the card. 'He's handsome enough,' she said.

'Is he?' April said indifferently. 'I'd say they're well able for each other.'

Two days later, just before lunch, there was a resounding knock on the door and a tall, tweed-clad woman swept in. She could have been any age between forty and sixty, with a high colour – possibly the result of wearing tweed in June – and bright darting eyes.

'Thomasina Longbottom,' she announced. 'Sorry, don't have an appointment. In town to have my bitch served. English setter. Nervy beast. Left her off with the breeder and thought I'd order some new tweeds in Ackroyd's when I saw your plaque. Well, I've never had time for marriage before, between Papa and the dogs, but Papa's gone to his rest now – won't suit him, he liked to be busy; he used to say to me, *Thomsy, darling, I jolly well hope there's hunting in heaven* – anyway, the house is dashed quiet apart from the setters, and I thought, well, I'm not utterly past it, am I? Shouldn't mind a whirl at the old marriage. But I wouldn't have a notion where to look for a chap myself, so if you gels can do the heavy lifting . . .' She stopped for breath and looked from Martha to April, suddenly less self-assured. 'Oh dear. You both look rather dumbstruck. Don't cater for veterans, eh?'

April recovered first. 'Divil the bit,' she said cheerfully, an expression Martha was sure Thomasina Longbottom had never heard before. 'We cater for everybody here at True Minds. If you'd like to sit down, we can have a wee chat.'

'We have a range of gentlemen with, er, your interests,' Martha said, as Miss Longbottom, beaming, arranged herself at the desk, folding her long, capable-looking hands in her tweed lap.

'Och, we've only the one,' April said.

Later she apologised to Martha. 'I shouldn't have said *only the one*,' she admitted. 'But I couldn't believe our luck.'

'It only takes one,' Martha said. 'Anyway, I've written to the Colonel, so keep your fingers crossed.'

The fingers worked. The meeting took place. The Colonel pronounced Miss Longbottom *a damn fine woman* and she said he reminded her of Papa, and they'd had a super chat about gundogs. They were going to meet again at the Coaldale and District Agricultural Show the following weekend. 'My new tweeds will be ready,' Miss Longbottom said. 'I've gone for rather a natty lilac.'

Angela Avery and Herbert Gee, in a meeting in the downstairs office, found a great deal to say, perhaps not exactly *to* each other – it was rather a case of concurrent monologues – but at any rate they agreed to meet again.

'Everybody's getting matched up,' April said with satisfaction. 'There must be something in the air.'

'We're just good at our jobs,' Martha said, and wondered why, instead of gratified, she felt rather empty. Like the time at school, she remembered, when everyone's parents came to take them out for half-term. Hers couldn't – she had forgotten why – and her chum Letitia Arnold had offered to let her tag on with her family, but she had been reluctant to butt in and too proud to show she cared, so she had let herself be left behind with Matron for the afternoon, and Matron had made her turn sheets side-to-middle for hours.

Really, Martha, dear, Mother said, *You must stop this foolish dwelling.* And she knew Mother was right, but it was easy for her to say, stuck up there on her cloud.

Twenty-nine

Fabian, leaning against a drystone wall, shouted with the last of his breath, 'Nearly there! I promise it's worth it.' He prayed his breathing would return to normal before April arrived; at one point he had thought he would have to suffer the ignominy of her overtaking him, but the cycling he had been doing for the last week or so was starting to pay off. Or perhaps it had been his pride that had pushed him up the hill.

Below him on the road April was digging down into her pedals and bending forward over her handlebars. *It had better be*! said her scarlet face. Prudence's bicycle drew level with her, Prudence's legs pistoning. Both young women redoubled their efforts, almost standing in the pedals, but it was April who had the glory of reaching the top of Shippards Hill before Prudence, who had gone hell-for-leather at the start of the long drag and now run out of energy.

'Phew!' April bent over to catch her breath, clearly too exhausted to dismount for the moment. She wiped her sweaty hands on her skirt. Quite a short skirt, green cotton; she looked almost as girlish as Prudence.

'Well done,' Fabian said. 'Come and see what all the effort was for.'

She leaned her bicycle against the wall and came to join him. He was aware of her breathing hard beside him, warmth radiating from her.

'Worth the climb?' He did not so much look at the view as feel it rear up in front of them. The ground fell away in front to a steep green wooded valley, a few stone buildings huddling together at the bottom, but up here all was purple and dun moorland and blue and white mottled sky. April whirled her arms around and breathed in the keen upland air. 'Oh!' she said. 'It's glorious. It's like the Sperrins – the hills near home.' And then she was quiet in a way that he knew was uncharacteristic.

'Homesick?' He had little idea of her life in Northern Ireland, or why she had left.

She shook her head. She turned round and called to Prudence, 'Come on! You're nearly there!'

Beetroot-faced, Prudence huffed out, 'You'd – better – have – the picnic ready!'

'Save your breath!' Fabian said. He smiled at April. 'She's so much happier,' he said in a low voice, 'and so much nicer.'

'I told you Miss Dunn would be a good influence. It's a pity she's going abroad – well, not for her of course.'

'And what about you, April? Would you like to travel?'

'Sure I am travelling.' She sat down and undid the straps of her knapsack; they had carried picnic provisions between them. Fabian had wanted to do it all, but she had said she couldn't allow that. Before marriage, Serena would have expected him to take charge of the picnic; afterwards she would have done so without discussion. He hoped it was a point in his favour that he had shared the task with April, who was a modern girl for all her quaint homely sayings. That skirt! He mustn't keep looking at it – or rather, at the long, shapely legs in fawn lisle stockings.

'But you're happy in Easterbridge?'

'Aye.' She gestured at the scenery. 'But standing here admiring the view won't make the baby a new bonnet.' On a low rock she spread out the old oilcloth he had brought and set out packets of sandwiches. 'Those are cheese, and those are cheese and pickle.'

'Lovely.' Fabian took one of each.

'Don't start without me, you big meanies!' Prudence said shrilly. She flung her bicycle at the wall and collapsed on the ground beside them. 'That's – the furthest – and the highest – I've ever – cycled.' She gulped in huge ostentatious breaths between words.

'You did well,' April said. 'You'll be flying up and down to that High School like nobody's business.' She found the flask, uncapped it and organised cups.

'I don't want boring old tea,' Prudence said, sitting up. 'Did you bring lemonade, Daddy?'

'In my knapsack. There's chocolate too. And apples.'

Anyone passing, Fabian thought, would have taken them for a family. April, hair pulled into a short loose tail, cheeks ruddy from exercise, long legs folded under her, was too young to be Prudence's mother, but nobody would work that out on a casual look. And Fabian, out of doors, the wind ruffling his hair, legs stretched out in front of him in old flannels, felt younger than he had for ages, and hoped he looked it.

April pushed her front hair out of her eyes and leaned back, lost, as far as he could see, in admiring the view. Behind them, ewes and their half-grown lambs bleated, some gruff and grumbling, some high-pitched and indignant. April plucked a daisy from the grass and twirled it in her hands.

'Penny for them?' Fabian proffered an apple and the chance for a confidence.

She accepted the apple but shook her head at the other offer. 'Just silly thoughts,' she said and when he waited for more, she said, 'About home and that sort of thing.'

'You must have left friends behind you in – sorry, remind me what your hometown's called?'

'Lisnacashan.'

Prudence looked bored and said that she had nature samples to collect for Miss Dunn. She wandered off, head down, occasionally diving importantly for a flower or a piece of moss, and April gave her attention to Fabian's question.

'A few friends,' she said. 'I *knew* plenty of people, och, the whole town really. But close friendships . . . mainly just Evelyn. But she got married.' She sounded wistful.

He looked into the middle distance, a half-eaten apple in his hand. 'And anyone . . . special?'

She raised her eyebrows. 'You mean was I courting?' She pronounced it *coorting*.

'Er, I suppose so.' He was taken aback by her candour, but Prudence, scattering lambs as she galumphed over the fields, was well out of earshot. 'Of course, you work in the marriage business. You're not going to be shy about talking about those things. It's like me talking about wills and money and so forth.'

'Or doctors talking about people's insides.'

'Indeed.' But the banter didn't deter him. 'So were you?'

She shook her head. 'No interest,' she said lightly. 'That's why I'm so suited to my job. The one before me set her cap at all the best men. Well, Martha's no worries about me on that score.' She was protesting too much. He hoped. 'In Lisnacashan,' she went on, 'there's these two pubs. Well, there's seven pubs, but there's these two in particular, McCoy's and McKay's, next door to each other. Mr McCoy's a rare one for the drink; Mr McKay never takes a drop. Guess which pub's better run?' He shook his head. He didn't want to talk about pubs in obscure Irish towns. 'Not that I've ever been in either one,' she assured him, 'but you know how everybody knows everything in a small town.'

240

Something flickered over her face when she said that – a shadow. Or he imagined it. He was probably looking at her too intently; he didn't mean to, she was just so lovely. But he must be gentle. She was clearly very innocent, despite her job. Her deeper feelings as yet untouched. He mustn't scare her off. He had been regarding her as a sort of jolly head-girl type but now he saw her more as a nervy young creature, like the lambs who frolicked and jumped in adventurous gangs, exploring the edges of their field, but who ran crying for their mothers when Prudence climbed over the wall and startled them.

But he must say *something*. Gosh, he was so unpractised at this! There had been nobody before Serena and obviously nobody since.

'April,' he said. 'I've come to, well, value our friendship.'

'Oh,' she said. The red in her cheeks deepened. 'That's nice. I do too. I haven't met many people here yet. Except the love-lorn of course. And Felicity and Martha.'

'I haven't enjoyed a day like this for years. Prudence isn't much of a companion and Felicity's always busy. Sometimes I've worried that it was the wrong thing, coming back here. But it was supposed to be a fresh start. For one thing, there aren't any memories of Serena here. She never liked the north – thought it was all clogs and cobbles. If she hadn't died I suppose we'd have stayed in London. Strange, where life takes you.'

'It is, aye. I'd never even heard of Easterbridge until four months ago.'

'Well, I'm glad you did hear of it.'

'Tell me about Serena,' she said.

'Oh. Um.' Surely you didn't woo the new – well, he couldn't say wife, that was hideously presumptuous – by talking about the old one? He shouldn't have mentioned Serena.

'Not if you don't want to.'

241

'I've got out of the way of it. When she first died, I longed to talk about her, but nobody would let me. People would jabber on about anything but Serena. The stock market. The Thames flooding. The Flying Scotsman. Anything but the one thing that filled my whole being.'

'Och, people are embarrassed by death. Sure don't I know rightly.' He remembered that her father had died not long ago.

'And they assume you can't bear to hear the person's name,' he went on. 'They think they're being tactful. Not wanting to upset you. Not wanting to remind you, when you've hardly forgotten your wife has died.'

'Och, I'm always in trouble for being tact*less*.'

'I imagine you're just very honest.' He smiled.

'Maybe. So, Serena . . . what was she like?'

'She was very womanly I suppose. Didn't want much outside marriage and motherhood.' He remembered that April considered herself a career girl and said quickly, 'Of course it was different times. We met when we were very young. Our families were old friends; we stayed with them whenever we went to London.'

She nodded.

'We'd have liked more children,' he went on, 'but it wasn't to be.' Gosh, he shouldn't talk about that sort of thing. 'And then of course she became ill. Cancer.' April's face twisted with discomfort – he had learned, long ago, not to say that word, but something about April's blunt candour made him want to be straightforward. 'She was a city girl,' he said to lighten the mood. 'London born and bred.'

'I've never been to London,' April said. 'Evelyn went one time with her husband. They saw two shows, *The Cat and the Fiddle* and *The Merry Widow*, and went all over London on top of a bus.' Her face brightened and he thought of how much fun it would be to take her to London, to see it from the top of a bus with her, enthusiastic and wide-eyed beside him. 'But she didn't like the Underground railway. I don't think I would either.'

'You get used to it,' he said airily.

'Mammy says you can get used to anything if you have to. D'you miss London? When I was talking about it there, you looked like you did.'

'I miss . . . aspects of my life there.' He did not say that what he missed was being married, having a home with a wife at its heart, instead of merely a house. 'Just as you must miss aspects of your old life.'

'Och, you know,' she said. 'Life's about moving on. If you worried too much about missing people, sure you'd never go anywhere.'

'Yes,' he said. 'I'm starting to see that.' And was this, could it be, an invitation to woo? An acknowledgement, albeit clumsy, that it was time for him to move on from Serena? 'I'd like,' he said tentatively, the words feeling thick in his throat, 'for us to get to know each other better. If you didn't find the idea too repulsive?'

She looked down at her skirt. There was a smudge of oil on it from her bicycle chain. 'I – I don't . . . I'm not . . . maybe just as friends,' she stammered.

'*Friends*?'

She nodded. 'I don't want . . . I'm quite happy . . .'

'I wouldn't want to rush you. I know you're very young.'

'Och, Fabian!' She laughed and for a moment the air, which had become very tense, softened. 'I'm not young at all. I'm not a kick in the ass off thirty. But I told you I wasn't interested in courting.'

'But, would there be hope for me?' Oh dear, he sounded like someone in one of those dreadful romantic weeklies Mrs Perry stuffed behind cushions and that he sometimes glanced over.

She bit her lip and he should have had the sense to leave it there, to say of course they could be pals, to have more days like this and to let her gradually come round to it, to *him*, but he didn't. He forgot that he was supposed to be a cautious, middle-aged provincial lawyer and blundered on.

'I was a good husband,' he said. 'I'd like the chance to be again. I don't expect you to *love* me' – his cheeks flared at the word (April's were as red as strawberries and no wonder, he hadn't meant to leap this far ahead) – 'but I think we could get along very nicely. You'd be so good for Prudence. And Felicity thinks the world of you; she's told me so. And in time, maybe . . .'

She was shaking her head. 'No,' she said. 'I'm sorry, but no.'

'Oh gosh, I've rushed you, haven't I? I didn't mean to. I only meant . . . but you're so lovely. And I'd be good to you, I promise. We could have your mother to live here if you wanted, I mean, if you were worried about her.' Good lord, what on earth was he saying?

'Fabian,' she said gently. 'You're a lovely man. I know you'd be good to me. Any woman would be lucky to have you as a husband; I've often thought that.' (Later, going over the conversation in his head, this was the phrase that gave him hope.) 'But not me. When I said I wasn't for getting married I really meant it.'

'I know you're a career woman, but—'

'Don't say you wouldn't mind if I kept on working. You want a nice wee woman to make a proper home for you and Prudence. You'd be mortified at your wife going out to work. I can imagine all those fusty old solicitors talking about it and you letting on not to mind. And it's not as though I'm doing anything so very special. Not like Felicity. You might not mind your wife being a writer or an artist.'

He seized on this. 'So if you don't think it's so special, maybe you wouldn't mind giving it up?' He leaned towards her and she shied away, not so much lamb now as skittish pony. Even her nostrils were flaring.

'I don't want to marry you.' She was every inch the head girl now, but not the jolly one. 'I don't want to marry anybody.'

And then she grabbed her bicycle, jumped on, and flew back down the hill.

Thirty

She had flounced. Like a wronged heroine in a film. Like a toddler. She had always been impulsive, always had a temper, but she had never stormed off like that. (She did not count the escape from Johnson.) It felt good at first, freewheeling down the hill, cheeks cooling in the wind, and then, as the town rushed to meet her and her wheels started to joggle on the cobbles, it felt bad. Childish and embarrassing. She felt everything that had ever been meant by the word *scundered*.

But what else could she have said?

Why, when she said she didn't want to marry, did nobody believe her? Why did nobody listen when women explained what they wanted?

She stopped by the river, not ready to go home yet, and looked down into its depths, still straddling her bicycle. Chicks of some sort – moorhen or duck – bobbed along its edge, in and out of the green weeds that softened the bank. She picked at the stain on her skirt. Blast. Oil didn't always come off. This skirt was old but a favourite, and she could not easily afford a new one. If she married Fabian, this would not be a problem. No more scrimping. And she would have a home that wasn't just a room in another woman's house.

But you couldn't marry a man for a nice house and a new skirt. Fabian deserved better. He was kind and interesting – she would have happily cycled all over Yorkshire with him and eaten picnics and admired views. He was solvent and sensible and any woman would have a comfortable life with him. Prudence would go her own way in due course. He was perfectly eligible, as she had always known, and she liked him enough to want him to be happy and not lonely. Sure hadn't she tried to get him to sign up with the bureau? Hadn't she thought he'd do grand for that wee Miss Murrell? Hadn't she half hoped he would fall for Jenny Dunn?

He wasn't meant to fall for *her*! She ran her fingers through her hair, which felt sweaty and had come out of its make-shift 'do'.

In books, the heroines often said no to the first proposal only to give in afterwards. Look at Lizzy Bennet and Anne Shirley! But Jo March had said no to Laurie and meant it. Aye, and then married that beardy old German professor! This made her think about Felicity and her German friend – what was his name? Felicity had jouked away from talking about him that night at Fabian's, as if there was a story there.

She wished there was someone she could talk to. But there wasn't. She couldn't tell Felicity when it concerned her own brother. Martha, well, possibly, but she'd have to wait until Monday. And she certainly couldn't jump on a train to Manchester. Mammy would think she was mad in the head to say no, and Aunt Kathleen would be all tight mouth and folded arms. She could imagine her: *You're not getting any younger, April . . . It's not like you've had any other offers . . . You said no to a solicitor?*

And it wouldn't be enough to say she didn't love him. Aunt Kathleen had married for love and where had it got her? To a Manchester backstreet and a life of hard work and unhappiness.

Mammy – yes, Mammy had loved Daddy, once upon a time. And look what had happened to them.

But that wasn't something she wanted to think about right now.

What she wanted was to sit in a café with a pal and drink a huge pot of tea and eat fish and chips and talk and talk and talk the way she and Evelyn used to. She remembered how nice it had been, walking home with Felicity that night, the easy chatter, the feeling of having a pal. Well, why not invite Felicity out for supper? *My treat*, she'd say, and if Felicity asked what the occasion were, she'd say, *Och, just for the craic*. Sure, Miss Connaughton and Miss McGlone, who had shared a home in Lisnacashan, you used to see them in Tiernan's Tea Rooms all the time. April always thought they were lucky. It was what she'd planned with Evelyn, sharing rooms, going out for tea, having fun. Only Evelyn didn't want it once Maurice Kenny came along. Ugh! Did *all* roads lead to marriage?

It was only when she got off her bicycle outside number eleven and put it away in the shed that April realised how tired she was, and how stiff her muscles. It was a long time since she had cycled as far or as strenuously. She rotated her aching shoulders and decided to have a good soak in the bath before anything else. Physical discomfort was a good distraction. She felt the need to minister to herself – nobody else would! The geyser was temperamental but could generally be relied on at this time of day. Felicity bathed at night. Up in her room she had lemon verbena bath salts which Mammy had sent for her birthday and which she hadn't opened yet.

Felicity was, most unusually, mopping the kitchen floor when April came in the back door. She had taken off her cardigan and hung it over a chair, and was sweating in a short-sleeved blouse. She had a bright red spotted scarf tied round her curls and was singing what sounded like a German song.

'*Die Gedanken sind frei,*' she sang, '*wer kann sie erraten?* Oh, hello April. Don't step on the floor. *Sie fliegen vorbei wie nächtliche Schatten.*' She had a hoarse singing voice with a kind of crack in it. Rather appealing, April would have thought if she were not desperate for a bath and being scolded for the innocent and unavoidable crime of standing on a floor she had not expected to be wet in the middle of a Saturday afternoon.

'I can't levitate.' She looked down at her dusty shoes. 'I'll take my shoes off and tiptoe, will that do?'

'Well, don't slip in your stocking feet. I don't want bloodstains on my lovely clean floor.'

Only people for whom cleaning was a novelty made such a fuss about their lovely clean floors.

'Have you used all the hot water?' April asked, after she had removed her shoes. 'I'm desperate for a bath.'

'This water's from the kitchen tap via the kettle. It's nothing to do with the bath water.' She frowned at April. 'Are you all right? Did my brother wear you out on those hills?'

April shook her head. 'I'm fine, just grubby and tired. But why are you cleaning the floor? On a Saturday?'

'I've sacked Mrs Gibney,' Felicity said. 'She wasn't much good.'

Better than nothing, April thought. 'We've a great wee char at the office,' she said. 'She's always looking for extra hours. I could ask her.'

'I mean I've sacked her because I don't want a char any more. I'll do it myself.'

'But—'

'But what?' Felicity tilted her chin.

But you don't have time. *But* you'll forget. *But* I'll end up doing it. *But* I should have a reduction in my rent.

'Why?' she asked, since she couldn't say any of that.

249

'I need to make economies. There isn't enough money coming in for . . . for everything it needs to cover.'

Despite the singing, there was something agitated about her. She hadn't the air of someone who wanted to go out for fish and chips and girlish gossip, and though April hadn't asked her, she still felt rejected.

Felicity was mopping and singing again, under her breath, but sort of warily, as if she wanted April to keep out of her business. '*Kein Mensch kann sie wissen, kein Jäger sie schießen.*'

April didn't know a word of German and this made her feel even more annoyed than if Felicity had been singing in English. The indignation that had sent her flying down the hill away from Fabian flooded her now. Don't tell the lodger anything, keep her in her lowly place with fancy foreign words. Well, she, April McVey, wasn't an eejit, and she wasn't going to be palmed off like that any longer.

'I imagine it'll take a quare bit of money to fix the damp in the hall?' she said innocently. Felicity stopped singing, and looked stung, but April pressed on. 'And the bath – the enamel's all worn off under both taps. And my window's still not closing right. We . . . *you'll* need to get that sorted out before the winter.'

'I'll ask Fabian to look at your window,' Felicity said. 'The rest will have to wait.'

'Why?' April demanded. 'I thought you'd a new Forest Fay out next month. Won't that bring in some money?' She hadn't the vaguest idea how publishing worked but surely to God if you published a book, you got paid. And she'd smuggled a registration form home to Felicity too – wasn't that meant to have inspired her to write a bunch of her profitable stories?

Felicity leaned on her mop and said nothing. Her hair, springing madly up from the red scarf, looked rather like the mophead, but there was no amination in her face, only anxiety.

'Felicity? I don't understand. Why this need to save money? Why isn't there enough coming in? Where's it going? You're working all hours, you get well paid for your stories, I pay you a decent rent, you seem to have sold a lot of pictures lately – I don't mean to be nosy, but I do live here and, well, it looks to me as if there's something strange going on.'

Felicity lifted the mop bucket and began to pour the dirty water into the sink. Her short sleeve slipped back and, with a sick horror April saw, right round the top of her arm, a ring of yellowing bruises. 'I don't think it's any of your business, Miss Marple.'

April ignored the slight. Anyway, Miss Marple was a great wee soul. 'Look, I know I'm only the lodger, but—'

'Is that how you see yourself?' It wasn't like Felicity to sound so unsure. 'I thought we'd become sort of friends?'

There was so much April could have said to this. She would have liked to say, Och surely they were friends. But she hardened her heart. She wasn't an eejit. Felicity wasn't really offering friendship, she was using the *idea* of their so-called friendship as an excuse not to take April into her confidence. An excuse to get away with not fixing up the house.

'If we were friends you'd trust me more,' she said instead.

'Trust you to what?'

'Are you being blackmailed? Or do you have a dope habit?' Both sounded ludicrous as soon as the words were out, so she pressed on, 'Because your money is going somewhere while the house falls down round you. Round us.'

And what about those bruises? Just who, or what, was she involved with?

Felicity laughed but she blushed too, and the blush stayed long after the insincere tinkle of mirth flickered and died. 'Dope? Blackmail? You should stick to matchmaking and leave the penny dreadfuls to me.' And then she said, in a different, more

251

serious tone, 'Did you and Fabian . . . I mean, how did you get on?'

'Grand,' April said. 'The hills were grand. The picnic was grand. It was all grand.'

Even to herself she sounded false. And the bath, after she had tiptoed, not particularly carefully, over the drying kitchen floor and up the stairs to the bathroom, was disappointing, the water lukewarm and the lemon verbena redolent not merely of luxury but, painfully, of home. Which might have been what Mammy intended but she would not have intended April to lie in a lukewarm bath with tears cooling on her cheeks, wishing she was somewhere else. Only she didn't know where.

Thirty-one

It was absurd to imagine that weekends were getting longer –
time was supposed to speed up when you got older, not slow
down – but it seemed to Martha that Saturdays and Sundays
dragged as never before. Beulah's parents were visiting, so she
had no Billy to distract her. She spent Saturday gardening and
doing dull chores, like cleaning Mother's old china, and went
to bed early with P. G. Wodehouse and a feeling of vague
dissatisfaction. Mother opined that *it would not do*, and Martha
could not disagree.

On Sunday after church she gave herself a good talking to and
set off for a walk through the park. She preferred country walks
really, the park was rather manicured, and she had a sudden
desire to strike out over the hills with haversack and stout stick,
neither of which she possessed, but she would never do so without
a companion. Really, was she becoming a frightful old spinsterish
stick-in-the-mud? She thought of Miss Longbottom sweating in
her natty lilac tweed – now there was a woman who wouldn't
think twice about striding alone over hill and dale, setters at her
heels. Only Miss Longbottom might at this very moment be
stomping along with the Colonel, if their visit to the Coaldale
Show yesterday had gone well. Jolly good luck to her – to them.

And she, Martha Hart, was not a stick-in-the-mud! As if to prove it, she left the park, with its neat rows of delphiniums and begonias, crossed the Sunday-sleepy town centre and took herself right over the bridge and up Riverside Road, an area she never ventured into. It was true that the houses were much shabbier than she was used to; she felt quite daring walking past The Queen's Head, and her breath caught at the prospect of passing the rusted gates of the closed-down Shaw's Mill. But April lived here, despite Martha's reservations, and said it was grand – though Martha had learned that the Irish *grand* conveyed less approbation than the Yorkshire one. If she could remember what number house April lived in, she might even call. Braced by this thought, she strode past the mill gates as boldly as if she were Miss Thomasina Longbottom herself – or indeed April, who presumably skipped up and down this road without turning a hair. After all, what was so frightening about an empty mill?

Only it wasn't empty. There were people in the grounds; Martha saw them as she passed the gates. *Children, up to no good*, Mother suggested, but children were not so quiet. Her natural interest in people made her slow down and squint through the gates. It was a couple, hand in hand, deep in conversation, looking up at the mill and then towards each other, swinging their arms companionably. What an odd place for a walk, but when you were in love you didn't mind much about your surroundings. Why, she and Gordon had often had to make do with strolling the squalid streets around railway stations, just to squeeze the last moment out of his leaves. She had swung his arm in just that way as if to keep hold of it for longer. At least this couple, whoever they were, wouldn't have their lives destroyed by war.

Not *destroyed*, she amended. She had made a jolly good life, even if it were not the one she intended.

She was almost past when some twinge of recognition made her look back at the couple. It was Sybil and Henry Barrett. How odd. Why should they be walking around a derelict mill? She was about to call out, to say what a lovely photograph they had had in the *Easterbridge Recorder* – she felt the nannyish interest in them that she had in all 'her' couples – but something about the intensity of their talk, something in the way they bent towards each other, told her that they didn't want to be disturbed. Something in the clasp of their hands made her chest feel hollow, as if she had been winded. So silly.

And it had been even sillier to think of calling on April; she wouldn't want to be disturbed at the weekend. She would take herself back home and finish cleaning Mother's Wedgwood tea service. Mother, from her cloud, passed no remark about this plan, not even to say thank you.

By eleven on Monday morning she could ignore April's sighs no longer. The girl sighed as she did most things, with gusto, but these were not the sighs of someone fed up typing invoices or frustrated with filing. These were the sighs of someone begging you to ask what is wrong.

So.

'What's wrong, April?' And she remembered the last time April had confided in her and sent up a swift prayer for more empathy and insight this time.

'Och, nothing.'

'Nonsense. You have a face like a wet weekend in Whitby, and if you sigh any harder you'll blow those envelopes through the window.'

This raised a reluctant smile. 'Och, I suppose it would be good to hear your opinion.'

'I can generally oblige.'

'Well.' April set down the brochures she was meant to be

putting into envelopes for the post and leaned forward across her desk. 'I got a, er, a proposal at the weekend.'

'A proposal? You mean' – Martha gestured round the office – '*our* kind of proposal? A marriage proposal?'

'Aye.'

'And you said . . .?'

'I said no.'

'Because . . .?'

'*Because* I don't want to get married. Amn't I never done telling you?'

'And this is . . .?' But she knew. The landlady's brother. The solicitor.

April blushed. 'Fabian Carr.'

'And you said no?' So why blush at his name? But – *gently*, Martha reminded herself.

'Aye.' April's voice was weary. 'I told him I'd be happy to be pals but nothing more. But he wouldn't listen' – Martha's face must have sparked in alarm because April rushed on – 'Och no, nothing like *that*. He was, is, the perfect gent.' She rubbed the end of her nose. 'I acted like an eejit. I said no and ran away.'

Martha's mind flew back to Gordon. They had known they wanted to marry from the beginning. She couldn't remember a proposal, just a certainty that this was the person she wanted by her side throughout life. But the war had made it so difficult – he hadn't wanted her to commit when he might be killed, and she *had* wanted to. *I want to belong to you!* she had cried melodramatically, and they had quarrelled, and it had been fraught and tearful and desperate but also rather romantic. And of course they had married and he had been killed.

So Fabian Carr and April had quarrelled too. She had run away and now she was embarrassed. But that didn't mean she didn't want to marry him.

256

'I must say,' Martha said gently, 'I quite thought you were interested in him.'

April turned a shocked face to her. 'I'm not and I never was.'

'But' – she tried to think back to what had made her suspect – 'when you went to his house for dinner a few weeks ago, you were *glowing*. And you'd done your hair and worn such a pretty frock. I remember—'

'You thought I'd done a Hilda on you,' April said drily. 'Well, I hadn't and I wouldn't and . . . ah for dear sake, why does nobody believe me?' She sounded genuinely distressed.

'I'm sorry. But sometimes people say they aren't interested in a chap, even most sincerely believe they aren't, but deep down—'

'Deep down I don't want to marry Fabian. Or anyone.' She hunched over her work again, as if weary of the subject, and Martha was silent, scared to say the wrong thing. She had introduced so many couples, and seen so many happy endings, but she didn't see the bits in between – the misunderstandings and uncertainties.

'I'll make a cuppa,' she decided, and she popped out to the bakery on the corner for some ginger biscuits while the tea was brewing. When she returned, April had not moved, and she accepted her cup and biscuit absently.

'Martha,' she said, cradling the cup in her hands and looking like an earnest rabbit, 'd'you think there's something wrong with me? Like, really wrong?'

'Of course not!' But perhaps the reassurance was too pat; April looked unconvinced.

'It's just, when I say I've never wanted to get married, I'm not making it up. I never have.'

'Well, then, you haven't met the right chap. Honestly, my dear. Once you do, you'll know.'

'But I've never met a fella I could imagine feeling that way about.'

Perhaps it wasn't so strange, Martha thought, that out of all the chaps in Lisnacashan, there had not been one to please her. It was a small and, by all accounts, unsophisticated town. April was not sophisticated, but there was something about her, a lively spirit, that might indeed recoil from the boorish farmer or small shopkeeper types that were probably all she'd encountered. If she were a client, what sort of chap would Martha match her up with? She contemplated her assistant, nibbling abstractedly at her biscuit, a little line between her eyebrows, a lock of fair hair falling over her forehead, and could not come up with an answer. Not because there was anything wrong with April; she wasn't remotely unlovable, rather the opposite.

It's because you don't want to lose her, Mother said tartly, and Martha knew she was right. Still, she couldn't bear to see the girl unhappy. There was something terribly unnatural about it; April was made for spring sunshine and hope, as her name suggested.

But April had showers too. And – she felt very clever remembering this, because she'd never got on with Eliot, always felt there was something going on that she would never be clever enough to grasp, that he didn't *want* you to grasp – there was that poem about April being the cruellest month. What cruelties had April seen, perhaps, to put her off marriage and men?

Ah. Of course.

'Do you think' – Martha chose her words carefully – 'that frightful cad put you off? Because, honestly, my dear, most men aren't remotely like that. I'm sure this Fabian chap—'

April shook her head. 'Fabian's a dote,' she said. 'Honestly, Martha, if I could make myself love him, I would. But even I know it doesn't work like that.'

'No.'

'And this is nothing to do with that . . . with Mr Johnson. I've always felt I wouldn't marry.'

Martha asked a question she sometimes asked nervous clients. 'What was your parents' marriage like?'

'Oh!' April whooshed out a breath. 'Complicated. Daddy wasn't . . . easy.' She was quiet again and Martha worried that she had gone too far. And yet this was what the girl needed: to work out *why* she had this aversion to marriage. After all, her happiness – and possibly that of Fabian, who sounded a thoroughly good egg – might depend on it.

'He died recently, didn't he? Heart attack, you said?'

April nodded. 'It wasn't as straightforward as that sounds,' she said. 'Och, I might as well tell you. He dropped dead at a pub in the next town.' She looked up with defiant eyes. 'I know it's sordid. And that's not the half of it. He wasn't there for the drink. He was betting on horses. It turns out he'd been doing it for years; Mammy had no idea.'

Martha tried not to sound shocked. 'I suppose people do gamble.' Though not people she knew.

April shook her head. 'We're not talking a wee flutter on the Grand National. This was hundreds of pounds. He was in debt to half the country. It all came out after he died. He'd had a big loss and he started gambling more and more to try to win it back. Only he kept on losing. Mammy was disgraced. We sold the house and the factory and it just about covered it, but there's nothing left. That's why Mammy's gone to live with my aunty.'

'Oh, my dear!' She tried and failed to imagine her own family in disgrace. *I should think not!* Mother admonished, and if she had had pearls in heaven, she would have clutched them.

'I managed the office, so everybody thought I must have known rightly. Only Daddy never let me near the money side, so I never knew what a mess he'd made.'

'You didn't know about the betting at all?'

'No. He didn't do it for fun. At least, I don't think it can have

259

been much fun. It was more like something he was compelled to do. Mammy always said we were lucky, he never drank, he never hit her. Some of the men back from the war . . . och sure, you know yourself.'

She did. Not for the first time, she wondered if losing Gordon to death was not the cruellest blow she could have been struck.

'Daddy was hard to do with. Sometimes you daren't look sideways at him. Other times he was grand. But mostly he was like something tightly wound up. You were always waiting for him to snap. I got used to keeping the peace, only it was exhausting. You had to read him – the way he closed the front door coming in; the way he cut up his potatoes; the way he spoke to the cat – we were always waiting to see what kind of evening it was going to be. Mammy always said we couldn't be cross with him because of the war, because he'd suffered. But' – she shuddered and took a gulp of tea though it must have been cold by now – 'I don't know. It seemed like we were the ones suffering. So when he died . . . it was a shock, and it was mortifying – to die in a backstreet pub, among, well, low sort of people, and owing money to half the town. He'd even taken the subs from the church bowling club; he was the treasurer. God, Martha, we could never show our faces in Lisnacashan again.'

'It sounds horrid for you.'

'Worse for Mammy. But aye, it wasn't much fun.'

'And, my dear, it's no wonder you have a jaded view of marriage, if that was the model you had, but not all partnerships are like that.'

'It was no partnership.' She was quiet for a while and then said, '*Partnership*. That's a lovely word. Working with someone; having them on your side.'

Martha seized on this. 'That's what marriage ought to be.' She thought of Sybil and Henry Barrett in the grounds of the old mill yesterday, so intent, so involved. That was a partnership all right. One of their best success stories. She must tell April about them, but perhaps not right now.

Thirty-two

Next day there was a note for April from Jennifer Dunn, who was taking up a position in the South of France in the autumn. *It couldn't be more perfect*, she wrote. *The family are going to the Riviera for the sake of the daughter's health – she's had rheumatic fever and needs a year in a warm climate. But she's aiming for Oxford entrance after that, so I'll certainly not be bored. It will be more challenging than working with Prudence, at least academically. Prudence keeps me on my toes in other ways! But seriously, this position has opened up my life in ways I hadn't imagined and I'm so grateful to you. True Minds is well named – you almost read my mind. Honestly, you shouldn't just stick to matchmaking.*

Maybe I shouldn't, April thought, tucking the note into her pocket since it was not, strictly speaking, marriage bureau correspondence and certainly not for Martha's eyes. It was gratifying to be so appreciated, but the note pricked her recent vague discontent into definite restlessness. Or jealousy. Where was *she* going? And if she was meant to be so good at reading minds, why had she not realised what Fabian's intentions had been? And why could she not work out what was going on with Felicity?

Things were quiet in the bureau but Martha said this was normal for July.

'We'll be busy again soon. When August ends, people realise that another summer has passed and they haven't had anyone to go on a holiday with, or their children go back to school and the house feels too quiet. Or, for the younger ones, that they've spent the summer going to weddings that weren't their own.'

'At home,' April said, 'they're great ones for pinning bible verses to anything that doesn't move. There's one: *The summer is over and we are not yet saved.*' She saw it now, in red paint, nailed to the tree by the bridge at the bad bend on the Cookstown Road.

The word *saved* and Jennifer Dunn's letter made her think again about Felicity. She couldn't help believing her landlady needed *saved* from whatever bother she was in – if it was not dope or blackmail then *something* was draining all her money. Money didn't just disappear. Look at Daddy! All those years gambling on horse races and April had never even heard him say he fancied this or that horse for the Derby. If she and Mammy had known, could they have done something? How long was he at it? At what point had it become a problem? And there was something more worrying going with Felicity: how on earth had she bruised her arm? But April was too shy to tackle her again and risk getting the face chewed off her.

When Felicity said that evening that she had to go to a meeting in Manchester and would be away overnight, April fought the temptation to sneak about for clues.

Fought and lost.

She felt like a criminal, pushing open the study door. But it was in a good cause. If she'd snooped about more at home, maybe she'd have saved her family from disgrace. Maybe Daddy would still be alive even. That wasn't an altogether comfortable thought, so she set it aside and focused on Felicity's desk, which dominated the small room. It was neat, the Underwood typewriter empty and silent beside two thick manilla folders. April opened the first one, heart thumping though she knew her landlady was safely away. It wasn't fear of discovery that made her nervous but worry about what she might find.

One folder seemed to be the typescript of a Forest Fay book, the other stories of the shopgirl and brigand type. Nothing incriminating or secret. But then you wouldn't put such things on top of your desk, would you? There were two drawers, but neither yielded to pulling and she didn't like to hoke around for a key. There was no filing cabinet; there would hardly have been space. She let herself out of the room, feeling dirty and silly. You're an eejit, April McVey, she told herself. Full of daft notions.

But the daft notion, or evil spirit, or sheer nosiness, whatever it was, wouldn't be banished and she found herself, instead of going back to her own attic, gently turning the doorknob of the room next door, Felicity's bedroom. This was a bigger room with a high ceiling, long sash windows, and a fireplace tiled with green and white tiles. There was a double bed neatly shrouded in a coverlet patterned in what she thought must be Bavarian folk embroidery, and a small daybed by the window strewn with cushions and a messy, colourful pile of the old djibbahs and scarves Felicity wore around the house. The wardrobe doors and dressing table drawers were all closed, and she was about to step back onto the landing when she noticed, behind the clock on the mantelpiece, a bulging envelope. Bulging with what? You can't, she told herself. You mustn't. But by the time she was thinking this she was standing in front of the fireplace with the envelope in her hand. It was full of white five-pound notes; she counted – eight of them. Forty pounds! So it wasn't her imagination that Felicity had plenty of money. And it wasn't her imagination that something strange was happening to it.

She set the envelope back and, heart thumping again, crossed back to the doorway, but on the way her foot caught in one of the scarves streeling over the end of the daybed, and she stopped to free herself. And there, under the tangle of silk and cotton, was a large, hessian-backed scrapbook. She pulled it out and sat down on the bed to look properly. There was a photo gummed to the cover, a mountain scene, and when she opened it most of the pages were covered in what she presumed to be mementoes of Felicity's time in Germany – photos of wooden chalets, of a town square with oddly shaped rooves, of a smiling group on a mountainside, leaning on stout wooden sticks. A bright-faced girl laughed at the camera, a tall dark young man had his hand on her shoulder and the third person . . . April squinted to be sure but yes, it was Felicity, a younger Felicity with her hair plaited round her head in what April supposed was the German fashion. All three looked gay and carefree; looked, in fact, exactly like the newsreel she had seen months ago – those fresh-faced German young folk in their meadow. She flicked on through the book, but the remaining pages were full of what looked like newspaper cuttings, all in German. She saw the word *faschistisch*, but the Gothic print was hard to decipher, quite apart from not knowing the language. Towards the back of the book were more cuttings and leaflets, in English this time. She started to read the first one, but before she could get further than the words *Sir Oswald Mosley* and *British Union of Fascists* and *grand rally* – Sir Oswald Mosley: of course, *that* was who he was! – and a date scribbled in Felicity's writing, there was a knock on the front door. Very loud, it sounded, up here in the front bedroom, and though it couldn't be Felicity knocking like that, still it made her jump and shove the book back where she'd found it, heart battering in her chest. She ran downstairs, anxiety at who might be calling so late trounced by disquiet about what she'd found.

It was only a woman selling flags for Save the Children and apologising for calling after teatime. 'I'm busy all day,' she said, 'with seven kiddies and my old mam. It's hard to get the time for my good causes.' April gave her sixpence and closed the door feeling desperately inadequate. She hadn't done a tap for any good cause but her own all her life. And Mammy, she reminded herself, but she wondered now if helping Mammy stay out of Daddy's way, turning a blind eye to Daddy's funny wee ways, had been a kindness or a curse.

She lay in bed for a long time before she slept that night, wondering what kind of people Felicity was involved with at all. She had a notion Mosley's rallies attracted trouble. But how could she ask her? Felicity seemed a stranger now. When they met – by no means every day – they were merely polite: land-lady and tenant. The memory of that walk home, the helpless giggling, Felicity's hand on her arm, the sense that she had been about to confide something, that they were indeed halfway to being friends . . . och, sure, there had been drink taken that night.

And to think about *that night* was to think about Fabian, and that made her want to pull a heavy shutter down over another part of her mind. Not that it was easy to avoid thinking about him, working in a marriage bureau all day. And Martha knew, of course, and kept giving her concerned, curious looks – she didn't go as far as to ask if she'd had second thoughts, but April, gritty-eyed with tiredness the next morning, struggling not to yawn, could tell she was desperate to.

Maybe Jennifer Dunn was right and she should branch out from matchmaking? Maybe being surrounded by the lovelorn wasn't healthy? When Martha was downstairs interviewing a new client, she took the *Easterbridge Recorder* from her desk and scanned the *Situations Vacant*. There was nothing; she could have addressed envelopes at home for sixpence a hundred, or if she were a fourteen-year-old lad she could have become a junior office clerk, or an apprentice bricklayer, but there was nothing for an independent woman who had to support herself. She could look further afield, but the thought of starting over again in a new town made her want to put her head down on the desk and howl. She did, in fact, do the first of these, just for a moment, but was deterred from giving in to the latter by a brisk knock at the door.

'Come in!' She sat up hastily and pushed her hair into some sort of order. She hoped her face wasn't creased from the desk.

It was Sybil and Henry Barrett. Joy shone out of Sybil's face and Henry looked quietly satisfied. Their hats and coats were misted with rain, but that didn't seem to dampen their spirits.

'Miss McVey, we must share our news!' Sybil burst out. 'Seeing as we'd never have met without you.' She and Henry exchanged soppy looks. This was when they told her they were going to have a baby, she supposed. She remembered Evelyn getting like that before Robbie was born.

'It was Martha, really,' she lied.

Sybil waved her hand. 'It was True Minds. Anyway, we've just started on the most wonderful adventure. Tell her, Henry.'

Henry cleared his throat. 'We've bought a mill,' he said.

'A *mill*?'

'We won't run it as a mill,' Sybil said. 'But we've such plans!'

'You'd better sit down.'

They did so, Sybil leaning forward in the chair in her eagerness.

'It started with me looking for bigger premises,' Henry said. 'Business has been brisk and I need to be closer to town.'

'And I wanted something to do with my money,' Sybil said. 'Daddy settled quite a bit on me when we married – it's no use looking so coy, Henry, it's a fact – and I wanted to use it for something constructive. We don't need a huge house and we don't especially want to travel. I want to do something here in Easterbridge.'

'*We* want to do something,' Henry amended. 'Miss McVey, I think I told you I started out with nothing—'

'Like Daddy,' Sybil put in.

'—and I was lucky enough to be apprenticed to a wonderful man. But I look round today and I see so many lads like me, only without my chances. So many works closing; so many lads coming from families where the father's got no chance of a job.'

'Not just lads,' April said and Sybil nodded.

'Exactly,' she said. 'Girls too. So we've bought Shaw's Mill.'

'Och, sure don't I live right beside it!'

Sybil smiled. 'Henry's having part of it for his works. He's got a couple of men working for him now, and we're going to use the rest for, oh, all sorts of schemes!' She beamed. 'You know I love handicrafts?'

'I remember.'

'I won't make things to sell, it's silly when I don't need the money, but I could teach others. And there must be people, women especially, who would like to make money from the things they make. I thought of having a little shop on the premises.'

'It sounds wonderful.' It did, but she felt the same sense of inadequacy she had felt last night with the Save the Children lady. That energy! That sense of purpose. Where had hers gone?

'We'd run classes and help people learn skills. There's so many kids in this town hanging about on corners.'

'Aye, I know. In Lisnacashan, the town I come from— Oh, Martha! Wait till you hear Mr and Mrs Barrett's news.'

Henry and Sybil spilled out the story again for the newly arrived Martha's benefit, finishing each other's sentences, talking over each other and laughing, and April thought again of that word *partnership*. And a word Mammy used to use about her and Evelyn: cahoots. *Are you two in cahoots again?* She remembered what Sybil had said about Henry at the start, that it was like having the best chum, only more so.

'How marvellous,' Martha said when the Barretts left. 'To think I was reluctant to match them, and now they're going to do something that will benefit who knows how many others. That was your admirable instinct, my dear. Though I hope you don't mind my mentioning it, but you seem to have newsprint on your cheek.' As April, with a squeal of horror, pulled out her pocket mirror to check her face, Martha said, 'The *classifieds*? I hope you're not looking for another job.'

April laughed and said not at all.

'I should hope not. To think the Barretts were your very first attempt. You're a matchmaker born and bred!'

It was one thing to be cleaning the kitchen floor, but the scene that greeted April that evening was pandemonium. When she started up the stairs there was an awful hubbub above her – huffing and puffing and the scrape of furniture against linoleum, and both study and bedroom doors wide open.

'What—!' Her first, panicked thought was that it was a burglar. Her second, which was much worse, was that somehow Felicity had come home and found out about her snooping.

'April!' It was indeed Felicity's voice, breathless, high-pitched, relieved. Definitely not angry. 'Come up and help me before this bloody thing breaks my foot.'

When she reached the landing she discovered the source of the noise. Felicity was attempting to move the daybed from her bedroom to her study. It had got stuck in the doorway and Felicity was panting and wheezing in the dust which moving furniture scares up from even the cleanest floors. There were piles of books on the floor outside the study, an empty bookcase, and other odds and ends stacked here and there about the

landing: an Anglepoise lamp; a pile of what looked like manu-
scripts; an old teddy bear with one ear; a heap of clothes; a
bundle of letters tied up with brown ribbon. April tried not
to blush at the thought of how she had searched for something
like those letters only last night.

'What are you trying to do?' April grabbed the end of the
bedstead and lowered it carefully to the floor. 'Here, take a
break. Your back must be killing you.' The bed was small and
shabby, but heavy and awkward to manoeuvre. It would have
been better to have taken it apart and reassembled it, but she
supposed that Felicity was impatient and imagined she could
manage. Like herself. *Always going ram-stam*, Mammy said.

Felicity waved a grateful arm and sank back against the
doorjamb, coughing, eyes streaming. For the first time, April
remembered that she had a history of chest trouble.

'Are you all right?' she asked. 'You shouldn't have done this
on your own. I'd have helped.'

Felicity couldn't reply for some time; she was bent over,
wheezing. Eventually she had enough breath to speak. 'I know,
I know,' she said. 'I meant to have it all sorted before you
got home.'

'But what are you doing?'

'Moving this blasted thing into my study.'

'Why? So you can' – a phrase from a poem she'd learned at
school came to her – 'recline on it "in vacant or in pensive mood"?'

'To sleep on.'

'But . . .' She couldn't say that she knew that Felicity had a
perfectly good double bed, with a prettily inlaid mahogany
headboard. So she asked simply, 'Why?'

Felicity looked awkward. 'I'm moving into my study for
a while.'

April wrinkled her forehead. 'Why?' she asked again.

'I've other plans for my bedroom.'

'Not another lodger?' She asked the question idly; Felicity had said more than once that she had been reluctant to let out a room, and that it had only worked because April was so agreeable. And of course there wasn't space for one. So she was taken aback when Felicity said, 'Well, sort of. They'll have my room, so I'll bunk up in the study.'

'So will their rent cover the cost of fixing the damp?'

Felicity bit her lip. 'It's not exactly a matter of rent. We're friends, you see, and—'

'I see.' April became very businesslike. 'Right, can we get this bed shifted? I don't have much time.'

Felicity looked puzzled, but obediently took up her end of the bed, and with two of them, so they could lift rather than drag, they got it into the study, where it just about fitted, jammed between desk and window, looking ridiculous. No way was Felicity going to sleep on it. This was for show. For April's benefit – or Fabian's if he called. Even Felicity wouldn't want anyone to know she was sleeping with her lover. Because that was the only explanation. And this lover, whoever he was – *we're friends, you see* – must be where all her money was going. Maybe *he* was the one with an expensive dope habit? Or was he some sort of kept man? Did such a thing exist? She had heard only of kept women. But if he was draining all Felicity's money, for whatever reason, then he clearly wasn't worthy of her. And the bruises? She couldn't turn a blind eye to that kind of thing under her own roof.

But it wasn't her own roof. She was only the lodger. She'd no power to do anything. Except leave.

Thirty-three

The new room was in Pickering Street, in a dull part of town which lacked either the faded industrial grit of Riverside Road or the cosy grandeur of Parkgate. The landlady, Mrs Sadler, let out three rooms and kept a flat for herself on the ground floor. She seemed to spend her time going to spiritualist meetings, and when she met April in the hall always wanted to talk about her son Raymond who had died at Mons and would shortly be making contact from the other world. *Any day now*, she would say, her pale eyes glittering. The other tenants were Miss Dawson, an old lady who often seemed to open her door at just the same time as April, and a young clerk, Bleaney, with an uncertain moustache, who spent long hours in the bathroom and left obnoxious smells behind.

April's room, first floor back, overlooking a grey yard with a high brick wall, was much smaller than the white attic, and very much drabber. The day she moved in, she stood in the doorway and itemised it: brown furniture, brown lino, brown walls. The wooden furniture must always have been brown, but the streaked walls looked as though they had had brownness thrust upon them by years of tobacco and condensation.

There must be some nice shades of brown, April thought, but not in this room.

She knew from the first moment that she had made a terrible mistake, but she also knew that she could not have stayed in Riverside Road.

Felicity had been shocked when April said she was leaving. 'But why?' Her eyebrows had furrowed.

'I need a change.' God, she thought, remembering the conversation now, looking at the brown lampshade, it's that all right.

'I thought you liked it here,' Felicity had said. 'I thought we rubbed along pretty well.'

'It's nothing personal.'

'Is it because of the damp? Because I will get it fixed. I keep meaning to, only—'

April shook her head. 'It's not that.'

'I could ask Fabian.'

'Please, Felicity, don't. I've made up my mind. Sure you'll easily get another lodger. It's a lovely room.' Lovelier than any she had viewed – Pickering Street was actually the best. Those kind chintzy landladies she had snubbed first time round were all in Parkgate, and that was out of bounds now – sure she couldn't be bumping into Fabian every time she ran down to the corner shop for a packet of tea.

Felicity had looked knowing. 'Is it Fabian? Did you quarrel? He won't tell me. Look, if it's awkward for you, I'll tell him not to come here. I'll—'

'It's not Fabian.'

In Pickering Street she set out her things with none of the excitement and enthusiasm with which she had done so in the white attic and wondered how long she could stick it. There was no tenants' kitchen; she would have to make do with what she could manage in her room at the ring beside the gas fire. She saw a good deal of toast in her future. There wasn't a proper bookcase, just a shelf above the bed, and she would miss Felicity's library. Then she gave herself a shake. Sure there was a grand public lending library in town. And she liked toast.

'I'll stay and finish those notes,' she told Martha later in the week.

She much preferred staying late at work to going back – she couldn't say *home* – to Pickering Street. For a couple of evenings she had lingered in town, window-shopping, or calling into the Teaspoon Café for a tea she could ill afford, putting off the hour when she would turn her key in the lock and smell the hallway's ancient odour of frying and neglect. Easterbridge was not known for nightlife; when the offices and shops packed up around six, the town shut up for the night, the streets empty of life except for a few couples walking arm in arm.

Martha frowned. 'You stayed late yesterday. I don't want to take advantage of you.'

'You're not. I'm in no rush.' No rush back to Pickering Street to sit in the brown room, listening to young Bleaney flushing the lavatory and clearing his throat, or old Miss Dawson's wireless. She had not noticed noises in Riverside Road, except to welcome them as signs that Felicity was home. Nothing about Pickering Street would ever feel like home.

Thirty-four

Mother insisted it was nosiness, but Martha begged to disagree. It was concern. April was behaving jolly oddly. Leaving her lodgings! Of course it was all to do with this Mr Carr – the sooner she changed her mind about him the better. Martha would miss her, but who was she to stand in the way of true love? Or True Minds? All this moping around, working late, insisting on living in some ghastly rooming house, it must be stopped, and she, Martha, was the one to do it. So now, when April once again offered to stay and finish some filing, Martha said, 'I'll stay too.'

There was no need for either of them to work overtime, but Martha had a plan and the plan was to get April to confide in her once and for all. She would bring her to her senses, and then that nice solicitor chap would have a companion, and his poor daughter would have a mother.

And you'll be looking for another assistant, Martha Hart, Mother reminded her. Which was vexing, but perhaps they would have a long engagement and give Martha time to get used to losing April.

By dint of making a cup of tea, finishing some leftover biscuits, and doing some wholly unnecessary filing, she managed to eke it out until almost seven, but no confidences were forthcoming. April was not silent – *that* Martha would have worried about – but she would be drawn on nothing more personal than the excellent news that the Colonel and Miss Longbottom had gone to the Great Yorkshire Show together the previous week, which they both agreed was much more of an expedition – it had been in Bradford – than the local show at Coaldale.

'I wonder where they'll venture next,' Martha said. 'I suppose in the autumn there'll be shooting and that kind of thing.' She was rather vague about country sports. 'Good gracious, who can that be at this time?'

'I didn't hear anything.'

'At the door.' Perhaps she had imagined it. It had been, certainly, a very faint tapping, but Martha's ears were tuned to the knocks of the nervous. She opened the door. Primrose Lewis stood on the small landing, her hand half raised to knock again. 'Mrs Lewis!'

'Oh, Mrs Hart. And, er, oh yes, Miss . . . yes. I hope you don't mind. I saw your light, and I . . . you'd been so kind and so, well, I just . . . Oh dear.' Her face crumpled and she gave a little sob.

Martha took her arm and drew her into the office. 'Mrs Lewis, whatever's wrong?' Without waiting for a reply she settled her in her own chair. 'Look, you sit there, it's quite comfy, and I'll make you a cup of tea. The kettle's not long off the boil; it won't take a moment.' She bustled around with the welcome distraction of tea.

Mrs Lewis sat obediently, doing her best to gain control. She sniffed and looked about her for a handkerchief, which she eventually located in her sleeve. It had already seen hard use. What on earth had happened to change her from the buoyant, hopeful woman Martha had seen only a month ago? She looked ten years older. Had something happened to the daughter in

Australia? She had been so excited about going to see her, had hinted that she might not be going alone.

And then she remembered her conversation with April. April must have been remembering too because she said, tentatively for April, 'Mrs Lewis, has someone taken advantage of you?'

Mrs Lewis bent her head low, and tears dripped onto the chest of her peach-coloured blouse.

'I've been so foolish,' she said. 'I really believed . . . I don't know how I could have been so silly.' She raised her face to look Martha in the eye, while April, without being asked, took over the tea-making. 'I wanted so much to meet a companion, and as you know the best efforts of your bureau were in vain. I . . . I'd almost lost hope, and then . . . oh dear, I feel so idiotic.' She bit her lip and looked down at the floor. Then she took a breath and tried again. 'I met a chap. I . . . when things didn't work out here, I answered an advertisement – one of those Lonely Hearts things.' She blushed. 'It wasn't the local paper. Oh dear.'

Martha made her face kind and interested, which wasn't difficult as she felt both in abundance. 'Go on.'

'I bought the *Matrimonial Times*. I know people talk about white slave traders and unscrupulous characters, but I did think the *Matrimonial Times* would be safe. I'm not one of those silly impressionable girls who believe anything.' She gave a deep sigh and accepted a cup from April without seeming to be aware of what it was. 'I still can't believe . . . maybe he *was* genuine? Maybe I've judged too hastily?'

The burst of hope in her voice was heartbreaking and Martha said gently, 'Why don't you tell us from the start?'

It was, she supposed, a common enough story, the kind of deception so many women must have fallen for. You occasionally heard of such matters coming to court but mostly the women were too embarrassed and the men too clever for that

277

to happen. Primrose had answered a likely-sounding advertisement; she even recited it word-for-word, and Martha imagined her having learned it by heart: *Respectable, cultured gent, considered handsome, would like to meet lady for matrimony; widow preferred.*

Widow preferred: to Martha it was obvious that he was looking for a vulnerable older woman with money. Or rather, he was looking for the money, not the woman.

Primrose had felt rather dashing, she admitted, answering the advertisement by writing to the PO box, and very hopeful. Mr Edwin Montgomery sounded exactly the sort of man she had always hoped the bureau would find for her – Martha and April both refrained from saying that the bureau had in fact found several potential matches for her, men who had been as carefully vetted as they could manage.

Montgomery had replied by return, so pleased to get her letter, so delighted to hear from such a refined lady. He was not yet quite forty, but preferred an older lady of quiet, domestic tastes. His mother had lately died, which was why he was dipping his toes into matrimonial waters so comparatively late in life. He had been unable to leave her in her last illness, which sadly had been of a lingering nature. Having waited so long he was anxious not to waste time and he very much liked the sound of Mrs Lewis – *Primrose* if he may? He could tell by her means of expressing herself that she was as flowerlike and dainty as her name. He enclosed a photo and dared to hope that she would find it pleasing and would send him one by return. He already felt a sympathy between them. Her letter had given him so much hope, allowed him to dare to dream . . .

'And he really was handsome.' Primrose put her hand into her bag and showed them both a photo of a fair, conventionally attractive man; rather younger, Martha would have said, than

278

the forty years he claimed – but then, this was most likely some obscure actor. It was a professional studio photo, not a snap.

They listened without comment, with an occasional question for clarification, and the more Primrose told her, the more indignant Martha felt on the older woman's behalf. Montgomery – she didn't suppose it was his real name – had been so clever, knew exactly which buttons to push. He must have pushed them many times before: the dying mother devotedly tended, the diffidence, the anxiety about life passing by – all guaranteed to arouse sympathy, particularly in a woman who had already known love and loss. Even his eagerness to move quickly would have appealed to a lonely, no longer young woman. Montgomery, whoever he was, must have sent that letter and that photo to scores of women. How could Primrose Lewis have been so naïve?

'Such a gentle face,' Primrose said sadly, taking the photo back from April. 'He replied saying how much he longed to meet me, but he wasn't able to come up from London quite yet.'

'He lived in London?' April said. 'That wasn't too handy.'

'No, but he said he would be happy to begin again in a small town. He had holidayed in Yorkshire as a boy; he'd very happy memories of the area.'

Of course he had. He doubtless also had happy boyhood memories of Glasgow and Kidderminster and anywhere else he got a letter from.

'Mrs Lewis,' Martha said carefully, 'you're speaking as though you still believe this man was genuine. I'm assuming you've never actually met him?'

She shook her head. 'He was keen to meet. We arranged it.'

'That Saturday in the Willow Pattern? He didn't turn up?'

She shook her head. 'I waited until closing. It was most unfortunate. I got a letter next morning. He had been on his way – he was coming all the way from London, that's how

279

keen he was, or seemed, I mean – when he was robbed in the street; they took everything; he didn't even have the train fare left.' She stopped and bit her lip. 'Well, I suppose . . . I mean, I don't suppose it was true, was it?'

'I wouldn't have thought so.'

'Divil the bit,' April said.

'He said how disappointed he was; how he had been longing to meet me. And now he was laid up – he had fallen under a bus in the attack.'

'If I'd the hallion here I'd shove him under a bus myself,' April said. 'You poor cratur.'

Though unsure what a *hallion* was, and doubting that Mrs Lewis relished being called a *poor cratur*, Martha couldn't help agreeing. Under a bus with him! Along with all the other men who saw women as mere prey, who exploited loneliness and fragile hope.

'He said he'd been taken to a private nursing home; well, it would have been clear he was a gentleman,' Mrs Lewis went on. 'His leg was broken and there were complications. He needed an operation, but most unfortunately, he hadn't been able to lay his hands on the money – there had been some hold-up with the sale of his mother's house. It was only a cash-flow problem; he was keen to emphasise to me that he'd been left very comfortably off. He just needed me to—'

'Send him down enough money to pay for the nursing home? Promising to pay you back? Looking forward to coming to see you as soon as his silly old leg was better?'

'Well, yes.' She plucked at her skirt.

'And you believed him?'

'I'd no reason not to! He even telephoned me. He sounded so disappointed not to have been able to visit, so full of hope and plans for when the house was sold and we could be together.'

'How much money have you given him?' April asked.

She looked down at her lap. 'Well, most of my legacy. Something in the region of, er, four hundred pounds.'

It was not a fortune, but it was a lot of money. Several years' salary for a working person. Four hundred pounds would have left Primrose Lewis comfortable for the rest of her life, allowed her to visit her daughter in Australia, freed her from the hundred exhausting small economies of workaday life. That old aunt would have enjoyed thinking of the gift she was giving her favourite niece, and now the money was being enjoyed by a fraudster who didn't care a fig for Primrose Lewis, who had fed her with false hope. That was the cruellest thing. If she had gone to Doncaster races and put the four hundred pounds on a horse that fell at the first fence it would not have been so bitter. Martha remembered that April's father had done more or less that and decided not to voice this sentiment.

The rest of the story was depressingly simple. Edwin Montgomery had vanished. Become a ghost. Her letters went unanswered; she had no phone number for him – he had been the one to ring her; she had thought of going to London to check out the address he had given, because she did think what if he was ill, and nobody knew? Perhaps blood-poisoning had set in in his leg and he was lying there in a fever; he could even have died. London was such a lonely, cold place; nobody cared about you, it wasn't like Easterbridge. Her face puckered with worry, concern for this man she had never met, and Martha could see that she would rather think of him dying or dead than acknowledge that she had been deceived, that part of her, even now, still half believed in him.

'I don't think that's the case,' she said gently. 'I don't suppose he actually hurt his leg.'

'Sure there's no such person!' April said. 'It's made up, all of it – the dead mother, the attack. He's probably used the same story with a dozen different women.'

Primrose shook her head. 'But I spoke to him – he sounded so genuine, so gentle.'

'I'm afraid Miss McVey's right. It's part of the trick,' Martha said patiently. 'There's probably a gang of them. Of course they're going to sound genuine and decent, that's how it works. If he sounded like a cad you wouldn't have fallen for it.'

'So I've just been really stupid? And my money's all gone?'

'I should think your money's gone for sure. But don't be too hard on yourself – you haven't been any stupider than lots of people.'

'It's being alone,' Primrose said. 'It does things to your mind. You get so foolish, you'd do anything to ease the loneliness. To have someone to just be there. Be interested. Share things with.'

'I know,' both Martha and April answered at the same time.

There was silence for some time. Then Martha said, 'What would you like us to do?'

'Do?' Primrose sounded surprised. 'I don't suppose there's anything you can do. I just wanted to tell someone.' She made a visible effort to jolly herself. 'Now, you've both been so kind, and I've taken up so much of your time. You must be aching to get home.'

After she had drooped out, there was no chance of Martha and April leaving yet. They had to discuss it, and they could do that nowhere but in the privacy of the office.

April insisted on running out for fish and chips. 'I'll starve to death otherwise,' she said. 'I know you think it's common . . . look, I'll put them in this shopper, so nobody sees me with a parcel of haddock and chips.'

'You are resourceful,' Martha said, and though she fretted slightly about the office smelling of fish and chips, she had to admit they were welcome and comforting, though it felt terribly déclassé to be eating out of newspaper with their hands.

Still, there was no one to see, not even Mother, really, and she could open the window to chase the smell out.

'You were right to be suspicious,' she told April.

'I wish I hadn't been.'

'Poor Mrs Lewis. If we'd been able to get her suited, she wouldn't have been such easy prey.'

'Och, you can't blame the bureau,' April said, licking her fingers. 'We did our best. She wasn't the easiest to suit, God love her.'

Martha sighed. 'It just seems so cruel. And there must be so many other women out there just as vulnerable. It was nice that she came to us.'

'To you. She couldn't remember my name. But she knew you'd listen and be non-judgemental and unshocked.'

'Well.' Martha felt uncomfortable. 'I wasn't quite so good at that when you told me about, well, your own encounter with a scoundrel.'

To her relief April laughed. '*Encounter with a scoundrel!* It sounds like a penny dreadful.'

'I wish we could do more for her,' Martha said.

'I wish I could shove him under a bus like I said.' April sounded fierce.

It came to Martha in a flash. A way to help Mrs Lewis *and* April, and do some matchmaking into the bargain. She was about to tell April her plan, but something – perhaps it was Mother (*You were always so hasty, Martha, dear!*) – made her desist. No, this would take careful thinking through. She couldn't wait to go home and get started.

Thirty-five

A delicate matter.

Fabian read the letter again but it was carefully discreet. Mrs Martha Hart of True Minds Marriage Bureau would like to consult him professionally on a delicate matter. *I should welcome the advice of a solicitor.*

He set the letter down on his desk and rubbed a hand over his face.

'Can I get you anything, Mr Carr?' Miss Cooke hovered. She had been hovering more than usual lately.

'No, thank you. You may take your lunch.'

She gestured at the letter. 'If you want me to stay and type your reply . . .'

'Thank you, no.' He fixed a pleasant smile as he waited for her to leave, and then read the letter for the seventh time.

It must be a coincidence. What could it have to do with April? The woman wanted legal advice, and there were not many solicitors in town. Probably she wanted to make her will. No, that was scarcely a delicate matter. A lawsuit? One of her clients complaining of being sold a pig in a poke? He frowned; that was an indelicate way to put it. Anyway, he would ring her up; the number was on her notepaper.

Was he hoping April might answer? His heart speeded up as he dialled, but the voice at the other end was most definitely not April's. A softer, deeper voice announced, 'Mrs Hart's, er, I mean, True Minds Marriage Bureau, Mrs Hart speaking.' She seemed surprised but gratified that he had rung up so quickly, but reluctant to go into details. 'It's a private matter concerning a client, well, a former client,' she explained, fuelling his pig-in-a-poke suspicions.

'Would you like to come and see me?' He reached across and took his appointment diary from Miss Cooke's desk.

'I'd prefer you to come here.'

'It's usual for the client to come to the office.'

'I know.' She sounded apologetic. 'But it's rather private.'

'You don't want to be seen going to a solicitor's office?'

'Er, no.'

'But that's nonsense. You could be doing any number of perfectly innocent things. Making your will or settling an estate or . . .'

'This *is* perfectly innocent. But as I said, delicate.'

'But it's not delicate for me to be seen visiting a marriage bureau?' Gosh, women were odd. Look at Felicity this last week or so: cross as a weasel and hinting at some big change coming. No wonder April had left, though Felicity was convinced it was all his fault. ('You shouldn't have proposed to her, you idiot,' she had said.)

But Mrs Hart sounded genuinely contrite. 'I hadn't thought of that, Mr Carr. I'm so accustomed to people coming to my office. Could you really not bear it? It's very discreet.'

He didn't want to be thought of as a person who couldn't bear things. Imagine if this Mrs Hart told April, 'That solicitor's a poor sort of fish. Too self-conscious to come to the office.'

And if this were such a delicate matter, surely April wouldn't be there? And presumably this Mrs Hart didn't know that there

285

was anything between him and April? She would not, surely, have told her boss about his proposal? Or perhaps she had? You never knew with women.

He agreed to call the following afternoon at four, and could not decide, right up until the moment he was straightening his tie and smoothing his hair at the top of the two flights of stairs which led to the marriage bureau, whether he longed or dreaded to see April.

April herself answered the door to his knock. And there was no doubt she was astounded to see him.

'Fabian!' Colour flooded her cheeks. 'I thought you were Martha,' she said. 'I thought she'd forgotten something.'

'I have an appointment to see Mrs Hart at four.' Habit, or the need to look away, made him glance at his watch. It was just after four.

'You want to sign up?'

His turn to blush. 'Of course not! Mrs Hart wants some legal advice.'

'She's downstairs in the interview room. This is our private office.' She folded her arms across her chest. 'She normally comes out when she hears the street door and meets clients downstairs. I don't know why she didn't hear you.' She frowned. 'But I'll take you on down.'

'How have you been?' She did not look well. Not ill exactly, but dull, as if she needed a polish. Even when she stopped frowning, a line stayed between her brows. Had *he* made her look like that?

April fled down the stairs ahead of him and pummelled on the first-floor door.

Mrs Hart was a handsome, dark woman with a calm manner. 'How kind of you to come, Mr Carr,' she said, shaking his hand with a cool, firm grip. 'April, I think I mentioned I'd consulted Mr Carr to see if he can advise us about poor Mrs Lewis?'

A dim light dawned on April's face. 'You never said.'

'Didn't I?' Mrs Hart had very fine dark eyes and she widened them now in puzzlement. 'Gosh, how silly. I was sure I had. Remember when you said you'd like to shove the chap under a bus?'

April and Fabian exchanged baffled looks.

Martha continued, perfectly serene. 'Mr Carr, please do come in and make yourself comfortable.'

He obeyed her and took a seat at rather a nice walnut coffee table. He noticed that it was set for afternoon tea with the sort of pretty china Serena liked, and a vase of cheerful pink gladioli. April sat opposite him, folding her hands over her red-skirted knee, and Mrs Hart settled herself beside her.

'The fact is,' Mrs Hart said, 'that one of our clients – former clients I should say – has got herself into rather a pickle.'

'She's been swindled out of everything she's got,' April added. Sitting down, she seemed more relaxed, though she didn't meet his eyes.

Mrs Hart took up the story: a sad story, a widow falling for a con man who had disappeared once she handed over a considerable amount of money. He couldn't imagine being so foolish himself, but then he looked at April and saw a young girl who couldn't be remotely interested in him and wondered if he'd been just as silly and self-deluding as this Mrs Lewis. Really, loneliness could make a fool of you.

'Can you see any way of getting her money back?' Mrs Hart asked.

Fabian shook his head. 'I wouldn't have thought so. These con men aren't stupid. They don't leave traces.'

'Maybe not.' Mrs Hart sounded thoughtful. 'But I wondered if you might be able to send him a stiff letter.'

'Did she ask for legal advice?'

'No,' Mrs Hart admitted. 'I don't think she would go to a solicitor's office. She was so crushed. Wasn't she, April?'

April nodded. 'Aye, like a wee puppy that's been trampled on.'

'She was mortified. I think she could only bear to tell us because, well, she knew we'd understand. But she might agree to meet you if we set it up. Would you be willing to do it? A stiff letter on official notepaper? Maybe, I don't know, mentioning some offences and suggesting consequences?'

'It would have no legal standing,' he said, 'and I have to ensure I stay within the law – I can't go making threats. And surely this isn't even one individual, is it? It'll be a gang of them. It won't make the least impact.'

'It might on her,' Mrs Hart said. 'Just to know that someone is helping, that she's made some kind of stand. I think feeling helpless and . . . and so alone makes it worse for her.'

'Well, I could listen and advise,' he said. 'It'll be a change from wills anyway.'

'Splendid. And naturally you must charge your fee to the bureau.' Mrs Hart rose. 'Now, I'll make tea. We can't let you go without.'

He made a token protest, but the day was warm and the little table inviting, and he was not unwilling to stay. Besides there was April. If Mrs Hart left to make tea, they would be alone together. Which might be awkward but at least would give him an opportunity to talk to her.

Only it didn't. The moment her colleague had gone, April stood up. 'I've an awful lot to do,' she said. 'Yous'll not need me.'

'April.' He had to speak before she went. 'I heard you'd left Felicity's. I was worried that—'

'It was nothing to do with you.' She sounded brusque.

'But you seemed so happy there.'

She shrugged. 'She was desperate at doing repairs. The place was falling down round us.'

288

This was surely an exaggeration, but he tried a different tack. 'She misses you. She's always asking after you, wondering if I've seen you.'

'And now you have. Give her my regards.' And before he could object, ask her how she was, apologise – though he wasn't sure for what, really – she had swept out of the room. Never mind, Mrs Hart would be back in a minute; it couldn't take long to make tea, and she gave every impression of being efficient. But she did not return. Five minutes ticked by. He could not leave, it would be too rude. Ten minutes. He picked up a *Tatler* and was reading about the new hemlines when Mrs Hart came back bearing a tray and a bewildered expression.

'But where's Miss McVey? I'm terribly sorry you've been left alone.'

'She had work to do. Don't worry, Mrs Hart, I've been educating myself about something called the bias cut.'

She laughed and set down a silver teapot and a plate of small cakes. 'That must have been edifying.'

'My wife – my late wife – was very fond of fashion.' He had a fleeting memory of Serena's frocks and costumes hanging in their big double wardrobe, the bright silks and soft wools, her scent clinging to garments she had, months before the end, given up in favour of nightgowns and wrappers. He had been reluctant to get rid of them, thought of keeping them for Prudence, but Felicity had swept in and taken charge. 'You can't mope around with her frocks forever, Fabian,' she had said. 'It's unhealthy. And they'll be years out of date before Prudence has any interest in them.' He knew she was right, and had let her take them away, he had no idea where. The wardrobe was almost empty now, his own suits taking up little space. He thought of the swish of April's red skirt and tried to imagine it hanging in his wardrobe. He could not.

'I'm sorry April has left us; she's too conscientious,' Mrs Hart said. 'I've never had such a wonderful assistant. So bright and thoughtful and enterprising. Really, a dear girl.'

'Er, yes.' Did she *know*? She gave nothing away, pouring tea with precision, making sure it was drawn to his satisfaction, offering cake. She had elegant, well-kept hands with a gold ring on her wedding finger. He remembered April saying her boss was a war widow. She must have been very young. They talked, at first, about the lady who had been swindled, and then more generally of the bureau.

'I was wondering,' she said, 'if I ought to take some legal advice myself. Just to ensure we don't have anyone on our books who isn't what they appear.'

'I should imagine your methods are stringent.'

'I've always thought so. But we depend a good deal on mutual trust and, well, decency.' She elaborated on how the bureau worked, warming so much to her subject that she let her tea grow cold, which she failed to notice until she took a sip and grimaced. 'Ugh. That's what happens when I talk too much. I'm sorry, Mr Carr. You must think me a frightful bore. But this bureau means a good deal to me. After losing Gordon, it gave me, well, something to care about.'

'By no means. I can imagine how it would. And clearly you've helped so many people.' He gestured round the wedding photos which lined the walls, so many of them reminiscent of his own, all essentially the same and yet all unique.

She smiled. 'That's what makes it so worthwhile. And why I feel such a responsibility for poor Mrs Lewis.'

'Though you aren't in any way to blame for her situation.'

'One *feels* responsible. Do have another cake, Mr Carr. I made them myself but they're quite good.'

'They're delicious. I've a daily woman and she cooks, but she only bakes on a Friday and it doesn't last long, not since Prudence, my daughter, came home.'

290

'I only started lately. I have more time on my hands since Mother died, and it's an absorbing pastime. But if I didn't give some away I should be the size of the town hall clock tower.' This was a squat edifice to which the slim Martha Hart bore no resemblance, but he did not know her well enough to say something gallant, so he simply smiled, took another cake, and the talk moved on to the practicalities of his meeting with Mrs Lewis, should she agree.

'I wonder if she'd like you to come with her?' he suggested.

'Or April.'

'Whichever of you she feels happier with,' he said, and found himself hoping it might be Mrs Hart herself. April was clearly uncomfortable with him, and it would not do to have two awkward women in the interview. Mrs Hart would be better at putting Mrs Lewis at her ease. But he would leave it to her – she seemed a woman who liked to make up her own mind.

As he left – it had somehow become half past five – she pressed the last few cakes on to him, in a little bag. 'For your daughter,' she said. 'Young girls love sweet things. I always did.'

Thirty-six

'What a distinguished man,' Martha said next morning. 'I hadn't realised he was so . . .'

'Eligible?' April said drily, and busied herself typing out invoices, clearly not expecting an answer. Martha waited for her to start chattering but she was silent. Only the tat-tat-tat of the typewriter showed she was alive.

Well. She had done her best. It had been a good plan, but as Mother always said, you could lead a horse to water but you could not make it drink. And April had refused to drink even a cup of tea with that nice Mr Carr. Silly girl! If she had suffered as Martha had – as Mr Carr himself had, losing his wife so young – well, Martha didn't think she would be so stubborn as to let such a good chap pass her by.

But Martha was not easily daunted. Plan A had not worked, but there was always Plan B.

'Mrs Lewis has agreed to see Mr Carr,' she told April a couple of days later.

'Fair play to her, and to you. I never thought she would.'

'Only she's rather self-conscious, poor dear, so I said you would go with her.'

April groaned. 'Och, Martha, no! She doesn't like me. Sure she can't even remember my name.'

'Nonsense.' For Plan B to work, it *must* be April who accompanied Primrose Lewis to Mr Carr's office. Only she refused. Dug her heels in like the pony Martha's father used to borrow to pull the lawnmower. Tossed her hair and tilted her chin. And in the end Martha was obliged to go.

Primrose looked more than ever like a trampled-on puppy when she met Martha outside Mr Carr's office.

'I don't know what to tell Mabel,' she said. 'She keeps asking if I've booked my passage. How can I say I gave all that money to a . . . a con man?'

At least, Martha thought, she was admitting the truth now, and she murmured consoling noises as they negotiated a formidable receptionist and were shown into an office bursting with papers and ledgers and lined with brown and red law books. Martha's hands itched to tidy up. It would not have suited the bureau to interview clients in such a place, and it hardly seemed a fitting background for Mr Carr. But Primrose Lewis looked round in impressed satisfaction.

Mr Carr was courteous and sympathetic, encouraging Mrs Lewis to tell the whole story, interrupting only to clarify points. Martha, having heard it all before, sat back and watched. She noted that he behaved rather as she did when encouraging a nervous client, saying little but showing concern and warmth in face and voice. He had rather a good face, lean, with a strong chin and clear blue eyes. She liked the brisk way his hands moved when he made notes, and the whiteness of his cuffs. He was indeed eligible. The sort of chap they could jolly well do with on their books if April didn't come to her senses.

Really? Mother raised celestial eyebrows. *You'd like to find him a match? Are you sure?*

She found herself blushing and turned her attention back to the conversation, which seemed to have progressed very satisfactorily. Mr Carr was going to write a stiff letter to the address Mr Montgomery – 'or whoever he is' – had given her and hoped it might at least put the wind up him.

'At any rate, it will make me feel better,' Primrose said. 'I know you'll be terribly fierce.'

Mr Carr mock grimaced.

'And now,' Primrose said bravely, 'I'm going to tell Mabel. That will be the worst thing. Not seeing her after all.' Then she brightened. 'If we put him off enticing even one other woman,' she said, 'that will be good, won't it?'

'I can't imagine its having much effect on a hardened con man,' Mr Carr said with lawyerly caution.

'If only there was a way to warn other women,' Martha said. 'So they're less vulnerable.'

Mr Carr drummed his pen against his notepad. 'I've an idea,' he said. 'I don't know if you'd agree, or if she would . . .'

Both women looked at him expectantly.

'My sister writes. I believe she'd do a story for one of the London papers. Of course she wouldn't use your name.'

'Oh, Mr Carr! I couldn't possibly.' Mrs Lewis sounded as shocked as though he had asked her to dance naked down the High Street.

'I understand,' he said gently. 'It was just an idea.'

'Mrs Lewis,' Martha said. 'If you'd read a story like that, would you have been taken in?'

Mrs Lewis wrinkled her face. 'Oh,' she said. 'I see what you mean.'

Mr Carr and Martha held each other's gaze. Martha was willing Mrs Lewis to agree. It was a jolly good idea after all.

'It won't put the cads and con men off,' Mr Carr said, 'but it might make women more aware.'

294

'It would be an act of sisterhood,' Martha said, and then wondered if this sounded frightfully pi. Or rabidly feminist. She wouldn't really want Mr Carr thinking she was either.

'All right,' Mrs Lewis said at last. 'I'll do it. At least, I'll let you ask your sister. She might not want to. She might think women like me are fools who deserve all we get.'

'Of course she won't. She's keen on causes. Always marching for this and that. I think she'd be delighted to show scoundrels like this where they got off. You leave it with me.'

They were dismissed, and as Martha walked down the street with Mrs Lewis she thought that she seemed just a tiny bit brighter.

As for herself, she felt . . . *unsettled*. Which was jolly silly, and she didn't need Mother to remind her of that, thank you very much. Mr Carr was keen on April and she on him, whatever she said – for goodness sake, how could she not be! – and Martha's role was to help them get together. That was what she always did, for everyone, and there was no reason to stop now just because things felt a little complicated.

Thirty-seven

One evening in early August Miss Dawson was waiting at her door as April put the key into her own. Her excuse was a spider. It had been in her room for some weeks now, not annoying her, just hanging on a thread; she had become almost fond of it, but today she had got new spectacles, and oh dear, all around where the spider had ensconced itself was a mass of cobwebs.

'I felt one brush my face and when I looked up, the china cabinet was covered in them.' She shuddered. 'So horrid, like that poor Miss Havisham. Anyway, I've cleaned up best I could, but I haven't the heart to disturb the spider. Would you, dear? Not kill it of course, I shouldn't dream of it, but just move it on? There's a shed in the yard; it'd be quite comfortable there, spinning webs to its heart's content. I can't manage the stairs well.' She gestured down at the splayed carpet slippers which barely encased her swollen and veiny feet, a green-blue relief map of bumps showing through thick, neatly darned stockings.

April didn't mind creepy-crawlies, and was, as usual, in no rush to embrace the brown delights of the first floor back, so she quite enjoyed the challenge of finding a cardboard box – an empty Corn Flakes box from Miss Dawson's tidy wee larder – and luring the spider inside. It did not protest at being uprooted from its comfy billet in front of the china cabinet, but when she reached the shed, it lurked in the deepest recesses of the box. She could have left it to find its own way out, but what if it didn't? The shed, all dark corners and dusty shelves, was a spider's paradise, but if it hid inside the box forever it might never find that out. So she gave the box a shake and the spider scurried out, into a crevice behind an oil can, and there she left it to its fate.

Miss Dawson was waiting for her at the top of the stairs. 'I've put the kettle on. You'll stay and have a cup of tea, won't you? Just to say thank you.'

'I will surely.'

Sitting down in what was obviously the best armchair, April could observe the room properly. It was better than her own. Shabby, and brown underneath, certainly, but the impression was of colour and softness because every space was filled with Miss Dawson's things – glass cabinet full of rose-patterned china; bookcase stuffed with classics and romances (Ethel M. Dell and E. M. Hull); crocheted rugs and cushions in bright shades, and, as she had noticed before, a larder-cupboard, gas ring and kettle. The walls were covered in needlepoint pictures of the kitten and hay-wain type. In some moods she would have seen the room as cosy; tonight it felt sadder than if Miss Dawson, like her, had made no effort. But that was nonsense. For dear sake, she was becoming an awful old misery!

She asked Miss Dawson how long she had lived in Pickering Street.

'It must be over ten years,' she said. 'I was a teacher, you know. Not the High School, just a little private school – Miss Martin's. It's closed now. And when I retired, I was fortunate to have a small income, just enough to live on. I don't get about much, because of my silly old feet, but I don't do too badly here. Mrs Sadler is a lazy old thing but she's decent enough, though I don't like those meetings she goes to – interfering with the dead; it's not right, is it? Poor thing. I don't think much of that chap Bleaney, do you? I don't like a man who hides his mouth with that nasty hair. Now what do you do, Miss McVey? I know you're a business lady.'

It was hard to get away; Miss Dawson wanted to hear her life story, and April didn't mind, though she skipped out Daddy and was hazy about why she'd left her last lodgings. She grew used to the sour-sweet old-lady smell, and had no objection when Miss Dawson, looking furtive, offered her a glass of ancient sherry.

'Did you make the pictures yourself?' she asked, as Miss Dawson settled back opposite her.

The wrinkled face brightened. 'Oh yes, dear, and the cushions and the cross stitch. In my day, girls learned handicrafts and I always loved them. They were my favourite subject to teach, too.' April remembered Sybil Postlethwaite – Sybil Barrett, she should say. Could she find a way to introduce her to Miss Dawson? Age differences didn't matter when you shared a hobby.

'I used to crochet for my nieces and nephews, but they've all moved away now. Never mind, wool's got so expensive, it's as well I've nobody to make things for.'

What had Sybil said about running a shop? *There must be people, women especially, who would like to make money from the things they make.* Perfect! She opened her mouth to tell Miss Dawson about it, and then shut it again. No. She wouldn't go ram-stam for once. She'd do the thing right: talk to Sybil, get her facts straight. Imagine giving that old cratur hope and then snatching it away again if Sybil was looking for something a bit more high-end. Sure that would be cruel.

Thirty-eight

It was the fourth time he had asked – a nice little note, sent to the bureau. Would she care to join him for a country walk on Sunday afternoon? Martha was running out of excuses. She had used looking after Billy, catching up on paperwork, and an entirely fictitious Sunday lunch with an old friend, and now she couldn't think of anything else.

And besides, Mother suggested, *you do rather want to go out with him, don't you?*

It wasn't that simple. A decade, even a year ago, her main concern would have been Gordon. But for some reason Gordon, whose ghost – kind and wistful, not bossy like Mother's – had hovered in the shadows of her life for years, seemed to have receded, and what stood in her way was not her dead husband, but the girl who had shared more of her day-to-day life than anyone since Mother died.

She couldn't encourage Fabian Carr because of April. Because however the girl protested, it was clear that she had feelings for him. Feelings that perhaps she hadn't admitted to herself yet, but that were, Martha suspected, as wholehearted as everything else about her.

But how twisted and tangled they must be! Look how she

had moved out of his sister's house! As if to escape any reminder of him. So dramatic! Martha looked at April now, bent over some registration forms, frowning, the little line between her brows deepening and relaxing as her pen scratched and amended. She glanced up as if she felt Martha's eyes and smiled briefly before returning to work. She looked tired, the bloom worn off. But then August had been a long, stuffy month; sometimes there was hardly a breath in the office, and she had not had a holiday. Well, neither had Martha. How lovely to escape for an afternoon in the country – tea at a cottage, strolling through the lanes, three or four hours perhaps with company. Male company. Martha looked at the note in her hand and traced the firm slopes of his handwriting. Black ink, very classy; she liked the way he did his *M*s. She remembered his hands clearly, the long, sensitive fingers. M for Martha. M for Marriage. She blushed. Gosh, she was getting ridiculous in her old age.

But darling, you're not old at all. You're a comparatively young woman.

Unlike Mother to be so affirming! Or could it be that this time it was not Mother, but Gordon, stirred out of long repose? Perhaps that was what made Martha take out a plain sheet of notepaper and her good pen and write, quickly, before she could change her mind, *That would be delightful, Mr Carr, and as it happens I am indeed free this Sunday. Shall we meet at the park gates and take to the lanes?*

And she practically skipped along St Margaret's Lane to the postbox, an early scattering of yellow leaves scrunching under her feet as if to remind her of the promise of a country walk. Only as she was slipping the envelope into the postbox did she think, with a lurch, Well of course! He wants to meet me to talk about April. To see if I can help him win her. How foolish to have imagined it could have been anything else. To have thought such a decent man could move on so quickly

with his affections. Well. It was done now, the note posted.
She squared her shoulders as she walked back down the lane
to the office. She would do her best to help him, and thus
April, to put this nonsense behind them and get together once
and for all. It was, after all, her vocation in life.

But Fabian Carr did not seem to want to talk about April.
Perhaps he was shy. Well, he clearly was shy. From the moment
they met at the park gates – he was already there, and she was
grateful not to have to stand waiting – he was awkward. The
professional confidence he had shown with Mrs Lewis had
evaporated into a diffidence and formality that were at odds
with his sports jacket and flannels. They discussed the season
changing (she liked the autumn, he found it melancholy); the
recent Empire Games in London (she had little interest in sport
so this proved a short conversation), and the late wild scabious
and hawkbit along the riverbanks (which they agreed were
pretty . . . jolly pretty . . . really very pretty indeed). Though
they were quite alone, especially after they crossed a stile and
wound their way along a narrow lane fringed with long grasses
and dandelions, it seemed to Martha that April walked between
them, bumping their elbows, pointing things out in her gruff
Ulster accent. Almost, Martha could hear her. *Och, aren't the
wee flowers gorgeous?*
  She could bear it no more. 'I think,' she said, 'we should talk
about April.'
  'Oh.' He was clearly taken aback. 'Why?'
  'She's obviously on your mind.'
  He pulled a long grass from the hedgerow and started to pull
it apart. 'I'm not sure what you mean. She isn't.'
  'I know you proposed to her.'
  'Oh.' He did not, as she would have done, blush, but some-
thing tensed in his face. 'I didn't think—'

'She confided in me. Now don't look so worried, I shouldn't think for a moment she's told anyone else. But we work very closely, and I knew she was fretting over something. I wormed it out of her. I wouldn't want you to think she was indiscreet.'

'Well,' he said. 'I don't suppose it matters. She made it clear she wasn't interested. And I realise now that I . . .' He tossed the tattered remains of the grass into the ditch. 'It was a mistake to ask her.'

'But she's a splendid girl!'

He smiled. 'She is. But she made it very clear she had no wish to marry.'

'She's said the same to me,' Martha admitted. 'But I never quite believe people who say that. Surely everyone wants to, well' – she found herself feeling warm, perspiration gathering at her neck under her frock – 'be with someone. A soulmate.'

He nodded. 'Hence your calling in life.'

'How nice of you to think of it that way, as more than simply a job.'

'It must be very satisfying. Like me when I sort out a legal muddle for someone.'

'Oh it is,' she said. 'But not all my clients see it as looking for a soulmate. Often they're rather pragmatic. Perhaps not a bad way to be. The notion of romantic love being necessary for marriage is a fairly modern one.'

'I think when I asked April,' he said, frowning as if he found the subject difficult, 'I was being pragmatic. I was lonely.' He said it without embarrassment. 'I'd started to think about remarrying and she was, well, it sounds so insulting to say that April was *there*, but she was. I don't know many women, and she was lively and friendly and Prudence liked her. I allowed myself to think that that might be enough. The fact is, she doesn't have a scrap of romantic feeling for me. She made that clear. She's exactly what you said, a splendid girl. But she's not for me.

302

I feel foolish, to be honest. It's not like me to act so hastily. Normally I'm quite cautious.' He grinned and looked suddenly younger. 'Felicity, my sister, accuses me of being middle-aged.'

'I rather embrace middle age,' Martha said.

Careful, said Mother, *you don't want to sound past it.*

'My dear Mrs Hart, you aren't remotely middle-aged,' he said gallantly, but she frowned, wanting to be serious, or at least honest.

'When Gordon was killed,' she said, 'I felt old overnight. Before I'd ever even really grown up. *Widow* sounds so elderly. Even though there were thousands of young war widows. For years it was just about muddling through, looking after Mother, running the business . . .'

'You clearly did more than muddle through,' he said. 'And I know what you mean – *widower* sounds elderly too. Like I should be tending my roses and letting Prudence warm my slippers.'

'At least you have Prudence.'

'It's been the hardest thing of all, though,' he said. 'Coping with a girl that age. Everyone queueing up with advice: send her to school; keep her at home; talk to her about her mother; don't mention her mother; engage a housekeeper; don't engage a housekeeper. My head used to spin.'

'I remember one or two men from church losing their wives and it was exactly like that. Half the parish' – not, as it happened, herself – 'rallying round with advice and hot dinners. It's not at all the same for women. We're expected to get on with it. And they say we're the weaker sex.' She snorted, before Mother could admonish her for being unladylike. *You don't want to sound like a feminist, my dear!*

'I've noticed,' she went on, 'that men and women deal differently with being widowed. Men remarry more often. And more quickly. When I take a widower onto my books, it's often only a year or so, sometimes less, after the wife's death. But it seldom happens the other way round.'

He was quiet for some time, then asked, 'And in your case it's been . . . sixteen years or so?'

'Seventeen.'

'A long time to be alone.'

'Yes.'

'Forgive me, do you mind? I don't want to open old wounds.'

She shook her head. 'It was a long time ago.'

'Something dies in you, doesn't it? You keep walking and talking and working and eating and sleeping. But there's an emptiness. You grow round it, but there's still a hole.'

'Exactly. I filled that hole with my work, which I love, but it's not the same.'

'I feel,' he said, and then stopped, as if uncertain how to proceed. 'I mean, that is, we do seem to be rather in sympathy. I wonder if you'd care to do this again, or perhaps go for tea or dinner?'

'I . . . I'd like to,' she said slowly. 'But April . . .'

'I told you,' he said, 'that I fooled myself about April. I can understand your worrying that I could let my affections change so quickly' – she couldn't help glowing at the word *affections* – 'but I assure you—'

'That's not what I'm worried about.' And she knew enough of how men approached these matters to be confident of this. 'It's April herself. I couldn't hurt her.'

'But she was the one who said no.'

'I don't think it's that simple.'

'She made it very clear.'

Martha shook her head. She so far forgot herself as to put her hand on his sleeve. And oh, how lovely it felt, the sense of a firm, warm arm beneath the light tweed; she had to force her fingers not to caress. 'Mr Carr, I've enjoyed our walk so much, and I'd very much like to, er, get better acquainted with you, but . . .' Gosh, for the proprietor of a marriage bureau, she was not managing this at all well! She pulled at a thread on her skirt. 'I would need to know for sure that April didn't harbour any—'

'She doesn't!'

'I hope you're right. But I spend five days a week with her, and I know her much better than you. She's breaking her heart over something, and if it's not you I can't think what it can be.'

She had to stop speaking then as she realised they were no longer alone in the lane. A woman and a little girl were approaching, picking blackberries as they came.

'Not down there, Sally, darling,' the woman said, as the child dived into some fat low brambles. 'A dog might have cocked its leg.'

The child looked up in puzzlement. 'Cocked its – oh!' Light dawned. 'Done its weewees, you mean?' She giggled, her hand at her mouth.

'We don't want doggie weewees in our pie, do we?' The woman smiled at Martha, and it was only when they had passed that Martha recognised her as that nice Miss Murrell, one of April's first clients. And it was jolly satisfying to see her so settled – only it did, in the circumstances, make her feel rather more lonely too.

Thirty-nine

He had only himself to blame. If he hadn't leapt in with that hasty, ill-judged proposal to April, he could have set about wooing Martha without complication. How principled women were!

Could April have feelings for him? He ran the conversation on Shippards Hill over and over in his head. Every time, April was firmer in her rejection – but he had not wanted to believe her then, two months ago: now he did. So was he twisting the memory to suit himself? Was he missing something? He knew he could be dim about these matters, and maybe, as Felicity accused him, his mind was too legal and logical. But no. April had refused very clearly. She had said she was not interested in marrying. He could respect that; why couldn't Martha? All this scrupulousness about not hurting April – was it her way of dissembling, of letting him down easily?

But he conjured up Martha's open face with the serious dark eyes and heard again the simple honesty in her voice. *I rather embrace middle age . . . Surely everyone wants to be with someone. A soulmate.*

This was not a woman to play games. If she did not like him, she would say so.

As April had done.

But did April *mean* it?

He was back where he started. And the only thing he was certain of was that, when his mind was unguarded and focused on nothing in particular, especially on the border between waking and sleeping, it was Martha's face he saw, and the touch of Martha's warm hand on his arm that he remembered.

He might have consulted Felicity, but she was being so odd herself. He had asked three times about writing the article on con men, and three times she had said she was too busy.

'But the new book is just out,' he pointed out when she deigned to call the day after the walk with Martha. 'Surely you have a little respite now?'

She sighed and pushed a curl off her face, tucking it impatiently into the band round her head. Like April she was looking plainer, unkempt even. He couldn't help comparing them both to the immaculate Mrs Hart – Martha – in that smart green coat and her dark hair shining. 'I keep telling you it doesn't work that way,' she said.

'So you're busy with the next Forest Fay?'

'Not exactly,' she admitted. 'Other things.'

'Other writing?'

'Hmm. Can you hurry with that tea, Fabian? I haven't much time.' She drummed her hands – bitten fingernails, no rings – on the table. 'Can't you stir it to give it a move on?'

'Fee, what's the big secret?' He was fed up with women being so impenetrable. Surely his sister, at least, could be straightforward with him.

'What do you mean?'

'You're being very odd. Even for you.'

'I'm sorry.' The apology was unlike her, and when she looked at him her eyes were troubled and tired. For the first time in ages, older-brotherly protectiveness stirred in him. She ran a

307

finger round the rim of her waiting cup. 'I'd like to tell you,' she said. 'There is something – something I'm involved with – but it's not my story to tell. And I've promised to keep it secret until things are settled. I thought they would be, by now. I've been preparing for it, but things kept happening and . . . oh, don't look at me like that, Fabian. Can't you trust me?'

'Can you at least tell me what it's about?' He wasn't sure what he expected: something about her writing perhaps – was another Forest Fay story going to be on *Children's Hour*? But surely that would make her happy, rather than troubled? Memory stabbed him. 'Oh gosh, Fee, it's not . . . you're not having any medical explorations or anything horrid like that? Your chest—?'

She shook her head and, unusually for Felicity, patted his arm. 'Nothing like that. You don't need to worry.'

'Can't you even hint?'

She frowned and said slowly, 'Remember Erich?'

'Your German pal?'

'Yes. It's to do with him, but I honestly can't say more than that. It's not that I don't trust you, but he made me promise . . . You'll know soon enough, if everything works out.' She took a deep breath and a long sip of tea. 'It will work out,' she said as if convincing herself. 'It has to.'

Forty

Martha was being as odd as get out. Not in a bad way, but she kept looking at April thoughtfully. And she had done something different with her hair; those desperate old-fashioned earphones had given way to a flattering do that took years off her. Not only that, but she had appeared this week in *two* new frocks, one a soft heathery shade and one in burnt orange that really suited her dark colouring and the season.

'You look nice,' April said. 'I mind my pal Evelyn had a frock that colour. Like autumn leaves.'

Martha, usually so self-possessed, actually blushed. She looked down at the frock. 'Well,' she said, 'I'd not had anything new for ages. It's important to set clients a good example.'

April hoped this wasn't a dig at her own appearance. It wasn't as easy to do her ablutions in Pickering Street as it had been in the bathroom in number eleven, shared only with Felicity. She hoped she hadn't let standards slip, but she found it more and more of an effort to be bothered and now that her hair was longer, she tended to simply ram in as many grips as would hold it out of her way. She would have loved a new frock, but she had less money than before. Because she didn't have access to a proper kitchen, she found it much more expensive to eat,

309

and by the time she had paid the instalment on her bicycle and sent the few shillings to Mammy there was little to spare. She thought of Miss Dawson, unable to afford the wool she loved to work with. Those patient pathetic feet in their neat darns. Would that be her in thirty years' time, still living in rooms, still scraping by, still alone? She brushed the thought away. And, oh lord, she hadn't yet contacted Sybil Barrett.

I know, she thought, I'll join the library. Haven't I been saying I would for weeks? It would kill some time and give her something fresh to read. She felt a new sense of purpose as she tidied her desk, covered her typewriter and put on her soft felt hat.

The Carnegie Library, a red-brick-and-stone building rather like the one in Lisnacashan, was near the station. As soon as she went through the tiled hall into the big, hushed room, she relaxed. She should have come here weeks ago. Lost herself in the crucial but not heart-wrenching decision of which three books to take home. She did the necessary formalities with a young librarian and, with a calm sense of purpose tinged with excitement, walked up and down the aisles, breathing in the lovely aroma of books. What was she in the mood for? Nothing romantic. Nothing that would wring the withers. An old friend or a new adventure? Three books! What riches.

She was standing in front of *Adult Fiction A–E,* scanning the shelves to see if there was any E.M. Delafield she had not read, when she heard a voice cry, 'Miss McVey!' She turned to find Prudence Carr, in a neat grey blazer and tunic, standing beside another girl, identically dressed, tubby and earnest-looking. They were both clutching books.

'Och, Prudence,' she said and wasn't sure what to say next, especially as the librarian, while not exactly *shushing* them, had looked up from the desk as if sorely tempted.

'This is Susan,' Prudence hissed. 'My new pal. At the High,' she added with studied casualness.

Susan breathed loudly through her nose.

'What have you picked?' April asked.

Prudence looked important. 'One about tennis and one about hockey. Oh, and one about knitting. I'm going to make Daddy a blue scarf.'

'No stories?'

Prudence shook her head. 'Stories are soppy. Don't tell Aunty Fee!' She giggled and this time the librarian did *shush* them, so – April feeling like a naughty schoolgirl herself – they slipped into the *Religion and Philosophy* aisle, which was both empty and hidden from the desk. Susan thrust out her books for April's inspection.

'*Emily of New Moon*!' April recognised an old favourite. 'Och, I loved Emily – even more than Anne.'

Susan beamed. 'I love reading,' she said in a nasal whisper. 'I've read every single Angela Brazil I can get my hands on. Only' – her face fell – 'she's banned at our school.'

'She was at mine too. Miss McCoubrey said she was frivolous and nonsensical. I thought she was great fun.'

Susan looked politely incredulous that April was young enough to have read Angela Brazil.

Prudence nudged her friend. 'Show her what else you've got,' she demanded.

Obediently Susan held out a handsome, green-bound book with a delicate watercolour of a fox and a girl in an idealised woodland scene. 'I know it's too young,' she said apologetically, 'but Prue *says* Cicily Rafter's her aunty.' She sounded unsure.

'*Forest Fay Faces the Future*,' April read.

'It's her new one,' Prudence said. 'And she *is* my aunty, isn't she, Miss McVey?' Anxiety mingled with pride in her tone. 'That's her pen name.'

'Oh, she is surely.' April flicked through the book – there seemed to be a faun, and a fox and a lot about friendship. Fay

311

and her new friend Eve Silversmith, who appeared to be some kind of sprite or fairy according to the illustrations, were organising all the woodland creatures to resist a machine that was going to chop down the forest. Rabbits and foxes on the same side. Ants and bees and birds and squirrels taking risks to help each other. Sweet but unlikely. She supposed it was an allegory or a fable; she was never very clever about which was which. It didn't seem any more like Felicity than brigands and ruined maids, but that only made her realise how little she really knew her.

She looked at the dedication on the first page: *To E.S. with love and fond memories. Die Gedanken müssen immer frei sein.* Whatever that meant. She closed it and handed it back to Susan.

'So you're enjoying your new school, Prudence?' she asked.

Prudence beamed. 'It's super.'

'And how's your Aunt Felicity?'

'Very strange. Stranger than usual. Nobody's allowed to visit. She's got a German man staying.' She giggled. 'Her chap.' She turned to Susan. 'You're not allowed to tell anyone that,' she ordered. 'Swear you won't.'

'Cross my heart and hope to die,' Susan rhymed.

'I heard her telling Daddy about their wedding,' Prudence went on, 'only I wasn't supposed to know. It's not fair – I could have been a bridesmaid; I'm her only niece. But it's going to be *quick and private.*' She looked disgusted. 'Or it was; I don't even know if it's happened yet. Nobody tells me anything.'

'I was our Joan's bridesmaid last year,' Susan said. 'I had a Bo Peep frock in yellow satin.'

So she had been right about Felicity's secret being a lover. But why all the secrecy? She pondered it all the way home, having grabbed three books without much thought. Was it to do with him being German? And all that disappearing money – it clearly wasn't to pay for a big wedding. Was *he* taking it for something? Those Nazis marching all over the screen, that huge rally, it must cost money. Fabian had said Felicity loved causes – always marching and rallying, hadn't he said? She remembered the leaflets and cuttings about Oswald Mosley and the British Union of Fascists.

She remembered the bruises.

She remembered the dedication on the book: *To E.S.* Erich someone?

Lord, everybody was getting married but her! Wasn't it the luck of God she'd no notion of it herself or she could be feeling very left out.

And Felicity wasn't the only one; as bright leaves quivered in the sharpening air, a flurry of application forms landed into True Minds. There were more women than men: Miss This, Miss That, and Mrs The Other, who had lost her husband in a boating accident. April paused at this one. The woman, Mrs Crisp, had been with her earlier that morning. She was in her thirties, fair and slightly plump-faced, pretty in a gentle way. She had been left with two young sons and enjoyed country rambles and gardening. She seemed kind and lively. She would be perfect for Fabian. And if Felicity's marriage was making *her* feel, well, left out, sure Felicity's own brother must be feeling even worse. Maybe now was the time to take action. She hadn't done anything for Miss Dawson yet – she made a mental note to see to that next – but here was something she could do right now.

Or at least, ask Martha to do.

'Martha?'

Her boss looked up from her own desk, where she was settling invoices. 'Hmm?'

April waved the form. 'I've a grand wee widow woman here,' she said. 'A Mrs Crisp.'

Martha sighed. 'It's men we need,' she said, as if April could somehow conjure one up. 'Though we've a retired bishop coming in at three – apparently Thomasina Longbottom recommended us; she's terribly well connected.'

'He'd be too old for this one.' April dismissed the bishop, though the underneath part of her mind was riffling through the files of their older, churchier women clients. 'But I was thinking – Miss Murrell is definitely settled with thon farmer?' she asked. She still had a wee notion about Miss Murrell so there was no harm in checking.

But Martha left her in no doubt. 'Oh, absolutely. We— *I* was walking past the farm a couple of weeks ago and saw her and the little girl blackberrying in the lane. She seems very much ensconced.'

'Right. So this woman here, I was thinking she'd be grand for Fabian.'

When Martha's mouth dropped open she clarified, 'Fabian Carr? The lawyer?' Martha couldn't have forgotten. 'I know he's not a client,' she went on, before Martha could object. 'But he wants a lady friend – who knows that better than me! And I know' – she could see that Martha was about to object – 'that we can't exactly match them when he's not signed up. But I thought you could contact him and maybe suggest a free consultation, you know, as a reward for sorting out Mrs Lewis.' April reached for her diary. 'Why are you looking like that?'

'You. Your determination to get Mr Carr suited.'

'Sure isn't that what you employ me for? Och, I can't help it, Martha – I see matches everywhere. You warned me I would.'

'But, does that mean' – Martha sounded very serious – 'that you definitely don't have feelings for him?'

'Divil the bit,' she said. For dear sake, what did she have to do to convince people? 'I'd love to find him a woman. But I can't suggest it so I'm asking you.'

314

Martha was silent for a long time. So long that April waved the form in her face. Martha batted it away. 'I won't need that,' she said.

'But how will you know what to say?'

'I'll think of something. Actually,' she said, 'I'll pop round and have a word now. His office isn't far away.'

'Martha!' For dear sake, *she* was meant to be the impulsive one. 'We're not that desperate for men. You could leave it till tomorrow.'

Martha stood up and took her green tweed coat and orange felt hat from the hatstand. 'No,' she said. 'I've been leaving it till tomorrow half my life.'

Forty-one

Martha felt about twenty-one. A bold twenty-one. The twenty-one-year-old who had run away to be a VAD. She marched into Fabian's office and told his cat's-bottom-mouthed secretary that no, she didn't have an appointment but she was quite sure Mr Carr would see her, and went on marching into his private office with such aplomb that Miss Cooke simply pursed her mouth tighter, clutched her files closer and let her go.

Mr Carr – *Fabian* – looked up from his desk and started, his pen skiting out of his hand. She bent down to lift it.

'It's not broken,' she said, and he said, 'Mrs— Martha!'

And then she didn't know what to say, she hadn't planned it properly at all, she simply crossed to his side of the desk, held out the pen and said, 'Um. I've changed my mind. I mean, I haven't changed my mind about what I wanted. I always wanted it. You. Oh dear.' She took a deep breath. (*Really, Martha, there is no need to throw yourself at him!*) 'What I mean is, and, gosh, I hope you meant what you said, but I've just found out that April isn't in love with you. Not in the slightest.' She searched his face for reaction and saw confusion, relief and finally, joy. 'But I think I might be,' she said. 'I hope that's all right.'

316

'It's . . .' He shook his head as if in wonderment. 'It's certainly all right. Extremely all right.' He reached out a hand and she slipped hers into it, the most intimate contact – especially since she had dashed out without her gloves – she had had with a man since Gordon. Gordon, who had been so young and so close to death. Fabian was no longer young: his hair was threaded with grey and when he smiled – he was smiling broadly now – the skin round his eyes fanned out into fine lines. As, she supposed, did hers. But there was no embarkation waiting for Fabian, no Passchendaele. He stood in his office, the untidy ledgers and heavily bound books piled behind him, and grinned like a boy.

From the outer office they could hear the clatter and ding of the secretary's typewriter.

'Come on,' Fabian said. 'We can't talk here. Let's go outside.' And he suited the action to the word, calling out, 'I'll be back for my three o'clock, Miss Cooke, fear not.'

In the street, he offered his arm and she took it, feeling terribly giddy and absurd.

'I'm sorry about having to be back for my three o'clock,' he said. 'I'd like to, oh, I don't know, tramp the hills for miles, have tea in a roadhouse, walk home by starlight.' He threw back his head and breathed in the crisp air.

'That sounds perfectly delicious,' Martha said, 'but as a matter of fact *I've* to be back for my three o'clock too. It's a new client we're keen to snaffle and I don't want to leave April alone.'

He laughed. 'Is this what it's going to be like, keeping company with a business lady?'

'Are we keeping company?'

'I hope so.'

She leaned into him, not too obviously – they were walking down Bridge Street in broad daylight, and they both had reputations to think of. Gosh, what would April think about

317

what she was doing now? She giggled, and Fabian looked at her quizzically.

'April thinks I'm signing you up for the bureau. She asked me to. That's how I knew for sure she wasn't in love with you. And I ran straight round to tell you. Isn't it shameful?'

'Shocking,' he said. 'But why didn't you just ask her?'

'I did. More than once. But I didn't believe her. I thought my intuition knew better. She's been most unlike herself. Rather mopey. Exactly what I'd expect from a girl who was in love and didn't want to admit it to herself. But she's not!'

'If you'd believed her, you'd have saved us both weeks of, well, uncertainty. Anxiety.' He stroked her hand, and it felt terribly strange but also absolutely right.

So he had been anxious too? Good. Not that she wanted him to know an unhappy moment, but a little disquiet was a positive sign. And this – walking through homely streets, with flurries of dried leaves scuffling round their feet, and Fabian handsome in a dark overcoat and inexpertly knitted blue muffler – was so perfect that the wasted days and weeks didn't matter. They had the deliciousness of *now*, and if it hadn't been for her misunderstanding April, they might have had this conversation some weeks ago, and by now the novelty could have worn off.

She gave a happy wriggle because she knew the novelty was not going to wear off.

'It won't be easy,' Fabian said. 'I can't pretend I don't have complications – well, one. Prudence.'

And the ghosts. Gordon and Serena. But what were ghosts compared to Passchendaele? What was one girl?

'It will be all right,' she said, and she stopped and turned to face him. His arms closed around her waist, and she leaned up and, in broad daylight on this extraordinary, ordinary October Tuesday lunchtime – *In the street!* Mother objected – they kissed.

318

Briefly. Gently, but with a confidence that made her feel as certain of him as of any of the matches she had made for other people.

'Well?' April demanded when she got back to the office. 'Did you get him to agree?'

Martha hung up her coat. 'I certainly did.' She smiled inside.

'So, will I book him in?' April waved the diary. 'Or would you rather deal with him?'

Martha bit her lip. 'I shall be, er, *dealing* with him,' she said, 'but there's no need to book him in. He's already— I mean, *we* are already suited.'

'*You?*' Confusion played over April's features. Then she shrieked, 'For dear sake!' and jumped up, upsetting a fortunately-almost-empty cup, and made for her partner's desk. There was an awkward moment when they both realised a hug was possibly imminent, and they were unsure whether to allow it.

Then April said, 'Och, Martha, I'm that pleased for you!' and threw her arms around her. 'And here's me thinking I was getting quare and good at the matchmaking.' She pulled away and looked Martha closely in the face, as if her appearance might have changed. 'Sure isn't it as clear as the eye in your head? I should give up if I couldn't work that one out. I've been trying to find him a nice woman for ages. Why didn't I think of you?'

'Well, I'd no intention of marrying again, as I told you,' Martha said, remembering that April had told her more or less the same thing, only Martha hadn't believed it. And there she went again – *marriage*, when they had only come together an hour ago! 'I honestly never thought I would. All the clients over the years, I never saw them as *men*. I suppose I was loyal to Gordon. But Fabian . . . well, it's different. I recognised something in him – that sounds fanciful, doesn't it?' How funny, she thought, that after a lifetime of matching people she should be so wary of sounding romantic!

'Divil the bit. Sure you've both been widowed.'

'I don't think that's enough in itself. But yes, there are things I don't have to explain. Like that I'll always love Gordon but it's a different love now, kind of' – she felt embarrassed to talk of such things – 'spiritual, I suppose. It can coexist with any feeling I have – might develop – for Fabian. And I imagine he feels the same about Serena. We needn't fear each other's past. I never expected to meet anyone, you know. It seems silly, doing what I do for a living, but honestly, it was enough to see other people suited. And then the day he came to talk about Primrose Lewis, you left in rather a hurry, and we chatted over tea, and I found him awfully easy to talk to. We just seemed to feel a sympathy.'

'He's a grand fella,' April said sincerely. 'But that was weeks ago. Why wait till now?'

'Because I thought you were in love with him!'

'Och, Martha, you're an awful eejit. Didn't I tell you a thousand times I'd no more notion of him than I have of going to the moon? And if you're worried about him asking me first, I don't think he meant it. I think he was only sort of practising. Och, that doesn't sound right. But I don't want you to worry that, well—'

'That he was on the rebound?' Martha shook her head. 'I understand. Men are different. Widowers often remarry quite quickly. They seem to decide they're ready and then start looking around. I don't mind that he looked at you first.'

'That's all it was,' April reassured her. 'Like you say, he was ready and I was there. But I wouldn't have suited him. I'm really not the marrying type.'

'You're the jolly decent type, that's what you are,' Martha said fervently. 'I'm relieved that you aren't . . . well, that you don't feel any . . .'

'I don't. I could have been tempted, maybe for a minute, because life is so much easier for married women, and he's a dear. But no, it wouldn't have been fair. He deserves someone to love him and be a . . . a real wife. You'll be perfect.'

'It won't be plain sailing,' Martha said. 'Prudence might be difficult. But we're not kids this time round; we know life is complicated.'

'Prudence is quare and improved,' April said, 'thanks to that nice wee Miss Dunn I found.'

'Yes, Fabian's mentioned her. What do you mean, *you* found her?'

'Oh, um, well.' April cast her eyes down furtively. 'I forgot you didn't . . . och, I don't suppose it matters now.'

'What doesn't?'

'She came into the bureau. Grand wee girl, awful smart. And I knew fine rightly she'd no more notion of marrying than I have. She wanted a job. Something to *do*. She only came to us because, well, that's what women are told to want, isn't it? Marriage? And it's as well for your business that they are. But some women want something different. And I could tell she was one of them. And I knew Fabian was near dead to find somebody to teach Prudence so I sort of . . . put them together. Now you're not cross, are you? At least I didn't set him up with someone he fell in love with.'

If April had confessed this even an hour ago, Martha would have been outraged. But everything was different now, and she only laughed and said, 'April McVey. I don't know if you're a matchmaker or a witch.'

April did not seem unduly perturbed. 'Will you keep on working?' she asked.

'I don't suppose so.'

'But you've worked so hard.' April sounded shocked. 'It's your life!'

'I suppose it is.' A marriage bureau instead of a marriage; hadn't that been how it was? She shook her head. Maybe April could take over – but she couldn't help knowing April's heart wasn't in the marriage business the way hers was. It didn't matter terribly, sending that Miss Dunn off to be a governess, but she couldn't be encouraged in too much of that, or it wouldn't be a marriage bureau at all. All very well for Mrs Hart's Matrimonial Bureau to be modernised into True Minds; she wasn't ready to let her life's work become some sort of employment agency. 'We haven't talked about the details yet. Give us time. We aren't even engaged.'

'But you will be.'

Martha nodded. 'I think we have what used to be called an understanding.'

'Understanding.' April sounded unusually wistful. 'Isn't that a lovely word?'

Forty-two

April assumed this new romance would move slowly. Martha had been on her own for a lifetime; there could surely be no hurry? But she was wrong. A fortnight later, Martha showed her a small diamond-and-sapphire ring on the third finger of her left hand. Her wedding ring, Gordon's ring, was now on her right hand.

'We don't see the point in waiting,' Martha explained. 'We won't marry until next spring, but we thought it would be simpler for Prudence if we were officially engaged, rather than have her wonder.'

April admired the ring, which was very dainty and pretty, and asked about Prudence.

'She's been very polite so far,' Martha said cautiously. 'She loves the High School so that's keeping her busy. She has a best friend called Susan and she's determined to get into the third eleven.'

'That sounds promising. I've met Susan, I don't think she'll lead her astray.'

'I honestly don't think she minds too much what Fabian does, as long as it doesn't impact on her,' Martha said.

'It'll impact on her when you move in.'

'She'll be used to me by then. And it's not as if I'm going to burn all Serena's pictures or change everything.' April noticed that Martha said Serena's name very naturally, as she supposed Fabian did Gordon's. 'And she told me she'd been worried her father would marry someone young, like you, and have more children. She likes me being an old lady.'

'An old lady!'

Martha laughed. 'If that helps her tolerate me, I don't mind.'

April looked at her partner with affection. 'Och, she'll do more than tolerate you. You'll be a wonderful stepmother.'

'She suffered when Serena was ill,' Martha said, 'and then I think – though she wouldn't say so – that it was rather a relief when she died. I understand that; I went through it with poor Mother, though I was older. I won't try to *mother* her, but I can be a friend and role model.'

'Och, you will surely.' She thought of Daddy's death for the first time in ages. It had been too much of a shock to be a relief at the time, but there was no doubt that it had set her free. Mammy had settled grand in Manchester, was helping with the sewing and had joined a missionary work class. April had gone to visit last weekend and Mammy, though pleased to see her, had been almost too busy to take much to do with her. There was no need to worry about Mammy.

It's me, she thought. I'm the one not settled.

It was hard being in the office with such a happy boss. Martha had always been efficient, good-natured and kind, and apart from their fall-out about Nigel Johnson, they had always got on the best. But now there was a glow about her; she seemed to get younger every day while April, with the prospect of Pickering Street ahead in the evenings, felt duller and older and sadder as autumn advanced. Easterbridge was a leafy town, and some October mornings, the air sharp and the trees yellow and gold against a cool blue sky, were so lovely that they hurt.

She found herself out of patience with her work. With herself. Over seven months she had been in Easterbridge now and she had failed in so much. For dear sake, she was pushing thirty, and what had she to show for it? She hated Pickering Street so much that she was forever poring over advertisements for rooms, but there was nothing suitable. As the evenings drew in, it was harder to spend them wandering the streets; she did not want to get the name of being an eccentric, like old Miss McCaughey who used to walk up and down Lisnacashan Main Street with a dolly, singing 'In the Gloaming' – that would do the bureau's reputation no good, and anyway, she didn't feel confident about walking in the dark. It wasn't like Lisnacashan where you knew everybody.

Was it time to move on?

Presumably when Martha married, she would give up the bureau or sell it as a going concern. April was not so attached to the work, or to Easterbridge, that she would want to carry on working there for a stranger, but neither could she leave while Martha was so caught up in her new hopes. She made up her mind: she would stay for the wedding, and then move on. That would be in May. She would have given Easterbridge over a year – nobody could say she had just quit. But May was far enough away for her not to think about it too much. She would hunker down for the winter. She needn't think seriously about her next step until maybe March. Which was a relief; she didn't have the energy to bother.

And that wasn't like her at all. Mammy would have said she needed a tonic. Evelyn would have said she needed a kick up the b-t-m. And she would have laughed.

Why was April not laughing these days? She seemed to have turned into a right wee Moaning Minnie.

At work she had to keep up the pretence of being happy and interested in Martha's plans; the last thing she wanted was for

Martha to think she regretted turning Fabian down herself. So she was resolutely cheerful, and it was exhausting. But she couldn't blame Martha. April had insisted often enough that she had no desire to marry, so she could hardly complain that Martha had finally accepted this. When Martha said how reassuring it was not to look at the future alone, when she said what fun it was to have someone to tell the little details of her day to, April smiled brightly and said *och aye* and *that must be grand right enough* and though she would not have said her teeth were gritted exactly, she did seem to be developing an ache in her jaw.

'We're planning an engagement dinner,' Martha said one day towards the end of October. How easily she had adapted to saying *we*. 'Nothing grand, just family' – Phew, April thought – 'which of course includes you.'

'I'm not family.'

'We'd never have met without you! You matched us, in a way. We wouldn't dream of celebrating without you.'

There was nothing April could do except smile and wonder how she could get out of it as Martha outlined the evening: a quiet dinner in the Royal Oak, Easterbridge's best hotel. 'Just ourselves and you, and Felicity. And Felicity's friend Erich.'

'Lovely.'

All couples, except her. And Prudence presumably. She would feel like an extra child, tolerated at the grown-ups' party but not accepted as a full member of their world because she was not one half of a couple. How cruel the word *couple* was; how it excluded people. She could not refuse the invitation; it would look exactly as though she really did begrudge Fabian and Martha their happiness.

And do you? asked a cool voice in her head. *If you don't want to marry him, or anyone, why do you feel that way?*

I don't know! she told the voice. *Shut up and leave me alone!*

So she accepted, and said she was looking forward to it, and appeared at the office on the designated Friday in her good blue frock with her hair done more carefully than usual in a sort of chignon. It reminded her of the evening she and Felicity had gone to dinner at Fabian's; she'd worn the same frock.

She worked with ferocious energy, opening two new applications and scanning them impatiently. Who were these eejits, so blithely confident of finding love, or at least companionship? She thumped both down on the desk and let out a long sigh.

Martha, who'd spent most of the day staring into space with a gormless expression, sparked into life. 'What's wrong?'

April waved the forms. 'These people are deluded!' she said. 'This girl with the big teeth, sure who'd fancy her? And she's the cheek to say she won't look at a fella with spectacles! Sure that'd be her best chance. Stone blind if we can get it. And this boyo here whose wife died six months ago – *six months*! Would he ever let the dust settle on the poor cratur's grave before sniffing round for a replacement? People need to catch themselves on.' And she ripped through both forms, letting them fall in a flutter of torn hopes, the toothy girl smiling up at her in black and white from the floor.

'April! What on earth?' Martha looked more shocked than she had ever seen her, even when she had told her about Nigel Johnson. 'Are you . . . you must be unwell!'

'I'm fine.'

'Is it, er, your monthly visitor?' Martha lowered her voice as though the good citizens of Easterbridge were crowded round the door to listen.

'No. I'm fine,' April repeated.

'Well, take your lunch early,' Martha said. 'And maybe you'll return more . . . more like yourself. You know I'm going to the hairdresser at two? Are you sure you can hold the fort?' She looked nervous.

April took a deep calming breath. 'Of course I can,' she said. 'I promise I won't match the wrong people or tell them they'd be better off with a cat or a nice hobby.' She forced herself to grin brightly and Martha, after a slight hesitation, smiled back and started to pick up the torn forms.

April went out for lunch, but in the chilly street, leaves gathering in rustling russet heaps at the kerbsides, her heart pounded and stupid tears pushed behind her eyes. She bought a bun, but her throat swelled against it and she let it fall to the street where a flock of pigeons descended on it. For dear sake, what sort of an eejit was she? She *didn't* begrudge Martha and Fabian their happiness; she *wasn't* in love with Fabian and never had been, so why did she feel so . . . so *wrong*?

The office felt different without Martha, emptied of not just her physical presence but her warmth and concern. I used to have that, April thought. I loved sorting out people's lives. I was interested. Kind. Bossy, but kind. She looked at the registration forms she had torn up, which Martha had placed on her desk, and began, painstakingly, to gum the fragments together.

Tears still kept threatening, and she had to dash them away every so often. Maybe her monthly visitor was indeed due? She remembered the last time it had taken her by surprise, when Felicity had been so kind. She heard feet on the stairs and fumbled for her handkerchief to blow her nose. How could Martha be back so quickly? She mustn't see her like this.

But it wasn't Martha. It was Primrose Lewis, full of having been interviewed by Felicity for the newspaper story – 'What a bright young woman she is!' – and keen to impart some news. Not a romance; it would be a long time, Primrose said, before she trusted another man, but she was going to rent her front bedroom to a refugee couple, so she would have company again, and their modest rent would help her save up to visit Mabel. It would take years, but it gave her something to look forward to, and the couple were dears, so grateful for a safe and peaceful home after the time they'd had, and they seemed to look on her as an older sister. She couldn't wait for them to move in.

An older sister. The words lingered in April's mind after Primrose left. That's what I used to be like, she thought, back home. Bossing the girls in the factory, but helping them too, listening, trying to be a good role model; running the club in the evening with Evelyn's help. She was glad those girls couldn't see her now. That wee lassie who had defended her when some people had said she must have known rightly what her daddy was up to. *Miss McVey wouldn't lie*, she'd protested, her cheeks flaming with self-consciousness. That girl had stood up for her and now April couldn't remember her name. She could recall exactly the way her tongue used to protrude through her front teeth when she was concentrating hard, and the smell of her cheap scent, but not her name. It had begun with an M. Maggie? Minnie?

She bent over her notes and just as her mind flashed with *Millie! That was it, Millie Nesbitt*, the door opened and Martha returned, with her hair cut and waved.

She looked relieved that April had not ransacked the office, but relief gave way quickly to concern.

'You really don't look yourself,' she said, 'Are you sure . . .?'

And the Miss McVey who never lied, who got into trouble for being too honest, seized the chance for escape and said she feared the shrimp paste in her lunchtime sandwich might have been off.

'I've been up and down to the lavatory ever since,' she said.

'Oh my dear!' Martha looked horrified. 'I wonder if you should see a doctor?'

'Och no, it's just a touch of the trots,' she said briskly, knowing Martha was embarrassed by bodily functions. 'But I'm afraid I won't be able to make your dinner.'

'You must go home at once,' Martha said. 'I'll order a taxi for you. But what if you take ill on the way? Perhaps I should come with you.'

'No, you've that shy wee Mr Innes coming later. You know how hard you've worked to get him to this stage. The fresh air will do me good. Honestly, Martha, I'll be grand.'

Keeping up the pretence of being well enough to cycle home, but too ill for a party, was exhausting. Even though a cold needling rain had started, she did not go straight to Pickering Street; she cycled up into the hills and, on reaching the tops, stopped and looked down into the valley, breathing in the sharp, damp air. Easterbridge was so familiar now – its hunched yellow-grey houses, the tall chimney and rain-slicked black rooves of Shaw's Mill, the spire of St Margaret's Church, the green oasis of the park – but it had never really become *home*. But what was? She would never go back to Lisnacashan. The white attic had felt more like home than anywhere she'd ever lived, but sure it had only been a room in someone else's house.

Home was something other people had. Like saying *we*.

She shivered in her thin dress, jumped back on her bicycle and pedalled hard back to Pickering Street.

Her heart sank as she rounded the corner to her own room to find Miss Dawson waiting. She had not exactly been avoiding her, but she was very aware that she hadn't yet contacted Sybil Barrett about her. The old April would have done so weeks ago.

'I wondered if you might take a cup of cocoa with me,' Miss Dawson said. 'Oh, my dear, you look chilled to the bone.'

'I'm not dressed for the weather,' April admitted, looking down at her mud-spattered stockings. 'I'd love a cup of cocoa. Would you mind if I just changed?'

'I think you ought. And give that hair a good rasp with a towel.'

Back in her room she felt shivery and exhausted and much in need of that lunchtime bun she had wasted on the pigeons. All she had was a packet of McVitie's digestive biscuits, so she brought it in to Miss Dawson's room, and was glad to see, along with the little cocoa pot bubbling on her gas ring, a tin of shortbread.

'Excuse the cut of me,' April said. She was wearing blue flannel pyjamas and her old tartan dressing gown. 'I dried myself and then I couldn't bear to change into proper clothes.'

'Not at all. It's like a cocoa party,' Miss Dawson said. 'We used to have them at college. Such fun!'

'This looks very festive,' April said, and Miss Dawson said, 'Actually, dear, it's my birthday. My niece sent the short-bread and such a pretty card.' She showed April the card – kittens and sunflowers – and April said how nice.

'I usually get one from Muriel Lowe – we were at college together, but it hasn't come this year.' She frowned. 'I do hope she hasn't died. I don't suppose anyone would think to let me know.'

'Tell me about your college days,' April said, and Miss Dawson's face broke into a delighted smile.

'I shouldn't like to bore you,' she said.

'I'd love it.'

There were many, many tales, of many, many girls, all of whose names Miss Dawson seemed to remember – and if the names did not come easily, she spent a great deal of time working through the filing cabinet of her memory until they did. 'Was it Verity who smuggled in the kitten? Or was it her pal Winifred? They were always very thick. *Double trouble* we used to say. Of course we were only joking, they were dear girls really.'

'They used to say that about me and my pal Evelyn. Joined at the hip.'

Everyone was joined to someone. Except her. Well, Miss Dawson wasn't, but the thought did not cheer her.

331

'You're shivering, my dear,' Miss Dawson said. 'Here, take this.' Carefully, breathing through her nose, she placed a crocheted shawl round April's shoulders. It was orange and yellow, soft and warm and light.

Look at me, April thought, with my shawl and my pyjamas and my cocoa. I must look exactly what I am – a spinster, verging on the eccentric, verging on middle age.

'Oh, we did have fun!' Miss Dawson said. 'Mind, it was hard work, and the staff were terribly fierce – talk about being chaperoned! People called it the convent, though it was a Church of England college. But it was the friendships, you see, that was the best part.' She smiled a little sadly, and April wondered where they had gone – the Muriels and the Winifreds and the Veritys, those modern, educated young women – whether they had taught all their lives, whether they had become respected headmistresses, escaped or settled into marriage, or, like Miss Dawson herself, spent birthdays alone in damp rooms in boarding houses.

It was a shock to both of them when the doorbell rang.

'Mrs Sadler's at her meeting,' Miss Dawson said, 'and that Bleaney never hears a thing up at the top.'

April jumped up. 'I'll go.'

'Oh dear.' Miss Dawson looked anxious. 'Look out and see who it is, will you? Just in case.' Obligingly, April went to the window, pulled back Miss Dawson's thick net curtain and looked out.

Felicity was below her, standing back and looking at the front door. She was wearing a little black hat but the aureole of curls escaping from it was unmistakeable. April's breath stopped. She was barely aware of Miss Dawson behind her.

Felicity pushed the doorbell again and then turned round and said – April could hear her perfectly – 'No answer. Not much of a house, is it?'

And a tall, bearded man stepped out of the shadows and said, in a foreign accent, 'Come, she is probably asleep.'

'I'll just leave a note,' Felicity said, and April watched her take something out of her bag and scribble on it. She bent down low to place it through the letterbox and then left. The man offered her his arm and she took it, walking away with him down the street.

A *couple*, April thought. She had known, of course, but to have it confirmed . . .

'Who is it, dear?' Miss Dawson's voice brought her back to herself.

'Oh, someone with a tract or something. Nothing to bother about.'

Miss Dawson sighed. 'The world's gone mad,' she pronounced. 'Tracts about this and that. Vegetarianism. Spiritualism. Communism. Sometimes I think that chap Hitler isn't doing so badly, getting Germany into shape. Though as I always say, I never trust a man with a moustache.' Her face brightened. 'Though I confess, my dear, I do rather like that Mr Mosley – Sir Oswald, I should say. He's awfully handsome.' She giggled in a girlish way.

April told herself she would not pick up Felicity's note that night, it could wait until morning, but once she had escaped from Miss Dawson and had steeled herself for her routine evening ablutions in the bathroom, she couldn't resist looking down the stairs and there was the note lying on the doormat. She would just go and lift it in case in case Mrs Sadler or Bleaney picked it up. Not that it would be private.

It wasn't private but Felicity's bold handwriting gave her a start all the same:

Dear April,
We missed you tonight – what foul luck for you to get
a bad shrimp. Funnily enough I remember you telling me

333

you didn't eat shrimps and suchlike. Anyway, I hope you're all right. You're missed at number eleven too. As you know, I have had company – too complicated to explain in a note – but it's not the same as having YOU. Your room is still there, and you'd be welcome back anytime. Unless you're well suited where you are of course. Or just call and say hello some day.

    Warmest regards
    Felicity

Imagine her remembering about the shrimp! Or was that her way of hinting that she knew April was malingering – you can't be poisoned by something you don't eat? Och no, she was just being kind. And it was a pleasant evening; what harm in taking a stroll with her gentleman friend through the darkening streets after the family celebration? She saw again the way Felicity had taken Erich's arm, how they had walked off together into the night, looking, as their figures moved away down the street, like one being. A couple going home.

Forty-three

Nobody had ever called at Pickering Street for her before, so it was a surprise, next morning, to hear a knock at her door quite early. She wasn't even dressed; there hadn't seemed much point. It must be Mrs Sadler – her rent was due.

'Come in,' she said, running her fingers through her hair, and pulling up the counterpane over the rumpled sheets. It was a nuisance, having to do everything in one room.

It was Martha, looking like Red Riding Hood, with a basket over her arm. And, just behind her, Fabian.

'Oh!' She pulled her dressing gown tighter round her to hide her pyjamas. 'I wasn't—'

'We wanted to be sure you were all right,' Martha said, 'after your, er, indisposition.'

April, though she hadn't actually been ill in the sordid way she had feigned, felt herself blush. 'Och, I'm fine,' she said. 'Right as rain.'

Martha rummaged in her basket. 'We had a lovely cake,' she said. 'All the way from Germany – at least the recipe is. Felicity's friend made it.' She handed April a parcel done up in grease-proof paper. 'Felicity was most insistent that you try it. Wasn't she, Fabian?'

'She was. She was very disappointed not to see you,' Fabian said. 'She wanted to introduce you to Erich and—'

'Isn't that lovely,' April said. She opened the parcel and a rich, buttery, almondy smell wafted up to her nose. So Erich was a baker as well! What a paragon. Why did they call him *friend* and not *fiancé*? Hadn't Prudence talked about a wedding? Or were they all being terribly careful with April, handling her with kid gloves, not wanting her to feel like the lonely, aging spinster she was? She could see Martha taking in the horrible brown room, the stained walls, the grimy window. *I never set out to live like this!* she wanted to shout.

'Felicity was so sorry not to see you,' Fabian repeated. 'I think, between ourselves, she misses you. She seems rather lonely.'

She misses you! Nonsense. Sure, Evelyn had said that after she married Maurice Kenny. *I've missed you* – as though April were the one who'd made herself unavailable. People said they missed you to make *them* feel better for neglecting *you*. Probably they did miss you a little, but not the way you missed them, like someone had gouged a hole in your heart with a knitting needle. As for lonely! How could Felicity be lonely, now of all times? Indignation flared. What did these people with their engagement rings and their cakes and their homes and their casual *we* know about loneliness? She hoped they didn't expect her to ask them to stay for tea and cake.

But no, why would anyone linger in Pickering Street? Already Martha was glancing at her wristwatch. 'Fabian,' she murmured. 'We must go.' There it was – *we*!

'Of course.'

'Now, April, you're not to come in on Monday unless you are completely better,' Martha said. 'In fact' – she looked round the shabby brown room – 'I wonder if you'd benefit from a little break? Why don't you go away for a few days? You haven't had a holiday.'

'Bit of walking in the dales, perhaps,' Fabian suggested heartily. 'I know the days are short now, but the colours are lovely and the weather's set pretty fair.'

Wouldn't that be the quare craic, all on my own? April thought but didn't say.

Martha, more understanding about the life of a lone woman, said, 'Perhaps a short visit to your mother and aunt? A change of scene?'

'I'm fine. I'll be in on Monday.'

But, when they had gone and she had looked at the cake and wondered if she should invite Miss Dawson round to share it, she felt Pickering Street close round her like a damp brown shroud, and she knew she would have to get out, even though the streaked window told her it was raining. The thought of Miss Dawson reminded her that she had still not mentioned her to Sybil. Why not do that now? Doing something for someone less fortunate would take her out of herself.

She washed and dressed swiftly. Keeping busy, that was the way. Not moping and thinking about herself. She didn't know where Sybil lived. Never mind, she would go to the mill. Sybil would hardly be there, but she could leave a note explaining about Miss Dawson, asking if she might give her a chance.

To go to Shaw's Mill was to go to Riverside Road. She hadn't exactly forgotten that, but she didn't let herself think about it too much until she was cycling up it, head down against the driving rain, remembering the exact place where she needed to change down to first gear. Riverside Road seemed to have developed a few new potholes since she had left. Even so, she couldn't help feeling nostalgic – the occasional *plish* of a moorhen on the river below; the yells of children in the side streets; even the sour beery smell breathed out by The Queen's Head. Despite the chill wind and the worsening rain, a crowd of girls huddled at the end of Townsend Street. Were their homes so unbearable, that they would rather be outside? A giggle burst from the group; the girls grabbed each other in helpless hilarity. *That* was what brought them out of their houses to stand in the rain. Friendship.

Even though she was only meant to be going as far as the mill – a towering shell, its gates sagging even lower, a big maroon-and-cream car parked outside (something to do with Sybil and Henry's grand scheme?) – she found herself cycling past it, as far as number eleven, and it was almost a shock to see it looking exactly as she remembered. She braked and looked up, she couldn't help herself, at Felicity's bedroom window. The curtains were neat, the glass clean; there was nothing to suggest that the room was now housing a lover. *Friend. Fiancé.* Whatever they called him.

With a click, the yellow front door opened. She sat back on her saddle, hardly breathing. If Felicity came out now . . .

It wasn't Felicity. It was a man. The tall, dark, bearded man she had seen last night. Erich. He looked down the street, past April, and then turned back to the doorway. She heard him say something in what she supposed was German, and then lean right in, as if kissing someone goodbye. She couldn't see Felicity, but she heard her respond, also in German, and then there was a long pause as if they were kissing again. On the doorstep! Well, the porch, but even so. The man continued on up the road away from the town, so at least she wouldn't have to cycle past him.

Right. Time to be businesslike. Shaw's Mill in the rain didn't look inviting even with the posh car parked outside, but the gate yielded to her hand. Inside was like a separate world. The high walls screened the whole complex from the street. The chimney rose high into the sky, and around it the tall brick buildings formed three sides of a square. The ground in the middle was rough, puddled and pitted. It looked hopeless and abandoned.

But it was not. She heard voices and round the corner of the main building, deep in conversation, interrupting each other and gesticulating, came Sybil and Henry Barrett.

And Felicity.

April stopped. How could Felicity . . .? Hadn't she seen Erich kiss her in her doorway only a minute ago? Nobody could move that fast, and besides, the group looked as if they had been talking together for some time. All their coats were darkened with rain.

'Miss McVey!' Sybil called. 'The very person!'

They came to greet her, all smiles and handshakes and exclamations of delight. Felicity hung back slightly, until Sybil pulled her forward.

'I believe you know Miss Carr, Miss McVey?'

'Yes.'

'Miss Carr is going to help us with our scheme,' Sybil went on. 'She's going to run writing classes.'

April couldn't imagine Felicity doing that. Where would she find the time?

'And then there are your friends, Miss Carr,' Henry said. 'Oh, is it all right to mention them? I know you said . . .'

'It's all right now,' Felicity said. 'They're here at last, and married and, well, as safe as they'll ever be, thank goodness.'

'Miss Carr's friend is an artist,' Sybil went on, 'and we're hoping to sell her paintings. Miss Carr's been selling them through some London gallery, but they take a hefty commission, don't they, Miss Carr?'

'Yes,' Felicity said. She seemed unusually subdued, April thought. Not unhappy but sort of in the background. Watching. But how was she here when not a minute ago she'd been kissing Erich in the porch?

Sybil kept her attention on April. 'Miss Carr tells us you've got experience with girls? So maybe you could help out? I know you're busy with your work, and we know how important that work is' – she glanced sideways at Henry and they both laughed sheepishly – 'but you must have some free time?'

April thought of the long evenings in Pickering Street and agreed that she might spare the odd minute. She told them about the girls in the factory at Lisnacashan. 'I'm no good at handicrafts, or writing, but I could maybe run a wee club?' A little bud of purposefulness, tightly folded for too long, started to unfurl cautious petals inside her.

Sybil clapped her hands. 'A club! Like the Guides?'

'Oh lord, nothing uniformed.' Felicity gave a shudder. 'Like the Hitler Youth.'

'I'm not sure what you mean,' Sybil said crisply, 'but I won't hear a word against the Girl Guides. I was a most enthusiastic Bluebell in my day.'

Felicity breathed out. 'Sorry,' she said. 'I'm oversensitive about anything that even smacks of fascism. You would be too if you'd—'

'Ours would be different anyway,' April cut in, seeing Sybil look puzzled. 'Not so churchy. And for older girls, the ones who're too old to play in the streets and too young for anything else. Something to teach them skills and self-respect, maybe even self-defence, but where they can have fun too.' Already she could imagine it, the bustle of girls, their high spirits, their earnestness. The little bud blossomed into a deep pink rose.

'And something for older women too – oh, and men.' Sybil looked at Henry. 'There must be so many people who'd like somewhere to go and something to do.'

April thought of all the people she'd met through True Minds, who had time and knowledge and skills. Wasn't it a pity Jennifer Dunn had gone abroad! But she might write and ask her to recommend someone to teach folk dancing; sure, nothing could be healthier or more fun. In her mind she was introducing the

Colonel to a group of local lads eager to know about Cocker Spaniels . . . all right, that might be going too far, but what about the nice rabbit lady? Though the people around Shaw's Mill bred their rabbits for the pot, so that might not be such a good idea. Mrs Lewis could give baking classes – if she wasn't too busy with her new lodgers. The rose became a bright garland of blooms. And talking of blooms – there could even be space for a garden here. Now who did she know who liked gardening? That nice little Mrs Crisp . . .

'It's all coming true!' Sybil outstretched her hands and looked round the shabby buildings. 'I thought all I wanted was to marry. But it's not enough.' She looked at Henry and laughed. 'Don't worry, Henry won't take that the wrong way!' She patted his hand. 'But I don't want to stay at home and do the flowers and plan dinner parties – I'm not that kind of woman. Of course it'll be different when . . . *if* we have a family.' She bit her lip. 'But maybe by then someone else could run it.'

April saw herself running the whole outfit. Of course she would have to work at True Minds as well; she couldn't imagine the mill being a full-time job. But it would give her such a sense of purpose, keep her away from Pickering Street. And talking of Pickering Street . . .

She told them about Miss Dawson. 'She's not hanging about the streets of course, but she's lonely and she'd love something to do. I don't know if she'd still be fit to teach, but she could certainly make things to sell. Actually' – she remembered how Miss Dawson lit up remembering her teaching days – 'I bet she'd have a go at the teaching. She's not very mobile, but if we could get her here . . . .'

Sybil waved a hand. 'Oh, we'll send the car for her,' she said with the ease of someone who has always had a car at her disposal. 'That sounds ripping.' She leaned forward. 'So will you help us, Miss McVey? Henry's a genius with wood,

I'm not too dusty at the handicrafts, and Miss Carr is going to look after the artistic side of things, but we need someone who's good with people.'

'Och aye,' she said. 'Of course I will.'

Henry looked at his watch. 'Darling,' he said. 'If we're meeting your father at one . . .'

'Oh gosh, yes. Daddy and Henry adore each other.' Sybil's voice brightened. 'I honestly think he married me for my father. Oh, we must lock up. Sorry for rushing you out. Ugh, isn't this rain beastly.' They all went out into the street, where they said quick goodbyes, and the way Henry took Sybil's arm and handed her into the waiting car told April that, Daddy or no Daddy, money or no money, he had married her because he loved her. And she, April, had made it happen.

But it wasn't just love, was it? It really was True Minds – they had a project to bind them together, something to work on. A sense of purpose. That was what you needed in life; that was what she didn't seem to have. *The most wonderful adventure*, Sybil called it. Well, she could be part of that adventure too.

'They're marvellous, aren't they?' Felicity asked and before April could agree, she went on, 'Oh – are you feeling better?' Felicity asked.

For a moment April didn't know what she meant. 'Oh! That. Aye, I'm fine. Thanks for your note.'

Felicity narrowed her eyes at her, an expression so familiar that it made April's heart tremble. She seemed to need to hold onto the handlebars of her bicycle.

'Are you sure you weren't faking it? To get out of an awkward evening?'

April's face flamed. 'Why would I do that?'

'Fabian's engagement party? Fabian and Martha?'

It dawned on her, very slowly, that Felicity was making the same mistake as Martha.

'Ah, for crying out loud!' she said, so loudly that a skinny brindled dog nosing the gutter stuck its tail between its legs and whimpered. 'Why will nobody believe me? I don't fancy Fabian. I don't want to marry Fabian. I don't want to marry *anybody*. I never have. I thought you, of all people, knew that.'

'Why me of all people?'

'I thought you were the same.' The skinny dog scuttled away. 'You said *fearsome spinster*. But now you've got Erich.'

'Erich?'

'Wasn't the party for you too?' *You two*. 'Prudence said you were getting married.'

'Erich's married to Hanna.'

'Whoa. Hold on. I saw you last night, from the window. You took his arm.'

'We're old friends. I was worried about you and so after dinner we walked round to see that you were all right. Fabian and Martha took Hanna home because she's not terribly strong after everything they've gone through. They were married a couple of weeks ago.'

'Not . . . not *you*?'

'No. Why on earth . . .?'

'I don't know. I knew there was something big going on. And you were so secretive. I thought . . . och, all sorts. But when you said you'd someone moving in, well, I thought it must be a lover.'

'So you moved out?'

April shrugged. 'I didn't want to be in the way.' A rush of anger swept through her. 'Why didn't you just tell me?'

'Until they were safely here, I couldn't tell anyone. It was such an undertaking to get them out of Germany. They needed papers, guarantees, it all took a lot of money. And then they had to marry in a hurry . . . And getting them into England wasn't a piece of cake. I had to pretend they were coming to

343

work for me as domestic servants.' Her face was very serious now. 'And they were terrified. So scared of anything going wrong. They begged me not to tell a soul. Not even Fabian.'

'But why were they so scared?'

'Oh, April!' Felicity looked exasperated. 'I don't know why people here are so blind to it all! Haven't you heard what that bastard is doing to the Jews?'

April shook her head dumbly. Then she remembered the Nazis marching across the screen, hands and voices raised above the stamping of their boots, and she shivered.

'Erich's a poet – his books have been burned in the streets. Hanna's been sacked from the art college. Her parents have had their farm seized. It's the same for all their Jewish friends. For Jews all over Germany. And it's going to get worse. Evie's been taught in her science lessons at school that Jews are subhuman.' Felicity's mouth twisted. 'That's Nazi policy, April. That's happening in a civilised country only a few hundred miles away. And people are letting it. *We* are letting it.'

'I thought *you* were involved with fascists. Mosley and that crowd.'

Felicity looked disgusted. 'How could you?'

'You wrote to him.' She couldn't say she had seen other evidence that Felicity had attended fascist meetings.

'I wrote to protest! And I've been to disrupt some of his meetings. Him and his blackshirt thugs.' Her eyes blazed.

'Is that how you hurt your arm? I saw the bruises. I thought your lover must be someone, well, violent.'

'That was at Olympia. One of the blackshirts grabbed me. Bastard. But I managed to kick him where I'm pretty sure it hurts a man.' She grinned, but the amusement was fleeting and her eyes grew bleak. 'It's terrifying, April. Even to *think* of that fascist poison creeping into this country when you see what's happening in Germany. You think it couldn't happen here but

344

it could. It only takes people to turn a blind eye. To think it's not their business. That it's not quite *nice* to get involved. Some of the things Hanna and Erich have told me, you wouldn't believe. A bruised arm's nothing. At least I have the right to protest.' She shuddered. But then she gave a little cough and said, 'Anyway. They're here now, and they're safe. And I've sold some of Hanna's paintings for her – yes, those were all hers, the ones that went. I've got a gallery in London interested in her. And hopefully Sybil and Henry can sell some. She can give art lessons too.'

'So, they're going to board with Mrs Lewis? She said she had a refugee couple coming.'

'Yes. Fabian's taking them there today. They're welcome to stay with me, of course, but they're keen to be independent. And then I can use the room for someone else in need. I don't think there's going to be any shortage of refugees.'

She shivered in a way that was clearly nothing to do with her wet coat, but April noticed it. 'We can't stand about in the rain,' she said.

'Come home with me,' Felicity said simply. 'I'll put the kettle on.'

Come home with me.

Number eleven felt disconcertingly different. Boxes and suitcases stood in the hall and there was a sense of flurry and movement. Felicity called up the stairs, 'Hanna! Erich!' and then something in German. 'Sorry,' she said to April. 'They do speak English but we tend to speak German at home.' There was so little space to stand that April could feel the frizz from Felicity's damp hair tickle her cheek.

When Erich came downstairs, followed by a thin, brown-haired woman in a loose frock, Felicity said in English, 'Can I present my good friend April McVey? April, these are Erich Blumenthal and Hanna Silberschmidt.'

'Hanna Blumenthal now,' the woman said, coming forward to shake April's hand.

'Yous have gorgeous names,' was the first thing April thought of saying. *My good friend, April McVey.* She glowed.

'Haven't they? Silberschmidt, well, you'd guess that one,' Felicity said, 'and Blumenthal means flowery valley.'

'Nicer than McVey,' April said.

'Or boring old Carr.'

Something nudged at April's mind. Forest Fay's friend in the story, Eve Silversmith. Hanna's little sister, Evie? Immortalised in the story dedicated to her? *E.S.* Not Erich, then? For dear sake, hadn't she been an awful eejit, the conclusions she'd jumped to. And thinking Felicity was involved with some kind of fascist group when all the time it had been the very opposite.

The door knocked.

'This will be your lift,' Felicity said, and sure enough, Fabian and Martha appeared in the hall. It was like Paddy's Market, but April was glad of the distraction of helping to lift boxes and pack the car which was waiting outside. Glad to be busy and involved.

And then they were all gone, and it was just herself and Felicity looking at each other in the familiar narrow hall, and she was gladder about that than about anything. And desperate for it to stay that way for as long as she could make it.

'You said something about putting the kettle on?' she said.

The kitchen felt familiar, electric light making it bright against the gloomy afternoon that looked through the rain-streaked windows. Felicity switched on the gas fire and it hummed in a friendly way as she bustled about with kettle and teapot. They both took off their damp coats and hung them over the backs of chairs, where they steamed together, filling the room with the tang of wet wool. Felicity took a towel from a cupboard and threw it at April.

'You'll catch your death, as Nanny used to say.'

April scrubbed her hair and then handed the towel to Felicity.

'It feels very quiet without them,' Felicity said. 'I liked having company.' She rubbed at her damp curls. 'I missed you.'

'Oh.' April wanted to say *I missed you too*, she even got as far as opening her mouth, but something seemed to stick in her throat. Felicity might just mean she missed having someone around. She mightn't mean April herself, not in a special way.

'Fabian and Martha,' Felicity said, 'Erich and Hanna.' She sighed, not like the fearsome spinster she had said she intended to be, but more like someone . . . well, someone who felt left out. Like April. 'Feels like the world's full of couples.'

'You don't have to tell me,' April said. 'What d'you think it's like in my line of work?'

'But you don't want to be in a couple?'

'I don't want to get *married*. Doesn't mean I want to live on my own forever.' It was the first time she had said this aloud.

She watched Felicity wet the tea and stir the pot, deft and impatient, stopping to push back the odd unruly curl. Watched her take milk from the refrigerator and set down the teapot, two cups and the little yellow jug she remembered so well. She sat down opposite her at the table, as they had done so often in the spring and summer. She poured the tea and passed April's cup to her. 'Plenty of milk, isn't it?' she asked, and April nodded.

'I really did miss you,' Felicity said again. 'I'm sorry I was so impossible. I shouldn't have been so secretive, but—'

'I understand.'

She had said it twice now: *I missed you. I really did miss you.*

The third time, it would have to be April who said it. So what was stopping her? She blew on her tea. I want to stay here, she thought, drinking tea with Felicity forever. I'll even try coffee; you never know, I might like it.

347

'I missed you too,' she managed. 'Being here again's so strange. I feel . . .'

Say it, she ordered herself. Say something!

'You feel . . .?' Felicity prompted her.

It's like having the best chum, only more so, Sybil had said.

We just seemed to feel a sympathy, Martha had said.

I love her, she realised. I've loved her for ages. I want to live with her but not as her lodger.

But how could she tell Felicity when she had only just admitted it to herself? And what exactly was she admitting? The only time she had come close to this before was when Evelyn told her she was getting married and April had begged her not to. But that was different – Evelyn had been her best friend for years and her marriage was going to change everything. Maybe it had just been jealousy at being left behind; maybe it had been the conviction that she hadn't loved Maurice and that he wasn't good enough for her. She certainly hadn't said anything about love. And Evelyn had looked puzzled – not even disgusted, just puzzled, and said, *Honestly, April, why can't you be happy for me? And why can you not just want what normal people want?*

But this *is* normal, she thought. Here we are drinking tea in the kitchen. Here is the brown teapot and the little yellow jug. Nothing could be more normal. She looked at Felicity's hands clasped round her cup, at the familiar ink stains and the bitten nails, and the urge to cross the room and take those hands made her grip her own cup so hard that she almost broke it, and all the time she could not speak and the only sounds in the room were the tick of the clock and the occasional slurp of tea. Even the rain had stopped; a cold grey murk showed in the windows.

She would tell her. Now.

She moistened her lips, but at the same time Felicity cleared her throat, and said, 'Maybe I should try True Minds' services after all?'

'*What?*' The world tilted, not romantically, as it had for Martha, but the way April's world always did tilt, sickly and scarily.

'Remember you gave me one of your forms? For research? Wait here.'

She disappeared, and April sat on in the kitchen, numb, her heart suddenly too big for her chest, thumping in a very peculiar way, as if she had just cycled up Shippards Hill. Thank God she hadn't said what she really wanted to!

Felicity came back and handed her the form. She looked unusually self-conscious, her cheeks pink and her curls messier than ever.

April stared at her. 'D'you want me to read it?'

Felicity nodded, took her cup to the sink and began to wash it, even though she hadn't finished her tea. April unfolded the form; it was filled in in Felicity's familiar bold script and purplish ink, blotted here and there and barely dry. Her eyes glided over *Name, Age, Occupation to What sort of spouse are you looking for?*

I want to share my life with someone energetic and forward-thinking. Someone with whom I am in sympathy intellectually and politically. Someone who is their own person and allows me to be the same.

What is this? April thought. Her heart beat faster than ever.

In the space for *Income* Felicity had written, *Fluctuates wildly. I write books, which are well received but unprofitable, and stories, which are frightful nonsense but lucrative. I am independent but not well off. Recently I have been supporting a German Jewish family, helping them escape from the Nazi regime and to establish themselves in England. I intend to keep on doing this sort of thing, so it is imperative than any companion intends to keep on earning their living. And is in sympathy with such endeavours.*

And at the bottom, in the box for *Notes*, she had written and underlined, *I am not seeking a husband. I would prefer to spend my life with a female companion.*

April gulped. The world righted itself. Like Martha had said it would. She looked up and, again as Martha had promised, everything, though it looked the same, felt new. The little yellow jug glowed with sunshine. Felicity was drying her cup with the towel they had both used for their hair. She was clearly trying to look unconcerned, but her cheeks had darkened to crimson.

'Is this true? You want a female companion?' April asked. Her voice came out raspy and dry.

Felicity nodded. 'Not just any female companion. I told you I miss you,' she said. 'And I think . . . I hope you might miss me too.'

'Aye.' April jumped up from the table, crossed the room and took Felicity's ink-stained hands, grasping her fingers, feeling them close around her own. 'I do, Felicity.' And then, louder, 'I do.'

Acknowledgements

Mrs Hart's Marriage Bureau, though quite a jolly book, took a long time to write, mainly for the very appropriate reason that I was planning my own wedding at the same time. I do not recommend this.

I am hugely indebted to those who cheered me along the way, with particular thanks to Susanne Brownlie, always my first reader; Emma Campbell, who reassured me that my English characters didn't sound Irish, and especially Keren David, whose characteristically honest insights into an earlier draft were more illuminating than she can ever know. I wrote this novel mostly during lockdown, so the support of online writing pals was invaluable. Katy Moran, Emma Pass, Leila Rasheed, Rhian Tracey and Rachel Ward all gave an enthusiastic thumbs-up to the first chapter when I really needed it, and I am so grateful.

Ever since I read *Ballet Shoes* as a little girl, I have been obsessed with the 1930s, and it's been a joy to immerse myself in 1934 and in the fictional town of Easterbridge, which owes something to my memories of living in the north of England, but more to my imagination and reading.

The historically minded reader might well know that the first official marriage bureau in the UK was not in fact licensed until

1939, many years after my Martha started to ply her trade – how she would deplore such a vulgar expression. Penrose Halson's *Marriages Are Made in Bond Street: True Stories from a 1940s Marriage Bureau* is an entertaining and informative glimpse into a rather more metropolitan matchmaking world than that of Easterbridge. *Shapely Ankle Preferr'd: A History of the Lonely Hearts Ad 1695–2010* by Francesca Beauman reminded me why I have never been drawn to the dating scene and provided much inspiration. Virginia Nicholson's *Singled Out: How Two Million Women Survived Without Men after the First World War* is a book I have returned to often, and Juliet Gardiner's epic but very readable *The Thirties: An Intimate History of Britain* was invaluable.

I am, as always, deeply indebted to the wisdom, kindness and tenacity of my lovely agent Faith O'Grady, who has championed *Mrs Hart* from the moment I said I wanted to write about a matchmaker. Everyone at Harper Collins Ireland has been wonderful to work with. I'm sure there are people whose input I don't even know about, but I have been very privileged to have the expertise of Conor Nagle, Catherine Gough, Kerri Ward, Stephen Reid, Patricia McVeigh, Michelle Griffin and Flora Moreau at various stages of the book's journey. Many thanks to Jo Walker for the beautiful cover design. I am also extremely grateful to the Arts Council of Northern Ireland whose grant allowed me time to focus on writing the novel when I really needed it.

Of course the biggest thanks of all must go to my family, for accepting years ago that I live at least part of the time inside a story, usually in the olden days, and for not minding too much; and especially to my husband Seamus, who now knows more than perhaps he ever wanted to about the realities of living with a writer.

Sheena Wilkinson
Ballyronan
October 2022